Forcing Fate

Book One of the Fate Unraveled Trilogy

M. A. Frick

Copyright © 2023 by M.A. Frick

All rights reserved.

No part of this publication may be reproduced, distributed, or transmitted in any form or by any means, including photocopying, recording, or other electronic or mechanical methods, without the prior written permission of the publisher, except as permitted by U.S. copyright law. For permission requests, contact [mafrick.author@gmail.com].

Book cover by GetCovers.com

Prologue header art by Hmeluns on canva.com

Scene break art by GDJ on canva.com

Chapter headers by dewantoroo on fiverr.com

Rafe POV Header art by jamespaul77 on fiverr.com

The story, all names, characters, and incidents portrayed in this production are fictitious. No identification with actual persons (living or deceased), places, buildings, and products is intended or should be inferred.

No portion of this book may be reproduced in any form without written permission from the publisher or author, except as permitted by U.S. copyright law.

Also by M.A. Frick

The Fate Unraveled Trilogy:
Forcing Fate
Following Fate
Fulfilling Fate
***

The Dragon's Heart:
Between Flames and Deceit
***

Standalones:
The Petulant Princess

To Jessie.
Without you, I would have never spread my wings.

Prologue

Year 870 After the Alliance of the Dragon Men

The crowd gathered in the amphitheater. Excitement flitted across the multitude, each person restless for the main event. Bards led in happy choruses, which some of the crowd joined in, and jovial chatter filled the air. Stark rays of summer light illuminated the sandy arena, caressing the colorful globes huddled in the center.

Dragon eggs.

Each egg held its own distinct hue. Colors and shades ranged from the darkest black to the brightest scarlet and emerald. Some shadowed the deepest blue, a mirror image of the night sky, while others portrayed the purest white, untouched by flaw. Some were bright, while others were earthy and mottled.

In a wide circle surrounding the eggs, sat the young Dragon Men, humans schooled and versed in all things Dragon Kind. Years of training prepared them for this day. The Masters only selected those who excelled in every aspect of their schooling. They were the best of the best. Chosen to be Dragon Men.

They sat on the sand, hands folded and backs straight, waiting for the first crack of an egg. Adult dragons leaned over the rooftop, crooning down at the brood. Once in a while, a dragon would stretch its wings, crowding the others. Roars and screeches erupted as they settled back into place. Their claws scraped against roof tiles, just as anxious to witness the first signs of hatching.

A female dragon, the color of deepest purple, whined and craned her head, attempting to get a better view. Her Rider, a slight fellow with tawny hair perched beside her. He stroked her violet scales and spoke hushed, soothing words.

Crack!

The sound reverberated through the arena. Conversations ceased. All song and festive chatter came to an abrupt halt and every set of eyes fixated on the clutch, searching for the source, heralding a new generation.

A gray egg, mottled with mundane brown splotches, shuddered free of the rest. It wobbled a short distance from its siblings and soft gasps of wonder coursed through the crowd. Even the dragons held their breath in silent anticipation.

Crack! Crack!

Fractures split and spider-webbed its surface as it trembled with the effort of the cramped dragon struggling to escape its prison. People lifted onto their toes to peer over each other, all eyes trained on that single egg—the firstborn of the clutch.

Pop!

A small shard broke loose, revealing a petite, stubby nose. The grayish-brown snout halted as it hit the outside air. After a moment, its tiny nostrils flared as it took its first breath. A forked tongue flicked out, tasting the foreign world.

The egg lurched and a clawed foot broke through, tearing away pieces of shell. It let out a squeak in anger at its confines. Someone in the audience jested, claiming it to be a feisty devil. Polite, quiet laughter followed.

Stone-colored eyelids slid back, revealing golden eyes, as the new dragon shivered off the last bit of shell. It shook its fragile wings in awkward jerking motions, letting them stiffen and harden in the sultry summer air. After tucking its wings close to its sides, the dragonling turned in a slow circle, studying the ring of Dragon Men. With bated breath, everyone wondered which it would choose to be its Rider. Then the little dragonling did something peculiar that had never happened before. Its bright eyes flared as it snorted and backed itself into the clutch with cautious steps, cowering amongst its siblings.

It backed away... from the Dragon Men.

Murmurs spread through the onlookers. Above, dragons clicked in wonder. Perhaps the dragonling just needed time. New hatchlings were usually quick to single out a Rider, eager to begin the bonding that would last their lifetimes.

Never had a dragonling backed away from the would-be Riders.

One egg after another hatched. Brightly colored dragonlings of red, green, blue, and stark contrasting ones of pitch black and the purest white took the attention off the little one. They all squealed and waddled over to Riders, drying their wings and nuzzling eager hands.

The dragonlings were new to the bond, to this world, yet they had the instinct that drew them to certain Riders. These clutches always chose the next generation of Riders. They always bonded to the ones the Masters had chosen, the ones who had excelled in every aspect that would be a Dragon Rider's life.

As excitement over the new dragonlings subsided, if only marginally, focus once again returned to the first dragonling. The little golden-eyed hatchling stood in the center of the broken eggs. Its eyes flashed with distrust as it gazed upon the other dragonlings with their Riders.

One Dragon Man remained.

He sat cross-legged on the sand, his soft gaze sought the young beast. Riders never approached a hatchling. The newborn creatures had always come to the Rider. The Rider did as he had been trained—he sat and waited.

A bell chimed in the distance. Traditionally, this would be the time in which the Riders would take their young bonded dragons and feed them for the first time.

Yet, this year there was an anomaly.

A Master stepped from the side, approaching the would-be Rider, who still sat on the ground, dragonless. He gave a careful berth to all newly bonded, as was customary, to let them acquaint themselves with one another. Low and curious chatter filled the air, the crowd puzzled by the antics of the dragonling and Rider.

The Master bent low. His white hair fell over his face, shielding his mouth from prying eyes. He whispered something to the young man, then straightened, backing away with his fierce blue gaze trained on the back of the dragonling.

With a frown, the Dragon Man rose to his feet. He brushed the sand from his trousers and stilled, studying the hatchling. Slowly, the little beast turned his head, looking over his back at the Rider, tail thrashing with agitation. Its big, bright eyes took the Rider in and it whirled, facing the Rider head on.

The whole crowd cheered, sure that the young dragon would join its Rider, the one whom it would share its life bond with. Excitement thrummed throughout the arena, and the dragons on the roof howled their joy.

Then the small dragon roared.

Silence fell like a stone, sudden and complete. The crowd, who had been on their feet, fists in the air, cheering, froze. Horrified expressions passed over their faces, distorting their joyous celebration. The dragons arched their necks, looking down at the little one in puzzlement.

For that roar was not one of acceptance.

The dragonling crouched, flicking out its tongue, its burning gaze locked on the dragonless Rider. Its claws kneaded the sand and its tail whipped from side to side as sporadic hisses slipped past its lips.

Other dragonlings looked on from shoulders, laps, and between the legs of their Riders, heads tilted with confusion. A white dragonling with a sheen of blue, like a precious pearl, cooed to the solitary dragon in the middle of the empty eggs. Its Rider gripped it closer to his chest, as if worried it would mirror the lone creature's ferocity.

In response, the small beast spun and snapped its teeth at the pearl-colored hatchling. Its Rider recoiled in horror. Palms were lifted, covering mouths to stifle gasps as an air of trepidation hung heavy in the amphitheater.

The dragonless Rider took a careful step forward with placating hands outstretched toward the unruly creature. It whirled again to face him with a hiss. It dropped its head and pulled its lips back, baring teeth sharp enough to sever a limb.

The Dragon Man hesitated, a wrinkle forming between his brows.

The dragonling was refusing him. Spurning the bond. Denying the blood-magic treaty of the Alliance of Men and Dragons. This was not a choice that was thought, planned, and executed. These eggs were bred and laid for the next generation of Dragon Men. It bound them to men. To share their lives and blood-magic with the Riders who would care for them and be their ultimate companions.

The treaty's magic had never failed.

Yet, here was this small dragonling, roaring in defiance at its would-be Rider.

A woeful keening rang from the rooftops—the bone-chilling cry of a dragon weeping. Dragons keened during times of immense grief. When their Riders died, or another of their kind passed the Veil. Yet together, the dragons encircling the amphitheater joined the sorrowful lamentations for the little one. It would not know the love and connection shared in the bond. It would never know the joy of growing old with its Rider, never have a companion to share in adventures. The dragons deemed the little hatchling lost.

A deep, resounding roar cut off the mournful song. The great purple dragon, which had seemed so eager for the eggs to hatch earlier, snapped her teeth at the other dragons. The tiles of the roof cracked under the crush of her claws, sending shards of tile falling into the crowd below. Her Rider stepped back, giving her the space she demanded as she launched herself off the precipice. Those gathered below shrieked as the beast descended. Her heavy wings beat the air, flying above the heads of the onlookers. Dozens screamed, their fear rampant, as her claws and tail flew past heads, angling herself toward the defiant hatchling, seeking a place to land.

The dragonling brought itself upright, in a defensive pose. A second ground-shaking roar sent hatchlings cowering, and their Riders shirking back, covering their ears. They scattered from their circle until only the dragonless Rider remained.

Her weight shook the earth as the dragon landed roughly, planting her feet around the golden-eyed hatchling. It looked up at her with large trusting eyes and backed away from the Rider, ducking under her belly.

Bending low to coo at the dragonling and nuzzle it in assurance, her lavender eyes flashed in warning. When she raised her horned head, she snorted at the dragonless man, enveloping him in a cloud of sulfur. He backed away, shaking his head and blinking the dust from his eyes.

Two Masters stepped from the shadows, nearing the trio with heavy frowns. They stood by his side, staring at the purple dragon and the earth-colored hatchling. She nuzzled the young one again, then turned an imposing eye on the Masters before baring her teeth.

This dragonling would have no Rider.

It was deemed a Wild Dragon, and was only the first.

Chapter One

Summer of Year 895

My hands trembled as I ran the brush through my hair. I bit my lip, focusing on the mirror as if pure concentration could stop an involuntary movement. The tremors increased, and the brush tumbled from my grasp, hitting the vanity with a sharp crack.

Blowing out a breath, my head fell forward, and I buried my face in my hands. My stomach twisted painfully in response to my nerves. I skipped the first meal because I knew I would throw it up in front of everyone. Even a sip of water seemed too daring to attempt.

I dragged my hands down my cheeks, studying my reflection. Fatigue dulled the green in my irises. Worry thinned my pursed lips, tugging them into a frown.

Today was a big day—the biggest of my life. I had worked for twelve long and hard years to get to this point. The first four of my youth didn't count. Back then, I lived with my mother in a small village, Stonesmead.

My heart twisted at the thought of her. She was a larger woman, kind and soft. She teased about having a baker's body, claiming it came with the occupation. Flour dusted her hair and clothes more often than not. She always wore her brown hair in a knot on her head and had a smile for anyone who crossed her path.

Mother always said I was a mirror image of my father. I had his emerald eyes, white hair, and fair complexion. Any amount of time in the sun rendered my skin red and blistered.

My years spent in Stonesmead were peaceful, simpler times. No responsibilities or nerves weighed me down. I filled my days with playing in the sunshine and pulling on my mother's skirts for samples of her baked treats. I ran through the woods, climbed trees and splashed in the river with my friends. Life was carefree then, not a worry in the world.

Until news arrived that my father was killed in the war.

With that came the burden of my mother not being able to support a growing child. Our King had set a decree that when a soldier died in service, his children, and widow were provided for by the kingdom. It wasn't always easy, nor was it perfect, but it helped.

I was sent to one of the King's schools, Northwing, when I was nearing five-winters old. Here, the elders cared for the little ones. They oversaw my education, discipline, and training, and made sure all students were provided for. My mother received the relief she needed to get by, and with her baking, she had enough funds to visit me twice a year.

My stomach rumbled its protests of my fast as I glanced at the basket on top of the small table beside my cot. A white linen cloth hid the baked sweets beneath. Mother always brought me treats when she visited. If I still lived with her, my slight frame would have far more weight to it.

I took a deep breath and picked up the brush, resuming my attempt to smooth out the knots from my restless night of tossing and turning. If she were here, Mother would assure me that this was nothing to be worried about, that it would all be just fine. The rational part of me agreed, but one could not be calm on Hatching Day—especially one of the Chosen.

As I divided sections to plait my hair, my thoughts wandered to the history of Hatching Day. Over a thousand years ago, the War of Dragons and Men devastated the land. It was a bloody, unorganized affair of men hunting dragons in groups of militia, and the great beasts laying waste to entire cities in a single day. The fighting was endless, going back as far as our recorded history. Until a man, Zylan, found an orphaned hatchling. He connected with it, creating a magical bond.

The two understood each other to an unprecedented degree. Their thoughts were as one. They communicated on a rational level—and for the first time, man realized the great beasts were more than violent monsters. They had a conscience, a sentience. Together, they brought peace to the land, and through blood-magic formed the treaty still used on this very day. With the alliance came the Dragon Men—humans trained in fairness and battle, who fought for peace, vowing to never shed meaningless blood.

Throughout the years, the dragons slowly diminished to only lay the clutches to be raised by the Dragon Men. In the first years under the treaty, the Dragon Men were given eggs from the dragons themselves, as none of the eggs laid prior were bound by the treaty.

In the Dragon Men's care, the eggs determined the number of Dragon Men selected from the schools that would be Chosen. Because of the treaty, hatchlings never refused a chosen Rider. Until twenty-five years ago.

That fateful day, the first Wild Dragon was born in over five hundred years. It had no bond with any of the Chosen. It was a feral thing, unwilling to be tamed. Legend says a year after its hatching, it flew off, never to be seen again.

Every so often, another would hatch—the most recent being four summers ago. I was twelve then, not yet old enough to be a Chosen One myself, but I remember the slate-blue hatchling with silver eyes. It was wild and ferocious, attacking a Rider before another dragon swooped from the rooftop, taking it away.

Wild Ones spent their first year growing under the care of elder dragons, then in the night, they would disappear, never to be seen again. The Masters never tried to contain them, for they had the potential to grow into fierce fighters. No one wanted monsters chained to the schools.

Things amongst Dragon Kind changed since that first Wild One. Now, not only did the First Chosen sit in a circle around the eggs, but a larger circle of Second Chosen surrounded them. There were two Second Chosen for every First Chosen. The Masters theorized this gave the hatchlings more options to choose from and less reason to refuse the bond.

No members of Dragon Kind had any idea as to why some were wild. The breeding was the same every year. The blood-magic binding Dragon Men and dragons was still as strong as ever. There seemed to be no rhyme or reason to which would be wild or why.

I secured my braid with a leather cord and tossed it over my shoulder. Once again, I examined myself in the mirror, wishing I could hide the worry etched in my expression. As First Chosen, I would sit in the ring closest to the eggs. I wondered what dragon would hatch for me—if a dragon would hatch for me.

No.

With a firm shake of my head, I closed my eyes.

I had worked hard for this. My father died fighting the Shadow Men. As his daughter, I refused to let his sacrifice be for naught. I owed this to him, to myself. I would be a Rider and continue my father's fight, protecting our lands.

A dragon would hatch for me today. It would.

As the youngest of the Chosen, I proved myself with high marks in my schooling. The Record Rooms were practically my second home. I had no friends, no distractions. This day was the sum of my life's purpose. Everything would be fine.

Opening my eyes, I stared at the terrified girl in the mirror.

"It will be fine."

My boots scuffed against the cobblestone path that winded through Northwing's grounds as I made my way to the amphitheater. My stomach continued its threats to eject all non-existent food. I smoothed my simple gray dress for the umpteenth time. Peeking under my lashes at the other students, I spotted another First Chosen, Ruger.

At nineteen-winters old, he was tall and built like a warrior. He would grow into a fine Rider, yet even he seemed nervous. One of his friends clapped him on the back with a wide grin, saying something I couldn't hear. Ruger's worried frown broke into a smile as he punched his companion on the arm.

I dropped my gaze to my feet as I kept walking. Even after living here for so long, I had never made any friends. It wasn't for the lack of people trying. I simply had too much to study, too much to learn. I didn't have time for meaningless chats or hanging about with my peers.

Besides, the only thing girls wanted to talk about was boys—who had the best hair, the cutest smile. My nose wrinkled at the thought. Immature, smelly bullies were more like it. All of them behaved as if they were in an endless game of 'Who can do the stupidest things to prove some level of masculinity?' I shuddered. They called me an old hag, and that was the lot I accepted in life.

The amphitheater offered a cool reprieve as I stepped into its shadow. The structure was massive, seating over three thousand. Even with the immense space, people crammed in and stood wherever they could to glimpse the day's main event.

Giant wings blotted out the sun as an enormous black dragon coasted to a stop on the rooftop. Its claws scraped the tiles, shattering a few before it settled on its perch. It craned its long neck to peer at the eggs far below.

My nails bit into my palms as I clenched my fists in determination.

It would be fine. This is what I was here for. Once the day was over, the rest of my life would begin. I would avenge my father and continue his mission to banish the Shadows.

Trailing a distance behind Ruger, I paused as he said a final farewell to his friend. When his companion walked away, I offered a small smile as he held the door for me to enter.

"Avyanna," he said, inclining his head in a respectful bow.

"Ruger. Good day to you." I slipped past him and started down the hall toward the arena.

"Are you excited about today?" he asked conversationally, keeping pace with me.

We weren't friends, but that didn't mean I couldn't be friendly.

"Definitely. You?" I replied, trying my best to keep my anxiety buried.

"No." He laughed nervously and ran a hand through his hair. "There might be another Wild One."

"If there is, I'm sure it won't be you it refuses." My words were for him, but I used them to assure myself, as well.

"Easy for you to say. The hatchlings have never refused a female Chosen. I heard the Masters were thinking of trying a year of only female Dragon Kind—an experiment of sorts."

"They wouldn't do that," I scoffed, shaking my head. "It would be too risky." If it didn't work, an experiment like that chanced more Wild Ones, not less.

"I'm just saying, your luck is better than mine. So, don't worry." He offered me a broad smile that didn't quite reach the nervous glint in his eyes.

"It will be fine, Ruger, for both of us."

I hoped I was right.

We settled in our circles as the bell chimed nine times. The crowd murmured and the dragons on the roof snorted and clicked quietly. My mother was somewhere in the crowd, cheering me on. Her usual visits took place in the spring and fall, not in the middle of summer. She had scraped together her savings to be with me today. Suspense thickened the air, and I shifted, pulling my feet under myself.

The sun rose over the lip of the arena, caressing the eggs with warm rays. Every unique shell bore different hues and speckles. Some held distinct mottling and veining, leaving one to wonder what the dragonling inside looked like. My gaze landed on a beautiful gilded egg. I could almost see swirls on the eggshell as if it would have swirling patterns on its scales. I wondered what color eyes the dragonling would have.

A grown dragon, Aleon, had gold scales. I glanced up at the roof, spotting his gleaming hide right away. His dark, inky stare focused on the brood. Would that hatchling have black eyes as well?

The mother of the clutch, Esperna, a blood-red dragon, sat perched beside him, ready to swoop down if any Wild Ones emerged. Mothers did not love their young any less if they refused the bond. They treated them the same, keeping them close as they gained independence until they were nearly a year old and they flew off on their own.

Elgoth, a silver dragon, had sired this clutch. He was slain in battle shortly after their union. Esperna hadn't laid a clutch since and most suspected this brood to be her last.

We all waited patiently for the first dragon to pip their egg. Hatchlings took their time, only coming out when they were ready. There was always something magical about watching that first one break through. The crowd would erupt into awed whispers and hushed wonder, filling the air with excitement.

My thoughts drifted as I stared at the gold egg, almost willing it to be mine.

Dragons didn't mate for life. Their only lifelong attachment was to their Riders. In the days before the War of Dragons and Men, they lived for hundreds, if not thousands, of years. Now they averaged two hundred before they grew old and passed. Through blood-magic, Riders shared this longevity of life.

After passing the Veil, the dragon's bodies were guarded until they could be burned. The Shadows plaguing our borders were vile Shamans who used the blood and bones of dragons for foul magic. On the battlefield, Shadow Men descended on fallen dragons like hungry vultures, leaving nothing behind.

Their magics were black and poisonous, eating at their very own soul. The magic we knew was from Riders and the dragons. When a Rider bonded with the dragonling, there was an opening of minds, as if a bridge connected them. Emotions, feelings, thoughts, and even magic could cross that bridge.

Through this bond, though, Riders could not take magic from the dragons. It had to be freely given.

The Shadow Men did no such thing. They stole and polluted the magics for their own selfish desires.

Crack!

The sound of a dragonling pipping jolted me from my reflections. My eyes darted over the pile, frantic to see which egg it was. A little sea-green egg shook, and I relaxed with a smile, wondering at the thoughts going through its head as it tried to break into the world.

Dragonlings communicated with their bonded immediately after hatching. They couldn't speak words, but had intelligent thoughts. Their bodies grew at a rapid pace and within a year, they'd be the size of a horse. Their minds developed even faster, aided by their bond.

The hatchling's snout poked through his shell, flicking its navy-blue tongue as it sampled this new world and all the smells that came with it. With a faint chirp, the egg lurched, falling hard on its side. It cracked the rest of the way, and the tiny creature sprawled out on the sand.

The sea-green dragonling stood on trembling legs, shaking its body like a wet dog. Shards of eggshell went flying. Someone in the crowd giggled, but all the Chosen focused on the dragonling, wondering who it would bond with.

No bigger than a newborn calf, the tiny beast spread its wings wide. It blinked, eyes locked on the first Chosen that it had seen when first viewing the world. Estelle, a woman with dark hair and soft, gentle eyes, beamed at the young hatchling.

Anyone watching would know it was hers.

Egg after egg hatched, and my worry grew with each one. When only two remained, nerves had me gnawing the inside of my cheek. Out of the First Chosen, it was down to Ruger and I. There was an egg for each of us.

We were fine.

The golden egg I admired hadn't hatched yet. Slight cracks marred its surface from the struggle of the dragonling inside. Behind it, a dark sapphire egg wobbled. Surely that one was Ruger's.

The gold egg teetered, and a split ran down its side. I locked eyes with Ruger across the circle. He winked at me, nodding back to the egg. The blue egg splintered, demanding our attention. It was a race to see which dragonling would be the first out.

Lurching, a foreleg shot out of the gilded shell. Brilliant white talons glinted in the sunlight. I held my breath, waiting to feel some kind of connection. What would it feel like when I was bonded? I had read about it so much, but wondered what it would feel like on a personal level. After this, the dragonling would be my companion. I would have no need for any other friends. We would do everything together. We would fight side by side, forcing the Shadows back to where they came from.

A blue snout broke through the shell of the sapphire egg. The harsh motion sent it rolling across the sand. Ruger laughed, a huge smile lighting his face. Surely, that was his dragonling. After it freed itself from its confinement, the dark-blue dragonling wasted no time trotting over to Ruger.

I smiled at the golden egg, mentally cheering it on until it finally emerged. Spreading its cream-colored wings wide, it announced its arrival. Shivers ran over my skin when the gold dragon opened its crystalline eyes and blinked at me. I beamed as it shook itself and loped my way.

Then past me.

As if I was not even there.

Air rushed from my lungs as the world teetered and dropped from beneath me. My vision faded as the golden dragonling ran past me, and into the arms of a Second Chosen.

I struggled to keep myself upright. The rush of blood in my ears smothered all other sounds. The dragonling refused me.

I had been refused.

Twelve years of sacrifices and endless studies, trying my best to be selected as a First Chosen.

And I was rejected.

Passed up for a Second Chosen.

The crowd was probably on their feet, cheering for the dragonlings and their Riders. But I couldn't hear anything over the thundering defeat in my ears.

My father died so I could have this chance. I ruined it. I was almost glad for my blurred vision. This way, I wouldn't see my mother's disappointment when I walked away from Hatching Day without a dragonling.

I had failed.

Chapter Two

Winter of Year 895

Winter's sharp chill nipped at my cheeks and I shivered, wrapping my fur cloak tighter around myself. Snow glittered on the ground, freshly fallen the night before. Not a single pair of footprints marred the virgin path, aside from the tracks I left trailing behind. I traveled the path more from memory than actually being able to see it under the snow.

Heavy clouds pregnant with yet more flurries crowded out the dim morning light. No dragons were to be seen, having flown to Southwing, the new southern school of the King, during the harsh winter. Only a few older dragons and their Riders remained. They spent most of their time huddled in the caves below the school, soaking up the warmth of the hot springs. They remained in Northwing in case any threats arose. However, they rarely left the caves, choosing to enter a brumation-like state rather than face the bitter elements.

I was grateful for the respite from the dragons' presence. Seeing them served as a painful reminder that I'd been refused.

My foot slipped on a patch of ice buried beneath the snow, and I flung out my arms to steady my balance. Clutching my cloak about me as I regained my footing, I pressed on, trying to evade my sour thoughts.

I couldn't help but wonder what the first refused felt like. He left the school two years after that fateful Hatching Day. Most claimed he'd accepted his lot and moved on with his life. But how could he not be bitter and sore about it? He left the school, after all. At least I stayed for now, contemplating what I would do next.

There were still options. I could strive to be a Master. Perhaps learn to be a Records Keeper. A quiet life surrounded by books didn't seem too bad. Something where I could use the schooling that had been provided to me, and not waste twelve years of my life.

My stomach twisted in a knot as I thought about the idea of being near the beasts that rejected me. I couldn't put all the blame on the dragons. It wasn't their fault. Until that first Wild One, Dragon Kind thought everything had been settled by the treaty. The dragons were just as baffled by the change as we were.

Knowing it wasn't their fault didn't change how deep the refusal cut. The events of that day still plagued my dreams. I'd spent the better part of my life believing that I would be bonded to a dragon if I worked my hardest. So I did.

Now? It all felt like a waste.

Without the promise of a dragon, I floundered, feeling lost. I floated, like a leaf stuck in the current, drifting wherever it took me. The hold I'd had on my future slipped between my fingers, and I couldn't do a thing about it.

I looked up as I reached the Masters' quarters. The tall building loomed above me, instilling fear and intimidation. I had only been here a handful of times. Even though the structure with its sharp spires and dark brick was foreboding, the inside was warm and welcoming.

A set of guards posted outside the double doors waited for me to pull down my hood and reveal my face. One gave a brief nod, granting me access. The Masters requested this meeting; I assumed to discuss my future plans. I removed my cloak and hung it on a hook on the foyer wall. Wiping my feet, I made my way to the desk where a woman sat, her red hair swept up in a bun.

"Miss Avyanna," she greeted with a smile.

I nodded, returning the gesture. "Master Niehm."

"I see you're here for a meeting with the Council?" She glanced at a paper resting on her desk.

"Yes, ma'am." My hands clasped in front of me.

"I'll escort you." She stood and brushed her skirts out, holding out her hand to motion me down the left hall.

I started down the hallway, walking beside her.

"You've been quiet lately." A quick glance at her revealed a glint in her eyes.

"Quieter than normal, I should say," she corrected.

My shoulder lifted in a half-hearted shrug. "There hasn't been much to say lately."

"Avyanna, don't let a dragon's refusal sour the world for you." Her voice was soft as she gave a slight shake of her head.

She meant well, but the wound was still too fresh. I schooled my face, refusing to be anything but polite.

"It's all right, I'm fine." Assuring her, I looked back down the hallway.

Surely the meeting room couldn't be much further. I didn't want to talk about this. The last thing I needed was to deal with someone thinking they knew more about my future than I did.

"Dragons are not everything, dear," she said quietly.

Dragons were *my* everything.

Until Hatching Day.

I just smiled and kept my eyes pointed down the hall, refusing to look at her. She sighed and motioned to a door coming up ahead. Knocking twice, she opened it and motioned me inside.

The door swung open to reveal a large oval table, and a fireplace behind it heating the room. Upon entering, I noted the warm tapestries hung on the walls, depicting dragons and their Riders. I swallowed the emotion building in my throat. The door clicked shut behind me, but I didn't look back. I lifted my chin and crossed the room.

Thick rugs strewn about the wooden floorboards muffled any noise from my leather boots as I scanned the Masters in attendance. There were four, with Master Brann standing at the head of the table. He was a kind man, strong for his years. He kept his gray hair and beard trimmed and tidy, and his blue eyes sparkled with a constant glint of mischief. The other three Masters were familiar, all of them Egg and Hatchling Masters, though I couldn't recall their names.

My stomach dropped as dread filled me. Would they deem me unsuitable for Northwing? Would they shatter any hope I had of using the knowledge I'd gained through my years here?

This was about Hatching Day, I knew it.

"Miss Avyanna." Master Brann gestured to an empty chair, indicating I should sit.

Nerves tightened my throat as I settled on the edge of the seat, studying the Masters. I sincerely hoped I did not appear as insecure as I felt.

"You wished to see me?" Though my voice was quieter than I intended, I was pleased it didn't tremble.

"How are you, dear?" Master Brann asked as he took his place, sitting beside a hulking Hatchling Master.

"Well. And you, Master Brann?"

"As well as these old bones will permit in this blasted cold," he chuckled. "These are my colleagues, some of whom you may be familiar with. Master Hawkins, Master Zia, and Master Balloch."

A weight lifted off my chest, and I took a relieved breath. If Master Brann was at ease, perhaps this wouldn't be so bad.

"We've been hearing reports about you, dear," Master Brann said.

All anxiety immediately returned. What reports? I minded my own business and kept to myself. I stayed out of trouble.

"Don't look so frightened. We've not heard ill of you." The towering one, Master Balloch, waved a large hand, as if dismissing the worried look on my face.

"Unless we should have heard about something?"

Master Hawkins, an Egg Master leaned over the table. His cloudy eyes studied me intently, and I shifted in my seat. He was a slight man with a stooped back and a hawkish nose.

"I've done nothing wrong," I squeaked. My lips pulled into a frown at how pathetic the words sounded.

"Easy, Master Hawkins." Master Brann's brows lowered, scolding his colleague. "Miss Avyanna, we've been following your grades and activities for quite a while now. I'm sure you're aware that we scrutinize any student before we name them Chosen." His placating tone stilled some of my unease.

My cheeks burned with shame. I had been Chosen. I passed the scrutiny, tests, and trials... and through it all, the hatchlings still deemed me inadequate.

"Since Hatching Day, we've continued to monitor your studies and character. We have also consulted with the Master of Women, and the few students who call themselves your friends."

I arched a brow, but kept silent at that remark. Who on these grounds would name themselves my friend? I had none.

"'Friends' is a loose term with you, unfortunately," he added, noticing my quiet confusion.

Frustrated at being so easy to read, I chewed my cheek and clasped my hands in my lap.

"You're a hard worker, Avyanna." Master Zia, who had been silent till now, spoke up. Her unadorned raven hair draped straight down her back. The richness of her blue eyes hinted at wild violets. "Since the day you arrived, you've applied yourself to your studies and training with a tenacity that few other students could hope to match," she finished.

"Thank you," I murmured.

"Don't thank us just yet," Master Hawkins snapped.

Pressing my lips together, I glanced at Master Brann for reassurance, though it was Master Balloch who spoke next.

"Since the events of Hatching Day, we've deliberated amongst each other and have come to a conclusion. We have an opportunity for you, something that has never been offered to another student." Master Balloch scratched the scruff on his chin, pleased with himself.

"Think of it as an experiment." Master Zia nodded. "We have decided that if any student on the King's grounds is worthy of the title Dragon Kind, you, Avyanna of Gareth, are."

My lips parted in surprise that they used my father's name. Almost all the students of the King's schools were here because a parent or guardian died in the war. Why would they bring up my father?

She continued, "We have concluded that you will spend a second year as First Chosen on Hatching Day."

The room spun as those words rang in my ears. A second chance? As First Chosen? That was unheard of. It simply was not done. There were always two Second Chosen for every First Chosen. The First Chosen for the following year always came from the previous year's Second Chosen. It was a closed pool. No one else could get a chance at First Chosen. If, for whatever reason, a student refused, they were not given another chance. Ever.

My mouth hung open, but words evaded me. Each Master studied my face, waiting for my reply. I snapped my mouth shut, not having a clue what to say.

"We understand if you do not wish to accept." Master Hawkins folded his spindly fingers atop the table. "There are other Chosen who've been refused–"

"No!" The word rushed out, cutting him off. "No, I apologize. I am simply... surprised."

Master Brann winked, amused by my reaction.

"You will be classed with the First Chosen when lessons resume in the spring," Master Zia stated. "However, instead of the role of student, you will be assisting the Masters."

I watched her as she spoke, my eyes as wide as saucers.

"Young Avyanna, you know almost too much for your age." Master Hawkins' voice lowered, taking on an almost threatening tone.

My attention snapped to him. His words seemed a compliment, but the warning beneath them conveyed the exact opposite.

Master Brann cleared his throat, drawing my gaze back to him. "As the Masters' assistant, you will be expected to aid them throughout the year, and on Hatching Day you will be presented as First Chosen." An earnest smile lightened his features. "You have earned a second chance, dear."

"Next year's clutch is smaller than average," Master Balloch informed. "As of now, there are seven good eggs."

I bowed my head, holding my clasped hands up with gratitude. "Thank you. Thank you so very much." Emotion squeezed my chest, making it difficult to breathe.

This was hard to fathom. Second chances were unheard of. Perhaps it was because the gold dragonling didn't outright refuse me, but rather had a bond with a Second Chosen. Maybe, since it hadn't been a Wild One, they didn't completely write me off as refused.

"I won't disappoint you."

Looking up, I held each gaze, nodding my affirmation. I would study everything I could get my hands on and read every single parchment on dragons... for the fifth time. I would follow the Masters and learn all I could from them. There had to be more to the bond, something I missed. I wouldn't sleep, wouldn't eat.

I would bond with a dragonling.

Master Brann laughed, noticing the determination that played over my face. "I assure you, dear Avyanna. You could not disappoint us. You have already worked so hard. Try to relax, assist the Masters, and maybe even try to make a few friends."

Distaste wrinkled my nose before I could stop myself. Master Balloch had a good laugh at that.

Friends just took away from valuable studying time.

My mind was a whirl of frenzied thoughts as we said our goodbyes. On my way out, I noticed Master Niehm's frown. She had wanted me to give up on dragons, not hang my future on the acceptance of a hatchling. She must not have known what the Council planned for me.

Once again, my future was certain. Next Hatching Day I would have a dragonling.

"Friends!" I scoffed, plunging out into the cold with my cloak wrapped around me once again. The guards ignored me as I stepped onto the snow-covered path. Still, only my tracks led to the Masters' quarters.

Who needed friends when I'd have a dragon? We would share everything. It would be my best friend and I would never leave its side. Friends came and went, but a dragon was for life.

I shuffled through the cold, holding back from sprinting across the slick ice. Eager to write my mother, I rushed down the path. She'd want to be here for Hatching Day. If she skipped her visit in the spring, she'd have the funds to attend.

Last summer, she hadn't been disappointed in me at all when the gold dragonling bonded with a Second Chosen. My memories of that day were a haze. She had left that night, unable to stay longer, but I kept her letters, telling me how proud she was, regardless of my dragonless state.

My mother was my greatest supporter. Her faith in me outshined my own. I loved her dearly and wanted to do my best for her sake. I was her purpose in life, the reason she kept going. She never remarried after we lost my father, not even when the village blacksmith offered his hand. With no romantic interest in the men back home, she scraped by on her own. I would be one of the few female Dragon Kind and make her proud.

Though there were no gender boundaries concerning Dragon Kind, men were far more prevalent. Women didn't seem as interested in fighting a war when they could stay behind and care for their homeland. I wanted to fight. Not only to protect my mother, but to avenge my father.

As I neared the dorms, I took a deep, steadying breath, feeling the cold burn my lungs. Once inside, I shrugged off my cloak, turning to the women's wing with a nod to the secretary sitting at her desk.

"Miss Avyanna, I trust your meeting went well?" She didn't bother looking up from her papers.

"Very well, thank you."

Making my way down the hall, I passed the guards stationed to keep men out, and ascended the two flights of stairs to my floor.

Plenty of women lived here, displaced by the war, more than one would assume. Either their husbands died, and they had no form of income, or like me, they were young girls who'd lost their fathers. Few were attempting to be Dragon Kind, but all had a place. The Master of Women, Master Elenor, found something everyone could do. If one lived on school grounds, she would find something you were good at and set you to task. She did not abide idleness.

Down another hall, I came to my room. Entering, I hung my cloak on the back of the door and leaned against it, latching it shut. It was small, as was everyone's. These were not dwellings of luxury, they were the graces of the King. I couldn't complain. It was a roof overhead with free meals.

There was a cot tucked on the far side, with a minuscule table piled high with books beside it. On the right wall was another table with a looking glass and washbasin I used as a makeshift vanity. We had to fetch our own water, but I never minded. The women all shared public lavatories, but Master Elenor did not permit loitering, so they were mostly clear of people.

My room had little frills, something my mother lamented every time she came, but it was home. I earned coin here and there. Masters provided odd jobs for students, but there were too many seeking work for the Masters to supply our spending coin. Because of this, my coat rack bore only three dresses and a second cloak, more suitable for mild weather. The books were my decor, and that was fine with me. They were more useful, anyway.

Pushing off the door, I sighed and picked up the three books I needed to return to the Records Room. A smile lit my face as I left my room and darted down the hall.

I would be a Dragon Rider yet!

Chapter Three

Spring of Year 896

A crisp chill bit at my skin, pulling me from my sleep. Morning rays gleamed through my small window, and I groaned, throwing my feet over the side of the bed. The longer I put off getting up, the harder it would be.

The unforgiving wood floors were freezing against my threadbare stockings. My thin blanket did even less to ward off the cold. I stood and stretched, willing the blood to pump faster through my veins to warm my body. After folding my blanket, I straightened my pillow. Master Elenor did not tolerate messy rooms.

I padded over to my basin and splashed the frigid water on my face, holding in my gasp. Winter was over, but its chill still clung to the northern lands. I combed my hair, throwing it into a braid, and wound it about my head. Taking a drink of water to swish in my mouth, I examined myself in the mirror.

The dragons and their Riders would return soon—due in a fortnight. I was much more eager to see them with the promise of a dragonling next Hatching Day. I wanted to watch the dragons and Riders in my free time, observe them, and learn more about the bond. Even with all the books I read, studying them with my own eyes provided far more satisfaction.

Slipping out of my night shift, I dressed in my beige walking dress. My brown dress was for working in the gardens, my gray gown for formal events, and the blue for everyday wear. Today I'd serve with the Shield Master, and I needed something comfortable and easy to move around in.

It surprised me when I learned I'd be assisting soldiers and their Masters as well. Normally, students and soldiers were strictly separated until one was chosen as a Dragon Rider. Only then were they encouraged to learn the ways of the sword and spear. I assumed their reasoning for me tending to the War Masters was simply because they were taking more and more recruits. With the absence of the Dragon Riders, there were fewer bodies to help out in the barracks. They needed all the help they could get.

Slipping on my new spring boots that my mother had sent to me in celebration of my seventeenth winter, I admired the soft leather. I was eager to wear them even if it was still a bit cold. She did her best to send me sensible gifts, knowing I didn't care for frivolous things. Not that I wouldn't be grateful for them, I just appreciated practical things.

Grabbing my cloak, I made my way down the hall, mindful of my footsteps. I was an early riser. Some women were quite cranky in the mornings, and I wanted to avoid being the recipient of their nastiness. Ducking into the stairwell and down the first flight of stairs, I headed for the common room. Smells of freshly baked bread and bacon greeted me as my boots hit the second floor of the dorms. I would grab a quick bite before continuing on my way.

"Well, if it isn't the Masters' pet."

And with that, my morning soured like curdled milk.

"Good day, Vivian." I smiled.

'Kill them with kindness.' That was what they always said, right?

"Headed off to assist another Master? Maybe kiss some of their boots while you're at it?" She twirled a strand of raven hair around her finger.

Vivian was nasty—she had the personality of a snake. I gave her grace because she lost both her mother and her father when Shadow Men attacked her city. Maybe it was the lack of parental guidance that made her forget her manners so frequently.

She tried to block my way into the common room, but I managed to brush past her seething form.

"I heard you're going to the barracks today. You know what they say about those soldiers, right?"

I ignored her, looking at the long table on the far wall laden with food. There were ten tables set up with benches around them, a few occupied by older women. I made my way over, not bothering with a plate or napkin. I wouldn't be here long. Meats were reserved for the elderly and the Masters, not for students or younger workers. There were breads and a few preserves with some dried fruits as well. I snagged a warm roll and a handful of dried apples.

"They'll eat you alive." Vivian followed me.

Only a year older, yet she acted like that gave her permission to walk all over me. Her bitter attitude made me struggle to remember her fallen parents. Maybe that's why she was up early. She might have night terrors about losing them.

I refused to give in to her ugly words and let her twist my mindset. I was better than that. "Have a grand day, Vivian," I said, smiling and heading off to the stairs.

The other students had been particularly cruel since they heard the Masters granted me a second chance as First Chosen. That, combined with the fact that I was no longer a student, but a Masters' assistant. They assumed it changed me somehow or made me haughty. I was the same girl they always ignored before, and I didn't quite understand why this made a difference. They'd only see less of me, especially if I helped in the barracks. Wasn't that a good thing?

I scurried down the stairs and through the main hall, past the guards, and nodded to the morning secretary. "Good morn!" I greeted in passing, turning for the door.

"Oh, Miss Avyanna!" the secretary called.

I turned on my heel, hurrying back to her desk. "Yes, ma'am?"

"I've been asked to inform you that there's been a change to your schedule," she said. "Sword Master Elon will take a step back, as General Rafe ShadowSlayer is returning with the Dragon Riders. You've been asked to assist the General for two weeks' time, following your term with the Shield Master. Afterwards, you're to resume the current circuit of Masters."

"Is General Rafe ill?" I asked.

General Rafe had been at the front lines since my father died. Mother told me he had started in the same company as my father and rose to General in the short twelve years since. It was the fastest anyone had ever climbed the ranks.

"He has suffered a battle injury, yes, and will take time here to help teach the new recruits as he recuperates," she replied.

"Thank you for informing me." I gave her a polite nod and turned to head out the door again.

Lost in my thoughts, I nearly collided with the back of a young man.

"Oh, pardon me," I muttered, trying to take a step around him, but he held his ground.

"Ain't a pardon good enough for you, hag."

I blew out a breath at his harsh words. The boy, no older than I, turned and glowered down at me. These petty bullies were getting old this morning.

The secretary cleared her throat, and the boy smirked, unphased by her warning. "What did you have to do to get the Masters to give you a second chance?" he asked, clearly hinting at some form of bribery. He leaned forward to whisper in my ear before I could pull away, "You'll just be refused like last time."

I took a quick step back, glaring up at him. "I wasn't refused. That hatchling simply bonded with another Rider." I had been telling myself the same thing since Hatching Day. I almost believed it now.

A menacing sneer darkened his face, and he came closer.

"Distance!" A guard barked.

His eyes flicked to the guards stationed at the entrance to either wing of the dorms before he stepped away. Rules of appropriate distance between genders were strictly enforced. When so many children, teens, and unclaimed adults packed into such a tight place as Northwing, there had to be boundaries or tensions could rise. The King was determined to protect his people, even from each other.

"A dragon wouldn't be the first thing to refuse a girl as ugly as you," he snarled. "You look like an old woman with that white hair."

I shook my head and stepped around him. Bullies would be bullies, and I didn't have to give them any of my time. I had more important things to do.

Outside, sunshine warmed my face, chasing the chill out of the morning air. Mist rose from the grass as the sheen of frost melted away. The first spring flowers were already mid-bloom, letting their sweet fragrances drift on the breeze. It was a beautiful day.

I wouldn't let myself be bothered by the trivial nonsense of boys and bullies. One day, I would be a Dragon Rider, and my peers would be more mature.

I detested the immaturity of people my age. Even some of those older than me acted like children, fighting and squabbling over the simplest things. Things like fashion, and who would be whose life mate. Fashion was of no concern to me, unless it was the newest practical riding gear. And I had my whole life to find my life mate. I was in no rush. I didn't care what my peers thought of me. In the grand scheme of things, their opinions didn't matter.

Wrinkling my nose at the antics of boys, I walked toward the barracks. Boys were disgusting, smelly, and rude. Why anyone would dream of settling down with one of them—I hadn't the slightest clue.

Some men, like Master Brann, were gentlemen and I could appreciate ending up with someone like that as my life mate. Someone kind, fair, and dignified. In essence, someone who was mature. It was hard to imagine Master Brann as a ruddy teenager, but I supposed he had to have been at some point.

I strode through the giant wooden fence separating the barracks from the school grounds. The guard on duty stopped me with a lowered spear.

"Miss, you're entering the barracks," he stated, frowning.

It was all formality with the guards, but formality was to be respected. I produced a written order from a pocket in my cloak. It was a permission slip to enter the barracks, but only as the Shield Master's assistant. The guard took the paper and looked it over carefully.

"You know where you're headed, Miss Avyanna?" he asked, handing it back.

I shook my head. I'd been on this side of the grounds fewer times than I had fingers. It was always with a Master as a guide, during class. I had no reason to remember these paths, not when my presence was prohibited without a written order.

I looked around at some men milling about. They were all shapes and sizes—tall, short, lanky, burly. Some were all brawn, with muscles piled high. While others wore clothing that draped over their bones like poor, hungry skeletons.

"Wait a moment, if you will. I'll find someone to escort you," he said, scanning the men walking past.

While I waited, I took time to study the buildings on this side of the barracks' wall. Most of these structures were made of wood, versus the majority of the school buildings, which were constructed of stone and brick. I stood in the arms market, where dealers of swords, shields, spears, and bows hawked their wares. All manner of armor, tools, and weapons were out on display to be viewed with shining perfection. The space brimmed with a steady hum of voices and bartering, a lovely din. Nothing seemed amiss as men bustled about their duties.

I craned my head to see a knife stall with daggers out and gleaming in the early morning sun. Weapons were not allowed on the school grounds unless possessed by a guard. If we students were caught with a blade, it was lavatory duty for a month. If adults were caught with a weapon, punishment ranged from a fine or community work, to possible imprisonment.

The most dangerous thing I had ever held in my hand was a dinner knife.

"Hail! Willhelm!" The guard waved toward the shifting mass of male bodies.

A man with short black hair, streaked with gray, hesitated in his path and turned to look at us, jerking his chin up in question.

"Miss Avyanna here has orders from Master Damon. Escort her to the armory, would you?" The guard gestured from me to the man, Willhelm.

I offered a small, apologetic smile at the frowning man before walking over to him. "Begging your pardon for this inconvenience."

"I don't mind, miss. I'm passing by the armory office, anyway." With a nod to the guard, he gestured for me to walk beside him.

His long strides had me rushing to keep up with him. My sole focus diverted to my feet and not tripping when he spoke up.

"Miss, how long are you ordered here for?" he asked, not bothering to look at me, but rather at the surrounding men, offering nods of greeting here and there.

"Oh, I have orders to assist the Shield Master for the next two weeks. I'm sure I'll be able to find my way tomorrow," I assured him.

"No, ma'am. I'd rather not have that on my conscience." He drew himself to his full height, and the corner of his lip turned up. Slight wrinkles formed at the edge of his eyes, crinkling his skin. "Will you be arriving at the same time each morn?" he asked.

My eyebrows met in a frown. "Yes... give or take a few moments if I get delayed."

"I'll make my way to the gate each morning to escort you."

"That won't be necessary. I'd rather not trouble you."

"Miss Avyanna, I'd appreciate you trusting me on this."

I bit my lip and kept walking. I didn't need an escort. After today, I could find my own way. Surely the barracks were no danger to me. We were still on the King's grounds after all.

"A young lass like you might not understand it, but here in the barracks? It's a different world, miss." He insisted.

"If you wish to escort me, then so be it," I relented. "You have my thanks." I might not understand it, but I could trust someone in authority.

We kicked up dust as we walked. The barracks were vastly different. Where the school grounds were lush and soft, everything about this place was harsh and rough. The streets were unpaved and the scent of earth and sweat hung in the air.

Once in a while, between buildings and market stalls, I glimpsed men sparring or working. Most watched us with curious expressions as we passed. Subtle heat rose to my cheeks, sensing their stares. Bullies aside, I wasn't used to having so much attention directed at me. A bearded man stared at me so disconcertingly that I took a subconscious step toward Willhelm. He noticed, and glared in the man's direction before quickening his pace, forcing me to rush two strides for his one.

We soon arrived at a large weathered building with an expansive covered area. There, a blacksmith was hard at work, pounding his hammer into a piece of metal. Behind him, a forge sizzled, waves of heat rising from its depths. The hiss of steam and clang of tools created a strange discordance.

Shielding my eyes from the sun, I noticed a banner waving in the morning breeze. It depicted a mountain range with three shields in front of it.

"The armory office, Miss Avyanna." Willhelm took a step ahead, opening the door for me to enter.

Passing the threshold, the smell hit me first. The scent of man, metal, and leather. The mess greeted me next. Documents were tossed over most surfaces, the desk being the most disorderly. Various shields of all manner and make, stacked against walls and shelves. A few swords and other weapons I had no names for, laid haphazardly about the room.

I swallowed and slowly turned to the desk where an old man sat. Around his head, a leather band secured a thick glass over his left eye. He muttered gibberish, focused on the shield before him. It crushed a stack of parchments, scattering papers with each slight movement.

"Master Damon, Miss Avyanna," Willhelm called by way of introduction.

More papers drifted to the floor as the old man shifted the shield again. "What's that?" he shouted.

"Master Damon," Willhelm raised his voice, "this is Miss Avyanna, your assistant?"

"Ah yes, yes! The young lass." The Master looked up from his work. One eye was comically large, being magnified by the glass spectacle.

"What time will you be leaving for the school grounds, miss?" Willhelm asked at a more acceptable volume.

"I'm due back at the fifth chime. However, I will stay as long as Master Damon has need of me." I curtsied to Master Damon, who glanced between me and the current disaster that was his office, with an eager grin.

"Then I shall fetch you at the fifth chime," he replied, making for the door. I tilted my head, watching him as he left.

"Well, lass, I was told that you were to assist me with whatever I needed."

Now, I was almost positive that I was only to aid him in his teaching, but I would respect him enough to oblige.

"Therefore, this is your domain." He waved a hand at the room, as if indicating its state of disrepair was my doing. "These documents are to be organized alphabetically. They're all titled, so it shouldn't be too strenuous for a young thing like you," he stated, before turning back to his shield.

I raised an eyebrow at the papers overflowing from his desk, and his shield laying on top of it. "Would you rather I wait till you finish... examining that?" I asked.

"Ah, what did you say, lass? Speak up so an old man can hear you!"

I cleared my throat, then repeated myself in a manner far louder than appropriate for a lady.

"No, no, I'll be off soon. You just get started on those, there on the floor," he chuckled, muttering more nonsense as he set some kind of sharp tool to the binding on the shield's edge.

I took a deep breath, then knelt to pick up the papers. Surely this would not be so bad.

Chapter Four

Evidently, Master Damon did not get the message that I was supposed to help with his classes. Less than a chime after I arrived, he got up and walked out the door without a word. He'd been gone all morning. Well past midday, and I was covered in dust, grime, and ink.

I blew a stray hair out of my face and surveyed my work. All papers and parchment were piled into neat stacks in alphabetical order. I organized all shield designs and strategy drafts by category and title. I took my time with the drawings, and though they gave little insight concerning the Shadow Men, they did give me an insight into the war.

After bonding with a dragon, I would fight alongside men using these same shields and strategies. I would attack the enemy, but also protect these men. I then realized that this time assisting the War Masters was an opportunity for me to know what to expect when I became a Dragon Rider.

With all the papers and documents sorted, I stood there, not knowing quite what to do. The only chair available was at Master Damon's desk and sitting at a Master's desk was ill-mannered. He didn't tell me to touch anything else, and

I didn't want to upset him by moving something that he had organized in some obscure way.

I stood with my hands clasped in front of me, looking out the window. It was currently three chimes after midday. Two chimes remained until Willhelm came to fetch me.

I hadn't eaten anything aside from the roll and dried fruit. It was hardly enough to sustain me the entire day. With the school Masters, I took midday meals with them either before or after their classes. Master Damon left me with no instructions other than to sort through his papers. Normally, I was not one to complain, but I hated idleness. I could do so much more than just stand here without purpose. With only so much time a day, I wasn't one to waste any of it.

Leery but determined, I headed to the door. Willhelm hinted that the men here might not be the most friendly, but I needed to find Master Damon to figure out what I was supposed to do next.

The afternoon was pleasantly warm. I left my cloak draped on top of a pile of discarded shields and walked out into the sunshine. Taking a deep breath of fresh air, I smiled up at the sun.

A repetitive clanging drew my attention to the blacksmith, hard at work near the forge. I turned toward him, thinking he might be able to help me find Master Damon. I stood outside the fence, careful not to invade his workspace. He was a large man, as to be expected of a smith. Dark lensed goggles concealed his eyes.

"Pardon, sir," I called over the clanging.

He either didn't hear me or ignored me, so I waved my hands and repeated myself, leaning over the fence. He used giant tongs to put a circular piece of metal back in the coals and turned to face me, lifting his goggles.

"Miss?" he answered hesitantly, taking in my dress and hair.

"I beg your pardon, I was simply wondering if you knew where Master Damon might be?" I flashed him a bright smile, hoping it would encourage him to help.

Sweat beaded at his temple, running a trail through the grime caked on his face. The day was warm, but the forge was molten. Blacksmithing was brutal work.

"He'd be out teaching the first year cadets right about now." His voice was raspy, as if he didn't use it often. I assumed the metal didn't require conversational skills.

"Wonderful! Do you happen to know which direction that might be?"

Please don't escort me, please don't.

He jerked his head in a westerly direction and frowned. "Miss, you shouldn't go alone. Perhaps you should wait till someone fetches you. It wouldn't look right."

"I'm sorry, look right... how?" Pressing my lips together in a frown, I studied his serious face.

On school grounds, we had independence and could go where we pleased as long as it was in our free time.

"Ah... miss, a young lady such as yourself, wandering about without a chaperon in a place like this..." He took off a heavy glove and rubbed the nape of his neck, glancing back at the forge as if the metal would jump out and rescue him from this conversation.

"Please, sir. I don't understand. Is it because women do not frequent the barracks?" I asked.

"They're not allowed." He shrugged, putting his glove back on.

"Because there are so many men?"

His gaze returned to his forge once again, and I knew I wouldn't have him much longer.

"Aye, it's unseemly lass." He tugged his goggles back down over his eyes. "If you don't mind, miss, I'd rather be getting on with my work." And with that, he used his set of tongs to pull the metal disk out of the coals and hammer at it again.

Discussion over.

Alright, well, if it was unseemly, I'd just have to ask Master Damon for an escort or a list of duties. Or he could actually let me assist him, as the Council instructed.

Taking a deep breath, I turned and headed in the direction the smith had vaguely gestured. I kept my head high and put on an air of importance—as if I knew where I was going. At each crossroads, I checked either way for any sign of a class with shields.

A low whistle drew my attention to a man leaning up against a building near an alley. His dark eyes trailed over my body, taking their time in the most immodest manner. A heavy black beard covered his face and his sinister grin had my stomach clenching in disgust. I straightened and continued on my way, my pace quicker than before.

Hearing the clang of swords, I did my best to follow it. Turning down path after path, I searched for any sign of Master Damon when I noticed a man trailing behind me. The man from the alley.

Had he followed me?

No. He'd been going the same direction as me, that was all. Still, I dared not look him in the eye. Surely I wasn't in any danger. These were the King's grounds. And for all that was good and right in the world, it was broad daylight.

I turned down another path between two buildings and came up short, as it proved to be a dead end. Backtracking, I spun and almost collided with a large, towering frame. Fear tightened like a vice around my throat. The man followed me.

My heart beat faster, but I lifted my chin in defiance. I had no reason to be afraid.

"Pardon me." I tried to squeeze past him to the road, but he moved with me, blocking me. Taking a quick step back, I gave myself a bit of distance between us.

"What's a pretty thing like you doing, walking out here all alone?" His tone was low and quiet—menacing. "You could get lost, you know."

"I am Master Damon's assistant. I'm sure he's looking for me. So if you please–" I shifted to the left. Again, he blocked my way, this time stepping closer. I faltered for distance, stumbling back.

The man chuckled and ran a hand down his beard, with a wicked glint in his dark eyes. "Master Damon misplaced you, did he?"

He reached his hand up to my face. Though I was sure he was just reaching for my hair, I lurched away from him. My shoulder slammed into the wood of the building and I stumbled back as true fear sent my heart racing.

"Step away, soldier!"

A voice behind him rang out with clear authority. The man grimaced and turned to the side, revealing Willhelm at the mouth of the alley. My shoulders sagged with relief. Clearing my throat, I pushed off the wall and moved around the stranger.

"Sir Willhelm." The strain in my voice was clear, despite my attempt at keeping it steady.

"Miss," he spoke to me, but his eyes didn't leave the man behind me, "Master Damon wondered where you might be."

"Yes, I was on my way to see him. Would you be so kind as to escort me?" I asked, sincerely hoping he would say yes.

"As you wish." He gestured for me to move around him. Once he stood between me and the stranger, he lifted his chin. His voice dropped to a growl. "This won't happen again, soldier."

Willhelm offered his arm, and I took it without hesitation. He steered me off, confident his orders would be obeyed. I liked Willhelm. As a Dragon Rider, I wouldn't be so helpless. For now, though, his protection was a stroke of luck in this apparently uncivilized place. Some of the tightness in my chest eased, but in its wake, a strange sense of shame sank low in my belly. Frustrated, I shook off the feeling. I had nothing to be ashamed of. I'd done nothing wrong.

"Thank you," I muttered.

"I thought I made it clear this was not a place for young ladies without an escort."

The sharpness in his tone startled me. I wasn't a petulant child. It's not like I expected to be cornered by strange men if I ventured off on my own. "I apologize. Master Damon left me without instructions. I had only gone to find him when–"

"If Master Damon leaves you without instructions again, you simply wait for him. Don't go gallivanting off without warning." His frustration was evident as his gaze cut through the crowd. His strides lengthened into a ground eating pace. "I'll see you to Master Damon's current class, then meet you at his office at the fifth chime."

"Thank you kindly."

I, once again, struggled to meet his strides and was trying to hide my gasps of breath when we reached the training arena. It wasn't an extensive structure, but it was big enough to hold forty men, two rows deep in a semicircle. It was a roofed enclosure, though it had two giant doors on both its northern and southern sides, allowing a breeze through.

Master Damon stood on a rickety wooden crate that wobbled with each shout he threw at the men. Beside him, an archer with a quiver full of blunt, chalk-tipped arrows loosed shot after shot into the soldiers.

"Tighter! Get closer together! Oi, you redheaded oaf, use those muscles and lift that shield higher! If that wall drops, it will be on your head!"

I stood there in awe. A thrill of excitement buzzed through my veins. This was action. This was preparation for war. I would fight alongside these men. They would have my back as I fought against the Shadow Men.

"Woman present!" Willhelm shouted, causing me to flinch out of my daydream.

The wall of shields faltered as soldiers craned their heads, and Master Damon paused mid-shout to turn and look at me.

"Girl, I left you in my office!" he barked, clearly outraged.

I bit my lip. Masters were to be respected, but he needed to know I wasn't some dog to be told to stay. I was an assistant, not a servant.

"My apologies, Master Damon. I've finished the task you set me to, and simply wondered if there might be anything else you would like me to attend to while you're teaching, as my orders stated."

He ignored my question and snapped a glare at Willhelm. "Sir Willhelm, was she wandering about?"

"I'm afraid so, Master."

Master Damon heaved a sigh and rubbed his brow. "They sent me a girl, like I'm some nursemaid," he muttered.

I lifted my chin defiantly. I was not some child to be entertained. "If you'll not be needing me here, sir, I'm sure I can set to organizing the shields in your office." I grabbed a handful of my dress, turning to leave.

"No! Don't touch the shields! Sun above, no!" he bellowed. He gestured to a row of chairs against a wall. "Might as well take a seat till I be needing something," he grumbled.

I smiled at Willhelm, who gave me a brief nod before heading off. My grin disappeared when I noticed the layers of blood, sweat, and dirt splattering the chairs. I wasn't stuck up, but I was a lady. The last thing I needed was to worry about one of the few dresses I owned getting stained. I picked the chair that seemed the least filthy and gingerly sat on the edge.

"Well, get back to it, you bunch of daisy-headed bulls!" he barked.

Master Damon guided the men through several formations. I watched with rapt attention, having never had the chance to study the combat aspect of Dragon Riding. They worked laboriously and the stench of sweat filled the air. Their muscles trembled with effort as they lifted the large rectangle shields, trying to protect their fellow men from the chalk-tipped arrows. When struck, they removed themselves from formation and stood off to the side, leaning against their shields.

By the fifth chime, sixteen soldiers remained. As the chimes rang through the grounds, relief swept through them. Their shoulders slumped, and they wiped the sweat from their brows. Still, they awaited dismissal from Master Damon. He stepped off his crate and went through each man's weaknesses and strengths. He instructed those who struggled, suggesting different techniques and tactics to prevent gaps in various formations. After dismissing them, he motioned for me to join him.

Master Damon walked much slower than Willhelm. My stomach rumbled, and hunger weakened my knees. I was thankful for the steady pace.

"Miss Avyanna, did you learn anything today?" he asked. His thin lips darted upward as if he was doing his best to entertain me.

"I did, Master. I learned how hard the men work to protect one another."

"Eh?" He cupped an ear and leaned closer, eyes darting down to my lips as if to read them.

I took a deep breath to project my voice and repeated myself.

He nodded, pleased by my answer. "That they do, miss. They know their safety not only relies on their own abilities, but the abilities of their fellow man."

"And what of the Dragon Riders? How do they protect the soldiers?" Heads turned our way at my half-yelled question.

Master Damon regarded me thoughtfully. "Ah, you were the First Chosen that the dragon ignored last year, aren't you, lass?"

"Yes, sir." My words were firm, but I couldn't help but drop my gaze to my feet as I said them. "The hatchling chose a Second Chosen. Their bond is strong... the dragonling was not meant for me."

"You'll be offered as First Chosen a second time, will you not?"

"Aye." I smiled, letting the truth of that statement chase away my defeat. "That I will."

"It would be good of a Rider to think of how they can protect the men as the men work to protect the Riders," he said, returning to my question. "I suppose the dragons could protect the soldiers, but they're more useful for offense. They do too much damage to be placed elsewhere."

"But what of the dragons that defend the homelands? Why are they here if they're too valuable at the front?" I wondered.

"The Dragon Kind who safeguard our homelands are mostly older dragons with weaker fire capabilities."

"So if a dragon and its Rider are orderly and have no trouble with fire, would they be placed at the front?"

"You want to be placed at the front, girl?" he asked, baffled.

"I do." I met his incredulous gaze with a firm nod. "It's where I belong."

He stopped in his tracks and stared at me, waiting for an explanation.

"My father died on the front lines. I belong there—to take his place."

"Avenge him, you mean?"

My hands clasped in front of me. The Shadows took my father. They robbed me of ever truly knowing him. His death separated me from my mother and left her alone in a remote village. They stole the life I was meant to have, and I would make them pay.

"Regardless, I will take his place," I said, walking ahead.

Master Damon stared at me for a moment longer before chuckling and continuing on. "Women belong at home—Dragon Riders or not. The front lines are no place for the softness of women."

My lips twisted into a frown. "Women should be allowed to go where they want." The words flew out, and I bit my lip in an attempt to cut off the harsh retort.

It wasn't in my nature to talk back to authority, but his statement struck a nerve. My dragon and I would be on the front lines. We would slake our need for vengeance upon those who had not only taken my own father, but orphaned countless others.

Master Damon continued walking, but turned to me with a raised eyebrow in question. "If you knew a crumb of the things that happen there," he closed his eyes for a moment and shuddered, "you would not be so eager to join them."

It was true; I didn't know what happened at the front, but I could read. Shadow Men stole the dragons' magic and wreaked havoc against us. They unleashed it in sick and twisted ways, poisoning our lands. I had read stories of Riders separated from their dragons. Tainted by the magic that had been ripped from their dragons, they were the true monsters on the battlefield. They turned into empty shells of their former selves, somehow retaining the blood-magic of their dragons, and used their fouled gifts against those they once called allies.

I read stories of beasts that were once men being unleashed upon our armies. They feasted on soldiers, eating them alive. Once their victims passed the Veil, they left what remained of their carcasses to rot.

No, I may not have seen the horrors firsthand, but I knew the stories.

When we arrived back at Master Damon's office, Willhelm was waiting, leaning against the wall. I noted his easy confidence as he watched the passing men. "Master Damon, what rank is Sir Willhelm?" I asked.

"See those arrows on his shoulders? He's a Sergeant." He nodded at Willhelm across the way.

There were four crossed arrows on the sleeve of Willhelm's tunic, black against the off-white linen. It bothered me that I knew nothing about the ranks or how they were depicted. I would have to visit the Records Room to learn more about these men I would be fighting alongside.

It was half past the fifth chime when we arrived. I joined Willhelm's side with an apologetic smile. "Thank you for waiting for me."

"Miss Avyanna." Master Damon's low voice made me stop and turn to face him. "Never let me hear of you walking through the barracks without an escort again. You might be used to dealing with rebellious lads, snotty children, or petty women, but do not let yourself be fooled. These soldiers would like nothing more than to ruin a sweet girl like you." His tone brooked no debate. With a final stern look, he entered his office, leaving Willhelm to escort me to the school grounds.

Over the next few days, we settled into an easy routine. I woke, grabbed a bite to eat on the way along with a bit for later, and headed to the wall. Willhelm waited for me each morning, escorting me to Master Damon's office.

Willhelm was a gentleman, but not necessarily a sweet man. He was short and curt with the other men, expecting nothing less than obedience. By the end of the day, though, he was always more relaxed and easygoing.

I learned that he had been orphaned at a young age, as was the case with far too many soldiers. He attended Northwing, but at sixteen-winters moved to the barracks. He didn't aspire to be a great General or even fight on the front lines, though he would if he was ordered. The structure and routine of military life pleased him. He appreciated the purpose behind it and the lack of idleness.

After arriving at the office, I would organize documents, dust, and sweep. Under careful scrutiny, I was permitted to rearrange shields. A Shield Master had far more to do than teach people how to use a shield, which was my original assumption. Shields were Master Damon's life. He collected, studied, and designed them. He lived and breathed them. I listened to his endless rambles about where each shield came from. He gave rigorous details of why a design differed from others, and whether that design could be implemented or useful to our army.

It was usually around the eleventh chime that he left for his scheduled rounds. He did not teach all shields-men classes. Instead, he rotated through the outfits to troubleshoot their lessons and make sure they performed as expected.

Around midday, I ate what I had brought from the dorms that morning. I went out more often to watch the blacksmith work, whose name I learned was Elib. He was a rather quiet man, which I found so striking because of his large stature.

He crafted different, private shield designs for Master Damon and worked from sunup to sundown. On warmer days, I'd fetch him water from the well a few paces away from the office. Surely that didn't count as gallivanting off on my own. Elib was always pleasantly surprised and thankful when I did. I noticed he often got so involved with his work that he skipped midday meal. The least I could do was remind him to drink.

By the third chime, Master Damon sent someone to escort me to the arena. There, I watched him instruct his classes for the next two chimes—the highlight of my day. I learned more and more about formations used against arrows, catapults, horses, armed men, beasts, and many others. Master Damon was thorough and worked the men rigorously through their paces.

It was two days until the end of my term with Master Damon when the first Dragon Kind arrived. I was in the armory office, studying a particular shield from the southern lands, when I heard the first bellow. Familiar exhilaration flooded through me, and I rushed to the window.

A great blue dragon swooped low over the buildings with a delighted roar that shook the bubbled glass panes. A smile spread over my face as I glimpsed the Rider harnessed on its back, whooping with the same elation. It was a younger pair, clearly excited to be home.

Dragon Riders trained at the King's schools for three years before they left for the war front. There, they studied under experienced Dragon Riders fighting the war. They were kept out of harm's way as much as possible until their fifth year, when they joined them on the battlefield. Because of the Shadow Men, a Rider was lucky if they made it past their first year of actual combat.

Sunlight shone through the dragon's opaque wings as it glided over the armory office, and I ran outside to admire it. Its white talons flashed in the light, and its glittering tail lashed from side to side as it flew. It circled a few more times before heading to the Dragon Canyon, where all dragons and Riders lived.

It was a thick gorge, straight through an enormous mountain, with natural caverns hollowed and dug out further by Dragon Kind. They provided shelter from the elements and stayed cool in the summer. During the winter, those who remained retreated to the hot springs below the school.

Still smiling, I returned to my task. Hatching Day was a few months away. The idea of flying like that, wind tugging at my hair, tearing through the sky—a shiver of excitement ran through me. The freedom and liberties it would allow me were hard to fathom.

I went back to attempting to organize the shields but was suddenly absent minded, as I could only think of which hatchling would be mine in just a few short months.

Chapter Five

Willhelm led me back to the barracks' gate at sunset. The sky, painted with hues of golden orange and pink-kissed clouds, took my breath away. Its glow highlighted the magnificent dragons teeming above. Most of them thrived for this seasonal change, especially the beasts who protected the homelands their entire lives.

Two young dragonlings who were too small for their Riders, weaved beside each other, racing and testing each other's skills. They were the size of large horses and taunted one another with mock roars and little bursts of flame. This was perhaps their second Hatching Day coming up, and they were showing good growth.

"You're assigned to the barracks for another two weeks?" Willhelm asked.

Men still milled about, wrapping up tasks before dark. Now accustomed to my presence, most barely gave me a second glance.

"Yes. I'm due to assist General Rafe tomorrow morning. Originally, Master Elon was next on my schedule, but I received word of the change weeks ago. Perhaps the General's injury has something to do with it."

Willhelm grunted, and I glanced over to see him frowning. We'd built up quite a friendship during my term with Master Damon. I looked forward to his pleasant company. Though sometimes it felt as if he treated me like a child, there was a mutual respect between us. He was kind and gentle, nothing like my peers at the school.

When his sullen demeanor lingered, I prodded. "What is it?"

"General Rafe hasn't been here in the homelands for quite some time. I've heard some rumors about him."

"Like what?" I asked. When he didn't answer, I moved into his path, causing him to pull up short. With an encouraging grin, I raised a brow. "What rumors? They might be helpful if he's a prickly soul."

His eyes sought mine before he grimaced and stepped around me. "I won't gossip about a General. All I'll say is when someone is absent from proper company for a length of time, they tend to forget what proper company requires."

"Ah, so he's rude. I can handle that." I laughed, gesturing to the men bustling about. "These past weeks have supplied me with plenty of practice dealing with impudence."

In truth, my time in the barracks left me happier than expected. Sure, I was out of place, as if a bright sign that read 'Look at me!' was plastered to my forehead. I didn't even see laundry maids or female cooks anywhere. I was alone in my femininity, yet it still felt more like home than the school grounds ever did.

These men—well, they were men. They weren't insolent boys or devious girls, or cranky old women who had nothing better to do than critique your life. Yes, they were brash and sometimes absentmindedly vulgar, but despite their rough edge, they were honest. The few who escorted me throughout the weeks proved to be quite polite in their own way. It was like they knew their purpose in life, and weren't squabbling over what someone else was doing, or that someone else wanted the same thing they wanted.

"You'll be fine, I'm sure. You're a resilient one." Willhelm broke from his reverie as we neared the gate and offered me a faint grin.

Though the smile was small, it delighted me to see he was at ease in my company. With Willhelm, or even the blacksmith, Elib, it felt as though I were taming a wild horse. I had to be gentle and friendly to urge them out of their stoic, closed-off, man-made shells. Elib even took brief breaks during my midday meal just to sit and make quiet conversation about the things that happened on the barracks' side.

"General Rafe was due to arrive today, but I didn't notice a caravan. Do you think he's late?" I asked, pausing at the gate.

"Oh, he's here. He doesn't like to make a scene."

This surprised me. I thought perhaps there would be a small gathering or something of the kind when he arrived. I hadn't heard of anything, but students were not often invited to such functions. Perhaps his injury left him incapacitated for the time being.

"After being away for so long, you'd think a celebration would be in order," I said, taken aback.

"Miss Avyanna," Willhelm waited until I lifted my eyes to meet his before he finished, "be wary of him."

"Of course."

I tucked Willhelm's warning away in my mind. Although it excited me to have another few weeks in the barracks, I wouldn't allow that excitement to cloud my judgment or affect my behavior.

"Thank you, Sir Willhelm," I said, turning to leave.

"You're welcome, Avyanna."

My steps faltered a bit, but I kept walking, crossing to the school grounds. He had never addressed me without a title before. No one really had, besides my peers, who couldn't care less about titles. Something about the way he said it conveyed friendship. Was it even appropriate for one as young as I to be friends with a man so much older? If I was asked weeks ago, I'd have said a friendship between a woman and a man was improper. Yet the easy connection and respect we shared was far better than any relationship I had with the girls on the school grounds.

Willhelm was my first real taste of friendship, and it thrilled me to death.

In all honesty, his age didn't bother me. I'd rather be friends with older people, who were more worldly and knowledgeable. I seemed to have more in common with the older generation, anyway.

After stopping by the secretary to return my order for Master Damon and retrieve my order for General Rafe, I skipped dinner and headed straight to my room. It was only a little past the eighth chime, but I wanted to rise early and be fully awake and prepared when I met Willhelm in the morning.

I didn't know what to expect from General Rafe, but it delighted me that I would learn under a real General in the army. One day, he may fight alongside me on the battlefield.

I readied for sleep and climbed into bed, dreaming about flying and fighting on the front lines with my dragon-to-be.

I woke just as the sun brightened the sky. Smiling, I rolled off my cot, stretched, and let out a yawn. As I folded my blanket, I hummed a happy tune, glancing out my tiny slit for a window. The sunrise lit the sky with beautiful colors, where a black dragon flew in lazy circles amongst the sparse clouds. I fluffed my pillow and walked to the basin to rinse my mouth and wash my face. I was eager for today to begin, to see Willhelm, and meet an actual General.

After changing into my blue dress, I sat on the stool in front of my vanity, debating what to do with my hair. What tasks would a General need help with? I didn't have the slightest idea, but I hoped it was hard work, therefore my hair went into braids yet again. If this General was in fact a prickly soul as Willhelm alluded, I needed to get on his good side. I had dealt with rude individuals before, and the key to avoiding outbursts was quite simple; find out what made them angry and do the opposite.

A wise Master once told me not to look at people as bad, but look at them as broken.

I was sure this General had seen many horrors on the battlefield and was probably scarred inside and out. Until I figured out what made him comfortable, staying quiet and reserved seemed like the best idea. I was determined to make a good impression. I wanted him to remember me when I joined the ranks as a Dragon Rider.

Finishing my hair, I nodded to myself, pleased with my reflection, and pulled on my boots. Today was promised to be warm and sunny, but sandals didn't seem reasonable for chores on the barracks' side. I grabbed my order to enter the barracks, glanced over my room one last time, then headed out to the hall, shutting the door behind me.

In the common room, I helped myself to a piece of bread and dried apple. Fresh fruits were not in season yet, so dried was my only option. I pocketed extra for later in case this General did not take the midday meal, I wouldn't go hungry.

On my way down the stairs, I smiled at the few elderly women I passed at this early hour. Buzzing with excitement, I sped past the secretary, carefully avoiding the group of younger men huddled in the foyer. This morning started so well, I wanted to avoid anything that might spoil it.

Holding myself back from sprinting down the path, I breathed deeply. Flowers were in full bloom and their perfume wafted through the air. The trees were budding as well. Soon, their leaves would thicken enough to provide shade over the benches and workshops. The birds chirped, singing their songs as they prepared nests for the little ones soon to come.

A smile spread over my face as I thought about the little one that would come for me. I refused to think about the worst-case scenario. A dragonling would hatch for me this year. I just knew it.

When I arrived at the gate, my brows furrowed as Willhelm's usual spot was empty. He'd always been here before me, waiting to escort me. As I showed the guard my new orders, I stretched onto my toes, scanning the crowd in search of him. When I spotted him making his way toward us, I noticed the deep crease on his face, pinching his features into a scowl. I couldn't help but wonder what delayed him.

"Good morn, Willhelm." I braved the use of his name without a title, tilting my head at him as the guard handed me back my orders with a nod.

The guards frowned at me less as the days went on, getting used to my coming and going.

"I'm not sure that it will be a good morn, but morning nonetheless," he muttered. After a deep breath, he straightened and nodded to the guards.

I took my place at his side and he led us east, toward an area of the barracks I hadn't been to. "What's happened?" I asked, trying to figure out what upset him.

"Our newly returned General has shaken things up a bit is all."

Frowning, I tilted my head as I peered up at him. Willhelm was not one to lose his temper, or talk ill of anyone without reason, as I had been learning.

"Oh? What did he do?"

He watched me for a moment, as if judging whether he was required to share this knowledge, or if by friendship or acquaintanceship, he would tell me of his own will.

"He's demanded the companies to be ready at first light and will personally inspect our training. Every bit of it."

"That doesn't sound so bad. Surely he's just checking the progress of the companies."

"You don't realize what he's ordered." He cast me an incredulous expression. "He's asked the soldiers to go through everything they know about the battlefield in one morn. From riding to fighting, to hunting, and even bathing–" Willhelm bit it off with a curse.

My eyes rounded as I had never heard him curse, and I pressed my lips together. Surely, bathing was an important subject on the war front. People would get filthy, and proper hygiene was important to promote the health of the army. Without proper hygiene, something as simple as a foot fungus could incapacitate an entire company. However, I could assume being overseen as to how thoroughly one bathes would never be taken without offense.

"He's just finished with the first company of cadets. He's given half a chime reprieve before the second company."

"That means I'm already late," I groaned as my shoulders drooped.

Had I already made a terrible impression? Tardiness was a flaw in a person's character and the punishment was harsh on school grounds. I could only assume it was far worse in a military setting.

"No, he's just early."

"Which means I'm late," I said, dejected.

"You didn't know. He was told that you were coming and never sent for you earlier, therefore I can safely speculate that he didn't want to see you any earlier."

I nodded, trying to let his words assure my heart that I was not in the wrong. There was a bustle of activity around me and, for once, not a single soldier eyed me. They were all far too preoccupied with whatever task they were set to.

"Avyanna, you understand there will be times you will not be of assistance and asked to leave?"

"Aye."

I had read of company inspections, though they were usually one per company, per day. There were many reviews a commanding officer oversaw, yet I could guess at the ones that Willhelm implied I would be absent for; the evaluations of physical fitness and hygiene—in which the men would be immodestly dressed, if at all.

I had no quarrel with being sent away for those. I had no more desire to see a naked man than I had to clean the dung pits of the Dragon Canyon. However, I hoped to observe as much of the other inspections as I could to better acquaint myself with the men I would be flying over and fighting alongside.

With a sure nod, Willhelm led me through the throng. He pressed closer than would normally be appropriate, trying to shield me from the surge of other soldiers. Soon, we entered a large opening between two buildings that led to an expansive field crowded with soldiers, war horses, and fighting hounds.

My pulse quickened, gazing over the multitude. Nervous energy hung thick in the air, and I wasn't sure that General Rafe 'shaking things up' was such a bad thing. It kept people on their toes and forced them out of their trivial routines. Regardless of whether it was an inconvenience, the soldiers hurried about with purpose.

"The General has taken his respite in that tent." Willhelm indicated a large canvas tent off to the side of the crowded field and walked me to the entrance. He stood only a pace away as he stepped forward to the entryway to announce my arrival. "General Rafe, your assistant, Miss Avyanna," he barked out.

The corner of my mouth lifted. I hadn't heard Willhelm use that tone before. It was all formality and respect. The cadence of a junior officer.

A grunt of acknowledgment sounded from inside, and nervous butterflies flitted through my stomach. I would finally meet a real General, a real ranking officer who fought the Shadows firsthand—and lived to tell the tale. A General who would lead soldiers under me as I flew on dragonback.

Willhelm held the tent flap open. Worry crinkled the corners of his eyes. He jerked his head toward the entrance, and I gave him my biggest smile as I stepped inside.

I entered and had the briefest moment of shock when my eyes landed on bare skin. A gasp escaped my lips as I looked at the back of a man. A man, or a mountain, I couldn't be sure, to be honest. He was massive, with broad shoulders tapering to a thick, muscled waist that I wouldn't be able to get my arms around. Scars littered that expansive back like stars in a night sky, some long and jagged and others small and smooth, as if from an explosion.

My line of sight was quickly blocked by Willhelm's strong form as he stepped in front of me. "Female present, sir," he barked.

Tension radiated off of him, presumably offended for my honor upon seeing a man immodestly clothed. My cheeks heated with shame, realizing now how blatantly I stared. I had stood there *gawking* at a half-naked man.

The General did not reply at first and Willhelm shifted, using his body to block my view as he walked about the tent. A tense moment lapsed, and I thought perhaps he would not respond at all.

"I am well aware the title 'Miss' implies one of the female gender."

That *voice*—his deep timbre stroked my very soul, sending chills down my spine. There were no words to convey its power. The depth alone was enough to intimidate anyone who heard it. His tone purred with confident authority.

Willhelm stiffened in front of me, coming to the same understanding I did. The General did not care that I was a woman, and he was immodest. So, the rules of society would not matter to this man, I gleaned.

"I would stay till you are clothed, sir," Willhelm bit out.

I clasped my hands, palms clammy and ears burning, as I stared at the floor. Muffled shouts came from outside as officers ordered their men about. Horses whinnied and dogs barked at each other. I knew the General was moving about as Willhelm continued to block my view, yet there wasn't a sound. How could someone so massive move so silently?

Finally, after a few long awkward moments of wondering if he would ever dress, Willhelm stepped aside. I dropped into a quick curtsy, unable to meet his eyes. Staring at the floor, I waited for him to say something... yet only silence reigned.

I cleared my throat and dared to look up at him. Opening my mouth to greet him, all words died in my throat as I took in his behemoth frame. He wore black boots and black cloth trousers. His untucked white tunic hung loose about his thighs. The sleeves were ripped at the seams, revealing solid arms lined with thick muscles that were crossed over his broad chest. His head was shaven, and his jaw was devoid of the beard that was commonplace on the King's grounds.

His top lip was raised in a slight snarl. When my gaze finally moved to meet his, I schooled my surprise, snapping my jaw shut, seeing the scrap of black cloth over his left eye. That was his injury from the Shadow Men. He lost an eye then, perhaps more, to them.

One eye did not diminish his glower, however, and it silenced any greeting I might have offered.

"Sergeant. Pray tell, why have you brought me a girl child?" he growled, looking me up and down unabashedly—probably the same foolish way I assessed him.

"She is your assistant, sir, to assist in any tasks that you may need of her."

"And to learn what you have to teach," I added, bristling that he called me a child.

His glare sharpened on me before snapping back to Willhelm. "Who put you up to this?" he snarled.

In a few strong strides, he was across the tent, drawing up to his full height before Willhelm. I was short, but Willhelm was an average man's height, and even then, he only reached the General's thick neck.

"Sir, she is tasked with assisting you." Willhelm held his ground. "This is no scheme."

I bit my lip, affronted that my being here would seem like some foolhardy trick. It was unusual, no doubt. However, the Masters wanted to give me the best fighting edge they could before my dragonling hatched. Unable to join the other yearling Dragon Riders in their combat training this year, the Masters granted me this small boon.

"General Rafe," I started, drawing his withering glare, "I have assisted Master Damon before you and was due to aid Master Elon. However, I was assigned to you upon the announcement of your arrival." I managed to get it all out, though my heart beat like a rabbit's when it sighted a hawk.

"Tell me," he moved toward me menacingly, crowding me, "what good is a girl like you to a General?"

He was so much taller than me, the top of my head barely met his chest. I took another step back. He kept coming, prowling in my direction like some animal. A dangerous glint flared in his eye.

"I—I don't know yet, sir. I can assist with paperwork, or organizing, or—"

"Enough!" he roared.

My back collided with a shelf, knocking its contents to the floor.

"General Rafe!" Willhelm shouted, voice laced with silent warning.

The General was far too close for comfort. I craned my head to meet his glare, his chest a mere breath from my face.

"I have no need for an assistant." His lip curled in disgust. "Get out," he ordered, not moving an inch.

I swallowed hard, hating that my nerves made the movement so noticeable. "It is my duty—" I breathed.

"Go!"

His bellow sent me darting out from under his looming body and into the middle of the room. Willhelm glanced at me, apprehension clenching his jaw as he stepped to my side. He could not stand up to a General without punishment, but perhaps I could. After all, I was not a soldier under his command. I was a Masters' assistant. General Rafe was intimidating and frightening, but I would not allow him to rob me of this opportunity.

I worked to collect my thoughts. "Sir, ignore my presence if you wish. I will make use of myself where I can. As I have stated, I am not here only to assist, but to learn."

He scoffed over my last words. "First off, I might be able to ignore your girlish presence, yet the men will not. Second, do I look like some school teacher, ready to help you learn your manners and etiquette, girl? No. I teach men, not children." Thankfully, he kept his distance this time, boots rooted to the ground.

Gritting my teeth, I took a calming breath. I would not be humiliated anymore, but I would leave with him knowing I was more than just some simpering babe.

Squaring my shoulders, I lifted my chin. "I, Avyanna of Gareth, have the right to learn of combat as First Chosen of the King's School. Combat I would see, if not partake in its practice."

Something akin to recognition flashed in his eye when I spoke my father's name. They had served together, though I wasn't sure if he remembered him. As it was, his name was the only chance I had.

"Of Gareth?" His voice softened a fraction, though it was nowhere near a normal man's pitch.

"My father, Gareth, gave his life for the King and homelands thirteen years ago," I said quietly, though as firmly as I could manage. I was willing to be taught, but I was not willing to be tread upon.

I followed his gaze as it moved to my hair, then my face and my eyes. His frown deepened, as if he was considering my statement. Would he remember my father? I was sure that between then and now the General had lost countless men. Still, I clung to the hope that his name would mean something.

"Combat is no place for a girl." General Rafe glowered, though his words held less bite.

"I will not be a girl, but a Dragon Rider, when I see the Shadow Men in combat." I glared, back rigid and feet braced beneath me. If he rejected me now, I would count my losses and leave, but I'd do so with my head held high.

Resignation crossed his face, but disappeared as quickly as it came. "You will stay out of sight. If you distract the soldiers, you will regret it."

I stifled my sigh of relief. "What would you have me do?" I asked.

"Whatever it is that girls do." Contempt burned in his stare.

That statement was like a slap in the face, but I had no time to retaliate as he stormed out of the tent before I could tell him as much.

"Sergeant!" the General barked, his shout making me jump.

Willhelm cast another glance my way, probably concerned I would wander outside. He headed out, following the General, and I heaved a sigh, deflating and losing all the false pride I had mustered.

Perhaps he remembered my father, perhaps not. He hadn't dismissed me, though. But he left me in his tent. How often would he return? He gave me no task, but I had to prove I wasn't an insignificant child. I was more than a servant or a footstool. My gender did not dictate my value, with or without a dragon.

Chapter Six

I soon learned that General Rafe was more than cold, hard, and brash. His personality bordered on cruel.

I tidied up the tent, which took the span of a few breaths, then stood there wondering what to do. I secured the tent flap to the post so I could see outside and watch the inspections. Barely half a chime passed when a soldier glanced my way with a wide grin. He was young, perhaps younger than his twentieth winter. I offered a small smile back, and within a blink of an eye, General Rafe stood before the entryway.

He cut off any greeting I might have offered. "Do you want to put on a show for the soldiers?" he demanded as his eyes wandered my body with rakish abandon.

My stomach turned at his insinuation. "No, sir," I bit out.

"Then make yourself scarce."

He spit the words with such venom, I could almost feel them singe my skin. I shot out from the tent, squeezing past him and toward the mill of soldiers.

"Girl!" he growled.

Taking a calming breath, I forced myself to stop and face him, heat nipping at my cheeks. As I turned, he tossed a bundle of black fabric. I fumbled to catch it as it collided with my chest. Without another word, he walked off for the training field. My jaw clenched tight as I examined what he'd thrown at me. A cloak. I shook as I put it on. Whether my trembling was due to fear or anger, I didn't know. Probably both. The heavy cloak was far too big on me and reeked of sweat. Disgust wrinkled my nose as I pulled up the hood and wrapped the garment around myself. As I started for the nearest building, I kept my head down and tried to hide the hem of my dress from peeking out.

Shadows concealed me from curious stares, and I slumped against the wall. Should I go back to the dorm secretary and let her know I was not welcome here? That General Rafe refused me?

My spine stiffened as soon as the thought crossed my mind. A dragonling already rejected me. I would not be spurned by a General—especially when my only task was to assist him. I refused to fail. My mind raced, seeking something, anything he might need, any way that I could make myself valuable.

The midday chime rang and several men looked toward the dining hall with longing. That sparked an idea, and I left the safety of the shadows to walk to the main street. I had a rough idea of where I was, thanks to Willhelm's intensive descriptions of the area. The parchments I studied during my time aiding Master Damon helped as well.

I headed down the road, keeping my head low and the cloak wrapped around me. If anyone thought it odd that someone would wear an over-cloak on a warm spring day, they were too busy to stop and question me. My quick and purposeful pace brought me to the armory office. At the sound of clanging metal, I rounded the building and found Elib at the forge.

"Good Day!" I called.

Elib lifted his head, goggles concealing his kind eyes. "Miss Avyanna?"

He returned his work to the forge and pulled up his goggles as I drew back my hood. Soot and grime covered his face, except for two moon-shaped circles around his eyes. I smiled and leaned over the gate to his work area.

"Elib, could you tell me where I could fetch some food for General Rafe? Would I be able to get him a tray at the dining hall?"

He looked at me as if I had grown a third head. "He sent you to fetch his meal?"

"No, I wish to fetch it for him of my own accord."

"He won't eat it, miss."

I shrugged. "If he's not hungry now, maybe he'll eat it later when he has a chance."

"No, you misunderstand." He came to stand closer to me, as if the distance kept me from hearing well. "He won't eat anything he doesn't prepare himself. He doesn't dine with the men."

I tilted my head, puzzled. Why would he distrust food so? Perhaps he had been poisoned once, though surely he knew there was no reason to distrust the people here. They would serve with him. We were united in the same goal.

"What does he eat? Only what he can hunt?"

"That, and what he forages," Elib agreed.

So even if I brought him bread and water, he would probably deny it. He had so many duties as a General already. To add the task of providing his own food to that list seemed ludicrous. I didn't want to give up. I latched onto this idea like a dog with a bone. If he had to work that hard for his food, in his free time, no less, I wanted to help him. I just had to think of a way.

"Elib, are there markets in the barracks?"

"Aye, the arms market by the gate."

"No, a food market?"

He shook his head and the corners of his mouth pulled down in a frown. If there was no food market on this side of the gate, then there wasn't one on the grounds at all. I only had one other option if I was going to find something for this General to eat.

"Thank you, Elib." I pushed off the gate and secured the cloak over my hair. The smith looked at me as he often did, as though I was a curious creature, before he shrugged and lowered his goggles.

With one hand, I hitched up the hem of my dress, and with the other fastened the cloak shut tight around me. I enjoyed the independence of walking around without an escort, however, I did not want to end up cornered in an alley like last time.

After showing my orders to the guards, I passed through the gate back onto the school grounds. I made my way down the paths, past the dorm and beyond the Masters' quarters, hoping they would not see me.

As I rounded the last bend toward the amphitheater, a sense of inadequacy twisted my heart. The towering building was the focus of so many of my night terrors. The reason I had to hide while slinking around the barracks, the reason I was not in classes with my fellow students or Riders. I shook my head and continued to the far edge of the school grounds. It took me half a chime to get this far, and it would take me even longer to get back. I could only hope this was worth it.

At the edge of the grounds, I pressed into the woods. Twigs and undergrowth grabbed at the cloak as I trudged through the thicket. This part was always the worst, but it opened up further in. The air was damp and cool, musty with wood rot and new growth. The thick canopy blocked the sun's warm rays. Nearly twenty paces in, I looked up at the tall trees, searching their trunks for a telltale plant. Spotting a vine with a small blue flower, I hurried toward it.

A prickleberry vine. It grew around a cluster of older trees. The vine itself was harmless to the trees, but sharp curved thorns decorated its main stem, waiting to latch onto any innocent passerby. I crept closer, looking for the bluish-gray pods I hoped were still there. Inside the pods were sweet, blue berries, the only fruit in season this early. The dorm cook would sometimes send erring students out here to fetch them as punishment.

Hope fluttered through my chest when I spotted plenty of them clustered amongst the tangle of thorns and vines. Evidently, no one had recently offended the cook. I released my hold on the cloak, letting it fall to the forest floor. Careful to avoid the thorns, I reached up and plucked a pod from the vine, pinching it off at the main stem. Surely the General would have no qualms eating them if they were still sealed inside their pod. I smiled to myself, more determined than ever that I would convince him of my worth.

I subjected myself to the prickleberry thorns for a quarter of a chime and was rewarded with two pockets full. My hands were cut to ribbons, regardless of the extra care I took. Grimacing at the swollen scrapes, I slipped into the heavy cloak and lifted the hood over my head. On the main path, I walked as briskly as I could without attracting attention. At the gate, I showed my order. My lips thinned, noticing my blood smeared on the parchment.

These guards weren't as familiar with me and looked curiously at my order and back to my hands. I bit my lip and shoved them inside the cloak. The one holding my orders shrugged and jerked his head, indicating I could move on.

I headed east, moving with the throng of soldiers, trying my best to keep the cloak shut. Someone bumped into me and panic speared through me, till I realized it was merely a coincidence. I darted between the gap in the buildings that Willhelm had taken me through, and I strode toward the General's tent, my steps quick with purpose.

The tent flap was closed, though when General Rafe sent me away, it was open. I stood there for a moment, unsure how to proceed. The training field didn't seem orderly enough for an inspection to be taking place. Also, with no sign of the General, it would be wiser to announce my presence before entering.

I cleared my throat and opened my mouth to do so when the flap jerked aside. A Commander almost barreled into me. I yelped and jumped out of his path as he cursed and spit on the ground. My heart cringed at the impropriety of spitting in the presence of a woman, but the cloak kept me hidden. He had no way of knowing.

The Commander stormed off, and I looked back at the tent's entryway, now filled by General Rafe's hulking frame. He stood stiff and silent, seething at me. He gave me the cloak I was hiding in, so of course he knew who I was. I swallowed and licked my dry lips. I could do this. He was a bear of a man, but he wouldn't hurt me. At least not physically… I didn't think.

"General Rafe, I come with refreshments," I said, giving him my bravest smile, though the corners of my mouth trembled with the effort.

He reached toward me, but I gave my brain no chance to retreat. I ducked under his arm and into the tent. Instant regret flooded me as I spun to face him, seeing the tent flap fall. To be alone with a Master was one thing. Being alone in a tent with a man who had the attitude of a wild boar was another.

Spying a small tray on the desk, I started for it, turning so that my back was never to the General. He was practically frothing at the mouth; I assumed because I dared come back. Yet he made no move to order me away.

I removed the cloak, draping it over a spare seat before emptying my pockets. An overripe pod had burst and a deep purple splotch stained my dress. I cringed. It would be near impossible to get out. I placed the pods on the tray as neatly as my trembling hands could manage.

That settled, I retrieved the cloak to secure it on the rack. There, I noticed the wash basin was stained red. With blood? I spun to face the General. The black swath of cloth still covered his left eye, but the injury did not appear aggravated. My eyes scanned his body, and for the first time, I noticed the dragon tattoo on his right shoulder. The dragon would normally be the General's insignia patched into his tunic. With his apparent distaste for sleeves, he must have just had it tattooed on.

His knuckles were red and bloody, as if from a fight. I frowned, though I made no move toward him. He didn't seem like the type of man who'd appreciate someone trying to play nursemaid.

"I'll fetch you fresh water for washing," I stated.

I grabbed the basin, heaving it with all my might. He didn't move as I neared the entryway and I had to squeeze past him to get outside. Grunting, I hauled the basin further away before emptying the contents.

The General was exactly where I left him. His dark eye watched me as I returned the basin, then left to retrieve fresh water from a well to fill it. I did my best to ignore the heat of his stare as I looked about the room. There were no rags or bandages to be seen, so I took it upon myself to find him something he could bind his hands with.

"I'll return momentarily. I just need to fetch something."

I turned to exit the tent. Tension radiated off him and I wondered if I had gone too far. Yet as I squeezed past him, he didn't move to harm me. I left for the field, leaving him to his brooding anger.

Still no words. Perhaps he didn't trust his tongue in his gratitude.

Surely, if we were on a field where inspections involving swordplay were held, there would be a Healer about. I scanned the crowd for the bright white and blue robes, but saw none. However, a soldier snared my notice. He looked me up and down, then back at General Rafe's tent with a smirk. In my ignorance, I wondered what he was thinking when a flash of white caught my eye. Without thought, I ran and rounded a corner of a building where I saw a Healer walking away.

"Hail! Healer!" I rushed to him as he turned toward my call.

"Child? What are you doing here?" The older Healer glanced around, likely searching for a Master or escort, anything to determine why I'd be there.

"I am under orders to assist General Rafe. I am in need of clean wrappings. His hands have suffered an injury," I pleaded, clasping my fingers in front of my chest in a show of respect.

"His hands have dealt more injury than—child, what happened to your hands?"

He drew my hands apart, studying the hundreds of tiny scratches. My marred skin burned with inflammation, but I knew it would soon go away. Though the open, deeper wounds would take more time to heal.

"Only prickleberry scrapes. Nothing to concern yourself over," I assured him.

"Child, I will give you bandages for your wounds, but nothing for that scoundrel of a General unless he asks it directly of me." He jerked his head with a sharp, defiant nod. "You pass that along."

He shuffled through the bag strapped to his shoulder. The pouch held potions, wrappings, and a few fresh herbs. The Healer passed me clean bandages and a small vial of liquid.

"Rub this tincture on the lacerations. It will not speed the healing process, but it will lessen any pain and inflammation."

"Thank you, very much." I bowed my head before turning away.

Upon arriving at the General's tent, I noted the open flap and ducked inside, taking that as an invitation. My steps stumbled to a halt. Prickleberry pods littered the floor and the tray that I had set them on was thrown across the room. General Rafe was sitting at the desk, with his back to me, studying a piece of parchment.

My pride stung as much as my hands as I gawked at the terrible mess.

"Learn your place," he muttered the words in that deep voice of his, and though he never looked away from the parchment, I knew they were meant for me.

I gritted my teeth and stormed over to his desk, smashing the bandages down. My hand remained on top so he could see the results of the effort I went through to retrieve the berries.

"My *place* is to be your fire-blasted assistant!" I snarled. "The Masters have ordered me to assist you, and assist you, I shall."

"I've no desire to play nursemaid to a child," he said cooly, ignoring my wounds.

"I am no child!" I hissed through clenched teeth. "This will take the sting out of your hands, but not your words." I slammed the vial on his parchment and whirled to start on the mess.

A steel arm wrapped around my waist, jerking me back. An iron hand clamped over my mouth. It muffled my scream as my body crashed back onto his muscled chest, leaving no room between us. My heart rose into my throat, and the blood drained from my face. I had never touched a man. Ever. This man took that experience without consent, General or no. I bit at his hand and stomped my feet on top of his, seeking freedom.

His deep laugh vibrated through his chest and against my ear. "At least I'm only using my words."

He released me and I stumbled forward, sprawling to the floor. Prickleberry juice stained patches on my dress. I spun and sat up in a crouch, eyes wide with terror. My heart hammered a panicked beat in my chest that resonated through my ears. Every instinct screamed for me to run.

His dark eye narrowed. Bitterness and hatred were almost tangible as he stepped around me to the entryway. "Oh, and one more thing." He paused, turning back. "Clean up this thrice-cursed mess."

And with that, he stormed out of the tent, leaving me quaking with fearful rage.

Chapter Seven

I stood inside General Rafe's tent in my stained, filthy dress, wondering if I could take any more of his foul mood. He hadn't returned since he... *assaulted* me? Assault was a good word for it. He didn't hurt me—other than my pride—but he certainly put the fear of the Shadows into me.

On his departure, he left the tent flap down, so I couldn't see the training fields, and I wasn't eager to open it and peer out. Maybe tomorrow I would be braver, but today I had exhausted my mental stores of valor.

"Sergeant Willhelm to fetch Miss Avyanna," he called.

I took a deep breath to calm my frayed nerves and ducked under the flap. Willhelm's eyebrows rose as he took in the stains covering my dress, and I bit my lip to keep from tearing up. I was relieved to see him, but just wanted to head back to the dorms. School ground bullies were monsters I knew how to cope with. General Rafe was a whole different beast.

Willhelm didn't say a word. He simply motioned me to his side, and today I crowded a little closer to him as we walked away. When we reached the main road, he broke the silence.

"Do you wish to talk about it?" he asked gently, studying me from the corner of his eye.

I refused to meet his gaze. If I acknowledged his concern, I would only end up weeping like a babe. Perhaps if I replied with one-word answers, my voice wouldn't break. "No."

"Avyanna?"

When I didn't respond, Willhelm took a sudden turn and led me beside a building. It didn't hide us from those passing by, but it was private enough to speak more freely.

"Did he hurt you?"

I closed my eyes, trying to hold it together. I felt every bit the seventeen-winters I was—weak and helpless, and Willhelm was not helping that.

"Avyanna, I need to know if he hurt you." His voice held an edge of anger. Not at me, I was sure, but at General Rafe.

I shook my head and gathered enough courage to peer up. The concern blanketing his face tightened my throat. "Nothing but my pride," I assured him.

His eyebrows snapped together in a harsh frown, and he dipped his chin, accepting my answer. "Remember, even a General is not above the law."

I nodded and looked past him toward the crowded road. I just wanted the safety of my room. He seemed to understand that and led me back. We traveled to the gate in silence. I held out my order to the guards and heard a hiss from Willhelm when he saw my hands.

"It was my own doing," I murmured.

"And what exactly were you doing?" he asked.

"Picking berries. It was completely unrelated to my duties today." Which was the truth. Partly. I had tried to go the extra mile, and be better than what was required of me—look where that got me.

Willhelm grunted and nodded to the guards when they passed my orders back.

"I'll see you tomorrow, Willhelm," I said, crossing onto school grounds.

"You don't have to. Go, tell the Masters what happened," he urged.

No. I couldn't let the General beat me. There was no way I'd give up now. "I'll see you tomorrow," I repeated, turning away.

Tomorrow was a new day. Tomorrow, things would be better. Today taught me a lesson, yet I wouldn't let that defeat me. Yes, I was discouraged—I was angry and hurt. However, I had dealt with similar situations my whole life. My peers thought me nothing more than a bookworm and a prude, doomed to be a dusty old hag.

When the bullying began, I learned how to deal with it or hide away. Very few sought my friendship, and I had nothing to offer those who did. I lived my life for myself, my mother, and to avenge my father. Today, I might have lost a battle, but I would win the war.

The next morning, I rose with a hunger in my belly. I had skipped dinner again last evening, and I was ravenous.

After tidying my room, I stared at my blue dress with an ache in my chest. Those stains would never come out. I could at least wear it while doing hard labor, though the purple splotches stood out so much—I'd look foolish. Still, the dress was intact and served its purpose. I wouldn't throw it out.

I dressed in my only other acceptable clothing, my beige working-dress, and laid the ruined one by my door. Last night, I hadn't quite felt up to being around the gossiping women, or anyone else for that matter, to tackle the stains. It would have to wait till tonight.

Foregoing my usual braids, I settled on a simple bun and slipped my boots on. I didn't have enough coin for a new dress. I'd been saving to buy my mother a gift for the next winter. Perhaps I could get by with my beige dress if I washed it often. It would wear out sooner, but I had no other options. I would have to apply myself for more odd jobs from the Masters.

Upon entering the hall, I nearly bumped into a woman bustling down the corridor. She glared at me as she hurried past, ignoring my muttered apology. I took a deep breath. Today would be better than yesterday. If each day was what you make of it, I would make today a fine day.

In the common room, I snagged two rolls and stopped to put a dab of butter on them. I reached for the dried prunes, but a shrill voice had me pulling my hand back.

"Feeling gluttonous this morning, are we?" Vivian called, walking into the room.

Food wasn't scarce here on the King's grounds, but it was a precious commodity. With the King providing for so many of his subjects, the butter was spread awfully thin.

I made a face at her and grabbed a prune, anyway.

"You take enough for two people," she sneered. "One would wonder why you still resemble a stick."

"Vivian, leave her be," an older woman chided over her cup of tea. "She hasn't even come to dinner the past two nights."

Vivian gave me a shrewd scowl, and I slipped past her, rushing down the stairs.

She supplied me with yet another reason to enjoy the company of older generations.

As I passed the secretary's desk, I paused, thinking she might tell me I was excused from my assignment assisting the General. A strange part of me hoped she would. Would it still be considered a failure if General Rafe requested my dismissal? When she looked up, it was with a question as to why I stalled, not an order.

"Good morn. I trust there has been no change to my assignment?" I asked.

"Good day, Avyanna. There's none that I am aware of. Should there be?"

"No, no," I said quickly. "I was only checking."

She raised a skeptical brow, but nodded just the same.

Outside, the overcast sky did a magnificent job of mirroring my mood. Dark and looming, with the promise of rain. I shuddered and lifted my chin. Today would be fine. Would they still have the inspections if it rained? Battle waited for no weather. Though, one risked catching a plague. If they were just training, I didn't see why they would risk illness for an inspection that could be accomplished any other day.

General Rafe didn't seem like the type of man to put things off, however. He didn't seem like any man I had ever known.

At the gate, a small smile crept over my face when I saw Willhelm waiting for me, leaning on the gatepost.

"Morning!" I called, handing my papers to the guards.

Willhelm didn't move, but his eyes tracked my hands. The swelling had gone down, though the scratches remained. It felt... different to have someone other than my mother be so protective of me. He cared, and knowing that made me feel just a little better.

"Good morn, Avyanna." He straightened as the guards handed my papers back.

"Inspections still going on?" I asked.

"For the next week, I'm afraid." He fell into step beside me. "My company is due for review today."

"Oh, is it? I'm sure you'll do well!" I smiled and glanced over, noting his frustration.

"I can only hope," he sighed. "He's set grueling tasks for those who don't meet his standards."

"What time is your inspection?"

"At the fourth chime. Though I might be late to pick you up today. Yesterday, there was a brawl that delayed things."

I thought about the General's bloody knuckles. "Did General Rafe assault someone?"

Willhelm looked at me, then back at the ground, perhaps figuring out how he could word it without sounding like he was bad-mouthing a General.

"He came back to the tent with bloody knuckles," I explained.

"If you determine who starts a fight by who throws the first punch," Willhelm scratched his jaw, "then he didn't start it. Though he finished it."

I smirked. Apparently, I wasn't the only one that General Rafe tried to draw out the worst in.

"He's in a worse mood than he was yesterday," he warned as we rounded a building toward the training field.

"I do believe he lives his life in a foul mood," I muttered.

He grunted in agreement as we neared the tent. Unbound by the same principles as Willhelm, I generally thought well of people, but General Rafe was the exception. I couldn't manage a single pleasant thought of the brute.

"Sergeant Willhelm, announcing Miss Avyanna," Willhelm called, standing at attention.

Today I stood further back. I would take as much distance from the General as I could get.

There was a sound of acknowledgment, and Willhelm lifted the tent flap, peering in before motioning me inside. As I entered, I stayed close to his side. He wouldn't be here with me long, as he had to ready his company, but I would take any sense of security I could get.

General Rafe was washing his face in the washbasin with his back toward us. He wore the same type of clothes as yesterday; black pants with a loose white tunic with the sleeves torn off. There was no cloth wrapped around his head, and I wondered if he would attempt to frighten me with his battle wounds.

He finished washing and bent down to tie a wet cloth around his head, covering his missing eye before he faced us. Water dripped from the cloth to his shirt, and he stood there, staring at us as if daring me to make the first move.

I dropped into a deep curtsy and lowered my gaze to the ground.

"Well, Sergeant, are you going to stand there and babysit her all day?" he asked, smirking between us.

As I straightened, my lips pressed together to hold back my retort. I was no child to be entertained. I was there to help him, if he would only allow me.

"I'll escort her to the gate after my company's inspection," Willhelm ground out. With a slight bow of his head, he turned and left.

General Rafe glared as Willhelm took his leave, and my pulse took off like an arrow. I contemplated whether or not I should have come, or if I should have stayed at the dorms. What could I learn from this man anyway, besides how to be intimidating without saying a word?

"You sew, girl?" he asked, stalking in my direction.

"I mend," I breathed. Yesterday's events flashed through my mind in horrifying detail as I took a step back.

To my relief, he turned to a small table and retrieved a black tunic with detailed stitching worthy of a General, but well beyond my capabilities. He tossed it at me and I barely caught it before it hit my face. I examined it, seeing the sleeves hadn't been torn off, but it had been sewn without them. Some seamstress had custom-made this for him.

"Maybe having a girl assistant won't be so bad," he sneered.

Normally I would have taken a remark like that as progress. However, the tone he used made it an insult.

He started toward the tent flap to leave, and I inspected the tunic. It was torn at the yoke where decorative flaps were buttoned in place. It looked as though one had been torn loose and the black wooden button was missing. I opened my mouth to tell him I needed the button, or to admit that the stitching was beyond me.

I must have made some sound, because he paused and shot me a glare. "Now be a good girl and fix it," he said, then stormed through the tent flap, leaving it waving behind him.

I bit my tongue and gripped the tunic tight. The way he spoke to me made my blood boil. I closed my eyes and tilted my head back, teeth bared in a silent scream.

This was progress. It was definitely progress. He had a task for me, and I would do it.

It took me all morning to locate thread, and even longer to find a wooden button. I managed to find one of similar shape, but not black. Procuring ink to dye it, I sat in the General's chair while it dried on a piece of bark I'd found lying about. The tent flap hung open just enough to allow me to see the inspections through a small crack, though my attention was never on the field for long. It was enveloped with the cursed stitching.

As all girls in the King's school, I'd been taught how to mend. It was useful when trying to earn extra coin, and even caring for your own clothes. However, I was no seamstress. The woman who had sewn this tunic hid all her stitching. I struggled to figure out how she had managed it.

I was bent over in the chair, making a minuscule stitch, when suddenly the tent flap whipped aside. I yelped and jerked back from the entryway. My sudden movement toppled the chair with me in it. My hand held fast to the needle and thread, and my stitches bunched with the tension of my fall.

A string of curses climbed up my throat, but I bit them back as I straightened. It did not surprise me in the least to see General Rafe standing in the entryway with a smirk on his face. I glared at him and righted the chair, pulling it toward his desk as he walked in. He didn't say a word to me, and I watched him out of the corner of my eye as I picked up the tunic and tucked the needle in.

I turned to ask if he needed any assistance when I saw him tugging his tunic free from his trousers. My mouth went dry with panic as he walked straight to the washbasin and jerked his tunic off in one smooth motion. I stood there, horrified at the sight of bare skin, before scrambling out of the tent to stand by the door, gasping.

If another soldier had walked in and seen his state of undress with a woman present, our reputations would be ruined.

He could have ruined me.

I ground my teeth together as I stood there, tunic in hand, watching the hundreds of soldiers pass by. Any one of them could have happened in, and General Rafe had not a care in the world. Had it been any other man in his tent, it would be of no concern, but I was a woman. And he had yet to notice that I had a reputation he so carelessly jeopardized.

Almost a quarter of a chime passed before the sky opened with a crack of thunder and rain fell to the earth. I mentally cursed every single curse I could think of as the heavy droplets soaked my dress. The soldiers groaned and cursed aloud, but went about their tasks. I shivered. The spring air was still far too cold to be out in the rain without an over-cloak.

The downpour plastered my dress to my bones, and I sighed. I didn't have extra coin to buy the luxurious multi-layered or padded gowns. My clothing was simple and thin. And now, it clung to my hip bones and ribs, making me appear less like a woman and more like a skeleton.

General Rafe took that moment to exit his tent, squinting at the sky, then down at me. He offered a cruel smile, eyeing my dress before walking off. I noted that he had replaced his tunic, and wondered if he was just waiting for the rain to start, knowing I wouldn't enter with him inside.

I dodged back into the tent and my bun chose that moment to fall, sending my frigid hair slapping down on my back. I gasped and pulled it over my shoulder, setting the General's tunic on a table. My hair was longer than most women's, falling to the top of my thighs. I rarely wore it up unless braided. It was one of the few things I found beautiful about myself. The white blonde mass was such a different color than anyone that I had met, and the women in the dorm often commented on its uniqueness. It was the one thing I allowed myself to be prideful of.

I pinned my hair back up and dragged the chair to the tent flap before retrieving his tunic. Sitting down in the puddle of my wet dress, I wiped the raindrops from my face and watched the field through the crack. They began a physical inspection of another company, and I sighed, returning to my sewing.

Not that I had time to look, even if I wanted.

The tunic took all day to mend, and even then I wasn't thrilled with my work. Anyone else might see nothing amiss, yet I knew every mistake I made. At one point, when General Rafe came in, he threw the drying button to the floor—under some guise of it being in his way, I was sure. I had learned my lesson and never stayed in the tent while he was present. Whenever he entered, I left and waited outside. He might not care about his reputation, but I had one to uphold.

We settled into a routine for the next few days, starting my mornings with his mending. He always seemed to have something torn. I even noted he ripped a seam on one I had previously mended. How he damaged so many of his clothes, I had no idea.

When he started wearing the black tunics, I was both proud and afraid. Proud because I had mended them, and he thought well enough of my work to wear them in public. And fearful because they were tailored to him. They outlined every single bulging muscle. When he wore them, he looked every bit the fearsome War General.

On rare occasions, I finished the mending early. Though more often than not, it took me all day to finish. Especially when he had lost buttons. A man might not think buttons were that difficult to sew, and they weren't, but they were elusive. Buttons were a fine detail, one that most people couldn't afford. Commoners used ties to fasten their garments, not tiny whittled pieces of wood. Buttons looked so much better, but if you lost them, they were much harder to replace.

After I completed any mending, I replaced the washing water. And if I had any time left over, I observed the inspections.

Willhelm's company met General Rafe's standards, for which I was grateful. Willhelm kept his men in top shape and worked hard to make sure they stayed sharp. I didn't want him suffering for his men, though I knew he would in a heartbeat.

The soldiers' abilities left me in awe. Whether it was archery on horseback or sword fighting, or brute strength—they applied themselves completely to their tasks. They did nothing halfheartedly.

I wondered how it would feel when I was trained in archery or sword skills, if there was something I'd be more adept at. Martial skills wouldn't be my priority, but they'd still be something I'd attain. Learning to control a dragonling's blood-magic was of the highest importance for a Rider.

The week passed quickly—faster than I would have thought. My nights ended with splitting headaches from being bent over the mending, but I was able to see so much more of the army than I ever had.

I was thankful I had not given up after that first day. General Rafe treated me no better, yet no worse. Perhaps he knew it was because I helped him by mending his clothes, or perhaps he was finally just getting used to me. We barely spoke. He usually just glared and tossed whatever clothing at me that required mending. I didn't mind. The less he spoke, the less he could hurt me.

Chapter Eight

I woke feeling like I had just fallen asleep. Rubbing my eyes, I rolled over, burrowing into my blanket as I counted the chimes. The thin scrap of fabric did nothing to fend off the morning chill. Seven chimes meant it was time for me to rise, though I had no motivation to.

Yesterday had been the last of the company inspections, and I had no desire to ask General Rafe what he planned for today. I assumed Willhelm would escort me to the General's rooms or wherever he trained—if he was even up this early. Of course, he'd be up already. I had never risen earlier than him. By the time I made it to his tent, his daily activities were always in full swing.

I groaned and pushed my feet over the edge of the cot, stood, and stretched. My body ached, every muscle tight and sore, though not from physical activity. The constant hours bent over, mending his blasted clothing destroyed my back and neck. How did a General manage to do so much damage to his garments? I didn't know. I was thankful that I would be a Dragon Rider and not a seamstress for my trade. What a miserable job, bent over all day and go to sleep with terrible headaches.

The cold floor bit at my feet as I shuffled over to my glorified vanity. I washed my face and rinsed my mouth out, looking at myself in the mirror. Dark circles hung under my eyes, physical indications of my lack of sleep. My night terrors of bonding with a dragonling were getting worse. They'd likely reach their peak right before Hatching Day. I knew when a dragonling chose me, they would pass. Shoving those thoughts aside, I threaded my hair into a quick braid down my back.

My beige dress was still damp from last night's washing. I refused to wear my battered brown working-dress to the barracks, and my gray gown was far too formal for any kind of strenuous activity. With longing, I glanced at my blue dress, the prickleberry stains still evident. I wondered if I would ever bring myself to wear it again, knowing the pain and disappointment I went through to get those stains. I should pass it to some gardener, cook, or maid who would wear an apron over it. That would cover the majority of the ruined fabric, at least.

After dressing, I tucked my orders in my pocket and reached for my sandals. Yesterday was rather warm, and by the day's bright sun and cloudless sky, I assumed today would be as well. As I picked them up, I noticed a strap hanging on by a few threads. Dragging my hand down my face, I set them down. I would either need to mend them or buy a new pair, as they were a bit small on my feet.

Pulling on my boots, I did my very best not to think about today. Once I completed my assignment with General Rafe, I was due to assist the barracks' Horse Master. I was excited about that. I could safely think about what the horses had in store for me while ignoring the immediate day in front of me.

Outside of my few riding lessons, I rarely had reason to be around the large creatures, but they were always calm and kind. From the finely boned riding horses to the thick and strong workhorses, they all seemed to resonate with their own beauty and grace.

When I entered the common room, I grinned at the fresh berries that were on the tables. Finally, we had reached harvest season. I took a roll and a handful of red berries and seated myself at a table beside a familiar face.

Meredith was an older woman with faded gray hair. Hidden among the many wrinkles lining her face were the deep crinkle marks of smile lines around her mouth and eyes. She was one of the few women I enjoyed being near.

"Good morn, Meredith," I greeted.

She looked up with an answering smile. "Good morn, Avyanna. What brings you to grace an old woman with your presence?"

"I thought you might grace me with the answer to a question," I replied with a playful wink. "Do you know where Master Elenor might be?"

The old woman took a sip of her tea, peering over the rim of her cup before answering. "What is it that you need, dear?"

"I just wanted to let her know I was in the market for some work to earn spare coin," I explained, eating a few berries.

"Ah, it seems as though everyone is in the market for extra coin these days. There simply aren't enough jobs to go around."

I frowned at her response. That meant the students who inquired before me would have the first choice of any available work.

"Don't look so gloomy, I'll pass on your request if you would like. Master Elenor is currently upbraiding the laundry maids for batting their lashes at the men who bring them laundry from the barracks."

I grimaced in disgust, and Meredith gave a good chuckle. "I know, dear. Can you imagine flirting with a man who brought you their sweat-stained under-breeches?" She cackled, and I joined in.

Already my chest felt lighter. When was the last time I had a good laugh? If that was some form of flirtation, to bring someone your dirty under-breeches, I had no desire to bat my eyes at any man.

"If you would pass that along, I'd be happy with any job, no matter what they might be," I said. "Thank you, Meredith." I finished the last of my berries and stood.

She lifted her hand in a small wave. "Have a good day, dear. Don't get into mischief."

"I'll do my best not to." I grinned and ducked out of the room, then down to the foyer.

I nibbled on my roll as I started for the gate, noting the students as they darted to and fro. With my mood now elevated, I smiled, thinking of the ones I had helped when I assisted the Masters on the school grounds.

In potions class, a poor boy tried to make a healing salve, but instead of plantain, he used snakeweed. His salve had been so smelly and potent, we deemed it a new potion used to keep people at bay.

In reading and writing, a girl read words at a lightning pace in her head, but when she read aloud, she stuttered endlessly, taking all morning. The Master of Letters told me that she did not sound out the words or read them aloud in her mind, which caused her to falter while reading aloud.

In art, a boy would constantly use the wrong colors for things. He painted a red sky, purple grass, and yellow leaves. At first, I thought him a terrible artist, but the Master of Art corrected me. The boy did not see colors. To him, everything was varying shades of gray and black and white.

Every student on these grounds was different. Everyone had their strengths and weaknesses. Even I had my own shortcomings. My lack of friends made me vulnerable. I also had a tendency to think violent thoughts about a certain General.

At the gate, I reached into my pocket to retrieve my orders for the guards. I smiled at Willhelm as he caught my eye, talking to the men with his arms crossed over his chest. The morning guards didn't bother checking my orders, but ushered me in with a rough jerk of their heads. I grinned at them and turned to Willhelm, catching the end of their conversation.

"This is not the front lines. We're training. We need sleep to train," one guard groaned. "He expects us to perform at the highest levels, yet he doesn't let us prepare."

"It doesn't matter what we think. It's what has been asked of us, and so we will do it," Willhelm said in a firm tone, motioning me to join him. "I understand where you're coming from, soldier. You weren't the only one he woke last night. Stand tall." He nodded in parting, and we headed off.

"What was all that about?" I asked.

"General Rafe."

I waited, but no further explanation followed. Was that the only reply I was going to get? I was sure that the name 'General Rafe' was an appropriate answer for many situations. What could cause any soldier to groan? General Rafe. What was the bane of my sanity? General Rafe.

However, in this instance, his name did not answer my question. "What did he do now?"

Willhelm rubbed his neck, and I noticed dark circles under his eyes as well. "He put forth a new training exercise."

"How is that bad?"

He paused, casting a baleful stare my way before continuing, "He decided, at the third chime of morning, to blow a Shadow Men's war-horn, then storm through the bunkhouse on horseback."

I slapped my hand over my mouth, but not soon enough to stifle my giggle.

"You think it's funny, but you weren't there." Willhelm leaned close and dropped his voice to a whisper. "Grown men pissed themselves."

At that, I laughed freely. It wasn't hard to imagine being dead asleep, and the sound of a horn jerking me awake. A demon the size of General Rafe swooping through the dorm bunks would be quite a terrifying sight.

"He tossed cots and bunks and fought off at least twenty men before someone realized it was him. He announced that we should be ready for an attack at any moment, then walked out of the bunkhouse."

I smiled at the story as we neared the training buildings. The General was already up and active, then. Would I have another shirt to mend from his adventures last night?

"He takes his job of training the men quite seriously," I commented.

"I don't think he realizes he's no longer on the front lines. I'm all for men learning, but he's expecting first year cadets to be in fighting shape as of yesterday. Captains over the first and second years can't train their cadets fast enough."

All jesting aside, Willhelm was tired and worn. This week having the General back was rough on him. When he wasn't escorting me back and forth, he was training his cadets. Or he was with the other company commanders, trying to wrap their minds around the General's antics.

I stepped close to Willhelm, and he raised a brow in surprise. "You're a great Sergeant. Your company has done amazingly," I assured him, knowing he was thinking of his own men who were in their fourth year.

Nearly a month after Hatching Day was Recruitment Day. It was the time in which both fourth year Dragon Riders and fourth year cadets would leave for the front. In their stead, more soldiers were recruited and added to the ranks to fill the voids made by men who would probably never return.

Recruitment Day saw the companies and their Captains shipped off. Willhelm had never been offered the title Captain, and would likely never seek it out. He was happy in the homelands, training soldiers. He never shirked his duty, but he never pursued battle either—something I could respect. Willhelm was more valuable here, instructing the cadets, than killed on a battlefield where he couldn't train anyone.

He smiled before he stepped away, putting distance between us. I admired Willhelm for many things. His gentleness toward me, his regard toward others, his fierce loyalty. He always respected me, and I cherished that. Even as a girl of seventeen-winters, it meant so much to me. He treated me like a proper lady, even though I hadn't received the title yet.

The title of 'Lady' was granted at twenty-winters. That was not when most girls married, however. Life mates were often sought at a younger age, from sixteen to eighteen. Most girls within that age bracket flirted and tested their mettle against men, seeing who might make a good spouse.

If one made it to twenty-winters without a life mate, they were considered a spinster, which made no sense to me. Even if I were not destined to be a Dragon Rider, and only lived the average life span, I would never rush into a claiming. A life mate should be someone who I would enjoy spending my life with. How could I look at the boys in the school and think any of them were mature enough to appreciate growing old with?

I shuddered. I would take my duty as Dragon Rider over the drama and emotions that plagued other girls my age any day.

Willhelm stopped, and I glanced up, seeing we arrived at a training building. Within was a small company of third year cadets. There were perhaps twenty of them, all holding wooden practice swords and shields, gripped tight as if their life depended on them.

General Rafe strode calmly through their ranks, swinging a wooden shortsword nonchalantly. The Captain of the company stood off to the side, back rigid and jaw clenched. Wincing in sympathy for him, I looked at Willhelm, who nodded his goodbye, not willing to speak and break the soldiers' concentration. As he left, I moved to the large open door. This structure, like so many others, had two immense doorways facing east and west. The breeze whipped through and caught the edge of my dress, lifting it off the ground, tugging it along.

A soldier glanced over, and in the mere blink of an eye, the General was on him. With a sharp thwack, the wooden sword slapped against the soldier's temple. I cringed and gathered my dress in my hands, hoping it would prove less distracting.

The soldier spun to face the General and staggered a step back, trying to give himself space to think. General Rafe grabbed the shield and yanked it from his hand while the soldier tried to slash at him with the sword. General Rafe parried the blow easily and threw the shield to the ground, advancing on the man.

"Never take your eyes off the enemy." His menacing tone sent chills down my spine.

He never talked to me that way. It was not a loud statement, but rather one that he growled so low it barely carried on the wind. Spoken in a voice that demanded obedience and threatened unspoken consequences.

I frowned, noting the dangerous glint in the General's eye as he singled out the soldier. Backing him into a corner, the soldier's gaze flickered to his comrades, but even they seemed too frightened to assist. The soldier's back hit the wall, reaching his snapping point. He lashed out in fear, swinging his sword wildly.

I had no combat experience, but even I saw that he left himself wide open.

General Rafe, almost teasingly, batted the weapon aside before rapping on the man's ribs with the flat of his practice sword.

"Dead," he grunted.

The soldier crumpled in on himself, defeated and embarrassed.

General Rafe turned toward me, swinging his sword up to rest on his shoulder, flat edge down. "You distracted him."

Fear tightened my throat. A sinister threat simmered in his dark eye. His iris was the deepest brown, like a tree in a shadowed forest. The first few days of my assignment with him, I thought it was entirely black, before I glimpsed it in the sunlight, seeing the light illuminate the warm color.

Not that anything about his gaze was warm.

How was it that when I was away from this man, I was fine? I had no trouble dealing with others, whether they meant me ill or not. How could he, with one glance, send my nerves scuttling away in fear?

He prowled toward me, slowly but purposefully. I could see it in his eye, and in his movements, he expected me to retreat as the soldier did.

Somewhere inside myself, I found the bravery, or stupidity, to lift my chin and stare him down. "I hardly take responsibility. If all it takes is a stray wind blowing a girl's skirts to distract your soldiers, perhaps you could teach them to be more focused."

The Captain choked, but I ignored him. I schooled my features into defiance, intent on holding his gaze. He came to a stop in front of me with complete disregard for my personal space—our chests a mere breath from one another. I was beginning to understand his tactics. He used his size to intimidate people, and once he had them cowed, he ordered them about like he was their better.

"If you weren't here, they would be more focused," he said lowly.

Courage or idiocy flooded my veins. I could hardly tell which. "Are we talking about them, or yourself, General Rafe? Am I distracting you?"

Something flickered across his face. Oh, I hit a nerve. I wondered if I should press my case, or let him be. This General got under my skin and pushed me to react with a rashness that I normally kept under firm control.

I pitched my voice low so that it would not carry. "In the mere moments you have talked with me, your men could have attacked you, while your focus was... otherwise detained."

His hand shot out so fast I didn't have time to even blink in surprise. He snatched my jaw between his thick fingers. My breath hissed between my teeth as fire licked my bones. This man had now stolen two touches from me. I had not given them. Touch was a woman's to give. It was never for a man to take without consent.

The men shifted and murmured behind him, yet I could only focus on his dark, hateful glare. His fingers dug into my skin, but I didn't fight it. He was stronger than I, and if he wanted to hold me, he would, regardless of my attempts. Despite the pressure, his grip was not bruising. It was as if he simply held my jaw to prove to me he could, as if he knew it was not proper, and this was something he could take from me to humble me.

I refused to let my glare waver for even a moment, though every nerve in my body screamed for me to run or fight. I gripped my dress so tightly that my fingers ached. Still, I made no move to push him away. It was as if we fought for dominance like common dogs.

"Your mending is on the table," he drawled, not taking his eye off mine.

"Did you damage your clothing from midnight rides in the dorms?" I asked, working my jaw against his grasp, daring him to respond. "Sneaking under cover of darkness, tossing cadets out of their bunks like some brute?" The words slipped out of my mouth, urged on by the fire in my veins.

Rage curled his lip. He shoved my face away from him, and I stumbled back. I fought the urge to hold my jaw, knowing the imprints of his fingers would linger on my skin. I straightened and glared at him for all I was worth. If looks could kill, he would be a dead man ten times over.

"Your ignorance of combat is showing," he said. "A girl knows nothing of the battlefield."

He turned, walking back to the company, who looked completely horrified that he had treated a woman that way. The Captain himself was as pale as a ghost, looking as though he might faint. I offered him a reassuring smile, even though my pride took a hit at the General's words. He was right. I didn't know anything about combat. It wasn't as if he would teach me, either. He only wanted a seamstress to tend to his mending.

I walked over to a table against the wall where one of the General's black, sleeveless tunics lay. It was torn along the side seam as if someone had pulled at it harshly. I picked it up and folded it neatly over my arm, taking time to gather my nerves. I knew the soldiers watched my every move, wondering what I would do next.

Would I demand a soldier to take up for my honor? Would I choose the Captain to fight for me as a Lady would if her honor had been impugned? They were no match for the General, who was a mountain of muscle, quick as a snake and just as vile.

No.

A slow, mischievous smile spread over my face as I turned to look at the General, holding his tunic to my chest. "I beg your pardon, General Rafe. I must retrieve my sewing notions. I will return your tunic by this evening."

He sighed heavily and waved me out, as one might shoo an errant child. Pride still stinging, I left with my chin held high. I would not let him win this fight. After all, even a girl could get under a General's skin.

If he treated me as though my only worth was as a seamstress, I would be a seamstress.

Chapter Nine

Somehow, I ended up on the school grounds, safe and unscathed. It might have been the rage that was written on my face that deterred the soldiers, or they simply chose to ignore me. Either way, I breathed a sigh of relief when I crossed the boundary under the guards' frowning gaze.

I made my way to a school workshop under the shadow of the dorms. There, Master Elta taught the art of sewing. Many of the lesser Masters had workshops outside of the main school. The structures were small, holding around ten students. Master Elta was a kind soul, an older woman whose hands shook so badly she could no longer hold a needle. Her eyes, however, were as sharp as an eagle's. She could guide a student's stitching from across the room without ever leaving her rocker. She taught me how to mend years ago. I feared if she saw any of my recent work, she would be ashamed.

I held General Rafe's tunic close to my chest and knocked on the wooden door. A hobbling figure moved past the dusty windows. After a moment, the door swung open, revealing the old Master. Wrinkles creased the edges of her eyes as she squinted against the sunlight. She leaned on her cane, and I hurried to explain my presence.

"Good morn, Master Elta. I was wondering if you might help me with something?"

"Eh? What's your name, dearie?" she croaked. She didn't have the best memory. I served as her assistant during my very first assignment, but that was months ago.

"My name is Avyanna, Master. I was wondering if you might help me with a project I'm working on?"

"Ah, yes, yes. I have a free moment if you need it," she replied.

She hobbled back in, leaving me to grab the door before it slammed shut on me. Inside, she headed toward her rocker near a table covered with sewing notions. Items littered the entire surface, yet everything was in its place; needles tucked into pin cushions, fabrics wrapped and folded, and skeins of yarn wound and arranged by color. Everything was in order, as it always was.

Master Elta took her seat and sighed, as if happy to be off her tired feet. "Well, what is it?"

The bolstering fire I had felt earlier had abandoned me and cold anxiety took its place. This was wrong. Part of me wondered if she could read the guilt written all over my face.

"Let's see it." She held out her palm, waiting for the tunic. "What did you do?"

Biting my lip, I gave it to her, trying to hide my trembling hand.

She held the tunic up and as it unfurled, a deep frown crossed her face. "I know this." Her thin lips pressed together as her bony fingers brushed the seams. "I know this, because I made it."

Fear ricocheted through my ribcage. I swallowed. This was a mistake. My mind whirled, calculating how I might backtrack, get the tunic and leave when Master Elta's harsh gaze snapped up to mine.

"Why do you have this?" she demanded.

I blew out a breath. "I beg your pardon, Master Elta, but I am mending General Rafe's uniforms." The words sounded steady enough, despite my stammering tongue.

"General Rafe is on the front lines. Where he has been for some time, fighting the good fight." She lifted the tunic, as if I wasn't aware of what it was. "Why do you have his garments?!"

"Master Elta, he is here. He has returned with an injury."

She studied me for a long moment. Those all-seeing eyes danced over my face, and I was no longer the fiery, defiant woman in the barracks, but rather a deceitful student, caught in the act of rebellion.

My shoulders sagged with relief when she relented and returned her sharp gaze to the intricate stitchings.

"He's here? How was he injured?" she pressed.

"I'm not sure, Master," I said, my heart racing. "I think he lost an eye on the front."

"An eye? Oh my, that's horrible." Her tone softened as she caressed the fabric. "He was such a sweet boy. I made these for him when he was promoted to General, you know."

Sweet boy? Were we talking about the same General?

"Perhaps it is fate that you help me mend it, then," I said, wringing my hands.

"I don't know about fate, dearie. You might not be thankful you brought this to me. This is a General's overcoat. Rafe didn't like to wear much, being the rake he was. I made him a coat and tunic in one." She looked from the tunic to me, gaze sharpening. "You have your work cut out for you. This was made by a Master Seamstress. You must mend it as though you are a Master, yourself."

I resisted a cringe, schooling my face and once again doubted my resolve. Taking a deep breath, I pulled out a chair and sat next to Master Elta as she rocked, ready to learn all her secrets... and perhaps humble a General.

It was dark when I finally left Master Elta's workshop. The eighth chime rang out some time ago, and though I tried to hurry the mending, Master Elta would have none of it. Willhelm was probably looking for me, and I had to return the General's tunic.

I hurried down the path as quickly as I dared. The full moon illuminated my way, and I rushed toward the glow of the fires beyond the wall. No torches lined the paths here, yet from what I could see on the barracks' side, they had torches and fires lit everywhere. The school grounds had a curfew, and apparently, the barracks did not.

Master Elta accepted my request to write a note pardoning my late night adventures, conceding that I take the General's tunic back to him straight away.

I hurried to the guards who stood near the gate, closed for the night. "Hail, I seek entry!" I called.

A guard peered through and frowned, opening the gate for a closer look. I handed them my orders for General Rafe, as well as my note of pardon from Master Elta.

"Ah, you're looking for the General?" the guard asked, running a hand through his hair anxiously.

"Yes, I must see this to him," I said, holding up the tunic.

He winced. "I'm afraid he's indisposed."

I tilted my head, waiting for an explanation. He shifted his feet and raised his brows at the other guard, silently asking for backup. The second guard mouthed something, then shook his head, relenting.

"Yeah, you can't see him." Clearly, the other guard wasn't as bright as the first.

"I have to get this to him. He's expecting it tonight," I pressed.

"Nah, we can have someone give it to him, though," said the second guard.

And rob me of the satisfaction of seeing his face? Hardly.

"You must understand. He will be upset if I don't get this to him." Where was Willhelm when I needed him? "Is Sergeant Willhelm about?" I asked. Perhaps I'd gain entry through him.

"He would be in the dining hall or his quarters. I could send someone to fetch him," the first guard offered.

I almost refused. I'd gotten by just fine without an escort earlier today. But, noticing the soldiers drifting here and there, drinking what I assumed was ale or mead, I thought better of wandering about the barracks alone.

"Yes, please. That will do," I conceded.

The first guard called over a cadet to fetch Sergeant Willhelm, and off the young man went, eyeing me as he left.

"A word of caution, miss." The first guard lowered his voice. "I wouldn't leave the gate. Wouldn't seem proper with a man and all."

I frowned. Fire-blast it all, he was right. It wouldn't look good for me at all to be seen walking around the barracks at night, even with Willhelm's escort. In fact, that would probably be worse. With as often as the soldiers witnessed us together, showing up late at night and being seen with him walking the streets would appear inappropriate. Frustrated, I kicked at the dirt with my boot and bit my lip.

I wanted the satisfaction of being there when General Rafe saw his mended tunic. Perhaps I could just wait till the morning. But now what would my excuse be for interrupting Willhelm's meal? To apologize? To say goodnight? That would be even more unseemly.

"Miss Avyanna?"

I looked up at Willhelm's voice as he made his way to me. The torchlight threw his face into shadows, making his features seem sharper.

"Willhelm!" I greeted, stepping out of earshot of the guards.

He came to stand beside me with a frown. "I was worried about you. General Rafe said he sent you off with no escort."

Even in the dark, I sensed his relief that I was safe and sound. "I set off to mend his clothes. I needed new thread," I hedged.

"One of the cadets said you looked angry enough to burn the building down around him," Willhelm teased.

"I was angry at the time, but all is well now," I assured him, holding out the tunic. "I wanted to give this to him, but the guards say he's indisposed."

Willhelm nodded, glancing at the bundle. "He makes himself scarce at night. I can find him if you'd like, but I can't take you from the gate," he explained.

"I know." Biting my lip, I ducked my head. "I'm sorry I didn't think of that. I only wanted to see his face."

"See his face when you gave him his mending? Have you not seen it before with other mendings?"

I kicked at a loose pebble on the ground. "This one is different." My cheeks warmed. Saying it out loud made me seem childish and ridiculous. "I had to go to Master Elta for help."

"Ah, so it was more effort? I'm sorry, lass, I'll give it to him if you want me to."

Reluctantly, I held out the tunic. Guilt gnawed at my insides as I watched Willhelm fold it under his arm.

"Are you well enough to get to the dorms alone?" he asked, glancing over my shoulder at the dark school grounds.

"I am. I know the way like the back of my hand." With a final glimpse at the tunic, I turned to leave. "See you tomorrow."

"Good night, Avyanna," he called.

Looking back, his puzzled expression fueled my guilt. I waved and rushed off into the dark. Lately, I had been so exhausted I couldn't wait to return to the dorms, yet tonight I was reluctant. I lifted my chin and picked up my feet. General Rafe would still get the tunic, and his pride would still take a blow.

With that happy thought in mind, I hurried my pace and headed back to the dorms.

I woke the next morning and rushed to ready myself for the barracks. Willhelm wouldn't be there any earlier than the eighth chime like he normally was, but I was still eager to see General Rafe's face.

Eager was one way to put it, anyway. My stomach knotted with nerves, rebelling against the excitement. He would retaliate somehow, but I was finding new satisfaction in the back and forth we had. I was never the type of girl to pick a fight, or even participate in one, yet General Rafe's arrogance had me itching for one.

Perhaps it was because before he had arrived, I placed him on a pedestal as some great General who would teach me all the things I needed to learn about fighting. Perhaps I had thought too much of him. For one thing, I expected him to differ from a boar. I envisioned a General who was polite and distinguished. A gentleman.

I scoffed. There wasn't an ounce of propriety in that brute.

I headed with my breakfast to the barracks. Willhelm was at the gate waiting, and he froze when he saw me, a mischievous grin lighting his face.

"Good morn, Willhelm."

"Morning, you little devil." He crossed his arms, staring me down with a smile. "I have to warn you, General Rafe is in a foul mood today."

His playful tone had me beaming. It was obvious something had put him in a good mood.

"Oh? And why is that?" I asked, feigning innocence.

"It appears as though he has had a wardrobe malfunction."

"Hmm. That's peculiar," I stated, tilting my head at the guards. They nodded me on without asking for my papers.

"He's been cursing and throwing things all morning. He also might be in a state of undress when I escort you to him. I'll stay with you if he is."

Usually, once I crossed the gate, Willhelm fell into step beside me, but today he lingered. Beneath his mirth was an underlying hint of warning.

"Oh my. Is he running about naked?" I taunted.

"Not quite, though the men have teased about him eating too much lately."

"The men teased him?" My hand covered my heart in mock horror.

"Oh, they wouldn't dare say it to his face. However, I have the sinking feeling a certain young woman might say something like that."

I grinned and shrugged, batting my lashes. Willhelm's humored spirit settled some of the anxiety clawing into my chest. I let out a contented breath. This morning was turning out just fine.

"Shall we?" I asked, gesturing to the road.

His smile faltered. "Are you sure you're ready?"

"Is one ever ready to face an angry viper?"

Willhelm gave me a slight nod as he conceded. He seemed to accept the fact that I knew the General was no more than a dangerous animal.

We walked in companionable silence to a different training field, one I had never been to before. It was littered with multiple obstacles and walls, low fences, nets hanging in the air between poles, and mud—lots of mud.

As we neared the soldiers standing at attention, Willhelm cleared his throat. "This is a physical training field. I forewarn you, the men will stay in a state of dress only because of your presence. If the General prods them, they may strip their tunics."

I offered a faint nod and stiffened as General Rafe rounded the corner. He wore a tunic, yet had one bunched in his fist. A black swath of fabric concealed his missing eye, but it did nothing to lessen the ferocity of his anger when he spotted me. His fierce gaze narrowed, sealing my fate as he stormed over.

"Sergeant! Dismissed!" His tone cut through any mirth and rang with authority.

Willhelm went rigid beside me. He was obligated to heed the order, yet with the fire in the General's glare, I sensed his reluctance.

"I hear and obey," Willhelm growled and spun on his heel, meeting my eye in passing.

With that single look, I knew I could call for him if needed and he would defend me. I gave him a thankful smile as he marched past.

"You," the General spat.

That one word held so much fury, it lifted the hairs on the nape of my neck. He stalked closer, taking his time, seeking to intimidate me.

"Fix it."

He threw the bunched tunic at me, and I made no move to catch it, letting it bounce off my chest to the ground.

I lifted my chin. "I did."

"You did more than fix it, girl," he said lowly.

He crowded close enough to make me crane my head to look up at him. The sun behind his back caused me to squint, trying to maintain eye contact.

"I assure you, I simply did your mending, as you have required of me. Me being a simple *girl* and all, incapable of assisting you in any other way," I snapped.

"Fix it," he hissed through gritted teeth.

"I already did." I glared, refusing to back down. "If my mending needs altered, perhaps you should seek out another seamstress."

"You refuse?"

I swallowed, not liking how his tone had gone from threatening to challenging.

I especially didn't like the wicked glint in his eye. "I don't know what you're asking me to fix." Dread settled low in my belly as I shirked the question.

"Pick it up."

I scowled, but made no move for it. Instead, I squared my shoulders, puffing out my chest like I was a dragon defending her space.

"*Pick it up.*" He emphasized each word as if they were each a threat on their own.

He reached toward my face, giving me the opportunity to move. I shied away from his hand, stepping to the side and giving myself space. I snatched the tunic off the ground, losing that battle. Over my shoulder, I glimpsed the company of men. They stood at attention, every pair of eyes scrutinizing our display, Captain included.

When I looked back at General Rafe, all the blood drained from my face. He was undoing the buttons on his tunic. I swallowed, watching him push each button through its hole at an excruciatingly slow pace. Mentally slapping myself, I snapped my gaze up to his eye.

He wanted to win this mental battle, but I wouldn't back down. Propriety be cursed.

"Sir?" The Captain's voice cracked as he spoke.

Tension was thick in the air. This was immensely inappropriate. I was within my right to call on any of the men to defend me. But this was my battle to win.

General Rafe ignored the man's inquiry. Deftly, his fingers loosened the buttons one by one. His challenging glare never left mine. I clenched my jaw and put every bit of my rage into my gaze.

He *smirked*.

My face burned as my vision tinted red. Anyone watching would have confused the blush for embarrassment. They'd be wrong. I was flushed with ire. I was so angry at him for making this a public humiliation, for risking my reputation as a woman in front of so many men.

Yet, I was not just a girl. I was not just some female that abided by the social rules and guidelines. I was to be a Dragon Rider, forged of fire and steel. I might as well start acting like it.

Guessing that he had loosened the last button, because I dared not take my eyes from his, he shrugged out of his tunic with a leisurely roll of his massive shoulders. My mouth dried as some unknown feeling curled low in my belly. My breaths came fast with the concentration it took to maintain eye contact and not look away as I caught sight of tanned skin.

He dropped the tunic to the ground, sneering at me.

"Give it to me," he said, reaching for the one I clasped tight.

Blindly, I shoved it at him, refusing to leave his glare.

"Sir, I really must protest—" the Captain started.

Of course, he could protest now. There was a half-naked barbarian towering over an unclaimed woman. If I were of any social standing, his actions would have plunged so far from social graces that I would never regain them.

"You'll protest nothing," General Rafe snarled, not offering him so much as a glance.

My teeth ached from clenching them so hard. And finally, thankfully, he pulled on his black tunic. He tugged on the hem, settling it over his broad shoulders, leaving the front hanging open. I knew why he didn't bother with the buttons, though I dared not say a word.

"Do you approve of your handiwork?"

I swallowed audibly, and a shiver went down my spine. "I simply mended the seam," I choked.

"You and I both know you did far more than that."

My fingers gripped handfuls of my dress, attempting to hide my trembling. I had done more than that. I fixed the side seam, but also took them in. His tunic was now a size too small, unable to be buttoned over his broad chest. I also knew that with it being custom-made, having it replaced would not be an easy endeavor.

It might have been a petty act of revenge, though at the time it had made me feel quite accomplished.

"You'll not be leaving my side today," he said, smiling. "I believe I can find a great many tasks for you."

And oh, how that smile was vicious.

I stood so straight I was sure that I would faint. Isn't that what I wanted—a chance to see the soldiers in action, to learn even just a tiny bit from him? My honor would pay dearly for it. He wouldn't change back into the tunic that covered him. He might even tell the men to strip during their physical training.

It was so inappropriate, yet I was more than a *'girl'*. Resolve flooded through me and I stood a little straighter, taking on his daring glare. I was First Chosen to be a Dragon Rider. Surely I'd see far more horrifying things than a man's skin on the battlefield.

"I can't wait to begin," I bit out.

General Rafe, I accept your challenge.

Something akin to approval flashed across his face right before he finally broke our stare-down and returned to the company. I dropped my gaze to the ground and took a quick breath, relieved that the battle was over, but also mortified that others had witnessed it.

When I dared to view the soldiers, they only had eyes for the General, though the Captain scowled at me. Whether his scowl was disapproval of General Rafe's actions, or my own refusal to call on a man to defend my honor, I didn't quite know.

Either way, I wasn't there to impress him. I was there for my own gains; to help General Rafe and learn what I could from him. I wouldn't be bothered by a man whose disapproval did not affect my duty.

Chapter Ten

I had been correct. The sun was high and hot in the sky. I spent my morning averting my gaze as men walked about, bare of their tunics. Not all soldiers paraded around half-naked, though. When the General offered them the option, some sent nervous glances my way and remained clothed.

True to his word, General Rafe found many things for me to do. I fetched water for the soldiers and fixed any obstacles on the training course that came loose. Most of the men ignored me after they adjusted to my presence.

It didn't take long till mud drenched the hem of my skirts and smeared my skin. Even so, I enjoyed it. I worked hard, completing each task he threw at me with utmost diligence. Through it all, I kept my attention focused on General Rafe's instructions for the soldiers, absorbing any details I could.

He dictated various challenges for them to tackle, such as completing an obstacle with their eyes closed or their hands bound. And he gave pointers on how to increase speed and dexterity through different courses. When a soldier had improper form, or used the wrong set of muscles for a task, he taught them a better way to accomplish it.

All in all, I was learning, and I would take that without complaint.

In as few words as possible, General Rafe revealed that the Shadow Men often attacked using potions and poisons. Some of which caused temporary blindness, or even interim paralysis. He explained that no matter what havoc they unleashed, soldiers could either keep fighting or retreat. To halt and nurse any wounds was not an option.

I squinted against the sun, pushing a log that had been knocked out of place by a cadet, when the Captain called for midday meal. General Rafe glared at him and I half expected him to give the company some statement about how a soldier on the battlefield had no time to eat. Just as the thought came to my mind, a wicked smile crossed his face. I straightened, wiping the sweat from my brow, and shaded my eyes from the sun.

"Attention!" he barked, his frown falling back into place.

I trudged through the mud pit, holding my dress as high as I modestly could, making my way to the line of soldiers. A young lad, a bit on the heavier side, was the most recent to run the gambit. He gasped for air, trying hard to stand up straight. Sweat drenched his tunic. He had refused to strip out of it, for my sake, and I was sure that wearing it contributed to his heaving breaths.

Dropping my muddied skirts, I stood to the side, trying not to draw attention to myself. The soldiers and their Captain waited for General Rafe's instruction with curious expressions.

"You'll have your midday meal," he stated, and a few cadets dared to sigh their relief, "but not from the dining hall."

That snapped all their attention back to him. The Captain frowned, as did I. The cadets had a grueling morning, exhausting so much energy. The dining hall had plenty of nutritious food to replenish their reserves. If not there, where else would they get it?

"You will eat what you hunt or forage. Meet back here by next chime."

My stomach dropped, and the men groaned. General Rafe's glare cut through their ranks.

"On the front, you don't always have the courtesy of a dining hall. You never know when your limited store of food has been tainted by the Shadows. To survive, you must rely on your wits and prowess." He spread his arms, gesturing to the open field. "Anyone who complains will remain here and run the course till sundown."

The soldiers trudged off, clearly disheartened, and I shifted on my feet, unsure what to do next. I looked at the ground when General Rafe's gaze met mine. I had managed to avoid looking at him during the morning and was sure he would either dismiss me for my midday meal or order me to do another task.

"Well?" he inquired.

When I looked up, he stared at me with a questioning brow raised.

"Begging your pardon. Did you ask a question?"

"That order was for you, too."

My eyes narrowed. What game was he playing? All week he treated me as if I were a worthless girl, and now he ordered me about as if I was his soldier. I gave a tart nod and spun on my heel, walking a few paces before noting his shadow looming behind. He was following me. I glanced over my shoulder, scrunching my face up in confusion.

"Proceed," he said, smirking. He waved ahead, urging me on.

I wasn't sure if his presence trailing me through the barracks put me at ease. Surely, with him as my escort, no man would bother me, yet his unyielding attention set me on edge.

Glancing at the sun for guidance, I headed to the southern edge of the barracks. The forest that bordered the school grounds had to reach this far. At least, I hoped they did. I had no prowess with a bow or knife, and I knew next to nothing of trapping. Yet even a girl such as I was not helpless when it came to finding my own food. I had served in the kitchen often enough to learn what I could and could not eat from the woods.

I crossed the empty training fields with the giant mountain of a man close behind. With an inward cringe, I thought of the prickleberry incident. Familiar anger stirred, tightening my chest, and I peered back to see General Rafe eyeing the treeline ahead, before his gaze slid to mine. Another confident smirk curled his lips.

What I would do to wipe that smirk off his face.

At the edge of the woods, I scoured the thick brambles for the easiest entry. A small game trail opened in a thinner section and I took a step toward it before stopping and turning.

"I hope you know how inappropriate this is," I said, gesturing between us. "Following a woman into the woods during midday meal? People might think ill of you." Maybe if I appealed to his reputation, he would turn back.

Instead, he scoffed and folded his arms across his chest, his stare deliberate. He wasn't going anywhere.

"I'm not following a woman," he said, unaffected. "I'm following a child. No man would think a thing of it."

He stalked toward me, and I took a hesitant step back before I could think better of it. His wolfish smile grew, and he came closer, amused by my nerves. I swallowed and glanced behind him, searching for anyone, any other soul who might witness this colossal mistake. Nothing. No one. I turned and pressed into the thicket before General Rafe could get any closer.

As I followed the trail, I pushed branches out of my way in hopes they'd swing back and hit him. At one point, after letting a particularly thick branch fly, his low chuckle stiffened my jaw. I was glad he was amused by this. At least someone was.

It was far cooler in the woods, as opposed to the shadeless field. Though it lacked the stirring of a breeze, making the air heavy and stagnant. I studied the trees and stumps, and the forest floor, slowing my steps to orient myself with this part of the forest.

I wasn't familiar with this section of the woods, but I knew how to identify the edible leafy plants near the school grounds. This being the same woods, I should be able to find them here as well.

I lifted the corner of my dress to use as a makeshift pouch and plucked leaves from low-hanging branches and shrubs, and even a few flowers. General Rafe's eyes burned into the back of my head, watching my every move. I took a calming breath, beyond irritated. He hadn't foraged a single thing. It wouldn't surprise me if he intended on taking everything I'd secured for himself.

I bent to pick some narrowleaf plantain and caught sight of him staring at the lifted corner of my dress. Pursing my lips, I spotted a small purple flower with a bright yellow center sticking out like a pike. If he planned on stealing my food, I'd at least have a good laugh over his paralyzed body.

"Hold."

General Rafe pushed against me to pick the flower himself, and I was forever thankful for the step he took back. He held it up and twisted it by its stem, looking at me with... was that disappointment?

"Do you know what this is?" he rumbled.

I narrowed my eyes at him and nodded.

"What is it?"

I frowned, thinking he caught onto my plan. "Nightshade."

He kept twisting it and stared at me, obviously trying to understand what I was playing at. I didn't want the poor man to bruise his brain attempting to figure it out.

"I know my plants, General Rafe. Almost as well as I know you were eyeing my harvest."

"You thought to poison me?" His voice took on a dark tone as he dropped the flower.

Someone had definitely poisoned him in the past. I made a mental note to stay away from that subject in the future.

"I thought if someone were to steal my hard-won harvest, they would pay an appropriate price."

A proud grin tugged at the corners of his mouth, and he inclined his head. "How wise of you."

I stood there staring at him, waiting for further comment. When he grew bored, he folded his arms across his chest and looked about the woods, still rooted in place.

"Well?" I lifted the makeshift pouch. "Are you going to take my harvest?"

He scoffed, "Girls eat leaves. Men eat meat. Have no fear, little rabbit, I'll not eat your dinner."

Satisfied, I returned to my task.

"But I might eat you," he added.

I whipped my face to him, sending a harsh glare his way. Knowing he was only trying to intimidate me, I pressed on through the woods with a sigh.

After I'd gathered enough to sustain me till the evening meal, I spied the telltale bushy leaves of a wild carrot. They were more bitter and grew in odd shapes, but the only other things I had were soft, stringy plants. Something with a bit more crunch would be welcome. I knelt down on the ground, set aside my leafy harvest and went to work, using my fingers to loosen the soil around the carrot. Just as I worked my way around the taproot, I heard an exasperated sigh, and I felt, more than saw, General Rafe crouch beside me.

"Move over."

He nudged my side with his thick thigh, and I scrambled over, taking my stash of food with me. He balanced on the balls of his feet where I had knelt and pulled out a wicked-looking knife from his trousers.

My eyes drifted to the center of his stomach, where his unfastened tunic displayed bare skin. Uneven muscles bunched and swelled with every movement as he stabbed at the forest floor. I had never seen so many muscles so well defined, and wondered if the muscles running down everyone's middle were so lopsided. My mouth was suddenly dry, my jaw fell ajar at the sheer power behind every small movement.

"There's eight of them."

My gaze shot up to meet his, and I snapped my mouth shut with a click.

"Something I doubt you would know, being a skin and bones girl, is that eight muscles run down your midriff." He stood, and I watched in sheer horror as he stuck a thumb in the front of his trousers and jerked them dangerously low on his hips, revealing the hard muscles. "Fighting will bring them out," he added. With a spark in his dark eye, he dropped back into a crouch and resumed digging.

My cheeks flamed, and I clasped my hands together, dropping my eyes back to the safe sight of his knife in the dirt. Not only had I just looked at a man's naked chest and stomach, I had ogled his abs. I acted every bit of my immature seventeen-winters. And to make things worse, he not only acknowledged that I had stared, but rubbed it in my face as well.

I couldn't help but wonder if all the men had such clearly defined muscles, or if only his body looked like it had been carved from stone. My face and ears burned with shame as I reined in my wayward thoughts and watched him loosen the dirt with his knife. In mere breaths, he pulled the taproot free, revealing a decent sized white carrot.

He held it out to me, and I took it with trembling hands, not daring to make eye contact. I had embarrassed myself enough for one afternoon. Gathering my harvest, I stood and turned to head back to the fields.

General Rafe straightened and wiped the knife on his leg, and I winced, hoping for all I was worth that he didn't slice his trousers. That would be a pain to mend. He tucked his knife in a hidden sheath under his belt. Without a word, he pushed in front of me, back down the trail toward the fields. I followed him, keeping a safe distance as he let branches swing back at me, just as I had done to him. We walked in silence and I had a moment to gather my wits about me again, clearly having lost all sense of sanity back in the forest. Who knew retrieving a carrot could be so dangerous to one's reputation?

Suddenly, General Rafe veered to the side, and I stood on the game trail, staring at his broad back as he pushed through the woods in an eastern direction. I started to ask where he was off to, but thought better of it. Biting my lip, I headed after him.

We advanced into the brush without a trail, other than the one that he made. The foliage was thick, and my dress kept snagging on brambles and shrubs. I sighed, thinking of the state it would be in when this adventure was through.

My skirts snared on a thorned bramble and I wrested it free with a frustrated grunt. Taking a step forward, I collided with General Rafe's back. He glared at me over his shoulder with his good eye. I bit my lip and tried to be as silent as possible, as it was clear he was listening for something. He looked straight ahead, and I waited as he tilted his head a fraction before pressing on. We traveled deeper into the forest, and I was grateful I wore my boots. Between the mud I dealt with this morn, and the briers and brambles I dealt with now, if I had chosen my sandals I would have regretted it.

A small jangling, like that of a bell, rang faintly through the woods. I stopped and tilted my head, trying to understand where it was coming from. General Rafe noticed my hesitation and looked back at me with a bored expression. I thought about telling him about the sound, but surely that was what he had been listening for before. I just hadn't heard it then.

I continued following him as he pressed on. Was he investigating the sound? Did he know what it was? It sounded like a small bell a trapper might use, but I was unfamiliar with them. I knew the louder, more prominent bells that farmers used to trap wild boars, but this was a faint jangling.

The sound grew clearer, though it was never loud. General Rafe slowed and held up a hand to tell me to stop. I halted as he dropped to a crouch and crept forward. He peered under the brush just as the jangling stopped and I waited, watching in anticipation.

Faster than my eye could track, his hand shot out and grabbed something. A terrible scream rent the air. I couldn't help but jump, and he straightened, pulling his knife free again.

He held a rabbit by its hind legs and cut the twine tangling them together. He turned back to face me, and I watched as he jerked, slicing the rabbit's throat. It thrashed wildly, bleeding out. As it did, General Rafe lifted his eye to watch me, gauging my reaction, I assumed.

I looked him dead in the eye and tilted my head. If he expected me to scream, rage, or cry at the loss of life, he was wrong. I shrugged and turned back the way we came, heading to the game trail that led to the training fields.

Loss of life was nothing new to me. Whether it be animals to feed people here in Regent, or soldiers and Dragon Riders at the front, death was a familiar beast. I was not ignorant of the brutality needed to feed hungry bellies. During one particularly hard winter, even Northwing felt hunger's pinch. That was the only winter we ate horse meat, but filling the bellies of children was a higher priority than feeding an animal.

I broke through the treeline and General Rafe exited close behind. I didn't wait for him before starting across the training fields. He let me go halfway to the obstacle course when he cut across my path, heading to a gap between buildings. I stopped and stared, wondering if I should follow yet again, or leave him be. Curiosity got the better of me, and I followed.

Soldiers gave him a wide berth and offered me suspicious glances, though at this point, almost all knew I was assigned to assist him. Perhaps it was that I willingly followed him after his treatment of me. It was more than likely the whole barracks had heard of my plight. Soldiers seemed to gossip as much as the women on the school grounds.

General Rafe came to a stop in front of a small fire pit tucked away behind a few buildings and grabbed a log from the stack, throwing it onto the smoldering coals. He tended the fire with deft hands, coaxing the embers into crackling flames. No soldiers wandered back here, providing a sense of privacy.

There were three roughly hewn chairs around the pit, as well as a thick cut of a tree trunk that I presumed acted as a table. The slab of wood was as tall as my waist and almost as thick in diameter. Tilting my head, I studied it, having never seen such a table.

I turned my sights back to General Rafe and noticed the field-dressed rabbit. He must have readied it while we were walking in the woods.

Flames licked at the log as he skinned the rabbit with ease. He skewered it and placed it on a spit over the growing fire before sitting in one of the chairs, leaning on its back legs. I watched with a frown, as I was sure his weight on just two sticks of wood would splinter it, but it somehow managed to hold firm.

General Rafe glanced from me to an empty chair and motioned me to sit with a jerk of his head. As I took a seat, I rubbed a hand over the smooth surface of the makeshift table.

I placed my harvest before me, sorting through the collection. "I've never seen a table like this," I commented.

He focused on the crackling flames. "Used to be in the training fields," he grunted.

"Really? Did a dragon move it here?" I wondered aloud, checking each leaf and flower for any bugs or questionable debris.

General Rafe snorted at my statement and smirked. "I did."

This slab of tree was massive. No man could lift it on their own. No man, no matter how big. I raised an incredulous brow.

"Did you use a horse?" I prodded.

He rolled his head to peer at me, something between a sneer and smirk on his face, but didn't answer.

"You moved it? By yourself?" Surely not.

"You say that like it surprises you, girl." He threaded his fingers behind his head, and his tunic fell apart, displaying his muscular chest.

I turned away, unwilling to make the same mistake as before. After a pause, he got up to turn the skewer.

"How?" I finally asked.

"You tell me." He crouched beside the fire, muscles bunching and coiling under his skin. He looked over his shoulder at me, waiting for my reply.

"Not even you could lift it," I said, smiling at his affronted expression. "You must have rolled it."

After another smirk, he nodded, returning his attention to his meal. I pinched my lips together and rubbed the carrot with a semi-clean spot of my dress. Even rolling it would be a terrible feat. I would think only a dragon could move such a thing, not a man.

General Rafe pulled the rabbit off the fire and used a knife to cut off a piece of flesh. The creature wasn't large, and with its cavity being empty, it cooked quickly. He lifted the knife and meat to his mouth, taking a bite, and hissed around the heat.

I turned my attention back to my plants and ate a bite of clover. He had been far more prepared than I to forage for food. Though from what Elib said, he only ate what he caught or gathered himself, and was therefore more experienced. He took a seat across from me, bringing the skewered rabbit with him. We ate in companionable silence and I wondered how long it would last before he did something that would make me hate him again.

Not long at all. As I chewed on a mint leaf, he reached over and snatched a handful of clover. I frowned as he tossed it in his mouth, chewing with a grimace.

I should have kept the Nightshade.

Determined to ignore his rude behavior, I focused back on my meal. He reached over and placed a piece of meat on my side of the table, and I looked up at him skeptically. He motioned to it with his knife and shrugged. A peace offering? Doubtful.

He returned to devouring his rabbit, and I glanced between him and the meat before popping it into my mouth. He grunted in approval without taking his eyes off his meal, and I finished my harvest. My belly was full, but I wondered how long my meal of leafy greens and a smidgen of meat would last me. I had gone without meals before, but General Rafe was certainly putting me to work today.

Finished, he tossed the bones in the fire and tidied up. As I stood brushing some of the dried mud off my skirt, I groaned, noting the new tear near the hem. I hoped that Master Elenor would find some job for me to do so that I could afford to buy myself a new walking dress and sandals.

General Rafe took off, and I followed as he led us back to the training field. We arrived as the bell tower rang with the second high-pitched chime. Either General Rafe had an internal clock or he was incredibly lucky.

Looking around at the soldiers, I felt as though none of them had been very lucky foraging for their meals. They grumbled and muttered, standing from various seated positions as General Rafe arrived. He walked through them to greet the Captain and explain the next round of exercises, to resume the day's training.

I tried to hide the small smile on my face as General Rafe went back to ignoring me and casting insults about like rain. I might have to work hard, but I didn't mind it at all.

Chapter Eleven

By the time the fifth chime rang, I was exhausted—physically and mentally. I did my best to avoid looking at the soldiers in various states of undress, but the concentration that took wore down my mind. Mud covered every bit of me, and my limbs trembled with fatigue. Yet, I was the happiest I had been in a week. General Rafe might not have directly taught me anything, but I listened. He didn't put me through rounds as a soldier, or Dragon Rider, but he ordered me to lift fallen logs and climb to fix netting often enough to give me a good workout.

I was just pleased he wasn't treating me as though my only worth was as a woman—helpless and doomed to mend my life away. If he thought I was determined now, I couldn't wait to show him what I was capable of when I had a dragon at my side. I wanted to show the General what I was really made of.

I heaved a sigh, and sat on the dirt, too tired to stand while waiting for Willhelm to fetch me. After the Captain dismissed his cadets, they shot off, either to bathe or for the dining hall. I didn't know. But they were eager to distance themselves from the grueling General.

My fingers ran down my braid and I pulled it in front of me, playing with the ends. Willhelm would disapprove of me staying where men were dressed immodestly, but I thought perhaps he might approve of my determination. As I sat, pondering what Willhelm might say, a set of dust-covered boots came into view.

General Rafe had donned the tunic that fit him and actually buttoned it for some measure of decency. He threw the too-small tunic at me with a scowl.

"Fix it." He cut my attempt at a defensive reply short, holding up his hand. "Fix it, girl," he snarled and stalked off.

I smiled to myself. It was an easy fix, though I didn't know if he knew that. I turned it over, studying the side seam where Master Elta had taught me to tuck the extra fabric in and sew over it. She argued he might want to let it out again, and did not want to trim off the excess.

The detail that went into the garment was astounding. Master Elta told me she made him five tunics when he was promoted to General two years ago. They held up well, despite the wear he put on them. He probably bullied her into the job, yet she seemed to have a soft spot for the General. Which was completely baffling.

"Avyanna?"

Willhelm walked toward me, frowning. I was probably quite the sight, crumpled on the ground, slathered in sweat and mud. Yet I couldn't bring myself to care.

I forced myself to my feet and smoothed out my filthy dress. "Good Day, Willhelm."

"Should I ask what you were doing on the ground?" His voice held a tentative edge as he eyed me up and down.

"Resting. It's been quite a day."

"I gathered. The men have been talking." He frowned as we turned for the road.

I glanced at the soldiers walking about. General Rafe worked them hard. I was surprised they had it in them to gossip already.

"What have they been saying?"

"That either you or the General are going to lose it and someone is going to have to defend your honor."

I tilted my head back and laughed. "They're only worried about their own hides!"

"They wouldn't stand a chance against him, you know."

"Yes, I know. But I want you to know I'll not call on anyone to defend my impugned honor." I rolled my eyes. "I can defend it well enough on my own."

"Much in the way you mended that tunic?" he asked, jutting his chin toward the bundle in my hands.

I smirked. "Much like that. I might be a woman, but I have my ways."

Willhelm grunted and eyed me before his attention returned to the path ahead. I started up a festive tune as we walked along.

After a moment, he spoke again, "I take it today went well?"

I smiled up at him and told him all about my day and its adventures.

After I finished last meal, I found Master Elenor, and was disheartened to learn there were no jobs yet. I made my way below the school dorms, sandals flapping against my feet. The fastening strap finally broke and my toes curled on my right foot, trying to hold it in place. My filthy beige dress was tucked under my arm, as well as my sleeping shift and clean under-breeches. This dress needed a thorough washing, and so did I.

As I padded down the winding stairs to the underground springs, I watched my footing by the torchlight. I ran my hand along the wall, not that there would be anything to hold if I fell. Humidity thickened the air the further I descended. It often made the stairway slick, despite how hard the maids worked to keep it clean and dry.

This stairwell adjoined the women's side of the dorms. It was spacious enough for a human. There were other separate springs with passages large enough to be accessed by the dragons that lived in the canyon. This one, though, was used strictly by women for their laundry and bathing.

Finally clearing the stairwell, I entered the expansive opening where women bustled to and fro, finishing their laundry for the day. They scurried about, washing and gossiping—a happy thrum of souls.

An entryway to my left led to the washing rooms. To the right was a chamber that somehow had a constant breeze. It had something to do with where a natural cave opened, allowing fresh air through to the chamber. However it worked, it allowed the rows of laundry to dry quickly.

I continued to the room on the right, following a woman with an armful of barracks' laundry. The stench was foul. I wrinkled my nose and grabbed a bar of soap off a nearby supply table before pressing on.

All around me, women talked about their days, their hopes, and dreams, and their plans for the future. I frowned. They had each other to share their aspirations with, but I had no one. Willhelm and I were friends, but I couldn't imagine telling him everything.

I crossed to an empty spot near a hot spring and settled down to wash my muddied dress. After setting my spare clothes on a dry slab, I pushed the dress under the warm water and set to scrubbing, listening to the women as I worked.

A pair washing their garments beside me spoke of a farmer one had met and how she swooned over him. If I ever swooned over a man, I wouldn't be able to tell Willhelm. We would never be that close. He was a man—and much older than I. He'd likely look at me in disgust if I ever managed to swoon over a boy.

I had never been friends with anyone, really. Though, I remembered playing with kids when I lived back in the village with my mother, but I couldn't recall their names or what they looked like. When I was sent here, everything was too new and my pain was too fresh to make friends. All the girls my age were nursing their own wounds from the loss of a parent or loved one. Some bonded over mutual losses, and some even came from the same raided villages. Most girls created friendships a few years after they arrived, but not me.

Alone, I withdrew and applied myself to learning and books. I practically lived in the Records Room before I took on the assignment of Masters' assistant. I was the odd one, and I was easily ignored.

Most students ignored me, most women tolerated me, and the older women taught me. I went without notice—until I was announced as First Chosen for Hatching Day. That got people's attention, though it was not a surprise. The process of selecting the First Chosen was not based on favoritism. It was based on your marks from testing and your aptitude.

Dragons could not speak to anyone that was not their Rider, yet they could feel an openness, like a beckoning, in some people. This opening, this calling, we referred to as aptitude. It was what many speculated the hatchlings latched onto for the bond. It was as if there were two lands welcome to each other, but no bridge to join them. On Hatching Day, that bridge was made, and the bond solidified.

The emptiness I felt would one day be resolved with a dragonling. I didn't need human companionship. I only needed an egg to hatch for me in a few months.

I stood, wringing out my dress and checking it over. My fingers ached from scrubbing out the grass stains I gained from my venture into the woods during midday meal, but it seemed as if the pain was worth the effort.

"Missed a spot." Two teenagers giggled. They eyed me with judgemental sneers, then strutted off. Their whispers and laughter bounced off the stone walls.

I shrugged, retrieving my clean clothes, and left the washing room. After returning the soap, I started toward the drying chamber and secured my dress beneath another woman's. I learned long ago not to single out my clothing. To do so was just asking for mischief. Any girl who set their clothing aside from the others often returned to find them stained, torn, or stolen. Nobody messed with the older women's laundry, though, so I always placed my clothes somewhat under the other women's.

Making my way to the bathing chambers, I grabbed a clean bar of soap from the rack and pushed back the heavy curtain to the main pool. Inside, a welcoming crowd of girls splashed and played. Ignoring them, I took the stone path to my left and crossed over the wooden bridge to the carved hall of private chambers.

The main pool was where most girls and women bathed, and the private chambers were often used when a woman was at the end of her moon cycle. The mini springs drained faster than the large pool, providing more hygienic conditions.

When a mini spring was in use, most women closed the curtains that hung above the entry. More often than not, I had to wait for a woman to finish and hope that she was not at the end of her moon cycle. But today I was in luck. The chamber glowed in the soft lantern light—completely empty.

The spring water sparkled clear, and tendrils of steam beckoned me, calling to my aching limbs. I stripped quickly, stepping in with my bar of soap. Every muscle relaxed as the warm water lapped against my body. I loosened my hair from its braid and scrubbed at the mud caking my skin.

Then I dove, letting the water swallow me up. I held my breath as long as I could, willing the moment to last.

It was here and only here I could have complete silence. Even in my room, I could hear the girls nearby, and the constant bustle of the surrounding women. I tried to bathe every day, not just for cleanliness' sake but for the minuscule peace it offered me.

I sat on the bottom of the stony spring till my air-starved lungs burned with need. Pushing off, I gasped when I broke the surface. A wave of melancholy swept over me, like a weight setting on my chest. I moved to lay my head on the cool stone ledge and closed my eyes.

I missed my mother. I wished life here was easier. It was physically easy, that was absolute, but it was harder emotionally. The mental-strain was heartrending. The sickening truth was, if my father hadn't died, I wouldn't be stuck here, feeling all alone.

Tears burned my eyes, but I blinked them away. I rarely allowed myself to think such thoughts. Thoughts dictated emotion, and emotion affected behavior. Feeling sorry for myself wouldn't change anything. I was not about to leave Northwing and everything I learned, to run home to my mother and abandon my dragonling that was yet to hatch for me.

Nodding in agreement with my thoughts, I hauled myself out and dried using the sheet hanging in the room. After dressing and grabbing my things, I jerked back the curtain, leaving the chamber and my woes behind.

I pulled myself together and walked taller. I would be a Dragon Rider, and Dragon Riders did not cry to themselves in pools.

My week with General Rafe flew past far too quickly for my liking. It was hard work, and my muscles were so sore I often debated between a bath or dinner because I simply didn't have the energy for both. My body ached, but my mind was alive. I had a taste of physical training and I loved it.

General Rafe kept pushing me to do harder tasks, taunting me with statements about how a lowly girl couldn't accomplish anything. He would constantly throw in my face something about girls not knowing anything about combat. Yet, for all he said to me, he allowed me to test my mettle.

We foraged every day, and I learned he always had a plan, whether it was trapping an animal, or setting a bow out and knowing exactly where to hunt for doves. He was always prepared for a meal. During the midday breaks, we drifted into companionable silence, only speaking when necessary.

General Rafe was a man of few words, unless it came to insulting someone. He was hard and rough around the edges, and I still hadn't forgiven him for how he treated me, but I understood his tactics now. He was testing me, seeing how far he could push me and if I would push back.

He, thankfully, wore his tunics every day, though he sometimes left them open and I would flush, trying to retain eye contact. The men soon learned that I would not call upon them to defend my honor and I didn't mind them stripping their tunics. I was the intruder here, and I did not want to inconvenience them solely because of my gender.

On my last day as his assistant, I wiped the sweat off my brow as the soldiers were dismissed. I settled under the shade of a building and noticed General Rafe stalking toward me.

"You're not done, girl," he said.

I looked back at the obstacle course where we spent our week. I fixed every single obstacle and once again covered myself in mud from head to toe. How was I not done? Had I not said goodbye?

"Begging your pardon, it's been a pleas– It's been *informative* assisting you, General Rafe." I dipped into a curtsy.

He smirked at me and crossed his arms. "Got that off your chest?"

I gave him a puzzled frown and glanced away to look for Willhelm.

When my attention returned to him, my mouth went dry. His arched brow and smirk were daring me to object as he shrugged out of his tunic. My eye twitched in rebellion as I held his gaze. He held his tunic out, but I didn't take it. I cleared my throat and waited for an explanation.

"Mend it."

I stood there, not believing what I had just heard. Earlier today, I noticed the missing top button, the one at his neck that allowed a slight glimpse of his chest, but I would not fix it this time.

"I apologize," I said, finding my courage. "However, I am not your personal seamstress."

"Mend it, girl." He spoke as if adding the condescending 'girl' to the end of his statement would make me more inclined to obey.

I lifted my chin and glared. "As of the fifth chime, I was no longer your assistant," I bit out.

He just stood there, gazing at me with an almost bored look, holding out his tunic.

"No!" I growled and whirled to see Willhelm approaching. "Good Day!" I snapped, glancing back at him to catch him smirking, before I stalked over to walk past Willhelm.

He pivoted and walked with me, chuckling. "Good last day, eh?"

"He's a barbarian!"

I couldn't believe after all I had done all week he would still treat me like that, and dare to demand something of me when I was not obligated by duty to obey. Neither was it in my best interest.

The next morning, I woke with mixed feelings. I was happy to be done assisting General Rafe due to his arrogance and rude nature. But I was slightly disheartened, as well. He actually gave me jobs and expected me to follow through. It gave me a sense of importance... when he wasn't berating me because I was a simple girl, that is.

When I rose from my cot, I stretched and headed to my washbasin. I had just finished rinsing my mouth when a knock sounded at my door. I stopped and tilted my head, wondering who might need me at this hour. Throwing my cloak over my night shift, I cracked open the door to see Master Elenor standing there, jaw clenched tight, as if I had kept her waiting.

"Master Elenor!" I jerked the door open in case she was there to inspect my room.

She was a tall, strong woman. Even her gray hair obeyed her every whim and dared not escape the severe bun she had it pulled into. Her blue eyes were the color of the coolest waters, with a temperament to match.

"Miss Avyanna, I have a job for you."

I stood a little straighter. I was excited she found a job, yet worried it would involve something like hauling the dragon dung out of the canyon.

"There's been a request for mending," she said, extending a small parcel wrapped in paper.

I bit back a groan, though I pasted a smile on my face as I took the package. What I would do to be done mending! When I was a Dragon Rider, I would never mend another garment ever again. I would hire someone else to do it.

She towered above me with a frown that said she knew too much. "I was told to tell you it's expected back by nightfall."

I schooled the shock from my face. Someone had told Master Elenor to tell me something? Not even Master Brann *told* Master Elenor to do anything.

"I will find time to mend it. Thank you," I said, trying to hide my surprise.

"I also expect you to not neglect your room or your current assignment."

"Yes, ma'am," I replied.

With one last fiercely disapproving frown, she left down the hall, her back stiff, and straight. I sighed and closed the door, setting the package on my bed. I would at least get an idea of how much work needed to be done before heading off this morning.

I untied the twine that held it together.

"Curse him," I muttered as the paper fell away.

Tucked inside was a black sleeveless tunic with a missing button. I closed my eyes and hoped I would have enough patience to see me through this day. He couldn't order me to do his mending, so he told Master Elenor to make me do it.

I mumbled a thousand curses and picked it up, noting the needle, black thread, and button that laid under it. Next to the button was a solid gold coin. My jaw dropped.

A gold piece was worth almost as much as I had in my spare coin pouch. Normally jobs for students paid a few coppers—a silver if one was lucky. A gold coin? For simple mending?

I snapped my mouth shut with a frown and glared at it. I couldn't take that much for mending. It would be dishonest. Not only for my conscience, but also to all the other students that worked so hard for spare coin. I desperately needed new dresses and sandals, but I felt as though I was robbing the other students if I accepted that much.

Sighing, I took off the cloak and sat down in my night shift, threading the needle. It would take me less than five minutes to sew a button on. I could have it done and take it back this morning.

I hurried through the work, careful to only do my best. Wrapping the tunic back up with the notions and coin, I dressed and headed out the door. I contemplated skipping breakfast but thought better of it, grabbing a simple roll to eat on the way.

I carried the parcel under my arm and hurried down the path to the barracks' gate. Just as it came into view, the parcel was yanked from my hold. I whirled around, wondering what snagged it.

Vivian stood there with two other teenage girls, arms braced across her chest. General Rafe's tunic was still wrapped, but now in her hands. For some reason, a shot of annoyance ran through me at the fact that she was holding the General's tunic.

"What do we have here?" she sneered, turning over the parcel, and feeling it.

"It's a mending," I stated.

Normally, I treated incidents with Vivian and her type with feigned indifference. They could never really hurt me, so I let them rage. But today was different. That was General Rafe's tunic. He would have my head if anything happened to it. It didn't help that I was running late to meet the Horse Master. If I didn't get moving, I would make a terrible first impression.

"You've been spending a lot of time on the barracks' side." Vivian tossed the package in the air, then hugged it to her chest.

I held in my snarky reply. "I'm assigned to the Masters there."

"We've heard things." One of Vivian's minions offered her best fearful glare.

"I'm sure you have." Rolling a shoulder, I held out my hand, waiting. I faced down the Demon General. A little girl didn't scare me.

Vivian clutched the package, leaning in to whisper as if it was some terrible, juicy rumor set on destroying me. "Things about you being around men... things about you being immodest."

I didn't manage to stop the roll of my eyes, though I tried to keep my next words as placating as possible. "The men are soldiers. They're doing their job and I'm doing mine."

"They say the General slapped you around... put you in your place." The other minion curled her fingers, examining her nails.

"He did no such thing," I shot back, though the seed of truth to her words warmed my cheeks in a shameful blush.

"But he touched you." Vivian hurried to challenge.

I had no argument there. He did. And in public, no less. The soldiers witnessed our exchange, and word got around. I lifted my chin and calmed myself, reigning in my emotions. They had no place here.

"Give me the package, Vivian." I stared at her, daring her to make a move. I was angry, and I never felt angry during these confrontations. It was just Vivian's way of interacting with the world. She was a bully, but harmless. I had nothing to fear, and yet anxiety zipped through my veins, urging my fight-or-flight instinct.

"What else did he do to you, I wonder? I've heard—"

I moved as quick as a viper and snatched the package from her hands, silencing her. She threw her head back and laughed while her minions snickered. I just gave in to the bait. I cursed myself and spun on my heel, seeing red.

My strides were brisk and clipped. I showed my orders to the guards, wanting to slap them when they didn't take them, but just nodded me toward Willhelm.

Willhelm stood there, leaning in his usual place against the gatepost, watching me with hooded eyes. He had to have seen everything... maybe even overhead everything, too.

I knew my reputation was at risk when I didn't ask a man to defend my honor. General Rafe treating me so poorly in public didn't help things either. But I never thought there'd be rumors suggesting I slept with him, like some village prostitute.

Willhelm straightened and nodded to the guards before leading me through the streets. I stared at the ground and walked at his elbow, seething in silence.

"Well, out with it," he urged.

I glared at him, then back at the ground.

He chuckled. "What were they on about?" he asked.

Taking a deep breath through my nose and steady exhale, I put my mind back in order. "Rumors are flying about me," I stated, hating how those words sounded.

He nodded with a knowing look. "Yes, they are."

"You knew?" I asked, surprised that he would participate in gossip.

"I've heard bits here and there." He shrugged. "Some soldiers confirm it, others deny it, but what does it matter?"

"It matters!" I bit out, trying to rein in my ever-growing temper. "You might not care about reputation as a man, but as a woman, it means a lot!"

Willhelm stopped and faced me, eyebrows raised at my tone. "Do I hear that right? From the same mouth that has so often argued that she didn't want to be treated like a woman? That she is to be a Dragon Rider, and being a woman didn't matter?" he mused.

I ducked away from his intense gaze. How could I tell him that even though I said it didn't matter, I still felt like it did? How could I explain that I wanted to defy the odds my gender placed on me? Just because I didn't want it to define me, didn't make it hurt any less when people thought ill of me for it.

"Chin up. Let it go. If people aren't talking about you, they're talking about someone else." He continued his long strides. "Pay them no mind."

I focused on the road and tucked my emotions away. Willhelm was right. I couldn't do anything about it now.

"Master Aron is pleased to have you today," he said, changing the subject.

I cleared my throat. "Is he?"

"He is. He believes having a *female* presence," he gave me a pointed look, "will have a calming effect on some of the wilder horses."

I bit my lip and nodded, looking around as we reached the stable. It was a large building, one story, but it was longer than the school dorms. Horse stalls lined both sides. On the far side, all the stalls opened into sectioned paddocks.

Doors broke the stone wall that faced the front. Above, reed blinds were coiled, tied to the ceiling. I assumed they unrolled them and staked them to the ground during the rain and snow.

"Hail!" came a cheerful call.

A lanky man, barely out of boyhood, jogged toward us. His shock of red hair was as disheveled as his clothes, looking as if he just rolled out of bed.

"Master Aron," Willhelm greeted with a nod.

"Sergeant Willhelm, how's that mare treating young Fior?" he asked.

"Well enough. He's managed to keep his seat during training," Willhelm replied.

"Glad to hear it!" He turned to me with an amiable smile. "And you must be Miss Avyanna."

"At your service, Master Aron." I dipped into a curtsy.

"Oh my, please don't bother with curtsies. Might scare my stableboys into thinking they have to bow to me now," he laughed.

The sound relaxed me, rich and genuine. I would like this Master far better than General Rafe.

"Now, are you ready to see some real horses?" he asked with a dramatic hand on his hip.

"Absolutely." I gripped General Rafe's tunic to my chest.

For now, I would focus on the horses, not the nasty rumors going about. Horses didn't care about rumors anyhow.

Chapter Twelve

I soon realized there was a massive difference between a lady's mount and war horses. The beasts that called the barracks home were demon bred. They were huge. My head only came to their chests, and they had the temperament of wild boars.

Master Aron told me not to be afraid of them, and to be calm. Though even he appeared a bit worried while comparing my stature to the animals. At first, he watched as I led around an old broodmare before he had me brave any of the chargers. This way, under his careful scrutiny, he tested my capabilities of handling the creatures.

She snorted my hair and nudged my shoulder, though that playful shove sent me staggering. Master Aron ordered me to take a shorter lead on her. She stubbornly carried her head high like a carriage horse.

It didn't take long before I was able to lead her about. Master Aron was satisfied with my handling, even if it looked as though the beasts could chew me up and spit me back out.

It surprised me when Master Aron didn't send me to muck out stalls or clean up the paddocks, but instead took me through his rounds. He went about checking on maimed horses. He explained the malady, their treatments, and how to handle them with their injuries.

We were working with a gelding that had a bad limp. Master Aron said it was due to the horse's hock. He applied an ointment and wrapped it. The gelding tried to nip at him several times—I kept a safe distance away.

"Well, I'd say it's time for us to start with training, but it looks like it's almost time for the midday meal. Do you take your meals at the dining hall?" he asked.

I put the ointment back in its place inside the basket Master Aron hauled around. "I haven't yet had the opportunity." What I wanted to say was that I hadn't been allowed yet, but that sounded petty and childish.

"Eh, I'm not going to tell you what to do on your time off." He straightened and gave the gelding a rough pat on the neck before untying him.

However, I noticed the silent objection in his statement.

"Do you think it would be unwise for me to go?" I asked, shouldering the basket.

He rubbed the back of his neck with a half-hearted shrug. "I think some men don't know how to act in a lady's presence, is all."

I smiled and nodded at him. It wouldn't be a change of pace, anyway. "That's fine. I had enough to eat this morning. I have a package for General Rafe, though. Is there some way I might get it to him?"

The corners of his lips dipped into a frown at the mention of the General. "The package you left in my office? I can have one of my boys run it to his quarters."

"Ah, alright then. Thank you," I said, dismayed, as I wanted to talk with General Rafe about his overpayment for the mending.

"I could look for someone to escort you if you prefer to take it to him yourself, but he doesn't hang about during meals."

"Oh, I know." I smiled to myself. He was probably in the woods somewhere checking his traps or hunting.

"I wouldn't feel right sending you to his quarters, if you understand, miss," he added.

I tilted my head at his words. Why wouldn't he feel right about that? I was just sending off a package. If a stableboy accompanied me, what harm would there be? Perhaps it had something to do with the rumors going about.

"I understand." I frowned as we left the stall. "If it's alright, I'd like to send a note with it as well."

"Fine by me," he said, shutting the stall door and locking it.

In his office, I wrote a quick note and tucked it inside. A young boy with a head full of raven hair and eyes dancing with mischief took the parcel and ran off.

"Pike is a good lad. He'll see it there safely."

I smiled and settled down to help organize some paperwork, noting that Master Aron worked through his midday meal as well.

"Do you normally take a midday meal?" I asked, not wanting to impose.

A slight blush colored his cheeks. "I—ah. I do," he stammered. "But it wouldn't be right for me to leave you here and not take you."

He didn't act as though he was a Master. He acted like a young man—which, in all honesty, he was. But he was a Master and deserved that confidence.

"Don't worry, I'm fine here. I'll stay till you return." I waved at his thin frame before focusing on the papers. "Go, eat."

"I really shouldn't." He shuffled about the parchments littering his desk.

"Would you fetch me something, then? I'm actually feeling rather faint now," I teased.

With a lopsided grin, he relented. "Alright then, I'll go fetch us both something. I'll be back before you know it." He pushed out the door at a quick pace.

Master Aron was quite a pleasant fellow. He was funny and kind. I judged him to be in his late twentieth-winter. He didn't seem any older than that. He lacked the confidence that came with age, holding onto his boyish charm.

I shook my head, mentally slapping myself. Boyish charm? Since when were boys charming?

I sorted through breeding papers with a renewed passion. Clearly, I had too much time to think if I was contemplating the charm of boys.

※

Master Aron returned with a chunk of crusty bread, some cheese, and radish. After I finished my meal, we worked with a mare in a circular pen. Master Aron stood in the middle, driving the horse with a long stick and rope. I leaned against the fence, watching as he moved and guided her without muttering a word. The stableboy, Pike, ran up to me, red-faced and panting as he tugged at my dress.

"Miss, the big General told me to give you these." Between his heavy breaths, he held out his hand, showing two gold coins.

I bit my tongue, pushing down a wave of anger. "Did he say why?" I asked, unwilling to take them.

Pike shook his head hard. Those big brown eyes, once filled with mischief, now only held suspicion and a bit of wariness. "He just said, 'You get these to her, and don't be snatchin' 'em.'" Pike lowered his tone to his best rumbly voice, then kicked at the dirt. "Don't mind me sayin' miss, but he didn' like your words on the paper much either. He was all in a tizzy, throwin' stuffs."

I smirked at that thought and knelt to get on his level. "How about you take those coins then, huh? I don't need them, and I bet they could buy a lot of things a little boy like you could want."

At my words, he grabbed my hand and shoved the coins into my palm. "No, ma'am, he'll think I'm a snatcher. And I ain't! You know what he says they do with snatchers? Cut off their hands!" He backed away from me as if I were some wild animal. "I want my hands!".

I hid my frown. Of course, General Rafe had to terrify the boy and bring me back an extra gold piece. I wasn't going to win this battle.

"Alright, thank you, dear sir!" I called as he spun on his heel and took off running.

The gold pieces were warm from Pike's hand. This much gold would easily buy a dress and new sandals, and I'd still have plenty saved for my mother's Year's End Celebration. I still didn't feel right taking it, though.

For a moment, I watched the bay mare run laps in the pen. She cantered gracefully, hooves pounding the dry dirt in steady cadence.

Perhaps I would go talk to him and explain that this was far too much money for what he hired me for. I doubted that would get me anything but an argument, but I could try. At least if I explained it to him, I might not feel as bad.

With my mind made up, I focused back on Master Aron. I'd ask Willhelm to see me to General Rafe when he came to fetch me. Surely it wouldn't be that bad.

I was wrong. So wrong. How could I have ever thought it was a good idea to seek out this man again?

"I'm sorry, but you don't understand. The mending isn't worth this pay." I tried again.

General Rafe leaned against the side of a training building, glaring at me with his arms crossed over his chest. He didn't move a muscle or make any indication he heard me. He completely ignored my outstretched hand, displaying the coins. With one boot crossed over the other, looking to all the world as if there was not a soul in front of him, trying to talk to him. Willhelm shifted his feet, waiting to escort me to the barracks' gate.

"I can't take this." I pushed my hand closer to him.

Soldiers passed to and fro, but no one stopped to see my mortification. I bit my lip. If he would not take the gold back, or even talk to me about it, it wasn't worth the trouble of doing his mending. My sanity was worth more than spare coin.

I thought about trying to stuff it in his hand as the stableboy did to me, but my mind warned me of all the terrible things that might happen. General Rafe was not a man who could be forced to do anything.

I glanced at Willhelm, who wasn't even looking at us, but rather off to the side, where a Dragon Rider flew just above the buildings.

The dragon's peridot green scales glinted in the fading light, and something in my heart faltered. I would not be bound to this General forever. I pulled myself up to my full height, which wasn't much, and glared back at General Rafe.

"Well, if you're not going to at least converse with me concerning overpayment, please find someone else to do your mending. Many students are looking for jobs and are better at it than I am. I'm sure one of them will be far more delighted to mend your tunics," I bit out, and turned to Willhelm.

Willhelm glanced between us before he nodded toward the General and started for the road. General Rafe's amused snort erupted from behind. I lifted my chin higher and followed Willhelm, and the snort shifted into a deep chuckle.

Of all the condescending, arrogant, rude pricks...

I whirled and threw the two gold pieces at him. He tossed his head back, roaring with laughter. My cheeks burned as I stomped alongside Willhelm.

When we were a safe distance away, he peered over with a glint in his eye. "Don't look now, but your age is showing."

I threw him a glare and kept walking. It was immature, and I already regretted it. I was better than that. I didn't throw things like a petulant child. It wasn't like General Rafe behaved any better, staring off as if I hadn't said a word. He always seemed to get under my skin. His arrogant 'I'm better than you' and 'You're not worthy of my time' attitude was wearing on me.

I blew out a forceful breath and looked up to the sky for patience.

"Well, how did your day go?" Amusement tinted Willhelm's voice. "Did you enjoy the horses as much as you thought you would?"

I smiled, thankful for the change of subject. "I had a splendid day. Master Aron let me assist with almost everything. I appreciated his efforts at finding useful things for me to do. The horses are... intimidating, though."

"They're not the calm type you're used to, I'm sure," he agreed.

"How do you ride them? There was a stallion today that I was sure would kick Master Aron clear across the barracks."

Willhelm chuckled and nodded absently at a passing soldier. "Most of us don't ride the stallions. We ride the geldings or mares. Stallions are too high-strung and spend more time fighting us than doing their jobs."

I pressed closer to Willhelm as a soldier brushed past me, almost running into me.

He continued, "Stallions have their place, though, for breeding stock or for the more talented riders who need a stallion's recklessness."

"Do you ride a stallion?"

"I ride a very mild-mannered mare. She's as easygoing as they come," he said, shaking his head.

"What's her name?"

Willhelm looked down at me as if my age was showing again. Yet, something as personal as one's steed had to have a name, didn't it?

"We don't all have our own horses, Avyanna. That's a luxury afforded to few. I ride a mare that is shared between me and two other Sergeants." He rubbed at his chin. "We're not on the front. We have no need for our own steeds. Here the horses are used for training, and we don't schedule horsemanship training at the same time."

"I see."

That made sense, didn't it? Surely she still had a name, but I wasn't about to ask again and be thought of as immature.

The next morning, I was getting dressed when a knock sounded at my door. I paused, lacing up my dress to stare at the solid wood door as if it would show me who stood beyond it. Frowning, I finished my lacing and padded over to open it.

"Avyanna," Master Elenor greeted sharply.

I plastered a smile on my face, eyes darting down to the package she held.

Surely not.

"Good morn, Master Elenor. What can I do for you?" I asked as pleasantly as possible.

"You wanted a job to earn coin, did you not?" she arched a single, stern eyebrow.

I was certainly on her bad side this morning. "Yes, ma'am..." I started.

General Rafe did this. I just knew it.

"If you ask for a job to earn coin, then you'll take the coin that is given you." Each word was clipped in agitation. "You do not get to insult people by making them charity cases."

I clenched my jaw, angry at General Rafe, and yet fearful of offending Master Elenor. "Master Elenor, if you'll let me explain–"

"There's no explanation needed. Simply do the job, or let me know you don't need extra coin."

Dread slithered through me. If I told her I didn't want a job, she would be sure that I received none at all. Beggars couldn't be choosers. I needed that extra coin. I was already wearing out my beige dress, and the heat of summer was fast approaching, which would make my boots impossible to wear.

"Yes, Master Elenor," I said with a note of resignation. I wanted nothing to do with this General, and yet here he was, offering me the one thing I needed.

"Good. Now that we have that established, here is another mending to be done." She peered over my head into my room. "See that you tidy up as well. I'll not have you living in a pigsty."

She handed me the package, and I took it, holding it gingerly as if it contained a thousand serpents. I glanced behind me, where my blanket sat folded on my bed, and the rest of my room bare and spotless.

Looking back at Master Elenor, I plastered on a tight smile. "Yes, Master."

With a satisfied nod, she spun on her heel and walked down the hall.

I closed the door and placed the package on my bed. Inside was the same black thread, needle, and one of the sleeveless tunics I knew so well. I laid the tunic out, glaring at the two gold pieces underneath.

The man was infuriating.

I snatched the coins, muttering to myself about the stubbornness of men, and shoved them in my coin pouch.

Chapter Thirteen

Summer Year 896

The season passed quickly, and before I knew it, I completed my assignment with the Masters. I learned as much as possible, hoping it would give me an edge when I started my training as a Dragon Rider.

General Rafe continued to send me his clothes, though it faded to one mending a week. He still overpaid me, and I bought myself two new dresses and a pair of sandals, then saved the rest. It built to a hefty amount, and I considered buying myself a nice riding outfit once my dragonling was old enough to ride.

I was given two weeks before Hatching Day to rest and relax. I spent the majority of the time studying. I immersed myself in reading everything from the anatomy of a dragon to battle tactics on the front lines. Most of what I read was beyond my grasp, yet I hoped that by inundating myself with the information, some of it would sink in. Even if something made little sense to me now, it would when I needed it to.

I'd been restless all night, my stomach turning. This morning, my eyes itched with fatigue. There was no rest to be had when it was my second Hatching Day as First Chosen. It would be my last sleepless night, for tonight I would have my dragonling and it would put my fears at ease.

With so little to call my own, packing my room wasn't hard. I wanted everything to be ready, as when my dragonling hatched, I would move to the Dragon Canyon. I had only visited it once, on a tour during class. The caverns were huge, and me and my dragonling would grow into them. Most were big enough to house a dragon of five years and their Rider easily. The larger, older dragons lived in caves further in the canyon, so deep they were only accessible by dragonback.

On my way to the amphitheater, I noted the hustle and bustle of those around me. People walked here and there, laughing freely. This was one of the few days that common folk gained access to the King's grounds. It was quite a celebration.

Vendors sold roasted goods, or sugary confections. The old and young alike joined in festival games, and a few merchants hawked their wares, adding to the pleasant din.

A bell tolled, a bell that differed from all the others on the King's grounds.

The chime rang clear and deep, and the bellow of dragons followed. Dragons took to the sky, flying for the amphitheater roof. As they settled on their perches, they jostled and snapped at each other when another got too close. I could almost hear the reassuring murmurs of their Riders.

Anxiety flooded me, my heart lurching to my throat. My mother wasn't here, and I wasn't sure why. Her letters told me how excited she was, and that she would be here to see a hatchling choose me. When I left the dorms, though, no one had seen her.

I wondered if she was well. None of the commoners mentioned anything of poor weather delaying them or any other worries on the road. Perhaps she'd fallen ill and was unable to make the distance by begging rides from people headed this way, as she normally did.

Insecurity crept into my bones as I neared the amphitheater. I parted with the crowd lining up at the main entrance and took the smaller path to the side of the building where the Chosen entered.

Someone slammed into me, and I hissed as I collided with the brick wall. Straightening, I spun to see who shoved me.

Vivian.

Her sneer was vile, her lips curled, and nose pinched with disgust. Her arm was looped through Geran's, and she leaned in close, whispering something in his ear, keeping her narrowed eyes pinned on me. Geran was a First Chosen this year and apparently the next victim of Vivian's poisonous attention. They shoved past me and Geran turned a malicious smile my way. On second thought, 'victim' was incorrect. He and Vivian seemed a brilliant match, indeed.

I shuddered and stared at my feet as they passed. I wasn't quite up to a fight today. When all of this was over, I'd be better suited to take on bullies. Until then, my stomach would be an endless roiling pit.

They snickered, stepping past me toward the arena, and I followed a safe distance behind. I tried to reassure myself that my mother was fine, just delayed, and that a hatchling would choose me today. There was no reason for one not to.

A week ago, the silver dragon, Glormith, checked the Chosen's aptitude. He still sensed the emptiness and aptitude for the bond in me. We didn't know exactly what that meant, but the dragons seemed to correlate that with being a suitable candidate to be bonded to.

I entered the arena, fingers clenching the skirts of my gray gown. Nervousness thrummed through me, and I looked around at the other would-be Dragon Riders. My shoulders sagged with disappointment. There wasn't a friendly face among them. They scorned me for being a First Chosen a second time. The students treated it as though the Masters showed me favoritism. Which they had, in a way. But I had worked as hard as any other student here.

Master Brann stood in the shadows and caught my eye. He gave me a small smile and a nod of encouragement. I tried my best to return the gesture as I settled in my place on the soft arena floor. The sun-warmed sand heated me through, a slight comfort to the chill flooding my veins. Rays of sunshine peaked over the lip of the amphitheater, glinting off the eggs in the center.

There were seven eggs this year, all sparkling with promise. I looked up as a dragon trilled, craning its head. Elispeth, a white dragon. She was small by comparison to the dragons her age, about two wagons in length. She was not the mother of this clutch, but she had mated this spring. Her maternal instincts likely prompted her actions toward the eggs. Her Rider placed a hand on her shoulder, rubbing her scales.

The amphitheater grew more crowded as more and more bodies packed inside. The cacophony of music and excited clamor echoed in my ears. Nausea flushed my cheeks, and I bit my lip, trying to keep it together. I focused on the clutch, breathing in and out—in and out.

It would be fine, it would.

Time passed in a haze. Dragons shifted, anxiously awaiting the new arrivals. People chatted and laughed. The sun beat down on the eggs and us Dragon Men. This was the Summer Solstice, the longest and hottest day of the year. Sweat beaded along my temples, and I chewed on my drying lips.

Crack!

My eyes darted over the eggs, scanning for the first one to pip. I dared not even blink. All chatter died. Dragons sniffed and huffed in interest from the roof.

A small reddish-orange egg teetered and shook. From where I sat, I saw no crack, but that had to be the one that sounded. My heart beat so hard in my chest, everyone had to hear it. The tiny hatchling emerged, and somehow, I knew this was not my dragonling. Glancing over at the other six First Chosen, a large raven-haired boy beamed at the little hatchling.

Sharp pain jabbed my heart, stealing my breath. The dragonling was clearly his. I offered a small smile for appearance's sake before refocusing on the clutch. One after the other, they hatched till one remained.

The rest of the First Chosen cooed and coddled their hatchlings, and I sat on the hot sand, sweating from heat and raging anxiety.

Thousands of eyes stared at me, baring down as if the ground beneath me would swallow me whole. The blue egg trembled. The Masters' nerves descended on me, too. They wanted this. They wanted to prove their experiment had some merit, that it wasn't all a waste. Fearful thoughts bombarded me. Would this be a repeat of last year? Or would this be my year of redemption?

A small indigo nose burst through the shell. It gulped the fresh, clean air like a drowning man. My throat tightened, and I swallowed, attempting to rid myself of the sensation. A foreleg reached out, clawing at the shell, and an iron vice clamped around my heart, crushing it. My lungs constricted as the hatchling tore itself from its confines.

The dragonling shook like a wet dog, scattering bits of shell, and blinked at the group of Dragon Men, glancing past me.

My heart shattered.

The tiny beast whirled around, letting out a hiss. Panic surged. Horror raised gooseflesh across my skin as I struggled to breathe. Glistening white fangs flashed as it pivoted and spun, taking in all the Dragon Riders and dragonlings. Its wet wings slapped against its scales as it tried to raise them, to make itself appear larger, as if we were a threat. It completed its circuit and its terrified stare landed on me, pupils narrowing into slits.

A Wild One.

Beneath the peal of terror ringing in my ears, the crowd gasped and murmured. The hatchling's dark, almost black, eyes flared with anger—with fear.

A dragon keening beckoned me to look up as Elispeth, the white dragon, glided down, landing in the arena. She coiled around the hatchling, glancing up to her Rider she'd left on the roof. The other Riders and Second Chosen rose, distancing themselves from the two dragons, but I was rooted in place.

My limbs wouldn't move. My brain would not function past the fact that I had been refused.

Again.

Elispeth turned her great lavender eye on me. That eye, the size of a dinner plate, gazed into my soul. Her pupil dilated, trying to convey some emotion I couldn't comprehend.

A tear slipped down my cheek. Elispeth nuzzled the hatchling, watching me closely. The young one cooed and peered up at her with dark, trusting eyes. Staggering pain ripped through my being. I choked, pulling in a gasping breath. Tears streaked hot trails down my face, unhindered and unrelenting.

Somewhere in the recesses of my mind, I registered a hand resting on my shoulder, but my body refused to move to see who it was. The white dragon turned her head fully toward me, still coiled around the hatchling. She sniffed in my direction and let out a quiet keen. I shivered at the mournful cry, and she tucked her chin to her chest, huffing.

The hand on my shoulder gently pulled at me, and I pushed myself up on shaking legs. The haze of my tears blurred the world around me, and I blinked them away. Master Brann stood beside me, his face laced with pity. My weak smile wobbled, threatening to fall. He opened his mouth to speak, but I brushed past him and rushed out of the arena.

As soon as I cleared the crowd and entered the hall, I broke into a jog, hiking my dress high in my clenched fists. I knew the way by heart. The tears blinding me did nothing to falter my steps. I shot through the door and ran.

The few stragglers lingering outside the amphitheater dodged out of my path with shocked, disapproving glares. They meant nothing to me. I didn't bother with mannerisms or apologies. They witnessed my moment of vulnerability. Could they think any less of me than to be refused twice by hatchlings?

I cut across patches of grass and wildflowers. I didn't see where I was going, and my brain didn't register it though my heart did. My feet pounded on the hard earth as tears streamed down my face. My lungs gasped for air but, I refused to let myself sob. I ran past the dorms, past the workshops and gardens. I ran past all that was familiar to me.

An eternity later, I tripped and splashed into water. I stopped and blinked through the tears to see a lake lapping at the sandy shore in steady waves. Heaving for breath, I pushed myself upright, watching as the waves rushed over my feet, lifting the hem of my gown and pushing it past me.

I backed out of the water and fell to my knees on the bank of the Great Northern Lake. The sun glared down at me, its harsh rays scorching my skin. My face fell into my hands as sobs wracked my body. All the disappointments and failures hit me at once, and I curled in on myself.

I had lost everything. All my hopes and dreams were shattered. Dejected. Worthless. I'd been given not one chance, but two, and I ruined it. I tried my hardest to be someone that a dragonling would want to bond with. I placed my future on a little creature—a little creature that would take me places I'd never reach on my own, that would be my friend through it all. It would have made my life worth something.

Sobs tore me apart, and I wrapped my arms across my chest, squeezing as if it would be enough to hold me together. I thought about the father I never really knew—his love protecting me from so far away. For so long, I wanted to honor his memory, take his place on the front. I had convinced myself that if he were alive, he would have been proud of me.

Tears burned my eyes. My throat ached from sobbing, but it wouldn't stop.

For once, I surrendered. I allowed myself to feel all the hurt I bottled up and ignored. I let myself cry till there were no more tears. Then sobbed some more.

I sat on the sand, not bothering to move, when I heard distant footsteps near me.

Irritation sparked, but apathy and dejection snuffed it out. The sun began to set over the lake. There was no curfew on the night of Hatching Day, though I doubted I could have been bothered if there was.

The waves rolled, coming and going, oblivious to me and my struggles, just as the world continued on without a thought to me. No one's life was affected by mine, and they would all go about their merry ways, regardless of mine being ripped away.

Someone dropped to the sand beside me. I didn't bother to glance their way. I stared off, seeing nothing, feeling nothing.

I was numb, as though crying all my tears left me vacant. Void of joy, peace, anger, sadness... everything. As barren as the shells left in the amphitheater—hard, empty, and broken.

We sat there, me and whoever was beside me, as the sun descended and darkness blanketed the world. Dragons roared in the night, having their yearly fire-breathing competition. Distance muffled the crowd's praises and applause as they cheered their favorite dragon on.

I closed my burning eyes and pulled my knees to my chest, resting my forehead against them.

Whoever was beside me didn't move or say a word.

They were simply there.

The moon was high, and the night was deep when I braved a look to see who pitied me enough to find me.

Willhelm.

He sat there, with one leg stretched out in front of him, and the other bent, resting his arm on his raised knee. His dark eyes searched the waters. He seemed relaxed, as though all the world could go on without him and he wouldn't care a bit.

But he was here. He was here for me.

He turned to me, his features barren of any smile or pitying frown. He simply looked at me, then turned back to the water.

I was tired, so tired. Physically and mentally. I didn't feel safe, though. I felt unsure, uprooted. As if I allowed sleep to take me, I might wake to find everything gone. That little blue dragonling kept plaguing my mind, hissing and whirling. I saw Glormith touch his lips to my brow, and his Rider giving his approval of my aptitude. My loneliness, as the dragons would call it, the emptiness inside me.

I felt empty now.

Tears pricked behind my eyes again. I bit my lip and tried to focus on the crash of waves against the shore.

Dawn's first rays found me lying in the fetal position on the ground. Fatigue glazed my vision in a bleak haze as I stared out at the water. The sunrise glinted against its surface. It was beautiful, and here I was thinking it was the ugliest sight I ever laid eyes on.

A new day.

That meant yesterday's events were set in stone, recorded and etched in history. Avyanna of Gareth—the first female Dragon Kind refused. The First Chosen who was refused, not once, but twice. The biggest failure in all of Dragon Kind history.

Footsteps sounded from behind, but I didn't look up when Willhelm shifted and stood. They spoke in low voices, and someone sat much closer to me, pulling my head into their lap.

I listened to Willhelm's retreating footsteps. He stayed with me all night, never saying a word, just simply being with me.

The woman hummed a soft tune and unweaved the strands of my braid. Her leg was not thick enough to be my mother, nor would my mother be so silent. I didn't know who it was, nor did I care.

Birds chirped and flitted here and there and the distant sound of dragons bugling could be heard. The woman ran her fingers through my hair, combing and humming. I recognized the tune, a soft haunting lullaby. It was quiet and eerie, as if it alluded to my future—uncertain and hazy.

I closed my eyes. The melody of her song relaxed my tense muscles. If I could just listen to her, and ignore the day and what it meant, ignore the sunrise and the birds chirping, ignore the sound of dragons—everything would be fine.

My heart stung at that thought, bothered that I would push away dragons, yet what was I going to do? What life did I have left to live? I was almost eighteen-winters old. I had no other plan for my life outside of becoming a Dragon Rider. Once, I entertained the thought of becoming a Master, but I knew I never could. I lacked the patience, the desire, or drive to teach students. Teenagers and the attitudes that came with them grated on my very soul. I could never teach them. Even now, the idea seemed... *wrong*.

A sigh escaped my lips, utterly unsure of myself and the future.

"Avyanna," the woman whispered.

I didn't move, didn't flinch or twitch. I just laid there as if I was dead because that's what I felt like.

After a pause, she tried again. "Avyanna."

I still had no reply. If I spoke, it would be an acknowledgment, an acceptance to the world of what happened—a witness giving my own damning testimony.

The woman went back to humming. Her fingers threaded my hair, replaiting it.

In the depths of my mind, I registered this wasn't right. It was wrong of me to lie here like some weak, pathetic girl. But at the moment, I was helpless to act against it. There was nothing inside me. No spark or fire. Nothing.

Her hands eventually stopped braiding my hair and moved to my back, rubbing gently. My stiff muscles objected at first, then relaxed as she massaged the worst of the kinks out. My eyes were swollen and dry, and I couldn't seem to open them.

"Avyanna, your mother is here."

I stopped breathing.

My mother was here. Part of me was relieved. I had been so wrapped up in my own failures that I forgot about her being delayed, but she was here now. She would make everything better again. As soon as that thought rose, a nasty part of my brain smothered it. I was not some child anymore. I didn't need anyone else to make the world better again. The world was a rotten, cruel place. Life was unfair. I needed to accept that.

I was an embarrassment to my mother and my father would be ashamed of me.

"I don't want to see her," I croaked through dry, cracked lips.

Her hand stilled on my back, and her thigh stiffened under my cheek.

She let a moment pass before she spoke, "Avyanna of Gareth. You do not get to say you do not want to see the woman who bore you into this world. She is your mother and has traveled far to see you."

I recognized her voice, but I couldn't place who it was.

"I don't want to be in this world anymore." My words were breathy and lifeless.

I didn't mean it, not truly. But it came out anyway. I was just so... lost.

The woman shifted, moving her leg out from beneath me. She eased me upright just as I managed to open my eyes. Master Niehm brought her forehead to mine and looked at me with her intense eyes, sparking with life.

"You will not say such things that you do not mean." Her stern voice brooked no debate.

I closed my eyes again. That crumb of happiness this woman brought me moments ago vanished.

"Look at me, Avyanna."

I forced my eyelids open, and I felt so... dead, compared to her bright gaze, sparkling with fight and *life*.

"You will get up. You will see your Mother. You will go on. I told you not a half a year ago that dragons were not everything. You will not let them shatter your spirit. You will not." She spoke with such passion and fervor—almost as if she could speak with enough conviction to affect my dead heart.

"Avyanna, you will get up," she said, as if it were a matter of fact. She gently let go of my head and stood.

I crumbled back to the sandy shore. I didn't want to see anyone. Not my mother, nor this bossy Master.

"This is your final warning. Get up, Avyanna." Demand clipped her tone.

I heard her words, yet no amount of her determination could stir my limbs. The world was simply better off without me in it. What was I going to go back and face? All of my peers who would tell me I was a failure? All the Masters that had invested in me, who would now see me as a disappointment? Master Brann who offered me a second chance, and I managed to ruin that–

A sharp slap across my face jolted me upright. My crusty eyes snapped open. Master Niehm sat crouched before me. She pressed her hand to my throbbing cheek, and I glared with as much ferocity as I could muster. Masters never struck students. Ever.

"There you are." A pleased smile spread across her face as she searched my eyes.

I willed every ounce of my rage into my glare. How dare she hit me? Didn't she know what I just went through? And she had the gall to strike me?

"Let's go see your mother," she said, rising from her crouch.

I glared, ignoring her outstretched hand, and pressed my lips into a thin line before struggling to stand. She threw another smile my way and started walking toward the school grounds.

Chapter Fourteen

As I trailed behind Master Niehm, I felt emotionless, vacant. My brain vaguely registered that she took me around the dorms to the Masters' quarters. Even with my eyes trained on the ground, I felt the stares and heard the hushed whispers of those few who rose early the morning after Hatching Day.

Master Niehm slowed to match my dejected pace. I didn't want to see my mother. I didn't want to see a single soul. No. What I wanted more than anything was to curl under a rock and die.

We came to the Masters' quarters, and she ushered me in with a muttered word to the guards, then escorted me down the halls. The path was nothing but a haze. Strands of hair fell loose from my braid and trailed down my face. I took small comfort in the fact that it hid my eyes from others, not that they wouldn't recognize me.

She held open a door and gestured me inside. At a table in the center of the room, Master Brann sat with Master Elenor to his left and my mother to his right.

"Oh, Avyanna!"

My mother leapt from her chair, rushing to me. Her body enveloped mine in an embrace. My emptiness faded the tiniest amount, and tears stung my eyes. Part of me just wanted to be a little girl again, back when my mother's hugs made the world right again.

I stood there, stiff and unmoving, before I forced my arms around her, then let them drop again. There was no passion, no emotion behind it. I stared at Master Brann over my mother's shoulder, not caring that he saw the lifelessness in me. He frowned and clasped his hands together on the table.

My mother pulled back, holding me at arms-length. She smiled, but it didn't reach the concern burning in her warm brown gaze. "Oh, Avyanna. I'm so sorry I wasn't here sooner! I tried, I really did, sweetheart. Oh, sweetie." Her hand cupped my face, stroking my cheek with her thumb.

Tears welled in her eyes as I pulled out of her embrace. She didn't deserve this. In my heart, I realized I was being unfair. Yet I could not bring myself to do anything different. I just didn't have the energy or motivation to greet her as she deserved.

She brushed away her tears with the back of her hand. Despite my coldness, her gaze still overflowed with love and compassion. I looked at the floor and stood there, unable to show her the same.

"Ladies, please, have a seat." Master Brann motioned to the chairs.

Numbly, I took a seat beside my mother, across from Master Elenor and Master Niehm. My stare dropped to the wood grain of the table, refusing to make eye contact with anyone. If I didn't witness the alternating compassion and pity in their eyes, I could justify my behavior.

"Miss Annabelle, it is good to see you," Master Brann addressed my mother. "Are you well? We were informed that you intended to be here for Hatching Day. You were sorely missed."

Sorely missed because they probably hoped she could have kept me from making a fool of myself.

"Yes, I am well, my lord. I became ill, and no travelers were willing to take me along with them. I so wish I had been here yesterday." My mother placed her hand over mine in my lap and giving it a squeeze. "I would have given everything to be here for you, Avyanna."

I lifted my eyes, seeing her sorrow for me, her empathy. She couldn't know how I felt, but I was her daughter. Anything that hurt me, hurt her. Perhaps it was my physical exhaustion from not sleeping for two days, but I just... didn't care.

I stared at the table again, and didn't offer a reply.

"It's good to hear you're well. We were all worried for you," Master Brann started. "Now, Miss Avyanna, I know this is hard for you."

Anger flared, burning at the emptiness inside. My jaw clenched. He knew it was hard for me? What he knew was I failed. He gave me a second chance, and I blew it. He wouldn't understand how it felt to be the first in recorded history to be refused twice. My name would be sounded to every class of Riders from here on out as the one who was rejected. The one who the Masters chose and coddled and failed despite it.

"This was unexpected and we understand it will be a difficult time for you. I think it would be wise for you to take some time for yourself to come to terms with what happened," he continued.

"I disagree," Master Niehm stated.

The flatness of her tone drew my attention. Anger licked at my bones, and she matched my glare with her chin held high.

"I think Miss Avyanna should stay busy. Perhaps she can assist around the dorms for now."

For now. Until I made use of my life somehow.

"I agree," Master Elenor said. "Idle time does not do anyone any favors."

I didn't bother looking at her. I had no interest in seeing those cold, hard eyes showing no mercy.

"Miss Annabelle, what do you think?" Master Brann asked my mother.

I attempted to pull my hand from my mother's, but she held firm. Here they were, all discussing what to do with me, as if I was some dog that hadn't turned out how they hoped. What to do with the poor child now?

I had no future, but that didn't mean that I didn't want to have a say in my future. Realistically, I understood they only spoke of the next month or so. Still, I couldn't help thinking I would always be in this rut, where others decided what I did with my life. My choice was to be a Dragon Rider, and look how that turned out. Perhaps I was better off letting them choose.

"What would you like to do, dear?" my mother asked, her voice gentle and hushed as if she wished she could read my thoughts.

My blank stare wandered over each of them. "I don't know," I croaked through a sob torn throat.

My mother's arm wrapped around me, easing me close to her side. "I think she needs time. Just give her some time, and I'm sure that everything will right itself. A good night's sleep and a cup of tea can do wonders," she said with a hint of optimism. Optimism that I did not feel.

"What if Niehm and Elenor keep an eye on you just until you're feeling better?" Master Brann offered.

My shoulder raised in a weak shrug. I didn't care. Right now, I didn't care about anything. The only thing I wanted was my room, and a locked door. I wanted to lie on my bed and not think about a single thing.

"I think that's enough for now. Perhaps Elenor, you and Miss Annabelle can escort Miss Avyanna to her room?" Master Brann asked.

"Yes, of course."

I braved another look around the table. Master Niehm's frown was sharp with disapproval. Master Elenor's expression lacked the unmerciful sternness I'd expected. Instead, a touch of concern colored her eyes.

"Thank you for your time, Miss Annabelle." Master Brann stood, and the rest of us followed suit. "Miss Avyanna," his voice softened with a sympathetic smile, "rest."

My mother looped her arm through mine and we followed Master Elenor out. She escorted us through the dorms and to my room. Along the way, people chattered as we passed and it felt as though they all spoke of me, of my failure.

In my room, Master Elenor left, and I walked to my bed in a daze. I laid atop the covers, hugging my knees to my chest. Fatigue itched at my eyes, pulling them closed. I was so tired. So very tired.

The bed dipped beneath my mother's weight as she sat beside me. Her warm hand rested on my back, moving in slow circles. "I'm sorry I didn't bring you sweets."

Her voice was quiet, soothing, as she told me of the farmer she had hitched a ride with. How the treats went missing from her basket, and the farmer's eight children, covered in sugar and crumbs, all denying they'd taken them. She'd fallen ill not long after that, barely able to stand. With all the sickness plaguing the country and so few Healers, everyone refused her pleas for passage. Even the traveling blacksmith who brought her last year turned her away. Once she gained enough strength, she walked and walked, wearing holes in her thin shoes, just to get here one day late.

Her hand slid to my arm, rubbing my shoulder, then smoothing my hair. Heavy emotion thickened her voice. "I'm so sorry I wasn't here for you. No one could have known…"

Her words trailed off, but I knew what she meant. No one could have predicted the hatchling would be a Wild One. But it was. Somehow, more tears leaked past my lashes, dampening my blanket.

When she spoke of how proud she was, of how proud my father would be, an ache, heavy and smothering, burrowed through my chest. Because how could they be? How could they be proud of me when I had only failed?

"Gareth would have loved to see the woman you've become," she whispered.

No. My father would have expected more from me. He would have scolded me for placing all my hopes and dreams on a gamble.

When she moved to wipe the tears from my cheeks, I turned, hiding my face in my blanket. She resumed stroking my back and spoke about life in the village. How she snuck treats to children when their parents weren't looking. She told me she adopted a cat to keep away the mice, then laughed as she explained the creature turned out to be terrified of the vermin. It constantly scratched holes in the flour sacks and left footprints all about the bakery. But she loved it dearly and refused to get rid of it.

She rambled on about the less important things until my breaths slowed and I drifted into a dark, dreamless sleep.

When I woke, it was morning—a full day had passed. My mother couldn't stay, and when she came to say goodbye, her voice was thick with grief. She placed a kiss on my brow and promised me everything was going to be alright. She asked me if I wanted to come home with her, but our little village wasn't the place for me right now. I shook my head. She kissed me again, then left.

Chimes rang outside my window, one after the other, marking the hour, then the day. Then another day. I hadn't eaten, hadn't bothered to change out of my clothes. My few travels to the lavatory were a blurred haze.

A knock sounded at my door, and I blinked the bleary fog from my eyes as Master Elenor entered with a tray of food. She placed it on the small table beside my bed.

"Eat," she ordered, settling herself on the stool.

I glanced at the roll slathered in butter and the cup of fruit next to it. My stomach churned in rebellion.

"I'm not hungry." The words rasped out of my mouth through dry lips.

"Regardless, you will eat."

I had no energy to argue, but I wasn't going to eat either. I simply closed my eyes and rolled over, turning away from her, dead to the world.

There was a heavy sigh.

"Sit up." Her weight joined mine on the bed.

My knees curled into my chest. I was still so tired. I didn't want company and didn't want to eat.

"Avyanna of Gareth, this is beneath you. Sit up."

No. This wasn't beneath me. I felt like the lowest possible human in all of Rinmoth. The history books would remember me that way. Eating wouldn't change that.

Strong hands lifted me up by my armpits, forcing me upright. My vision spun from the motion, and she gripped me by the jaw.

"You are not a child anymore. You do not get to throw fits and starve yourself. That is petty. You are not petty. Eat."

Her conviction had me glancing at the food. Nausea sat like a rock in the pit of my stomach. I attempted to pull away, but she held me fast.

"I am staying here until you eat something. I have a great many things to do today, and if I have to sit here and watch you eat, that will take up valuable time." Her piercing blue eyes sought mine, and for once, I saw the compassion in them.

I believed Master Elenor to be hard and uncaring. She always acted as though her favorite dress was stained, yet here she was, trying to get me to eat. A small spark of emotion flittered into my icy heart. Not much, but just enough to make me grab the roll. I tore off a tiny piece and pushed it past my lips.

Master Elenor let out a faint, relieved sigh and relaxed her shoulders. "Do you know what I have to do today?" she asked. I stared, void of curiosity.

"I have to talk to Master Tegun. That man is unbearable." She raised a brow at my roll, and I tore off another piece. She was referring to the Master of Men, the man who oversaw the male side of the dorms.

My stomach revolted as I tried to swallow, yet my mouth watered at the first taste of food in days.

"Some boys thought it would make for a good laugh if they smuggled frogs into the girls' rooms on the third floor. Frogs!" she said with a note of resignation.

"I almost sent for Tegun, only because I thought it fitting that his men catch the confounded creatures. Could you imagine?" She clicked her tongue, lips pressed firm. "Men, chasing frogs and horrified women chasing them with brooms? I know of several women who would like nothing better than an excuse to maul an unsuspecting man with a broom."

Amusement wormed its way inside me—a tiny, frail thing in such a large, empty place that was my heart.

She continued to drone on about her day and the plans it held until I finished the roll. After which she eyed the fruit. I shook my head. I didn't have it in me to eat more. She nodded, content that I ate at all, then saw herself out, leaving me alone with my thoughts.

I curled into myself, trying to fall asleep. Noises drifted through my thin walls—joyous laughter, women chattering, and the distant bellow of dragons. I pulled the blanket over my head. If I could ignore the world, then perhaps, just maybe, it would ignore me.

Master Niehm came by with my evening meal and sat with me while I tried to eat. I played with the stew, not hungry in the slightest.

"Avyanna?"

I looked up at her, ready for her to demand I feed myself as Master Elenor had. Instead, her gaze was focused out my tiny window.

"Did I ever tell you I knew the first Chosen who was refused?" Her voice was quiet and reserved, lacking its usual fire.

I stared at her, dragging my spoon through the stew. There wasn't much to know about him. People said he eventually left the school after the hatchling refused him. That he moved to another village and lived in peace.

"His name was Valden." She turned to look at me. The strangest sense of longing gleamed in her green gaze. "He had blonde hair and the kindest brown eyes you'd ever see. He was a gentleman and always put others first. If anyone needed help, they knew they could go to him for anything."

Her attention returned to the darkening sky and went on. "He trained, studied and practiced harder than any other student. He even volunteered to help load the dragon dung from the canyon just to be close to the creatures."

I wrinkled my nose at that thought. Even I wouldn't volunteer for that job. It was the absolute worst—shoveling giant piles of dung into wagons. It made an excellent compost for the local farmers who supplied food for the King's grounds.

She glanced over with a smile, noting my disgust. "He was a funny one, too... always making jokes, trying to get people to laugh. He was a prankster, but he never took it too far, like some of the boys here. If he were still here, I'd wager he would have had a hand with the frogs Elenor dealt with."

I lifted a bite of cold stew to my mouth as I listened to her story.

"He was my promised."

I hesitated with my next spoonful. I'd never heard Valden was promised to anyone. Had he *left* her?

"He was so excited to be a Dragon Rider. He told me that if they chose him to fight in the war, he would find a spot for me at the front. A cook or something—though I am a terrible cook. I burn everything."

Tears glinted in her eyes as she turned back to the window. Her smile was full and bright, despite the trembling in her words.

"He said that if they ordered him to stay and protect the homelands, he would take me with him. We would go on grand adventures. See the world and explore it together. Us and his dragon."

Her voice cracked a bit, and she took a moment to collect herself before continuing, "I was there that Hatching Day, when the dragonling refused him. He didn't know what to do. The Masters were as puzzled as we were." She let out a sigh, her shoulders drooping with the memory.

"He visited it every day that year, trying to bond with it by feeding it, and reading to it. He treated it like a wild animal he could tame. But nothing worked.

Nothing won that little creature to him. It flew off in the middle of the night, never to be seen again."

She turned to me with raw hurt in her eyes. "He changed Avyanna. That dragonling took a part of him that I never got back. He didn't help anyone anymore, or try to make others laugh. He spent every waking moment with that dragonling, trying to convince everyone it only needed more time to accept him."

She took a steadying breath and straightened. "Avyanna, he let the dragonling's refusal define him. He let that be the one thing people remembered about him." She paused, as if unsure how to form her next words. "What do you know of the rest of the story?"

I set the bowl aside. This happened almost twenty-six years ago, and still Master Niehm's pain was palpable, filling my tiny room.

"It's said that he left for a normal village life," I replied quietly. My voice was rough with disuse.

Her gaze took on a sharper edge. "He killed himself."

I pulled back at the venom lacing her words. A strange numbness iced my veins and stilled my breath. Any response stuck in my throat.

"He took his own life, not seeing the worth in it anymore. He took his life from all those that loved him, everyone he had helped and befriended." Her voice hitched, and she pressed her lips together, composing herself. "He took his life from me."

Silence fell, a thick and foreboding thing. A haunted look came over her face, and her piercing gaze seemed to see through my very soul.

"Your life is not your own, Avyanna. You are not an island."

Chapter Fifteen

The next few days were more or less the same, a repetitive blur. I refused to leave my room, unwilling to face anyone. Every morning, Master Elenor brought me something to eat, then sat and told me of her tasks. Then every evening, Master Niehm brought my evening meal and spoke of her day. She never mentioned Valden again. I sensed that particular wound was still open and sore, considering she never took a life mate.

"There's a package for you this morn," Master Elenor said as she entered.

I rolled onto my side, seeing the parcel wrapped in brown paper tucked under her arm.

"Our resident General has requested you do his mending." She set it beside me. "Again."

Opening it hesitantly, I noted the trousers and sewing notions inside. "One would wonder what he does to ruin his clothes so often," I mumbled, jabbing a finger through the hole in the fabric.

"Oh, I have a vague idea." Master Elenor placed a roll and apple on the table and took up her perch on the stool.

"Really? Is he simply that rough on clothes?"

"I don't think it's possible for anyone to be that hard on clothing, darling."

I removed my finger from the hole and reached for the needle and thread. "What is it then?" I asked.

I was still rather depressed, but felt somewhat eager to set myself to this task. It was familiar to me at this point. The only sure thing in my life seemed to be that General Rafe damaged his clothes, then sent them to me for mending. I threaded the needle and started sewing.

"General Rafe is," she trailed off, and glanced at the ceiling as if searching for the right word, "disruptive."

"So I've noticed," I concurred with a nod, thinking back on every unsettling incident between us.

Master Elenor eyed me, and I wasn't sure if she'd heard of his actions toward me.

"He's volatile," I added.

"That he is." She pursed her lips. "Being as such, I'm certain there's ample opportunity for him to be caught up in... clashes of will."

Was she implying that he got into fights?

"When he inspected the companies, there was a fight, though I don't know any details," I offered.

She chuckled and stood to check over my mending. "I believe that involved a Commander who disagreed with the General's grade of his companies."

She nodded her approval of my stitching and sat back down. I thought Master Elenor would be above common gossip. She bristled, likely noticing the glint of mirth on my face.

"Oh, don't look at me like that." She waved me off. "I'm not a gossipmonger. I am the Master of Women. As such, I hear a great many things. For weeks, the ladies in the laundry rooms had nothing better to do than complain how dreadful the General was for destroying such a handsome face."

I kept my smile in check as I minded my stitches. Wasn't she gossiping about the General to me right now?

A fortnight passed, and my spirits fluctuated. Some days... a dark cloud smothered my heart, and I felt as though my life wasn't worth living—like Valden. And others, everything seemed alright, like I could brave the world. I would sit up in bed and talk with Master Elenor and Master Niehm about their days, and about the other women and students.

They never pressured me to speak of my future, and for that, I was thankful. They were just there. Master Niehm and I shared desserts after the evening meal. And every so often, Master Elenor came for a cup of tea, just to relax after a stressful day. The two of them were good friends who grew up in Northwing as I had. Master Elenor was ten years Niehm's senior, but they shared the same dry wit and humor.

Tonight, sleep evaded me. My mind was restless, wondering what the next day had in store. More of the same, I assumed. A crushing weight settled on my chest, and I was unable to escape the feeling that my life... was not my own. I had lost all control, watching as everything slipped from my grasp.

A dragon bellowed near the dorms, and I froze. I'd successfully ignored the beasts for the most part, as long as I avoided my window. Part of me wanted to dismiss the magnificent creatures altogether and discover what else life offered. Yet, after everything, I was still drawn to them. Every second was a battle to keep thoughts of them from my mind.

I now understood why no refused ever remained on school grounds. No one should have to live hearing the calls of their dreams, knowing they would never be fulfilled.

A second dragon answered the bellow and my mind launched into questioning why they called to each other. Dragons did not speak to one another like humans used the common tongue. They were far more intelligent than any living beast, yet they were bound by the language of animals. I imagined that was what saved us from them during the War of Dragons and Men. If they conversed like humans, we wouldn't have stood a chance.

Dragons relied on their Riders for communication. They had their own ways of showing their feelings, whether it was a snort aimed at insulting another dragon, or a croon to a hatchling.

So when the dragons bellowed, it had to be for a reason. If there was a threat, there would be more dragons joining the call.

What was the little blue dragonling doing?

My eyes shot open, staring at the wooden rafters above.

Maybe it was a fluke. It might have been scared...What if it was welcome to me, but here I was in my room, locked away from it? What if it was as lonely as I was?

Not thinking, I jumped out of bed and grabbed my cloak. I was just going to see the little dragonling. Just making sure it was alright. Elispeth would likely be caring for it, considering her maternal instincts, but I just needed to see. I laced my boots up quickly and pulled the hood up over my head.

Lanterns lined the dim, quiet corridor. Without a sound, I shut my door and padded down the hallway. I headed toward the common room on the first floor, knowing if I attempted the main entrance, the guards would stop me.

Every student in Northwing knew of ways to sneak out of the dorms at night, even if not everyone did. As an unspoken rule, no one dared breathe a word of the secret exit. I was sure that many older women used it at some point. And I could only hope the Masters hadn't learned of it in my absence.

I crept into the dark common room. No one would witness my failure if I didn't make it down. I crossed to the open windows and peeked through the gauzy curtains to the grounds. Not a soul walked about, which was a stroke of luck, even in the middle of the night.

I knotted my night shift and cloak at my hip to keep them from tangling my feet. Brushing the curtain to the side, I climbed over the sill. My boots scoured the wall for the unfamiliar footholds. The stone bit into my chest as I dangled over the edge. My toe nestled in a crevice and I dropped my weight on it, testing it. Confident it would hold, I scraped along with my other toe, searching for another.

Slowly, oh so slowly, I climbed down the stone wall to land behind the holly bushes lining the dorms. I peered out, sure that it took me far too long to descend and someone had seen me. I shifted my weight into a crouch, listening for the guards stationed just around the corner.

The crickets chirped in the night.

There were no calls of alarm or encroaching footsteps. I freed the knot, fastening my night shift and cloak, then darted off between shrubs and trees, keeping to the shadows.

Without using the path, it took me almost a chime to reach the Dragon Canyon. With each passing breath, the weight of guilt grew on my shoulders. This was a mistake, creeping around in the dark, wearing nothing but a cloak and night shift! If someone caught me, what would they think?

I shoved those thoughts down. Turning back wasn't an option. I hugged close to a tree near the winding trail that led down to the canyon. Elispeth and her Rider, Gaven, would be in one of the larger chambers for adult dragons, far along the eastern side. Those were only accessible by dragonback. I'd never make it.

A dragonling, however, could not fly. Not till they neared their first year. Unless Elispeth carried the blue dragonling, she'd be in one of the ground-level chambers with the rest of the young ones.

Some Wild Ones were so ill-tempered that not even their mothers could temper them. Some were more docile with other dragons, but ferocious toward humans. Each dragonling was different, and I was hoping I was right about this one.

Hoping.

Hoped.

I sprinted down the path as quietly as I could. If I just saw the dragonling, everything would be alright. It might recognize me from when it hatched. It might remember I had done nothing to harm it. Perhaps, with time, I'd gain its trust.

The moon's relentless glow threatened to illuminate my features, and I pulled my hood tight against my hair as I ran. At the bottom of the trail, I slowed and ducked into the first cave on my left. Those who cared for the young ones and their Riders frequented this path... and those who cleared the dung pits.

I paused, waiting for a sign of movement or a dragon's bellow announcing my presence. Moonlight lit the cool gray stone. Caves and chambers littered the massive crevice, so wide that many dragons could fly abreast and their wings would not touch the sides. Dragons often flew from one end to the other, visiting one another, and dragonlings learning to fly dove off the lip of the canyon, plunging into the abyss below.

My breath caught in my throat as I snuck down the path on silent steps. The dragonling would've been exhausted from hatching, so Elispeth wouldn't have wanted to take it far. If she and the dragonling were here, they wouldn't be too deep in the canyon.

Soft lanterns lit most caverns, others had strategic holes chiseled out to allow moonlight in. The young ones slept in the first caves. The adjoining chambers of their Riders were hidden out of sight.

I walked past young dragons laid about in a blissful stupor, clearly tired from whatever training they had done that day. Some were thinner, more streamlined, and others bulkier. I smiled as I passed a green beauty—so graceful and small. She would be a sight to see when she started flying.

Pushing those thoughts aside, I crept on, determined to find my dragonling. *My* dragonling.

I stopped and swallowed against the lump in my throat.

I shouldn't get my hopes up, I really shouldn't. But what if this was my second chance, and it accepted me? What if I could go down in the record books as the girl who didn't accept the refusal and went on to forge a bond? What if I wasn't just known as the girl who was refused twice? What if I was known as something more? Something that would have made my father proud? I took quick steps forward and peered around a corner to peer into a cave.

My heart took off like a startled rabbit. Elispeth lay curled in a tight ball, resting her slender horned head on the tip of her tail. Double eyelids closed in sleep hid her lavender eyes, and I held in my sigh of relief. The blue dragonling slept peacefully at her side, tucked against the back of her tail. Its bright indigo scales twinkled in the moonlight, still sparkling with the newness from hatching.

I contemplated my next actions, watching as it squeaked and tapped its tail in its sleep, dreaming of something, to be sure. I dropped into a crouch and crept forward, boots silent against the stone floor.

Barely three steps in, Elispeth's eyes snapped open. Her pupils narrowed on me in surprise. I stilled, but she didn't move—she watched.

"I just want to say hello." I scarcely breathed.

Elispeth was not a violent dragon. Yet, with her hormones being off kilter and the new little one she'd taken under her wing, I wondered if I could rely on her notoriously kind temperament.

She blinked, eyelids slow with sleep, and huffed a sigh. Her pupils relaxed and expanded, and I accepted that as tolerance, at the very least. I took a cautious step forward, and when she made no move to sound an alarm—or eat me—I crept closer to the little one.

When a few steps lay between us, Elispeth chirped quietly and raised her head, peering down at the dragonling. She gave it a soft nudge with her tail. Anticipation sang through my veins.

It let out a garbled complaint and shifted with its eyes clamped tight, pressing closer to Elispeth. She chirped again, giving it a firmer nudge. The dragonling yawned, showing tiny needle-sharp teeth, and opened its midnight-colored eyes.

With a startled squeak, it scrambled to its feet, backing into Elispeth. It hissed and spat, back arched with fear.

I glanced up at Elispeth nervously, but she made no move to remove me from her cave. I checked the entrance to Gavin's personal room, hoping he hadn't heard the commotion.

"Easy, little one," I whispered, not moving any closer. It bared its teeth and narrowed its eyes to slits. "It's just me. My name is Avyanna." If I was slow and gentle, maybe its fear of me would pass.

"I'm just here to say hello." I settled more comfortably into my crouch, clasping my hands together. "You're a beautiful thing, you know? I've never seen a dragonling as beautiful as you."

Its tail was on the longer side. Males had longer tails than females. Sometimes it was hard to tell at first, and generally, we had Riders to affirm if it was a male or female dragonling.

"You're a boy, aren't you? I should have known with you being so feisty." My laugh was soft, and I lifted my chin in the smallest of motions. "You're a fighter too, I can tell. I'm a fighter as well, or at least I want to be. My father was a fighter."

The dragonling closed its mouth but kept its wary eyes on me, snuggling close to the great white dragon.

"My father died. He was killed, fighting. He left me all alone, like you. I never had any friends, no one to play with. You deserve better than that. You deserve someone to care for you and play with you, someone to fight by your side, little one."

My smile was tight-lipped, not wanting to show my teeth in case it took that as a threat. I rambled on about my mother and her baking. I told it all about my solo adventures here on the school grounds, and how they would have been so much more exciting with a little dragonling.

After a while, Elispeth laid her head back down and closed her eyes. A nervous curiosity dampened the dragonling's fear. I sat there for half a chime, talking about the other dragons and what I knew about their kind, telling it all I could of my life. My legs long since fell asleep, but I refused to get up.

I unfolded my hands, and inch by inch, slowly extending my palm toward the little one. "So, what do you say? Are we friends?"

He made no move to jerk away or bite me, so I took a slow step forward.

The step was too much.

The dragonling's eyes snapped wide with fear, and it let out an ear-splitting shriek before launching at my outstretched hand. I jerked away, stumbling over numb legs. My back collided with the ground, and my head cracked against the rock floor. Stars danced in my vision from the impact, and I threw my arms in front of my face as the dragonling pounced. Elispeth roared, batting the little one aside to protect me.

I pushed myself up, scrambling back on my hands and rear toward the entryway. The dragonling whirled on me again, murder in its eyes. Elispeth whined, and I frantically looked at Gavin's door. If anyone found me here, I would be in so much trouble. No refused Dragon Kind was permitted to try to force the bond. It was a fundamental rule.

Strong hands snatched my shoulders in a bruising grip and hauled me up to my feet. Pins and needles shot through my legs, and I wobbled, trying to face the dragonling who was now charging at me.

Elispeth was up, snaking her head back and forth, rushing toward the little one.

A rough hand shoved me behind a tall, broad body. I stumbled as a giant took my place, stepping in the path of the dragonling's attack.

I would know that sleeveless tunic anywhere.

My heart dropped like a stone.

General Rafe.

He was saving my hide? No doubt all the Masters would know of my attempt at forcing a bond now.

"Go," he bit out, reaching up to untie the cloth over his eye.

I paused, wondering why he was removing the covering from his missing eye.

"Go!" he snarled.

I backed toward the opening of the cave on unsteady legs, not turning my back on the scene before me. General Rafe bent his knees, ready to run or fight. I wasn't sure which. He stared at the charging creature head on.

"Be still," he demanded, his voice low and rasping.

Elispeth froze. Her stare found his, and she hissed, recoiling from his gaze. The blue dragonling whined and skidded to a stop. It stared up at him with wide, hateful eyes. Its sharp claws kneaded the stone beneath it, grinding at the surface.

What manner of man could command dragons?

"Be silent." General Rafe's tone resonated with deep authority, demanding obedience.

The dragonling opened its maw, baring its needle-like teeth, but made no sound. Elispeth pulled back her pure white head and flicked her tongue out, tasting the air nervously.

"We were not here," he growled, turning to her.

His back was still to me, and I darted from the cave, hoping to hide near the entrance. I barely rounded the opening when he burst out behind me. Watching his hand wrap the cloth about his head, I stumbled as he crowded me. He glared down at me and my feet moved of their own accord as he rushed me.

Minding my footing on the ledge, I walked as quick as I dared. With my head ducked low, I had every intention of avoiding all conversation and eye contact. His long strides had no problem keeping up with me, however. Still, we made no sound as we hurried along.

His rough hand snared my elbow and shoved me into a small storage cave. I yelped as he tucked his big body against mine, pressing me against the rocks. He clamped a calloused hand over my mouth. I stiffened, panic surging as he tilted his head, listening for something. When he looked down at me, his eye blazed with anger and condemnation.

The rush of blood pounded in my ears, but despite it, I heard footsteps coming down the trail.

General Rafe leaned in close, placing his cheek against my temple. "Play along or you'll be tossed to the dogs."

He jerked up my hood to conceal my features and removed his hand from my mouth. I took a quick breath before he slammed his whole body against mine, crushing me into the wall, then buried his face in my neck.

I grabbed the sides of his tunic and held on for dear life, trying my hardest not to flail or fight. My heart lodged in my throat, choking off the threat of any screams at the vulgarity of this. General Rafe placed his lips to my neck, and even though he didn't move his mouth, it felt as though they seared a brand against my skin.

I barely heard the sharp intake of breath at the cave entrance over the deafening thunder of my pulse. General Rafe looked up leisurely, placing his hand over my cheek. In the back of my whirling brain, I wondered if he did that to hold me or to shield my face from whoever found us.

My breaths came in quick, rasping gasps. I clung to his tunic with a death grip. The person cleared their throat, and their footsteps receded.

"Who was that?" I dared ask, breathless and trembling, trying to get my mind back in order.

I sucked in a breath, desperate to steady myself. Wood smoke, forest, and man flooded my senses. An unfamiliar feeling spread through me, flushing my cheeks and weakening my knees. Another deep breath through my nose, and I inhaled his masculine scent again, letting it anchor me.

"Someone doing what we only pretended," he grunted, pulling back to look at me.

Embarrassment and shame warmed my cheeks at his insinuation.

He seemed angry, and I could understand why. He caught me breaking the rules—rules that protected both Riders and dragons. I was sneaking around at midnight in nothing by my night shift and cloak.

What I couldn't understand, however, was how he found me or why he helped me—how he helped me. Most military personnel had no reason to be in the Dragon Canyon, definitely not under cover of darkness.

He braced his hands on the wall beside my head, boxing me in. "What do you think you were doing?" Anger brought his voice low as he demanded an answer.

I dropped my hold on his tunic as if it was on fire and tried to sink into the stone behind me. I turned my face to the side, hoping to escape his burning gaze. He towered over me, closing me in. I was confined, trapped.

"What were you thinking?" He leaned close to my ear, growling each word.

"You wouldn't understand." My voice cracked, and I hated how pathetic it made me seem.

Tonight had been a mistake. A huge mistake. One that could cost what little of my reputation I still had. Tears pricked behind my eyes, but I held them shut. I would not cry in front of this beast of a man.

He let out a sigh, heavy and laced with irritation as he stepped back, giving me space. I gulped in breaths of air, filling my greedy lungs. Glancing up, I secured my cloak tighter around myself before looking at my feet.

"I will only tell you this once, so look at me."

The steel in his voice slid up my spine, brutal and demanding. I forced myself to meet his glare, even as my heart raced in fear.

"Gareth of Beor once saved my skin," he said.

I jerked my chin up a fraction at my father's full name.

He crossed his arms over his broad chest. "I never got the chance to repay him, so saving you from your little stunt back there, I consider my debt settled."

I opened my mouth, but his hand shot out toward my face. My jaw snapped shut before he could latch onto it.

"Good girl," he said, tapping a thick finger against my lips. "Let me finish."

My whole body shivered, fighting the constraint he placed on me with that tiny movement.

"I'm no rat, so the Masters won't hear about this from me. That said, if you make another dung-brained decision like this again, I won't be here to save you."

I swallowed my questions and glared. It might have been stupid, but I had to try. He wouldn't comprehend that, though. My teeth ground together and I gave a sharp nod.

"Glad we understand each other."

I shifted my feet and eyed the small entrance to the cave, hoping we could get out in the open. This man stole all the air out of the room. It was impossible to breathe or think straight. He made it seem like the storage cave wasn't big enough for the both of us.

"One more thing—" His tone took on a bored cadence as my eyes flashed back to his.

He took one menacing step forward, crowding me into the wall again. I gulped as he straightened to his full height, and I craned my head to look up at him. My breath hitched as his hand settled lightly over my throat. His thick calluses were rough against my skin. I gripped my cloak as tight as I could. My nails dug into the fabric as deeply as I wanted to sink them into his remaining eye.

"If you ever breathe a word about what happened in that cave, I'll kill you."

His hold didn't tighten on my neck, but it felt like a noose just the same. My eyes widened in fear, and my lungs wouldn't work. I couldn't breathe.

He looked down at me, and what I saw in that singular eye froze my heart. He would toss me over the edge of the abyss this very moment if I objected. His eye glittered with a silent promise. If I so much as breathed a question concerning it—he would strangle me right here and brush his hands off as if he just disposed of a rabbit.

It would be so simple, so easy for him to take my life.

I swallowed, my throat bobbing against his palm.

He didn't say another word, but walked out of the cave, leaving me to fall to my knees and tremble.

Chapter Sixteen

Master Elenor was giving me the stink eye, and I didn't know why. Surely she hadn't discovered my escapade last night. General Rafe was rude, curt, brash, vulgar, arrogant... I could go on. But he didn't seem like the type to lie. More like the type of man bound by his own twisted principles.

Like a messed up version of Willhelm.

"I was sure there was no lemon in that jam," Master Elenor stated, looking at my expression with an arched eyebrow.

Looking down at the roll slathered in preserves, I realized I must have made a face when I compared General Rafe to Willhelm.

"There isn't." I schooled my face to a more pleasant expression and took another bite.

She gave a heavy sigh and settled onto the stool. "It's going to be quite a day," she said quietly, looking out my window.

"Why is that?"

All morning, I tried to act as though everything was normal. My week had been getting better, with my spirit on a high note yesterday. Until I sneaked off and a certain dragonling sealed my fate.

I wondered if Elispeth would listen to General Rafe's command, and not tell Gavin, her Rider, that we were there last night. It appeared as if I had her approval to win over the dragonling, but Gavin had to hear the scuffle at the end, and I didn't think she would hide that for me. If he learned of my attempt, he would take it to the Masters immediately.

"There's been more raids." She pinched the bridge of her nose, a gesture of frustration she normally would not allow herself. She always seemed so composed, as if nothing ever got to her.

"Where?" I asked, thinking of Stonesmead where my mother lived.

Nestled between the King's Palace and the Wild Mountains of E'or to the east, the village was one of the safest locations to dwell in, far away from the war front. Northwing was the closest settlement to the front, on the northwestern border of the King's Land. Beyond us to the west was the realm of the great Sky Trees, giant trees thicker than the biggest dragon, and taller than the palace itself.

Beyond the Sky Trees lay the sweltering path to the Shadowlands. We forced the Shadows back to their borders a time or two, but every time the King called the retreat, they followed. They seemed to have an endless supply of manpower for their war and endless greed to fuel their attack.

"To the south, close to Southwing. I fear they may have somehow received word of the King's efforts to establish a breeding regiment for the dragons there," she said wearily.

The dragons laid fewer eggs with every passing year. Without dragons, we stood no chance against the Shadows. The King instilled a breeding program at the school to the south, on the border of the wastelands. For all his efforts, it was still an experiment, as dragons would not mate simply because they were told to. It seemed as though it was a fluke, or the stars aligned when a female conceived.

Even when dragons went into season, they might not mate. Or they mated with several, to not even conceive. The breeding of dragons was still unknown territory, but the King was determined to pioneer in.

"Did they attack the school?" I asked.

"No. Dragon Riders held them off, but now they know dragons are there," she sighed, and for a moment, I saw the weariness in her eyes. "I sincerely hope they're as spread thin as we are."

It was a hope we all shared. We wouldn't be able to fight a war on two fronts. We barely maintained the one front we had.

"There will be more refugees today. I have to find rooms for all the women. We don't have enough rooms as it is," she said, rising to her feet.

There was one room she should have had to offer. Avoiding her gaze, I felt the sting of her words, even if she didn't mean them the way I received them. I should have moved to the canyon by now.

"Master Elenor?" I clasped my fingers in my lap, and she tilted her head curiously. "I want to thank you for your kindness and patience during this time. I've been a poor example of how a woman ought to act."

She offered me a rare smile, and her eyes shone a little brighter. "Avyanna, you've gone through something no one else has. You must know there are people here for you. I support you. Niehm supports you. I've gathered Willhelm supports you as well." She tucked loose strands of hair behind my ear. "You need to understand you're not alone. You don't have to weather this storm by yourself."

Tears pricked my eyes. She was right. She and Master Niehm took time out of their busy days to come and sit with me—just to let me know that someone else was there.

If I named anyone my friend, it would be Master Elenor, Master Niehm, and Willhelm.

Master Elenor looked at me, her eyes searching mine, and she pulled me in for a hug. I stood stiff with shock, before my pride crumpled in my heart and I wrapped my arms around her. She smelled of peppermint and lavender. Sharp and delicate at the same time.

"Now," she started, pulling away to hold me at arm's length, "if you're feeling up to it, I could certainly use some help getting the new girls settled."

I understood what she was really asking, without voicing it. Was I ready to get back out there and face everyone? Face the peers that would laugh at me and call me a failure? Was I ready to ignore what people thought, and somehow make use of myself?

"Let me get dressed," I said with a small smile.

Children came in droves.

The masses were horrifying. Normally, after a raid, they sent all the children and women to one school to keep them together. Because of its size, they split this group of refugees between the two schools. The few able-bodied men who survived stayed back, as well as some women, to rebuild their villages and hamlets.

Fifty-four children and twelve women. We didn't have sixty-six extra rooms. We didn't even have fifty extra rooms.

I was tasked with the younger children. I washed them after the long road up north and changed them into clean clothes. I tried to feed those that looked as though they had no food in days. Despite how busy I kept myself, I still heard the whispers of the women. I saw the telltale empty stares of those who witnessed the Shadows face to face.

Survivors muttered that the Shadows knew too much, they came in too large of a force, and it was as if they knew what to expect. Too many villages were lost to them for it to have been a coincidence. A small group of Shadows might slip through the Dragon Guard that protected our homelands, but one this immense should have been found sooner. They should have never been able to destroy so many lives, so many homes.

I washed the face of a young boy, wiping away the remnants of his meal. His stare was vacant, as if he saw nothing before him. He refused to speak, and I had to spoon feed him even though he was nearly ten-winters old, give or take a few years. It was as if he witnessed something so traumatic, he could see nothing else.

I brushed his unruly brown hair from his brow and spotted Master Elenor speaking with an older woman from the new arrivals. I finished with the boy and made my way over to them.

The older woman shook her head and pursed her lips, watching the children huddled throughout the space.

"We will have to room them together," Master Elenor told her.

"It would be better if you did." She nodded, the corners of her mouth dipping in a frown. "They've been through too much for ones so little."

"Mrs. Grimee, this is Miss Avyanna, my assistant. Avyanna, would you be so kind as to help us get the children settled?"

I smiled up at Master Elenor's words. Something so small as her claiming me as her assistant, when I wasn't really, meant the world to me.

"I would be happy to," I replied.

It felt like a little bit of my heart was growing back.

Over the next few days, I kept busy with the new refugees. Many women stepped in and cared for the babies, little ones they would 'ooh' and 'aah' over. Master Elenor tasked me with overseeing the older children, and I did my best.

Through it all, my peers reminded me over and over again why I didn't get along with them. Vivian and her friends made a point to harass me as often as possible. I ignored her lot, not sparing a single glance or response. Regardless of my attention, their words pierced my heart and tore out bits with every hurtful remark. Every mention of being useless, a failure, a reject—every mention of what the dragonlings were up to, seemed to rip out a little more.

The teenagers in the refugee party lashed out with words and actions, too. They didn't know the details, but they quickly realized I was an outcast. I didn't blame them, though. They survived a terrible ordeal, and I was not one to judge how they processed their pain.

After all, that refusal had been the biggest failure of all time. Then I hid in my room for over a fortnight, depressed and wallowing in pity.

I carried a basket of diapers from the laundry room to the drying line behind the dorms. Off in the distance, women crowded around the barracks' gate. Frowning, I wondered what drew them there as I hung the diapers on the line.

The crowd of women shifted and churned, but stayed at their place by the gate. Curiosity nagged at me. What was the big deal? Didn't they have more important things to do?

"A bunch of daisy-brained floozies," an older woman muttered under her breath. She set her basket beside mine and pinned sheets up on the line.

I smiled at her comment and continued with my task. "What do you think has piqued their interest?" I wondered aloud, reaching into my basket to grab two pins and a square of cloth. I gave it a harsh shake before pinning it up.

"Fresh blood."

I squinted at her, studying her wrinkled face as she turned to wink at me. My nose crinkled with my confusion.

She let out a cackle as she reached into her basket for a tunic. "Don't you know what day it is? You should be over there eyeing the goods, lassie." Her feeble body stretched to pin the tunic to the line.

Realization dawned, and I turned back to face the crowd with understanding. "Recruitment Day," I mumbled, watching the mass of bodies shift and sway for a better view, like a singular beast.

"Aye, and they'd all like to find a nice young chap to spend the night with." The old lady tsked and shook her head.

I pressed my lips together as thoughts darted around in my mind like a rabbit escaping a hunter. I hurried to finish pinning up the linen and hung the last diaper. Looking once more at the crowd, I picked up my basket and propped it on my hip as my heart warred with my brain.

"Thinking of having a look for yourself, dearie?"

"I don't need a man."

She seemed to think that was the funniest thing she heard in her life, and I walked away frowning as her cackles echoed in my ears.

I spent the rest of the day getting angrier and angrier. Something set me on edge, and I didn't know what it was. Every time a refugee lashed out, I had to count to ten. Every time I saw one of my peers and they gave me a disgusted or pitying look, I had to sneak off and collect myself.

Seething at yet another refugee calling me 'hag', my fingers curled into fists at my sides. One... Two... Three... Four...

"Miss 'anna?" came a small voice, accompanied by a tug on my dress.

I peered down to see Ran, a little boy of five-winters. He held a stuffed doll under his arm and talked around his thumb.

The older women had been firm with him, saying he was too old to be sucking his thumb. They scolded him for his doll, claiming they were for girls. My heart ached for him. Everyone was too busy to consider why he found comfort in those things.

He watched the Shadows kill his sister and do unspeakable acts to his mother. The Shadows wore masks and headwear made of skulls, a trophy of the most fearsome thing they had ever killed. It was an outward sign of their rank. Ran had whispered to me late at night that a horse killed his mommy and sister. To watch a man dressed in a horse's skull slaughter your loved ones was a good enough reason for his self-soothing actions in my book.

"Yes, Ran?" I asked, taking a deep breath and dropping into a crouch beside him. I offered my hand, and he took his thumb out of his mouth and grasped my fingers, looking at me with big brown eyes.

"The mean old lady said I have to take a nap." He pouted.

"Yes?" I prompted, stifling my irritation. This little boy didn't deserve my anger toward others.

"I can't sleep."

"Could you lay on your cot then? Play quietly with your doll?" I asked. The nannies would let the older children skip nap time if they were quiet.

"I can't, I keep seeing it."

His words gripped my heart like a vice. I knew what he meant by 'it'. He saw the Shadows. He saw the evil, vile corruption they wrought.

I swallowed against the lump in my throat, and nodded. "I'll come and sit with you then." My soul shattered with the smile he gave me as he put his thumb back in his mouth and led me to his room.

His cot lay among four others, cramped inside a tiny space. The other children tossed and turned, trying to find sleep, or fighting whatever plagued their dreams. Ran climbed onto his cot and waited for me to sit and lean my back against the wall before climbing in my lap.

"It's ok, Gwyn. Miss 'anna is here now," he whispered to his doll.

My eyes pricked with tears, and I pulled him close. Gwyn was his sister's name.

As I looked around the room, a wave of fury crashed over me. These were children. Small, innocent souls who had no right to be attacked. They were helpless. They suffered the worst and were not even the ones the Shadows were after.

Ran would live with this trauma for the rest of his life. He would carry it with him as a black hole in his heart, never fully healing.

My father was gone, but I still had my mother. I was lucky. I hadn't seen the Shadows face to face or felt their terror. Ran was so young, so fragile, and yet, he faced each day despite his pain. He was stronger than me.

I hated the Shadows—hated them for the damage they wrought, for the childhoods they stole, for the innocence they ravaged from women. A weight settled on my chest and my jaw ached from grinding my teeth. I despised them for the fear they implanted in us. I loathed them with every fiber of my being.

"Miss 'anna?" Ran whispered.

I looked down, and a hot, angry tear fell down my cheek.

"You'll keep me safe?" His voice was so pure, so trusting.

"Yes, Ran, I'll keep you safe. I won't let it get you or Gwyn." I pulled him closer and stroked his brow.

A plan formed in my mind, and I latched onto it with everything I had.

I would keep him safe.

Dragon Rider or not, I would do my part.

Chapter Seventeen

I finished my duties with the children and leaned against a wall, watching the bustle of women and refugees. They were almost all settled, at least in temporary accommodations. Master Elenor looked up from the group of ladies she helped and spotted me. She frowned and made her way over, weaving through children and belongings. Coming to a stop before me, she peered down at me with one thin brow arched in question.

"I'm going to be indisposed for the next few days," I murmured.

She offered me this task as a temporary job to keep me busy and get me working again. We both knew she never intended for me to stay here and help her for the rest of my days. She wanted me to move on with my life, and this had been her way of helping.

Well, I was certainly moving on.

"Oh? What exactly will have you so indisposed?" she asked.

"I'm taking another job. But I'll help where I can if it's needed." Though, with the dozens of other women from the dorms, she wouldn't need me.

Tenderness softened her features. "It's good to keep busy. I'm thankful for your assistance, Avyanna."

"Thank you for getting me out of my room," I replied with a shy grin.

If it hadn't been for her and Master Niehm, I would have wallowed in self-pity for the rest of my days. I would have never seen the need to help defend the homelands, to protect little ones like Ran.

"Anytime, darling," she said with a small smile—as much of a smile as one would get from her in public. She turned, pulled away by someone calling her name.

My heart pounded in my chest.

It was now or never.

The sun was just touching the horizon, and I didn't have much time. I rushed to my room. Once inside, I changed into my gray gown, still the nicest one I had. I secured my coin purse around my waist, then slipped out the door. Hurrying through the hallway, I darted down the stairs and past the dorm guards before my courage failed me.

I eyed the setting sun as I made my way across the school grounds toward the dwindling crowd of women at the barracks' gate. My heart raced, and I swallowed against the lump in my throat as I melded into the mass. Some noted me and took a step back, eyeing me with wary glares. I ignored them and lifted my chin, heading to the guards.

They were as firm as ever, but a group of soldiers in the barracks called across to the women. They had fresh, youthful faces, ones that hadn't seen training yet. Maybe they thought they would get lucky with some girl on the school grounds. Though, if Master Elenor or Master Niehm had anything to say about it, the women's dorms would be locked down tight tonight.

Recruitment Day was notorious for the young women trying to sneak out. Inevitably, some girls managed to sneak past the Masters and attempted to meet up with some boy they saw join the ranks.

I pressed forward, and one guard who recognized me from my assignments frowned when he spotted me.

"Miss Avyanna," he greeted.

Women crowded behind me. Whether they were curious as to why I was there, or if they pushed closer to inspect the young soldiers, I wasn't sure. One or two younger men studied me with expressions I didn't want to think too long about. When I noticed their stares, my skin crawled with the glimmer of hunger in their gaze.

"Good evening." I never caught the guard's name and sorely regretted it now. "I seek entry to the barracks." I was proud of my voice for not trembling.

"You have orders?" he asked, glancing at the crowd.

Women murmured behind me, and I held my head high. "No, sir. I'm here for Recruitment Day."

Something dangerous flashed across his face. "So are they." He waved his hand at the throng.

"They're not here for recruitment," I stated. My body felt like it didn't belong to me, as if I watched this scene play out from someone else's eyes. There was no turning back after this.

His dark brows met in a disturbed frown. "I don't follow, miss."

Clearly, I had to spell it out. "I am here to join the ranks, soldier."

The women gasped and broke out in renewed chatter. The soldiers murmured and shifted nervously. Some of the younger recruits looked at the older ones for assurance that this wasn't really happening.

"I—You're—" He closed his mouth, aware that he sounded like a fool. "Someone fetch Sergeant Willhelm!" he barked, glaring at the soldiers till one shot off into the busy mill of men crowding the gate.

Obviously, the guard wasn't sure what to make of me. I didn't quite know what to make of my actions, either. This simply was not done. There was no record of any woman ever joining the army.

I was the first female to be refused by a dragonling. The only First Chosen to receive a second chance and the only First Chosen to be refused twice. I might as well carve the way and be the first female soldier, too.

"Make way!" The men shifted, parting to reveal a glowering Willhelm. His dark peppered hair was tousled, and he glanced over the gathered crowd with disgust. "Miss Avyanna?"

"Greetings, Willhelm."

"Begging your pardon, but there seems to be confusion as to why you're here. Care to clarify?" he asked. His tone was not harsh, but it was firm. He frowned at me, but seemed more puzzled than angry.

"I've come to join the ranks," I repeated.

The women erupted into nervous chatter once again.

Willhelm blinked slowly, his eyes boring into mine as he processed that. He straightened and looked down at me from his full height. "You came to be a soldier?"

I wondered if he asked that to buy himself time, or if he honestly needed me to repeat it. Surely, of all the men present, Willhelm would understand me well enough to accept me.

I didn't trust my voice, but gave him a firm nod.

His fists clenched at his side as he took a deep, steadying breath. "Well, let's go then," he said. He waited for me to cross the gate and take my place at his side before walking off.

The men followed us, more curious about the girl on their grounds than the girls that were forbidden to them. When the cat-calls began, I felt my first real ping of fear.

What had I done?

We hurried through the barracks to the large recruitment tent. On the way, soldiers called to their friends, informing them of what was going on. They all joined the parade, waiting to see what would happen. I resisted the urge to press closer to Willhelm, knowing he was there for my protection, but also not wanting to show the men that I relied on him too much.

We arrived at the recruitment tent, the biggest tent I'd ever seen, and approached the open entrance. Every single set of eyes inside turned, staring as we approached. All conversation abruptly ceased.

Rows of desks filled the area with grim-faced men seated behind them. Long lines of younger men stood before each one. They paused in the middle of taking names of the recruits before them, their attention on the girl in their midst.

My hands shook as every gaze settled on me. Someone behind me snickered, and I straightened, not allowing myself to appear any smaller than I felt. Movement at the back of the tent caught my eye. Huge and foreboding, I knew him anywhere—General Rafe crossed the room. Eyes shot between me, Willhelm, and General Rafe. He did not come to us but rather folded his arms and leaned his hip against a desk, eyeing me darkly.

I bit the inside of my cheek as Willhelm grunted and led me to the closest line. One would think I had the plague by the way the recruits scattered to find another line to join.

I found myself in front of a desk, facing down an aging man. He managed to look down his nose at me from his seated position as he replaced his quill in a pot of ink. He folded his fingers with the patience of a saint, never taking his eyes off me.

"May I help you?" he drawled.

All my life, I prepared myself to be a Dragon Rider. I had to find that strength inside myself somewhere.

"I'm here for recruitment."

Snickers and scoffs answered my statement, and my resolve crumbled a bit more. I had to do this. I refused to stop now. Determination flooded my veins. I couldn't let people think me weak. I was stronger than this, better than this.

"You can't join," the man stated.

I blinked, staring at him in surprise. "Why not?"

Open laughter greeted my question. Willhelm shifted beside me, and I took comfort in the fact that I wasn't alone. He was with me. I would be fine.

The older man smirked and rested his chin on his hands as if explaining something to a young child. "You are clearly a girl," he said in the most condescending tone I ever heard.

"Woman," I corrected. "However, I fail to see how my gender plays a role in recruitment."

"Girls and—*women*—aren't welcome in the ranks."

I arched an eyebrow. "Whether you welcome me or not is irrelevant. I'm here to join." Teeth clenched, I forced my brightest smile. "I don't require a welcoming committee."

He looked around the tent, as if seeking backup. "Women aren't allowed to join the ranks." His tone grew more clipped with each word.

"Says who?" I crossed my arms over my chest.

"The law."

"Where?"

Oh, I knew the laws, and I knew the rules. They omitted women from a great many things, though they did not forbid them. Women just never had the desire or courage to pursue tasks that were deemed for men.

"It—Well–"

That's twice today I stumped a man. I smiled, feeling victory within my grasp.

"Article seventeen."

The smile fell from my cheeks, and dread filled me as I turned to face General Rafe. "Article seventeen?" I asked, cringing at the squeak in my voice.

The men gathered wore confident grins now that they had their big bad champion to hide behind.

"You seem to know the laws well enough. Tell us what article seventeen is." His low growl ran over me, chilling me to the bone.

"Article seventeen reviews the handicaps that would prevent a recruit from joining." I lifted my chin, unwilling to go down without a fight. "I have no such handicap."

General Rafe looked me up and down with a patronizing smirk. "Your gender is a handicap."

Anger boiled my blood. Being born a woman was no handicap. I might not be as big as them, and I might not be as strong as some of them, but I had seen smaller men fight. At least being a woman gave me brains.

I had to be thankful for the little things.

"Nowhere in article seventeen, or any other article, does it forbid women to join," I growled, not caring that the others saw how much General Rafe got to me. He could get under the skin of any man here.

"What if I do?"

I forced myself to take deep breaths and not slap this infuriating man. "Do what?"

"Forbid you."

I inhaled sharply and glared. It was well within his right as a General to refuse me admittance to the army. It was also within his right to dismiss me if I joined.

Surely he wasn't that much of an oaf.

"Well, do you?" I snapped.

He got off on holding his power over others. I saw it over and over during my time in the barracks. He was the type of man that made everyone feel like they were below him. He had a way of belittling everyone, even if they were not directly under his authority.

He studied me and leaned his hip against the desk again. The older man looked between him and me, and the tense crowd awaited his verdict. Willhelm shifted behind me, the only movement in the tent. I stood there, fighting the tremble that threatened to shake my limbs. I didn't take my eyes off General Rafe's dark stare, not for one moment, as the pause lengthened.

"No."

A ripple of shock and disappointment went through the men, and Willhelm breathed a sigh.

The older man spluttered. "I have to object, General—"

With a single, threatening look, General Rafe's glare silenced him. His glower returned to me, brows darting up as he shrugged his massive shoulders, before he pushed off the desk and pressed into the crowd.

"Start the wagers!" His deep voice carried over the men as they all started talking at once.

My cheeks burned at the insinuation. He didn't think I would last long.

"Avyanna. Avyanna of Gareth," I declared to the old man, who glared fiery darts at me.

"Well, Avyanna. My wager is you won't make it through the night," he grumbled, writing my name on the parchment.

Fate decided that I wouldn't make it through the night.

"What are you thinking?!" Master Niehm demanded with a scowl shrewd enough to cut. Master Elenor was at her side, chasing every soldier off with the same sharp look.

We stood in front of the bunkhouse in the barracks as dusk settled into night. The recruits had been dismissed to their bunks, but most milled about with nervous energy.

"She wasn't," Master Elenor muttered under her breath.

They wouldn't understand. "It doesn't matter. I'm here now," I stated.

"You're not staying here. Come back to your room."

"No, you need that room, and they sent the recruits to the bunkhouse. That's where I'll sleep."

"No, you will not," Master Elenor bit out.

"I'm a recruit now. I'm not welcome on the school grounds without orders from my Commander."

"She—She–" Master Niehm couldn't even finish. She threw her hands up in the air, exasperated.

Master Elenor surveyed the area with her cold gaze. "Where is the General?"

"I don't know."

"Where is the General?!" Master Elenor barked at the nearest cadet.

He flinched at her harsh tone and pointed across the road. I turned around and saw General Rafe reclining against a post beside a group of lively men—keeping his eye on me. I frowned and threw a glare back at him as Master Elenor stalked over.

"Honestly, Avyanna," Master Niehm sighed. "This is no place for a woman!"

"Why?" I hissed. As of a few hours ago, she was no longer my Master, and my temper was getting the better of me. "The only reason this is not a place for women is because women have never made it so. There's no rule, no law saying we cannot."

"There will be after this."

"Then we should resist it! What is so wrong with a woman wanting to fight for her homeland?"

"Nothing! There is, however, something wrong with a girl of a mere seventeen-winters sleeping in a room with over two hundred randy men!"

I pursed my lips and glared.

"You are young and naïve, Avyanna. In some ways, you are wiser than your years, but in this, you are ignorant." Anger flashed in her green eyes. "They are men, you are a woman. You're asking for trouble."

"You act like they're animals," I said, my lip curled with disgust. I worked with these men. I knew how they behaved.

"Most act as if they are. You cannot trust them—not as far as you could throw them." She threw a threatening glare at a boy who looked her up and down with a low whistle.

I took a steadying breath, unwilling to give this up. "They'll respect me. I'm one of them now."

A bitter laugh escaped her mouth. "No. No, they won't. If you thought your peers were bad, just wait till you see the treatment they have in store for you."

I frowned and turned to find Elenor again. She stood rigid and unyielding, chin up, biting out words at General Rafe. In turn, the General watched me with faint amusement curling his lips. He made no reply, other than a one-shoulder shrug. With a nod to me, he said something to his little group and walked off.

Elenor stared after him as though her look could kill the man. She said a few short words to the men standing there before marching back to me and Niehm.

"You are coming with me," she bit out.

"No, I'm–"

"Yes, you are. If you say one more thing before we get to your room, I will drag you by your ear in front of every single soul here."

I snapped my mouth shut, eyeing the men drifting about. They watched me with open curiosity. Some stood nearby, staring, while others pretended to be busy.

She spun on her heel and carved a path to the gate, and I followed. Knowing Elenor, she would make good on her word.

We passed Willhelm on the way out. When he saw me, he ran a hand through his hair. He eyed Niehm and Elenor and frowned. I offered him an encouraging smile.

I would be back.

"You're not going back," Niehm seethed.

I sat on my bed and faced the two crones that blocked my door.

"She is actually."

Niehm spun around to face Elenor, who was glaring at me for all she was worth.

"Dear Avyanna has signed away five years of her life. She is due in the barracks at the sixth chime." Elenor rubbed her temples as if the words pained her. "She's a fool, but she will be an honest fool."

She took a seat on my stool and patted her graying hair as if during the bustle of activity, a strand dared to find its way loose of her bun. She heaved a heavy sigh and looked at me again. "Is this because of the dragon?"

I pressed my lips together and shook my head. They only meant well. They cared about me and I knew they would disapprove, but for once, I wanted to explain myself. Perhaps they would understand.

"I don't want to go back to my village. I don't want to be a Master, I struggle with students. I can't be a Dragon Rider. I cannot waste my life doing nothing. If I can make the smallest difference, I have to try."

"You can make a difference here, in the dorms," Niehm said with a faint sigh. Her softening implied she noticed my attempt to explain.

I pushed off my bed. "That's not enough. Not for me. I can't just sit here and watch refugees come, tired, worn, and weary. I can't only be the balm for their damaged souls. It has to stop." My tone pitched higher, and I took a breath, calming my rage. "I want children to stop coming here hurt and traumatized. I want to be part of the group that goes down in history for pushing the Shadows back.

"Do you know Ran? The little boy? They gutted his sister right in front of him. He watched them rape his mother." Tears burned my eyes, and I didn't bother holding them back. "He carries a doll and sucks his thumb. One day he might put away those visible scars, but he will always bear that trauma, that hurt. He will never get over that. It's not right, and I'm not content sitting here while others fight the war I want to win."

I let out a breath and squared my shoulders. "I'm more valuable at the front than I am here, leeching resources, taking up room. There's no other option. I can't contribute enough to make my stay worth it. Even if I wanted to return to Stonesmead, I have no skills to offer my village. The only option left for me is to join the ranks. So I did." I clasped my hands together and waited for their response.

Niehm's eyes were soft when she replied. "I understand. I need you to know that. Your devotion and desire to help do not go unnoticed. Do you believe we don't sympathize with the refugees that come? Do you think we are immune to their plights?" She placed a hand over her chest with a small shake of her head. "A woman's place is not in the army, Avyanna."

"Why is it not a woman's place? Why does that keep coming up? I cannot see how my gender would allow or forbid me from certain tasks if I can physically complete them!" Fire-blast it all, I had it up to my ears with the gender rules.

"Avyanna," Elenor's harsh tone drew my attention, "you've failed to think this through. Where will you sleep? In a room with more than two hundred men? Half of which are young and rash, still learning to control their urges. The rest are grown men that haven't laid with a woman in far too long.

"Where will you bathe? In their lake? Will you strip your dress for the eyes of lustful men? You always go to the private bathing chambers here, among women. Did you even consider your modesty or reputation?"

My cheeks burned with shame. I hadn't thought of those things. I assumed that because I was a woman, exceptions would be made.

"I didn't think–"

"Clearly not. I know the General better than you. Were it up to the Commanders, they wouldn't have let you join, period. The General allowed it to make an example of you. He will make no exceptions. You will be treated as any other recruit. You will be expected to act like the rest of them."

Elenor didn't give me a chance to respond. She pressed on, "And what of your moon cycle? What will you do with the rags? Did you think they would excuse you to change them? Did you expect them to offer you someplace far from the men to air them?

"You are bound by your word, and I will not let you go back on it. General Rafe will dismiss you if you prove yourself unfit. Or, by the love of all that is good and right in this world, you will serve your five years.

"You made this choice out of haste, and now there's no going back." Elenor stopped, looking at my stricken face. She sighed, softening her tone as she went on. "You should have asked. If you had simply asked, I would have helped you find a way."

Niehm's features held a sad, resigned look as she spoke up. "We were here for you and will continue to be here for you, Avyanna. I'm not against you fighting, if that's what you truly want. We're not incapable simply because we are women. I just don't want to see them break you." Her voice cracked, and she cleared her throat. "You're so young and have so much promise. You have your whole life ahead of you, and I refuse to see you crushed by the army or some man."

I bit my lip as the fight drained out of me and I realized that these two were truly my friends. I had friends—friends I could have gone to for help or guidance. Yet their title of Master blinded me from the women that lay beyond. I judged them based on their titles and sorely regretted it.

"Now," Elenor stood and brushed out her dress, "tonight you will rest here. We will find some way to remedy your sleeping situation before tomorrow night. General Rafe granted me a favor by letting you sleep in peace.

"You are due in the recruitment tent at the sixth chime. The guards will let you pass in the morning, but never again without orders. We will arrange for your belongings to be brought to you." She eyed my waistline. "Please do not take your coin purse. Leave it for us to get to you. The men will only see you as a sweeter target with it hanging off your hip."

Niehm gave me a fierce hug. "Girl, I love you," she whispered before letting go.

Realization of what I had done sank like a stone in my stomach as they left. I had perhaps not made the wisest choice. There would be consequences for my actions, and I would have to bear them. I'd suffer ridicule and pressure as never before, or walk away in shame.

Everything Elenor said was true. If General Rafe had anything to do with my training, he would expect as much out of me as any other recruit.

I fell onto my bed and curled up in a ball, not bothering to change out of my dress. I thought I'd made some grand choice that would alter my life. Well, I indeed managed to alter my life—I just didn't know if it was for better or worse.

Chapter Eighteen

My stomach twisted painfully, as if punishing me for my poor choices. Nerves had me skipping first meal. I didn't want to risk running into any of the women in the dorms. Their disgusted sneers were the last things I needed.

It was still dark, half-past the fifth chime, when I crossed the gate. I'd come this way dozens of times, and even though I knew he wouldn't be there, I glanced at the post where Willhelm usually waited. It was strange seeing it vacant, yet this would now be part of my life. I had to accept that.

As I entered the recruitment tent, I smoothed the fabric of my brown skirt. A soldier's uniform consisted of a light brown tunic and dark, nearly black pants. Though none of the new recruits received one yet, my work dress was the closest thing I had. This morning, I debated wearing my gray gown again, to make an impression, but settled on this one, just in case I was required to do physical labor. I wouldn't care if it got dirty.

Anxiety writhed like snakes beneath my skin as I surveyed the tent. They had rearranged since last night. They removed the desks and set up benches, facing a raised platform. There were probably close to two hundred seats, and I chose one in the back corner, not wanting to draw attention.

The few men that arrived before me peered over their shoulders as I took a seat. They spoke in hushed voices, snickering amongst each other. I focused on my hands clasped in my lap, doing my best to ignore them.

As we neared the sixth chime, the tent filled quickly. No one came to sit with me, all giving me a wide berth. I reached up to fiddle with the braid I had plaited my hair in, secured tight on top of my head. Today would be hot, and I would have no respite from the heat or whatever labor they put me to.

"Well, hello there."

The patronizing tone was enough to make my stomach revolt. A young, cocky man with light-blonde hair stood in front of three other men, all wearing easy, predatorial smiles.

Arrogance lit his sneer as he leaned forward. "I thought they were jesting when they said they let a girl in." He lifted his boot, planting it beside me on the bench and rested his arms on his knee. "Between me and you, I'm glad they let you in."

My eyes shot to his, skeptical. I dared not answer him, but raised a brow in question.

"You'll make the nights a little more interesting."

My hand twitched as I fought the urge to slap him. Rage tinted my vision red as my mind raced to plot my course of action. "I'll be making no one's night interesting. I'm here for the same reason as you. To learn to fight."

"Oh, good." His theatrical whisper was beyond belittling. "I like the fighters."

"Beat it." A familiar growl had me thanking the stars above.

Willhelm came up behind the recruits and shooed them off with a glare, but not before the blonde winked at me. Unease crept up my spine. He would be trouble.

Willhelm threw a leg over the bench and took a seat, chuckling at my wide grin. "They couldn't talk you out of it, eh?"

I beamed at him. "Not a chance."

It was obvious he didn't approve, but he knew that he couldn't change anything. I was happy knowing he wasn't mad, but rather still my friend.

Funny how I had friends now. None were my age, but did that matter? There were three more than I'd had in... well, ever.

"You know it will be hard?" he asked, resting his elbows on his knees.

"Yes, sir." I smirked. Of course, it would be difficult. I didn't think it was going to be rainbows and sunshine.

"You're going to stick it out? Be the first female to join, the first woman to make it to the front as a soldier?"

"That's the plan."

A smile spread over his face as he dipped his head. "You'll be fine, kid. I won't lie to you—it's going to be worse than anything you've ever tried. You got in because of the General, but it will be the General that will try to get you out, too. Don't forget that."

General Rafe had been a thorn in my side for a while now. I didn't expect that to change anytime soon.

A Commander stepped onto the raised platform, heading toward the center. My fingers trembled as I clasped them tighter and my mouth went dry. This was it.

"I'll stay with you for a half a chime, then I have to see to my men."

"Thank you for coming," I whispered. I meant it. It was so much easier to weather the stares and laughter when I wasn't alone.

He nodded, and we both watched the Commander take his place. His hair was short and gray, and he stood with the poise and stature of a man who had served many years in the military. He gave off the air of getting down to business and not taking anyone's attitude.

"Welcome recruits!" His voice boomed, and even though I was in the far corner, I had no trouble hearing him. "It's good to see you all made it safely through the night."

A few snickers followed that statement, and his sharp gaze flicked to the source. "You there! I am Commander Dewal. What's your name, recruit?"

A young man looked around before standing with cocky arrogance. "Name's–"

"No, I changed my mind. I don't need to know. You're dismissed, son. Perhaps come back when you're a real man." His chin jutted toward the entrance. "Sergeant Briggs, see him directly to the gate."

A mountain of a man, even bigger than General Rafe, marched down the middle aisle behind the young recruit. Undeterred, the recruit chuckled, casting an easy grin toward his friends. He started to say something else, but Sergeant Briggs reached around him, clamping his hand over his mouth. He wrenched his head and arm back and to the side. The recruit's eyes flashed as he struggled to free himself. Sergeant Briggs twisted his arm viciously and there was an audible pop. My jaw dropped in horror as the recruit's muffled scream filled the tent.

No one moved a muscle.

I don't even think anyone dared to breathe.

As Sergeant Briggs dragged the whimpering man down the aisle, I peeked at Willhelm. He was frowning, but didn't appear the least bit shocked. Was breaking arms an everyday occurrence? Is that how they enforced the rules here? I shuddered at the thought.

"Now," Commander Dewal started again as the two men exited the tent, "If anyone else is prone to giggling fits like a bunch of schoolgirls, you may leave. We don't need your kind on the front."

The Commander didn't glimpse my direction, though a few nearby did. No one dared say a word.

"This road will not be easy. It was paved with the lifeblood of other men—not for you to laugh at, or play soldier. Whatever issues exist at home, you left them. Whatever pretty lass you left back in the hay, you left her there. Forget about her, forget about them. You signed up to be soldiers, men. You signed your life away on a little scrap of paper." His tone carried indisputable authority.

"You're ours now. You belong to the King. If I tell you to lick my boot, you do so without question. If I tell you to walk east till your feet fall off, you do it." He jerked a finger, pointing upward. "If I tell you to jump to the top of this tent, you'll find a way to do it.

"You will live and breathe the army. When you wake, your first thought will be of your King. Your second will be how you can better fight the enemy. You will ache—you will ache until you think you will die, and then ache some more. You will learn to fight, and you will take pride in that.

"We are fighting the Shadows, recruits. They don't play around and tickle you with feathers. They will gut your friends in front of you. They will sever your limbs from your body and toy with you to see how long you last. They will cut out your eyes and shove them down your gullet."

He paused, arching an eyebrow high as his eyes passed over those seated. "Let me make this abundantly clear; if you're not cut out for this, leave now. Yes, I'll think you're a coward for it, as will everyone here. All the same, the option is there." He stopped his speech and clasped his hands behind his back. Rocking back on his heels, he waited. It felt as if his sharp stare landed on each and every person in the tent.

A few recruits slunk out, most being younger men. I would guess they were still in their teens. They allowed those as young as the tender age of fifteen to join the ranks, though most that young never made it to the front.

When Commander Dewal's gaze found mine, I shivered and held my chin high, staring straight at him. I would not back down. I knew why I was here, and I knew it would be hard. It would be harder still if I made it to the front in four years.

I could, and I would do this.

His scrutiny slipped to another recruit, and my breath rushed from my lungs. Thus far, the Commander had not singled me out or commented on my gender. I appreciated that.

He waited a few more minutes, allowing ample time for us to rethink our choice and leave.

"Splendid. Now that we've got the stupid ones in here, let's go through the trials, shall we? We will see if you're tough enough for the title of soldier. Step in line."

He stepped off the platform, with more spring in his step than I thought he would be capable of at his age, and headed toward the opening. Willhelm jerked his head for me to follow, and I stood with the rest and hurried to catch up.

The men shifted as if they were unguided. I simply followed the orders that he gave. 'Step in line.' I put myself a few paces behind the Commander and trailed him as he strode to the training fields.

I watched his posture and his steps, trying to mimic them. He held his chin high and marched with purpose and strength. He moved as if he had steel for bones, as if nothing ever brought him down. I wanted to walk with such confidence.

He led us to a training field I was somewhat familiar with. The logs, fences, mud pit, and climbing net were all things I fixed while assisting the General. I scanned the field and obstacles when I spied an unwelcome figure. General Rafe stood in the shadow of a building close to the course. He stood there completely at ease, his arms crossed, chin down, inspecting the recruits with a dark glower. His eye found mine and I swear my blood pounded just a little faster when a smirk lifted the corner of his mouth.

Today, an eye patch replaced the scrap of cloth he normally wore. The patch was much smaller, revealing angry, red scars that streaked in a sunburst pattern from where his eye should've been. I shuddered, imagining the force behind whatever brutality caused it.

"Soldiers!" Commander Dewal barked, pulling me from my thoughts.

I jerked to stand at attention as if I had a string tied to the top of my head, lifting me up. The Commander spun on his heel and did a second glance at me, but didn't falter.

"This will be the first test of your strength and determination. If you fail, you return to whatever rabbit hole you came out of." His crystal blue eyes flashed to me. "You're up soldier!"

What had I done?

Horrified, I realized I would be the first to run the gambit. All eyes would be on me, searching for weaknesses, watching my mistakes to make sure they did better.

I was in a dress.

For once, I felt as though my gender rendered me inadequate. How was I supposed to scale the netting twenty paces high, modestly? How was I supposed to climb over the chest-high log, or the wall six paces in the air without my dress coming up, or ripping?

Commander Dewal checked the hourglass hanging off the starting fence and noted the time. "Go!"

I didn't think—I ran. These recruits would see what I was made of. I would show General Rafe that I was strong enough to handle this. I could do this.

My heart beat a wild rhythm as I jumped the first small log. I threw myself at the second obstacle—the rope netting. I climbed as fast as I could, careful not to tear my hands. Reaching the top, I launched over and almost lost my footing, but managed to secure myself and climb down.

I hit the ground and shot for the balance beam. I bolted across it, not bothering to walk like most soldiers. If I ran, it would be over sooner and I could better control my slight balance.

Sprinting off the beam, I sped toward the rope danging fifteen paces in the air. I jumped as high as I could, latching onto it. I wound the rope around my legs to make a rest. As the rope entwined my boots, I was thankful I neglected my sandals, despite the heat. With the rope secured around my feet, I inched my way up, gasping for breath as I went, arms shaking.

I slapped the top beam and slid down. Fire scorched my hands as the rough rope shredded the soft flesh of my palms. I hissed in pain and dropped to a crouch as my feet hit the ground.

"Let's go!"

Commander Dewal's bellow tore my gaze from my bloody hands and I focused on the next obstacle, a series of logs raised to chest height. My lungs screamed for air as I sprinted for them, but I couldn't get a grip on the smooth wood. Frustration made my movements quick and angry. My marred skin dragged against the bark every time I tried and slipped.

"Hands on top!"

I threw myself at it again, jumping and planting my hands on top of the log. A wince twisted my face as I forced all my strength into my arms to lift myself. Willhelm's called advice worked, and I mentally thanked him as I swung my legs over.

Four more to go.

My chest ached as I heaved for breath. I had a stitch in my side, and sweat drenched my skin, but I kept going. I didn't think for a moment about modesty. If these men expected me not to flinch when they ran around naked, they could handle a little leg.

Ropes tore into my bleeding palms as I balanced on the supports, crossing a wooden bridge missing several planks. I leapt across the last bit, missing the end of the bridge. My knees collided with the ground, sending a jolt of pain through my body.

Groaning, I pulled myself up and charged forward. My strength was fading fast. Fatigue fumbled my steps as I completed the next hurdles. I tried to pace myself, even with Commander Dewal shouting at me to hurry.

The last obstacle was a thin bar raised high in the air. I was supposed to get up and flip over it... and I couldn't even reach it. I ran and jumped, hands seeking the cool metal, but my fingertips didn't even brush it. Positioning myself underneath, I jumped for all I was worth. Not even close.

I was short compared to most women, let alone men. Still, being unable to reach this bar was humiliating.

"Get on the bar, recruit!"

Commander Dewal and General Rafe stalked toward me. I had spent too much time on this obstacle. They could fail me for this.

I jumped again with all my might—and missed.

"Get up on that bar, or I will dismiss you!" Commander Dewal screamed in my ear. He held himself with such grace, yet his tone raged with such ferocity, as if I hurt his favorite puppy.

I leapt again. An exasperated whine tore out of my throat. I would never reach it.

"I'm leaving her dismissal at your discretion, General," he finally said. His lip curled with disdain as he inclined his head to the General.

I glanced at General Rafe, who stood there in the blaring sun, a bored look on his face. His arms were still crossed over his chest and he held himself with such arrogance.

"She's worthless if she can't get on that bar," he grumbled.

"Women aren't cut out for this," Commander Dewal agreed.

I swear my vision went red. Their words stirred the blood in my veins. "I have to get over the bar? That's it?" I growled.

General Rafe's mouth quirked up on one side as he dipped his head.

I threw myself at the bar's rough supports and scrambled up it for all I was worth. My nails tore, and my grip slipped as splinters bit into my raw palms. But I got up. I swung over the bar with as much modesty as I could manage.

I ran to the finish line and doubled over, gasping for air. Pain and exhaustion sent tremors through every limb.

"You did good."

I peeked through my lashes to see Willhelm crouching beside me. I flashed him a tired smile and closed my eyes, focusing on breathing.

"Twenty push-ups."

I jerked upright. General Rafe stood there—smirking. Commander Dewal had moved on to the next recruit. My jaw dropped, and General Rafe lowered his arms, bringing himself up to his full height. I was a recruit. He was a General. I couldn't talk back to him.

"Yes, sir!" I barked, and dove to my hands and feet, dirt stinging my palms.

I dropped my chest to the ground and pushed up as Willhelm rose and backed away. My muscles complained, and I bit off a groan. I kept going. If this was my punishment for doing the last obstacle incorrectly, I would take it.

After the agonizing twenty, I weakly pushed myself up, brushing off my dress.

"I didn't hear you, recruit."

My ribs felt too tight, squeezing my heart, which thudded painfully against my chest. "You want me to count them aloud?" I cast a pleading look at Willhelm, who stood to the side, his jaw clenched. Why didn't General Rafe say as much when I started?! My arms didn't have another twenty in them.

"Are you dumb or just deaf? Sound them out, recruit," he growled, glaring down at me.

I was going to kill him. "Yes, sir!"

I plunged into position and dropped my chest to the ground, pushing up with quaking limbs.

"ONE!" I yelled.

"Good girl," he muttered, and I watched as his boots carried him away.

"TWO!"

I hadn't assumed being a soldier would be easy, but I now fully understood why Elenor had called me naïve.

I stood on a training field as men pressed their backs to the ground. They pulled their knees up and laced their hands behind their heads. They had split up in groups of two, one to hold their fellow's ankles, and another to start on sit-ups.

This thrice-cursed dress! Whoever held my ankles would get quite the show.

Willhelm returned to his duties after the obstacle course. I would get no help from him. Every curse word I'd ever heard burned through my mind as I scouted the recruits for one I might trust not to peer up my dress as I completed the exercise.

The blonde from earlier caught my eye as he settled down with one of his friends. Seeing me alone, a wide grin split his face. With a word tossed back to his partner, he leapt up and started my way.

Dread pooled in my stomach as I searched the field, but everyone seemed to avoid me like the plague.

"Hello there, young lady. You need someone to... hold something for you?" he drawled, looking at my chest obscenely.

I ground my teeth in annoyance. "No, thank you," I bit out.

"Find a partner. Now!" Commander Dewal barked.

General Rafe lingered in the shadows, content to let his presence intimidate rather than use his voice.

Frantic, I grabbed at the sleeve of one of the last young men to partner up, and the boy had the nerve to jerk away from me. He looked at me as though I had some contagious disease that would infect him.

The blonde chuckled. "Name's Victyr. I think we'll be getting quite familiar with each other. Shall we?"

He waved ahead, and I bit my cheek. I had to do this. Regardless of my partner, I had to do this. He wouldn't try anything in public, anyway. Woman or not, the Commander wouldn't let a recruit attack another.

With a steadying breath, I followed him. When he motioned to the ground, I shook my head. "You first." I glared, dipping into a crouch.

"As you wish." His tone was snide, but he settled onto his back and bent his legs.

I sidled up to his boots, placing my knees on them and holding his ankles through his trousers. My face flushed. Aside from the General's crude, stolen touches, this was the first real close-contact I had with a man.

I was blushing, holding some lad's ankles.

Where had my self-respect gone? It was his ankles.

Victyr wiggled his hips to settle into position and looked up, winking at me. It was just his ankles.

"Set—Start!" Commander Dewal's voice carried across the field.

Men started the exercise, and he walked through us correcting forms. We were to do sit-ups until he ordered us to switch places. This was merely to get an idea of general fitness and rule out any handicaps.

Victyr was sweating and breathing heavily when he got to eighty reps. We were ordered to switch at eighty-five, and he groaned and collapsed back to the ground. Perhaps he would be too exhausted to make any awful remarks, one could hope.

"Move it!"

He hurried up, and I laid on my back, pulling my dress around my ankles.

"Hands over my dress, please," I said. I knitted my fingers behind my head and squinted against the unforgiving sun.

His hand slipped under my skirts and grazed my calf.

I didn't think.

Kicking out as hard as I could, my heel hit something hard. He cursed, holding his nose as blood dripped down his chin. All the recruits stared, mouths open in shock, and Commander Dewal started toward us.

Seething, I scowled at Victyr. "I told you–"

"I don't care what you told me, you whore!" he snarled. "I'll do what I want with you!"

He lunged for me and I scuttled back on my rear, putting distance between us when a shadow blocked out the sun. I craned my head back to see General Rafe's face clouded in anger.

"Name!"

"Avy–"

"Not you!"

I snapped my mouth shut and looked at Victyr, who still pinched the bridge of his nose. Splotches of blood splattered the front of his tunic.

"Victyr."

"Victyr what?!"

"Victyr... of Remeth."

General Rafe took two monstrous strides toward him and grabbed him by the tunic, hauling him to his feet. "You call me sir or General to my face," he hissed, though his deep rumbling voice came out more of a growl. "You can call me whatever you like behind my back, but to my face, you will address me with respect." With that, he threw him to the ground and watched as he scrambled back in fear.

"Get up!"

Victyr scrambled back to his feet, standing rigid at full attention. Blood streamed from his nose.

"What's your name?!"

"Victyr of Remeth, sir!"

General Rafe threw a meaty fist into his face. The blow had him staggering back to the ground. He cradled his jaw and glared at the General not saying a word.

"If I catch you feeling up a fellow recruit again, I'll skewer you and hang you on the gates, as an example to the rest."

"But she's a–"

He reached down and grabbed a fistful of tunic, jerking Victyr up to his feet before punching him in the face again. When he crumpled to the ground this time, he didn't dare look up at the General.

"You talk back to me, boy, and I'll do more than just dismiss you. I'll make your life a living dung-heap."

I couldn't tell from his breathing if Victyr was in pain or panting in anger, but his breaths came fast.

"Go!"

Victyr scrambled to his feet and tore off. I sought out some kind of assurance in General Rafe's dark eye, but I couldn't make it out against the glare of the sun.

That huge bear of a man dropped to kneel in front of me.

"Get into position," he grumbled.

My heart leapt into my throat. I laid back, pulled my knees up, and laced my raw hands behind my head. I tried to calm my racing pulse as his heavy weight pressed into the toes of my boots. He tucked my dress down and wrapped his large fingers around my ankles.

"Go."

I sat up. He had his face turned away, staring at the ground beside me. I laid back down and sat back up. He still didn't look at me. I tried to push out all thoughts of men or boys and focused on the burn of pulling myself.

I settled into the exercise, up and down, up and down. My abs burned. I didn't even think I had abs up till now, but I did. And they were on fire. By forty-three curls, I shook from exertion, my breaths rasped and gasping.

"More."

I fired a glare at the General and lifted myself. I sat up one last time before crashing down, choking back a groan.

"More!"

I gritted my teeth, and I fought to sit up once more, noting the dark eye that finally looked at me, daring me to quit. I lowered again and struggled to bring myself upright.

"Do it!"

His tone was sharp and cutting, demanding I keep going, but I just couldn't. I fell to the ground with a hiss, arching my back in pain as my abs cramped.

"One more!" The shout tore out of his throat.

Fear fueled my strength. I shot up, gaping at him.

"Good girl."

I groaned as I went down. This 'good girl' nonsense was getting on my nerves. I was not some animal to be praised. I was a woman.

His hands released my legs and his weight lifted off my toes as Commander Dewal yelled for everyone to get up.

Everything hurt. Everything. Muscles I didn't even know I had, ached. I struggled to stand, trying to place the Commander or the General, but my vision spun as my stomach roiled.

I plunged to my knees and threw up. Not that there was much to spew, but still my stomach rebelled against this new regimen of exercise. I heaved and heaved, expelling bile and mucus. Gagging, I collapsed onto my side.

Lights danced in my vision, and I closed my eyes. Men muttered all around me.

"Get some water and move on." Commander Dewal's voice cut through my haze, and I pried my eyes open to see a wall of feet.

Great, everyone watched me puke my guts out. I forced myself upright and someone shoved a tin cup in my face. Water. I downed it quick, taking deep, greedy gulps.

"Easy," a familiar growl warned.

I set the empty cup down and sat there for a moment. Nausea pushed the water right back out of me. I vomited, bracing myself against the force.

A low chuckle grated on me as I settled onto my hands and knees. The dirt bit into my open palms, and I gasped for breath. Another cup was set beside me, and I looked up to see another recruit retreating.

"Sip it."

I wiped my mouth with my sleeve and took the second cup, nursing it. My limbs trembled, and I felt empty. I had no more energy to give.

The men retreated, following Commander Dewal. I tried to stand and failed, falling flat on my rear. Water sloshed from the cup, splattering my filthy dress. I glanced at General Rafe, crouched next to me, eyeing me curiously.

I glared at him and tried to stand again. My weak legs folded under me, sending me sprawling. I laid my forehead on the dirt and sighed. I had to do this. I had to get up and finish. I could do this, I knew it.

Big black boots stomped next to my head.

"Up."

I turned, seeing General Rafe's outstretched hand. I groaned, using all my willpower to swing my hand up into his. He jerked me up, and I stumbled with the force of his momentum. He grabbed my elbow to steady me. But I staggered away from him toward the group of recruits.

"Pace yourself," he warned.

I nodded, heading to where the men were doing another exercise. I could do this. If I just kept telling myself I could, perhaps I would eventually believe it.

Chapter Nineteen

After a few more vomiting sessions and a brief blackout during push-ups, it was time to break for midday meal.

I was relieved to see I wasn't the only recruit stumbling along. Commander Dewal dismissed some, others gave up, and some were like me, running on sheer willpower.

A few older men were more defined and mature in both mind and body. They handled the training far better than most. One of which was riddled with scars and didn't speak at all. I heard a few recruits saying he'd been a bounty hunter before joining the ranks. I wondered why he enlisted here. As a bounty hunter, he was free to move about. It would have made sense for him to choose the biggest and the best barracks, not the smaller northern one.

There were three barracks throughout the kingdom. There was one here at Northwing, and another at Southwing. The largest, however, was deep in the homelands, adjoining the King's Palace. There, they always accepted recruits. Here, we had Recruitment Day once a year, pulling from the surrounding cities and villages.

As I followed the crowd to the dining hall, I watched the solitary man. I had an awful feeling I needed to make allies here if I wanted to keep creatures like Victyr a safe distance away. The bounty hunter was lean, tall, and moved with the grace of a mountain cat. He wore a long-sleeved tunic and leather trousers, fully covered, yet he carried himself with obvious strength.

I started in his direction, attempting to put myself closer to him without drawing attention. We settled in line with four men between us. He grabbed a plate and held it out to a server. They slapped a cooked potato onto his dish before jerking their head to get him to move.

The line shifted, and I plucked up my plate, watching him. The next server slopped some meat-filled gravy over the potato and he stood there, looking at it forlornly. He kept his plate extended, as if expecting more, but they barked at him to move on. We shuffled forward again, and I held out my dish as I watched the bounty hunter's lip curl in disgust at the beans and peppers added to his meal.

By the time he retreated to an empty table in the corner, I was grabbing a fork and heading his way. He attacked his food with vengeance and barely glanced up as I neared. I swung my legs over the bench, sitting gingerly beside him. He did a double take, and eyed me up and down, noting my dress, then my face—which was probably streaked with dirt. With a curious 'huh' sound, he went back to his meal.

I ate my beans and peppers, watching as he ate, picking around the vegetables. He observed everyone in the room—his sharp eyes not missing a thing. He had picked a table near the far wall, giving himself a view of the whole dining hall, with no space for anyone to come up from behind. Even if we wouldn't be allies, I could at least learn something from him.

He pushed his dish to the side, bracing his elbows on the table. My palms stung as I cut my meat and gravy-soaked potato in half, then reached for his plate. He raised a brow as I slid half of my potato and meat onto his, then scraped his peppers onto mine. My stomach still ached from its constant purging and I wasn't used to such heavy food. The women's dorms didn't get this much for evening meal, let alone midday. I relished fruits and vegetables, though I wouldn't pass up a little protein right now, considering I skipped my first meal.

I eased his plate closer to him and settled in to finish my food. Watching him out of the corner of my eye, I hoped he would take my peace offering.

"You got a disease, kid?" His voice was dry and raspy with disuse.

I looked up, noting this was the first time he'd spoken to anyone—that I had seen. "No. Not unless... you're afraid to take food from a woman."

He squinted, and I offered a teasing smile.

"Careful, my femininity might rub off on you."

The corner of his mouth lifted in a smile. "I've done far more than just take food from a woman. Ain't had femininity rub off on me yet." He accepted the offering and scarfed it down.

Satisfied, I returned to my meal and scanned the crowd. As the food sank into my empty belly, my body's trembles eased. Finishing, I pushed my plate to the side and watched men as they shifted around in their small groups of friends. I spotted Victyr with his goons at another table, glaring fiery darts in my direction. I frowned and looked away, determined not to escalate things.

"That one's got it out for you."

"I haven't an idea why," I huffed.

The bounty hunter scoffed. "Your very presence is offending."

"Begging your pardon?"

"You're a woman, a girl. Trying to play a soldier."

"I'm not playing."

He smirked at me before scanning the crowd again. "What do you think the women would do if I wandered down to the washrooms to take up the title of laundry maid?"

"They'd chase you out with rug beaters."

"Exactly."

My brows met as his words sunk in. Why was the idea of him becoming a laundry maid obscene, but my need to become a soldier was just fine? Was I as gender-biased as these men?

A sharp blare of a horn interrupted my thoughts. The noise signaled the recruits to return to the training fields. I stood, placing my plate and cup in a dirty bin before merging with the flow of men. A hand curled around my backside and I whirled to face Victyr. He gave me a terrible smile. Dried blood was streaked across his lips and chin. Someone shoved him forward. I watched him go as the bounty hunter sidled up next to me.

"If he had done that to another man, he'd be buried."

I glanced up at him. He appeared as if it was a mere coincidence we ended up beside one another. With his angled shoulders and diverted focus, it didn't seem as if he spoke or walked with me at all. I bit my tongue, happy to have made an... acquaintance.

I might have had little experience with friends, but I knew this was a place where only the biggest and strongest survived. I was too small, too weak right now to be without allies. Willhelm had other duties—he couldn't be my nursemaid and take care of me all day. I needed a recruit or two, someone nearby to help me, and I'd do my best to support them in return.

We headed toward a training field closest to the barracks' stables, and a thrum of anxiety rang through me. I'd only ridden sidesaddle, and in a carriage, never like a man. I had never straddled anything, let alone a giant war beast.

As we neared, I picked out Master Aron's bright-red hair standing tall above the crowd. He spoke with Commander Dewal. And General Rafe did as he always did—lurked in the shadow of a building, eyeing the recruits like a vulture ready to pick off prey. We lined up on the field, facing the group of stableboys who held two steeds each. Most of the horses stood there, placid and tame, yet my heart still raced at the thought of mounting one of the giant animals.

"Recruits! Attention!"

We all snapped to straighten our backs and push out our chests.

"You're here to prove that you know your right from left, and how to mount a horse. Each of you will get on a horse, ride in a circle to your left, then to your right." Commander Dewal marched in front of us as he yelled. "If you are stupid enough to get bucked off, you best get right back on or you'll be dismissed. This is a test of your horsemanship. These are warhorses—I don't want to see any fancy riding. You get on, ride two circles, and get off. Any more than that and I'll have you do fifty push-ups."

A few groans answered that, and he spun on his heel with a glare, searching for who made the complaint. "One hundred then!" he corrected.

No one dared make a sound.

"Master Aron will choose the riders."

The Master of Horses started down the first row of soldiers, the row I was in. He stopped in front of each man, then pointed to a horse. As he made his way down, my heart raced, wondering if he would order me to mount the giant gray beast just ahead. His eyes slid to me as he directed the recruit three men down. He faltered and froze, blinking in confusion. His mouth opened, then snapped shut again. He cast an incredulous look at Commander Dewal, who stared at him as though he didn't know what on earth caused the man to pause.

He cleared his throat and pointed the next recruits to horses then stopped at me. "Recruit?" he asked in a strange, high-pitched voice.

"Yes, sir!" I shouted, making him wince.

Please, please treat me like any other recruit.

"I—ah–" He looked at the row of horses, all giants to me, and back at the row of soldiers.

"Get on with it, man!" Commander Dewal barked.

Master Aron studied the horses again, then me. He pointed me down the line to a stocky bay. "Her," he said, then dropped his voice to a whisper. "She's the most mild-mannered."

I glanced at the bay before offering a curt nod and headed to her. Calm, perhaps... but as I neared, she just got bigger and bigger. The stirrups hung level with my sternum. My hands couldn't even reach over her back. Even if I jumped, I wouldn't reach her withers to grab a handful of mane. She had to be one of the tallest horses I had ever seen.

"Miss?" A stableboy peeked around the mare at me, worry written on his face.

"Recruit," I corrected.

There was no way I could get my foot into that stirrup even if I hiked my dress up to my waist. "Could you give me a leg up?" I hissed.

"Sure, when someone takes this one off my hands," the boy said, jerking his head at the chestnut gelding he held.

I sighed and wiggled my fingers, determined to wait. Scabs formed on my tender palms. Whenever I made a fist, they cracked and fresh blood trickled from the wounds.

Master Aron worked through the row of recruits, and I cringed when he pointed one of Victyr's friends to the chestnut gelding the stableboy held. Perhaps the young man wasn't as malicious. He made his way to us with an easy swagger, a grin on his face, and dangerous glint in his eyes.

"Up."

I twisted to see General Rafe standing behind me, jerking his head to the horse.

I bit the inside of my cheek to keep from screaming in frustration. "I need a leg up, sir," I replied with as much dignity as I could muster.

Please call someone else. Please don't be the one to help.

He grunted, dropping to a knee and lacing his fingers together. I closed my eyes for a brief second, wondering what I had ever done to deserve this level of mortification. With as strong as he was, I wouldn't have to worry about getting on a horse for the first time—I'd have to worry about the man throwing me clear over her back.

The mare snorted and nosed my shoulder.

"I'm going," I breathed.

I placed my boot into the General's hands and reached for the mare's mane. My stomach dropped as the ground fell away and I was lifted into the air. I grabbed her mane and threw my leg over her broad back. My very first curse slipped through my lips as I scrambled with my dress. The fabric snapped taut. It wasn't wide enough to accommodate straddling a barrel.

"Rip it," the General ordered.

"No!" I hissed.

I tugged at the hem, trying to pull it high enough that I could sit in the saddle. The mare shifted beneath me and I held in a yelp. I had a moment of horrifying realization that if I was going to straddle this horse, the hem of my dress would ride to the middle of my thigh.

The fabric's tension went slack as a ripping sound rent the air. I whipped my head to gape down at General Rafe as my rear settled deep in the saddle. He braced his hands on the horse's flank and shoulder, and between them lay my dress, ripped above my knee. My jaw fell open.

He had just ripped my dress.

In front of everyone.

I glanced at the stableboy, whose jaw hung open in shock.

"Go."

My teeth clacked together as I snapped my mouth shut and pursed my lips. I would deal with it. My calf was mostly covered by my boot, but the top half and knee were exposed to the bright sun—and every set of soldier's eyes.

So much for acting like I was one of them.

The saddle was sun-warmed under my rear and thighs. It was strange, feeling it move between my legs rather than sitting sidesaddle. How did men get used to this?

I squeezed my legs around what girth of the mare I could reach. The stirrups dangled uselessly, and I clenched the reins in my bleeding hands as the stableboy let go. She responded to my touch, walking forward. I gulped at the height I was from the ground but tried to keep my back straight and ride her with confidence. I tugged on the left rein, and she obeyed, turning in a tight circle. I coaxed her straight, then pulled on the right rein. Shouts jerked my attention from the mare's movement between my legs. Recruits stared at me with a mix of shock and open horror. A few sneered, but what snagged my attention was the man who rode his horse into the line of recruits. I gritted my teeth, ignoring the breeze against my bare knee, and continued my circle.

Well, they all got their show.

I rode back to the stableboy whose eyes were plastered to my calf. It was probably the most female skin he had seen since he was a suckling babe. I reached to tug my torn skirts over my leg, and the mare snorted as my weight shifted. I righted myself quickly. It wasn't worth me losing my seat. The damage was already done.

The boy gawked with his mouth hanging open, and General Rafe clapped him on the back of his head. He startled and lunged for the mare's bridle. She raised her head high in the air and took a step back, eyes rolling in mock fear. The boy muttered, reaching up slower, and she snorted as he secured her bridle.

How was I going to dismount?

If I swung my leg over the mare's neck, everyone would get another show. If I rotated it over her back, I would fall. At this point, falling seemed inevitable. I was too high up and the angle was too awkward for me to catch myself.

"Down."

I glared at General Rafe. Curse him and his one word commands. Curse him for *ripping* my dress.

"Yes, sir!"

I leaned forward, over the mare's neck, and lifted my leg over her back. My chest slid along the saddle as I let myself drop off the side. My feet hit the ground, but the force of my momentum pushed me down. I fell flat on my rear, looking up at the white belly of the mare. I cast General Rafe a deadpan stare, then shuffled to stand before rejoining the line.

"Well, that was embarrassing." The bounty hunter smirked beside me.

I glared straight ahead, watching the rest of the recruits perform their task. Several men needed a leg up, but none fell off like I did. Embarrassing was an understatement.

We finished up with the horses and headed to the Healers' quarters at the third chime. It was time for physical examinations.

By working us hard, the Commander and General weeded through most of the men attempting to hide their ailments. Still, all recruits needed to pass a Healer's inspection before they could officially join the ranks. The Healers allowed many things. Once, I saw a soldier with only one arm. He'd been born that way and could do everything a soldier was required to do. He compensated without compromising, and he was permitted to stay. If men had a disease or ailment, Healers appraised them. They inspected their overall health and had the final say if they didn't find their current state suitable.

We lined up, and General Rafe walked away from Commander Dewal as we readied for inspection. A Healer fastened his eyes on the retreating General's back and squinted. He said something to his assistant, and the young boy darted off to catch him. When the boy reached General Rafe, he stopped in front of him, but the General kept walking, barreling into him and shoving him to the side. The assistant called out to him and gestured to his eye, but the General ignored him and just kept walking. The boy shrugged and headed back to the Healer, who glared after the General but motioned for a recruit to come stand before him.

The row of five Healers had their stations set up in the shade of their quarters. Various instruments littered their tables, and each had an assistant at their side. One female Healer looked up and frowned when she spotted me. Though it surprised me to see another woman in the barracks, I didn't make a face. I had dealt with female Healers in the past, but I was shocked to see they were allowed in the barracks. I fixed my gaze straight ahead, standing at attention.

When a recruit at the first table removed his tunic, my jaw clenched tight. As he started for his belt, I focused on the building's wooden planks with all of my might.

Did they honestly offer no privacy? Did they make the soldiers strip right here? Resignation beat my spirit in waves as I realized that would be the line I was not willing to cross. I would not remove my clothing in front of a group of men. I would not bear my skin for their ridicule. I valued myself more than that.

"Recruit!"

Disheartened, I stared hard at that wooden plank and didn't notice a Healer had approached me. I straightened my spine at the harsh female voice and looked straight ahead.

"Recruit!" She moved directly in front of me. "What are you doing?!" she bit out. Her dark hair was tucked into a braid, and her green eyes flashed in outrage.

"Waiting for inspection, ma'am!" I barked.

"Waiting for—Commander Dewal!" She threw a hand at me in exasperation as she turned to face the oncoming Commander. "What is this girl doing here?!"

"Girl? This is a recruit."

"You're recruiting girls now? I thought the only women your kind recruited were the whores in the village."

I cringed, fighting to keep my face neutral.

"She has enlisted as a soldier," Commander Dewal ground out as he stepped closer.

"What kind of game is this?!" she demanded.

"It is no game. Complete your examination, Healer. Don't waste my time with useless questions."

"How old are you?" She spun back to me.

"Seventeen-winters, ma'am!"

"Seventeen—by the sun's bright light! Commander! A girl of seventeen?!"

He simply glared, making no motion to reply.

"I will fail her," she huffed.

Commander Dewal shrugged. "Then fail her. You would be doing me a favor."

"Surely, you have only strung her along this far for amusement's sake."

He cast her a bored glance. "Do I look like the type of man to be amused?"

"Of all the dung-heaps of men–" She turned her bristling gaze on me. "Follow me."

I stepped in line after her as she led me past the row of tables.

"Rashel! Where are you going with my recruit?!" Commander Dewal yelled after us.

"Wherever I please. Now go back to commanding or I'll pull inspection on you and fail you!" she shouted without turning around.

The Healer, Rashel, motioned to her assistant, a young girl with long brown hair tied up off her face. She hurried to walk to her side as we headed to the main doors of the Healers' quarters. Rashel flung them open and stomped inside. The guards stationed there didn't even flinch.

She led me down a hall and into a large room lined with windows. Sick cots lay in a row, with bright white sheets tucked tight. She marched to a corner and grabbed a curtain, yanking it closed around us. She turned, braced her feet apart, crossed her arms, and stared.

"Why are you with those men?" she persisted, as if she couldn't believe I would try to join.

Her assistant clasped her hands together and stood to the side, a picture of calm.

"I've joined the ranks," I stated.

"And I'm a cat. Tell me the truth."

"I just did."

Her sharp gaze shot to my skirt, and I fought against the urge to hide the long tear.

"And what of your dress? Was that your doing or one of the men?"

How was I supposed to answer that? "It was an accident." I shirked the question, biting my lip.

Her jaw flexed as her glare deepened. "Women aren't allowed in the ranks."

"There's no law saying they're not."

"There's never been a female soldier."

"Till now."

She clamped her jaw shut, taking a deep breath. "You really joined? They let you?" She seemed as though it was unbelievable. Which, to me, it had been, too.

"General Rafe allowed me."

"General Rafe?! That insufferable man? You're joking."

I shook my head in answer. This woman was volatile. I could practically see the steam coming out of her ears.

"He isn't kind to anyone. He hasn't a decent bone in his body."

"I never said he did, ma'am."

"He probably only allowed you in to make an example of you."

I wouldn't put it beyond him.

I pursed my lips, not daring to respond to that one.

"That, or he plans to make you the new barracks' whore."

My brows snapped together, but I held my tongue. Why couldn't people assume that I had a decent reputation?

She tapped a delicate finger on her lips, thinking. "You want to be failed? I'll get you out of this mess."

"No! No, ma'am. I don't want to fail."

"You would have stood out there and stripped for those men? You would have disrobed for the physical inspection?" She lifted her chin with a challenging glare.

"No, ma'am," I sighed. "I wouldn't have. I still will not. If you make me go out there for the physical inspection, I will request dismissal."

"Oh, so you have a sense of modesty?" she mocked.

"I have a sense of self-respect. My body is worth more than to be viewed by hundreds of men." I held my head high, knowing my value.

"You wish to fight with them? You will bathe with them, sleep with them. You think they will make exceptions for you?"

"They have not thus far, ma'am."

"Hmph." She withdrew into herself again, lost in her thoughts as her eyes darted over me.

I honestly wished she would inspect me here, in privacy. It would be special treatment compared to the others, but I wanted to keep going. I knew I was physically fit—as well as I could be. I could pass if given the chance.

"Well, strip then—everything off." She waved a hand over my dress.

I tried not to let out the sigh of relief I'd been holding and slipped out of my dress and under-breeches.

She eyed me up and down with a heavy sigh. "You? You, of all people, want to become a soldier? You're skin and bones." She tsked and circled me, searching for signs of disease or handicap.

I knew what she saw—the angles of my bones visible through my thin, pale skin. My lean and wiry muscles did nothing to bulk up my frame, and the spattering of freckles over my pale skin was my only distinctive feature.

She took note of the only deformity I had. The fingers of my right hand had been broken in the past, healing without any more damage than a slight crook. Besides that, I was as able-bodied as anyone.

She had me put on my under-breeches again and ran me through a series of tests. She measured my breathing, tested my reflexes and vision—my hearing. I passed everything.

I sat on the cot, dressed and waiting for her to dismiss me when she dismissed her assistant instead. I frowned as the small girl trotted off and returned my attention to the Healer.

She rubbed the bridge of her nose. "I will fail you if you want me to. I am not above writing something to spare you this misery of a life. You passed, however unlucky you are, and I could also report that to Commander Dewal."

"I aim to be a soldier, ma'am. The first female soldier."

"Paving the way for us all, yes, I know." She took a seat next to me on the cot. "Just how naïve are you?"

"Begging your pardon?"

"How much do you know about men and women? The birds and bees? The way of courtship? For all that is good and right in the world, do you know the way of a man with a woman?!" She seemed exasperated, and a blush crept up my cheeks as I shook my head.

Mind, I had a rough idea, thanks to the gossipmongers in the laundry room. However, I had never been with a boy, never kissed. Never desired to do so. Even in my wildest imagination, I couldn't envision ever wanting to.

She muttered and rubbed her face with her palm. "I'm going to explain some things to you—and before you say that you don't want or need to know—you chose this for yourself. The moment you stepped foot in that recruitment tent, and demanded that you, as a woman, had the same rights as any man, you painted a target on your back. There are men out there that want nothing more than to teach you a woman's 'proper place', which would be directly beneath their rutting bodies."

Blood drained from my face and an invisible vice gripped my throat

"Don't look at me like that. I don't want to talk about this any more than you. Your mother and father are not here, correct?" She waited for me to nod. "I figured. No parent in their right mind would let their daughter join the ranks."

I bit my lip, thinking of what my mother would do if she knew what I attempted.

"There will be men who will try to attack you. It's inevitable. I cannot have it on my conscience knowing that I did not prepare you for such an event." She took a deep breath as I ducked my head. "I'm going to tell you things you don't want to hear—things that will make you look at men with fear and disgust, but I'm going to say them all the same. And you will listen. You will listen because you put yourself in this position, and if, by the terrible chance one of them succeeds in having their way with you, you need to know what to do."

I sat on the cot, stiff and uncomfortable. My ears and cheeks burned, and I refused to make eye contact unless she demanded I repeat whatever she said.

She was right. I didn't want to hear the horrible, awful things she had to say. I didn't want to know how a man could purposefully hurt a woman, or even acknowledge that there were men out there that would attack me with the sole intention of hurting me.

I looked down at my hands, studying every scab, every smudge of dried blood, and tried not to think about her remarks too long.

I listened, though. I soaked her words up like a sponge and stored them far back in my mind. So far back, I would only pull them out if absolutely necessary. Everything she said, I needed to hear, and I was truly thankful for it—even if it was mortifying. If something like that ever happened to me, I would appreciate knowing what to do, where to go, and what to say.

There were distinctions between genders for multiple reasons. The King set clear boundaries, and they were not to be crossed. Now that I had found a way around one, I was without his protection. I threw myself to the wolves, begging to be made a wolf. I didn't know if I had it in me to stand up for myself and face down the pack.

She explained that if a man attacked me—it did not lessen my value. I had a strong sense of worth, if nothing else, and even if they violated me, I was still worth every bit I was now. I was worth every bit of pride and self-respect. Someone else's actions did not dictate that.

So, I sat there, listening in agonizing silence, because I knew it was necessary. It could help me in the future, regardless of if I wanted to acknowledge it.

Chapter Twenty

When the fifth chime rang, the bounty hunter and I headed to the barracks' dorms. Surely we were near each other strictly due to coincidence. I wondered if Niehm and Elenor moved my belongings. Most of the beds were likely claimed last night. Still, I hoped I wouldn't have a smelly bunkmate.

Lost in my thoughts, I noticed nothing amiss until the bounty hunter chuckled. I followed his gaze to the bunkhouse. Niehm stood at the entrance wearing a sword strapped to her hip.

A *sword*.

"What—how? I thought weapons weren't permitted except for ranking officers," I muttered.

"If that's a ranking officer, I'd enjoy her pulling rank on me." The bounty hunter rubbed his neck, cracking a small smile.

She looked fierce, to be honest. The gentle breeze teased her red hair and swayed her skirts. With her back straight and shoulders squared, she looked ready for anything. Her green eyes flashed in defiance as she gripped the pommel of her sword. As we approached, she leveled a fierce glare at the bounty hunter.

"Good day, Niehm."

She let out a sigh, and her expression softened as she met my gaze. "Good day, Avyanna. Elenor is inside, waiting for you," she said, dipping her chin toward the entrance.

"Niehm?"

"Yes?"

"Why do you have a sword?"

She gave me a blank stare before turning a predatory eye on the man beside me. "Because I have trained in swordsmanship and refuse to be taken advantage of. I pity the fool who tries to play with me."

"Ah–" I nodded and moved to the door.

The bounty hunter had the silliest grin on his face. "Friend of yours?"

"Yes." Yes... she was. I supposed I could claim her as such.

He made a sound low in his throat and stretched his shoulders back. "I like her."

He pressed in front of me, into the crowd, and I assumed he was going to his bed. The bunkhouse was two levels, with large open floors. Bunks were lined up in rows, stacked three high. Men crowded here and there, jostling with good spirits. The recruits were all in this specific bunkhouse, with the cadets and soldiers grouped by year in separate buildings.

I scanned the room, seeing Elenor off to the side near a desk tucked in the corner. A deep scowl darkened the secretary's face, but it was nothing to match the look of sheer confidence and haughtiness that Elenor wore. I made my way to them, dodging the men that stepped in my path and ignoring their looks.

I smiled. "Good day, Elenor."

"Good day, Avyanna. I trust your first day went well?"

"As well as could be," I said with a shrug, which my shoulders objected to.

She pursed her thin lips and kept her wary gaze on the men. "We have arranged your sleeping quarters."

"My bunk?" I didn't want to be set apart from the rest of the recruits by sleeping in another building.

"A cot, dear. Sir Ethan, I would like to show Miss Avyanna to her quarters. We won't be long."

She didn't wait for a reply. His breaths came in quick bursts as if he wanted to yell at her, yet somehow managed restraint. He turned his gaze on me, anger burning in his eyes. I took a small step back, wondering why he looked at me so. Quickly, I followed Elenor as she crossed the room, walking along the far wall. There were a series of doors, and I only assumed one was to the lavatory, and the others perhaps storage closets. At the last door, cleaning supplies were lined outside. Mops, brooms, buckets, and rags littered the floor and leaned against the wall.

Elenor opened the door, and I peered inside. It was smaller than my previous room, with a cot shoved in, and a tiny table crammed in the corner. There was enough space for someone to step in, barely shut the door, and stand there. If I stood still, perhaps I wouldn't bump anything.

My clothes were laid on the bed, and my sandals were tucked under the table. On top was a pouch, the letters from my mother, and my quill and parchment. My mirror and hair things were there, as well. However, my books were missing. They weren't truthfully my books; they belonged to the Records Room, and I assumed that's where they returned to.

"Please get a change of clothes and the soap on the table. I don't wish to linger," Elenor said, glancing back at the men who watched us with wary expressions.

"This is my room?" I barely breathed, moving to grab a dress and a pair of under-breeches. Assuming it was soap, I grabbed the pouch on the table, giving it a squeeze to be sure.

"No, this is a storage closet. However, it is where you will sleep. Now, you look as though you have wallowed with the pigs. Let us find Niehm."

As I trailed her out, I couldn't help but notice all the stares. We rushed out and Elenor gave a terse nod to Ethan, the secretary, before heading out the door. Outside, Niehm turned with us, and we walked together.

"Are you allowed in the barracks because you're Masters?" I asked. Niehm and Elenor were tense, walking quickly and with purpose. Niehm's hand didn't leave her sword.

"Yes. If any dare touch us, they would bring the wrath of all the Masters on their heads," Elenor said lowly as her eyes flashed to the surrounding soldiers. "Our title offers us protection, but not you."

My muscles ached from today, and I had to force my feet to keep up as they sped through the roads and paths. "Are we headed to the springs?"

Elenor cast a sharp glance at me, keeping her pace steady. "If you want to bathe with the men, you're welcome to it, recruit."

"I would rather not."

"I didn't think so. We were able to locate a place where you might bathe in peace."

"Thank you."

Elenor's face softened as she lifted her chin at someone approaching. I turned and grinned when I saw Willhelm joining us.

"Willhelm!"

"She sounds so much more excited to see him," Niehm grumbled.

"He didn't help her in the least," Elenor stated, looking between us. "Perhaps he should take her to bathe."

"I, eh–" He rubbed his neck, slowing his pace while he eyed Elenor.

I sensed the sarcasm in her voice, but Willhelm seemed to have missed it. Her piercing blue gaze lightened. "We could use a man like you if someone tries to follow us," she said in a gentler tone.

"It would be my pleasure to assist." He picked up his pace to match ours. "Where exactly are we sneaking off to, Master Elenor?"

I looked at him, surprised, though I shouldn't have been. Of course, he would know who they were. There were very few on the King's grounds who didn't.

"To a spot where Miss Avyanna can once again resemble a human being. Not a–" Elenor drifted off, inspecting me.

"A slug," Niehm offered with a carefree grin.

"A slug?!" I choked out.

"An awfully smelly one," Willhelm added. His eyes sparkled with mirth, giving me a small smile.

"What great friends I have," I muttered, feeling happier than I had in a very long time. I was surrounded by people who truly cared for me. My life felt as if it once again had purpose, like I was finally moving forward.

"We are fantastic friends. It would be terrible of us if we let you walk around, smelling up the barracks." Niehm crinkled her nose, feigning a sniff.

We all chuckled at that, and I walked with my friends toward the King's Lake.

The King's Lake, also known as the Great Northern Lake, was a good distance from the school grounds. There was a passage from the barracks, and it took us through a thin stretch of forest to a clearing at the lake's edge. Elenor insisted Willhelm stay in the woods and watch the path. He took up position, angled away from the water, and leaned against a tree with a clear view down the path.

As Elenor led the way to the lake, the sparkling waves beckoned me. What I wouldn't give to get off my aching feet and feel weightless in that water. I looked around, and whereas no one was in sight besides us, the open expanse offered little privacy. A steep hillside flanked the clearing on the left, and a cliff towered on the right. Anyone above who happened by could see someone bathing.

Elenor and Niehm moved straight to the water's edge, before taking a hard right around the cliffside. We formed a single file line on the narrow, raised path—the edges slick from the kiss of waves. Water lapped at my boots and I placed a hand on the wall of earth to steady myself as we rushed along.

"Here we are."

I glanced up at Elenor's words, and my jaw dropped. There was a cave inside the cliffside, hidden from all views except the water. The chamber was so deep that when I followed Elenor inside, it easily concealed us from all views. The light reflecting off the water illuminated the cave, showing off the sparkling stone walls and a clear pool near the back.

"This is beautiful!" I set my clothes on a dry stone and stooped to cup a handful of water. "It's warm, like the springs!"

"It's fed by one. This is as far out as the springs go to our knowledge." Elenor scanned the space, as if double checking we were alone. "It has been a closely guarded secret, only known by a few Masters."

"Do the Masters use it?"

Niehm shook her head before returning to the entrance. She leaned on the wall to stare out at the water. "It's too far from the school grounds to be convenient. We will come with you, though, to stand watch in case someone decides to follow us or join us," she spoke over her shoulder.

"Oh."

My heart fell. I had hoped to bathe every evening after training, but I wouldn't want to inconvenience them. They might be my friends, but they were Masters, and with that title came responsibilities.

"It will be nice to take such a delightful walk after a long day," Elenor said, sitting primly on a boulder near the entrance and folded her hands in her lap.

"Please, bathe. There is still curfew on the barracks' side, is there not?"

"There is," I said. At least for the recruits, anyway.

I stripped my tattered clothes and slipped into the pool. I couldn't have the solitude I had in the bathing chamber, but this place still offered a piece of stillness away from the bustle of the barracks.

Elenor and Niehm spoke quietly of things that happened on the school grounds and I commented when I had something to offer. I scrubbed off the layers of sweat and dirt caked to my skin, then attempted to wash my dress out.

"I think this has seen its last days," I said mournfully.

Elenor and Niehm turned to eye it with disdain.

"What on earth happened to it? And your hands!" Niehm turned over my left hand, seeing the raw, torn skin from the rope.

We started back to Willhelm as I recounted the events of my day, and when we joined him, he validated my story about the obstacle course.

"Is it common that recruits vomit? Is it so exhausting?" Niehm asked in wonder.

"It is fairly common, yes. Most aren't used to the strenuous activity. When they vomit, they normally drop out. It's hard to keep going when you've got nothing to fuel you," Willhelm explained.

"I should have eaten first meal," I groaned.

"You didn't eat this morning?" Willhelm's tone deepened with disapproval.

"I didn't want to face the hordes of questioning women," I replied dryly.

"Oh, you've caused quite a stir. They're all in an uproar over the proper place of a woman," Niehm mused.

"I've had to disband several gambling rings of respectable women placing wagers on how long you'll endure," Elenor sighed. "Meredith placed the largest bet."

"No!" I said, shocked that the older woman would do such a thing.

"She wagered you would make it to the front—if that is any consolation," she added with a smile.

"I guess it is. At least she has faith in me. What are my odds in the barracks?" I asked Willhelm. Back on Recruitment Day, General Rafe had all but demanded they placed the wagers on me, this side of the wall.

"Not so good." He grimaced. "I will not partake. But I have to say, someone high up has a large bet on you sticking it out."

"Really? I can't imagine anyone other than you believing in me."

"Speaking of wagers, and coin—Avyanna, do you have a place for yours?" Niehm asked, reaching into the pocket of her dress to pull out my coin purse.

"No," I said with a frown.

There was no way I'd leave it in my room. And carrying it on my person didn't seem wise. It would impede exercises and honestly, I didn't trust half the men not to pickpocket me.

"I could keep it for you, if you'd like," Niehm offered. "I don't mean to come across as rude, Sergeant Willhelm, but the barracks seem an unlikely place to leave your spare coin."

He nodded his agreement. "Most men do not leave their coin in the bunkhouse. Those that do, don't have spare coin for long. Mind you, thieving is a harsh offense if they're caught. The punishment is thirty lashes."

I stopped with wide eyes. "Flogging? Whipping? That's a punishment?"

"You didn't know that?" His brow furrowed at me before he glanced over at Elenor and Niehm.

"No. No, I didn't. I only brushed over the laws, not the consequences of breaking them. I thought they were up to the Commanders' discretion."

Would I ever do something by mistake that would get me whipped? I sincerely hoped not.

"Some are. The Commander of your company deals with private affairs and mishaps between soldiers. If your offense is against another company, or the army in general, it's handled by the Corporal on duty," Willhelm explained as we continued along. "They have more of an organized punishment in correlation to offense. They, more often than not, throw the book, so to speak, at the offender. It keeps crime to a minimum."

We entered the barracks' grounds as the sixth chime rang, indicating the evening meal. Elenor and Niehm said their farewells. I trusted Niehm more than enough to keep my coin safe. She was not only my friend and a Master, but she had a golden reputation for being honest—brutally so, it seemed, but honest nonetheless.

I followed Willhelm with my plate laden with food when I spotted the bounty hunter in the corner. He leaned back, watching everyone with his hawk-like stare. He locked eyes with me as Willhelm and I headed to a table accompanied by other Sergeants. I smiled and jerked my head in invitation. With a bored expression, he arched a brow before scanning the crowd again. I frowned, but kept walking.

"Willhelm!"

A beefy man called from the table. He was huge. I would call him overweight, but he moved with strength, as if he knew exactly how to control his immense stature and use it to his advantage.

"Rory," Willhelm answered, taking a seat beside the man. He scooted to allow room for me.

Two others sat at the table across the way—older men with their gray hair cut short. One tilted his head, curious. "Who is this young lady?" he asked, studying me.

The other man frowned. "She's the one we've been hearing about all day."

Rory leaned past Willhelm with an open smile. "Well, hello there! You've caused quite a stir! Name's Rory."

"Commander Rory," the grumpy man corrected.

"Eh, titles, titles," Rory muttered, face pinched with distaste.

With an easy grin, Willhelm nodded to the older men. "Recruit Avyanna, this is Corporal Bane and Sergeant Greyson."

The grumpier of the men was the Corporal then. Discipline suited his sober manner. Sergeant Greyson seemed more open and curious, but not quite friendly.

"Good day to you, Corporal, Sergeant," I leaned around Willhelm, "Commander."

"I heard a bit about your riding inspection. Care to enlighten us?" the Corporal asked, leaning over his plate.

"Oh yes! Please do! Showing a little leg to distract the other men?!" Rory threw his head back with laughter, pounding a hand on the table.

"Please, put it into context," Sergeant Greyson asked, his tone far more polite.

"My dress ripped," I said simply, shoving a bite of cooked carrot in my mouth. The stew in the bread bowl was hot and hearty. I ate with a passion.

Sergeant Greyson grunted. "A dress is hardly gear for a soldier."

"She'll be in uniform soon enough," the Corporal stated flatly.

My eyes flitted to him, and I straightened. "There are women's uniforms?" I asked. I figured my brown dress was the closest I'd get to a soldier's attire.

"No." Willhelm shook his head. "You'll be given a uniform tomorrow evening."

"If you pass your weapons inspections," Sergeant Greyson added.

A lump formed in my throat. "I can wear my dresses. I can get one similar to the uniform."

"Dresses?" Sergeant Greyson pulled back and glanced at Corporal Bane. "A soldier in a dress?"

"Pray tell, how did your dress get torn?" the Corporal asked, staring at me with intense green eyes.

"General Rafe tore it."

Willhelm choked on his stew, and Rory slammed a hand on his back while surveying me with a worried look.

Sergeant Greyson tilted his head once more. "Context again, dear. You cannot state something like that without men's minds going... places."

Places the Healer had warned me about.

I licked my lips and met the Corporal's cold eyes. He was dedicated to justice. He was first and foremost a law-keeper and I would have to be careful with the way I said things around him.

"I mounted a barrel of a horse, and to keep my dress from riding up too high, he tore it to the knee," I explained.

Sergeant Greyson nodded to Corporal Bane as if to say, 'See, all is well.'

"Please don't go around telling people a man tore your dress," Willhelm said, clearing his throat.

My shoulder lifted in response. They wanted me to tiptoe around to be sure I didn't say the wrong thing. Why was I responsible for the way men thought? Corporal Bane was different. He was law enforcement, and I didn't want to rile his sense of justice for no reason. Having to watch what I said simply because men were men. That, I didn't like.

"She won't have as hard of a time when she's in uniform like the rest of them," the Corporal said, shifting back on the bench.

"You think they'll make her wear trousers?" Rory asked in disbelief.

"I'll make sure of it."

I leveled a glare at Corporal Bane, who in response cast me a bored leer.

"You're far more distracting in a dress, and it makes you easier to single out." He mimicked my one-armed shrug. "Take your sense of morality back to the school grounds if you quarrel with that."

Willhelm made a thoughtful sound beside me. "You have a valid point, Bane. Yet, I can't help but think that it would be more distracting if she was in men's clothes."

I fumed, feeling like a child among a group of mothers. "Do I get a say in this?"

"Nope." Rory beamed at me, all honesty.

I heaved a sigh and stood, taking my tray with me. Willhelm watched me, his head tilted in silent question.

"I've grown weary of this conversation," I explained and swung my leg over the bench.

I made my way to the corner table, still occupied by only one man, and sat down beside him. Willhelm frowned and said something to Corporal Bane, who then scrutinized the both of us with a harsh glare, crossing his arms.

"Friends of yours?" the bounty hunter rasped.

I slid my remaining bread bowl to him, with most of the meat still in it. "One is. The rest, I'm not sure."

"Strategically speaking, it would be good to have a Corporal in your pocket."

"I don't think that Corporal would ever willingly be pocketed," I scoffed.

He snorted as he took my food, watching their table.

"My name is Avyanna," I offered.

"So the gossip says," he said around a mouthful of stew.

I waited, but he didn't offer his name. "Were the recruits right in saying you used to be a bounty hunter?"

His gaze slid to mine with a subtle glint of danger in his eye. I wondered if that was too personal a question and if I should have withheld it. He finally grunted in response before shifting his stare to a group of recruits getting rowdy. The young men, perhaps in their late teens, pushed and shoved in good humor, clearly more relaxed at the end of such a rough day.

We all wore civilian clothing, and it reminded me of what the Corporal said. "Weapons inspection is tomorrow," I mused, watching as an older soldier forced the rowdy group apart with a laugh.

"Mm-hmm."

"The most dangerous thing I've handled is a dinner knife," I admitted, glancing at the bounty hunter to see an amused flicker cross his face.

"Mighty dangerous, that is."

I grinned and looked down at my raw palms. "Do you think I should wrap them? Would it hinder my grip?" I wondered aloud.

With more gentleness than I thought him capable of, he held my hand and examined the damage. Despite the care he took, I flinched at the contact. I had to get over this moral barrier of touching men. If these men were to be my family, in essence, I needed to adjust to a little touch here and there.

"Plantain."

I perked up. I knew the plant was edible, but didn't realize it had medicinal properties.

"Narrowleaf. Broadleaf plantain will be easier to find, but not nearly as potent. Make a salve, and wrap it—or see a Healer."

I bristled at the thought of seeing a Healer over such a little thing. They had more important matters to handle than cut up palms. "I think I'll try the salve." I stood and placed my tray in the dirty bin.

When I glanced back, the bounty hunter remained in his place. Willhelm was engaged in a conversation with his friends, and so I left the dining hall.

I didn't need an escort now, anyway.

I thought perhaps being a recruit might have given me a bit of grace with roaming the barracks till curfew. Last spring I figured the barracks had no curfew—turns out recruits did not have the same freedoms as those in higher ranks.

As I headed to the forest, I realized just how right Healer Rashel had been. It indeed felt as if I had a target painted on my back. When I crossed the empty training fields, the hairs on the nape of my neck stood on end. I peered over my shoulder. A tall man with dark hair and a thick beard followed behind. He moved with predatory grace, stalking after me with no care of being seen.

I told myself it was a coincidence that we wandered in the same direction and tried to brush it off. This wasn't the same as before, when that man cornered me in the alley last spring. I was a recruit—one of them. The sun was still a few hours from setting, and although there wasn't anyone around, I heard soldiers milling about past the line of buildings. Surely, if anything happened, and I screamed, someone would come to help.

I tried to calm my breathing as I stopped at the edge of the woods, scanning the foliage. Plantain was easy to spot, and I figured this would be a good place to find some. Crouching down, I ignored the footsteps coming toward me and fingered a leaf of clover.

The booted feet halted directly behind me, not a pace away. Unease slithered through me, and I stood, turning to face the man. He was tall, much taller than me, though almost everyone was. Thick lashes framed his dark eyes. His uniform fit snug to his body, showing off a muscular form. Surely a lady or two would find him handsome.

Some other lady.

"Can I help you?" I asked, cursing my voice for shaking.

He didn't smile—didn't say a word. He came close, tucking loose strands of white hair behind my ear. I shuddered and turned my face from his touch. Everything the Healer warned me of rang through my memory. He shoved a rough hand into my shoulder toward the woods. I shook my head and sidestepped away from him.

"No." My throat tightened.

Panic enveloped me, flooding my veins. I couldn't fight him—couldn't run from him. If I screamed, would anyone come? My heart slammed into my ribs as warning bells joined my mental fray.

His fingers snatched my shoulder, and I jerked away with a running step toward the training fields. His arm wrapped around my middle, yanking me against him. I screamed, kicking and thrashing against his hold. His heavy palm clamped over my lips, muffling my terrified cries as he hauled me through the woods. I jerked my head to bite his hand, but he cupped it too tight. I screamed as loud as I could, flailing my limbs back at him, hoping someone, anyone, would hear me.

Shadows smothered the light of day as he dragged me deeper into the woods. He finally threw me to the ground. Stars danced in my vision from the impact.

"No, no, no!" I spun, jerking to stand. "Please, no. Don't do this."

Frantic—I scanned the thicket. I wouldn't make it far, brambles crowded around the small clearing.

He made no sound as he reached for his belt. I lost what little composure I had and threw myself at him, sinking my nails into his arms. He barked a curse, shoving me off. Stumbling, I collided with the brambles just behind. Thorns tore through my dress, leaving angry red lines speckled with blood. I cried out, bracing myself as he stomped closer. Bloody gouges streaked his skin. His eyes burned with menace as he jerked at his belt.

"Please, no. Please! If the Corporals find out–" I stopped at the smile on his face. It was almost as if the idea of them finding us amused him.

He whipped his belt from his trousers and looped it together, giving it a sharp snap. Tears stung my eyes, but I refused to look away. He took a step toward me and grabbed a fistful of my dress. I latched onto his forearm.

"Don't."

He heaved me into his chest with one quick jerk.

At the same time—he flew back.

I stumbled forward into the sudden void as the man let out a surprised grunt. A thick, corded arm wound around his neck, wrenching him away from me. His face reddened, starving for air as he sputtered. He scrambled and ripped at the chokehold, dragging him back.

Relief weakened my knees, and I dropped to the ground.

General Rafe.

He hurled the man into a tree, pinning him with his elbow against his throat "What. Do. You. Think. You're. Doing?" He bit out every word, slow and deep. His growl reminded me of a leashed bear, ready for the kill.

The man glared, fighting at his arm. Through my haze of terror, I noticed he didn't kick at the General, he only sought to free himself. He didn't attempt to answer or speak. The title 'General' still demanded respect from this soldier, even if I meant nothing.

General Rafe lost patience. His fist slammed into the man's face. He sagged, lip bleeding, and General Rafe landed another blow. Spit and blood splattered as he lolled to the side. When he doubled over, the General snapped his knee up, ramming it into his nose with a sickening crunch. The man crumbled to the ground, wrapping his arms over his head and curling his legs to his chest. General Rafe pulled his thick leg back and drove his boot into him as hard as he could—into his back, his neck, his ribs—over and over without mercy. The man's guttural, anguished cries filled the clearing.

I must have made some sound of horror because his furious eye snapped to me. I shrunk away from the rage in that gaze. He kicked the man one last time in the neck. The man went limp and silent.

General Rafe lunged my way and realization spread, deepening my fear. He was not going to stop. His heated gaze was trained on me. Rage stiffened his strides as he arrowed toward me without slowing. There would be no tenderness from him. He reached down, hauling me up by the front of my dress. My feet slid and slipped against the forest floor as he forced me through the thicket of thorns, snaring and tearing my skirts. My back slammed against a tree, knocking the air from my lungs. I gasped as he crowded in, crushing his body against mine.

He leaned down, his furious eye a breath from my face. "How stupid are you?!" The force of his words stung against my skin.

I flinched away, pressing myself into the tree as if I could become one with it and disappear from his sight.

"You asked for that. You flat out asked for it!" he roared.

I closed my eyes, tears falling as I squeezed them shut as tight as I could.

"What did you expect? That you'd make it through the wolf's den without getting caught?" Rough fingers caught my jaw, and he forced my face to his. "Look at me."

A sob tore from my throat and I shook my head as much as his bruising grip would allow.

"Look at me!!" His livid shout thundered, deafening and terrifying. Spittle sprayed my cheek.

Terrified, my eyes shot open to seek his dark gaze. He grabbed my wrists in one hand and pinned them above me. His hips thrust against my body hard enough that the rough bark stabbed into my back. I whimpered and my teeth sank into my lip. Blood seeped into my mouth.

"Is this what you wanted?!" he growled, squeezing my jaw. "YES OR NO! IS THIS WHAT YOU WANTED?!"

"No!" I sobbed, sagging against him.

Terror and shame consumed every inch of me. I was naïve even after the Healer's warning. I should have known better. Regret devoured me whole. I closed my eyes again, blocking out his glare.

His hulking form pinned me tight, leaving no room to suck in my sobbing breaths. He held me like that for what seemed like an eternity, his rigid body crushing mine. I cried against the tree, while he watched my suffering, my remorse.

He waited until my sobs slowed to a hiccuping stutter. I dared peer up at him through my tears.

"Do you understand what could have happened?" He dropped to a low whisper, his voice catching on syllables as he spoke.

I wanted to take comfort in that voice, but it was laced with far too much wrath.

"Yes," I breathed.

His pupil constricted as he looked into my eyes. "Do you know what he would have done with you?"

"Yes."

"Do you know how he would have left you?"

"Yes."

"Have you learned your lesson?"

I choked on a sob before responding, "Yes."

He released my hands and took a quick step back. I collapsed. Pure and unadulterated relief cascaded through me. My fingers dug into the forest floor, grabbing fistfuls of dirt, desperate to ground myself—assure myself I was safe. I was alive—my body unharmed.

General Rafe dragged a palm down his weary face. He pushed a hand under the cloth covering his eye, rubbing at the old wound. When he looked at me, he bared his teeth and dropped into a crouch beside me.

"This was your fault."

I nodded—I knew better. I knew the men I chose to surround myself with. My careless actions put myself in danger. That man, my attacker, wasn't the only one to blame. I'd given him the opportunity.

"Make a stupid choice like that again, and I won't save you."

I swallowed another sob and wiped the tears from my eyes with dirt covered hands.

"I will *watch*."

My gaze inched back to his. Dread flooded my soul.

"Make a decision like that again, and I will stand by and watch. I won't make a single move to help. I will make sure you see me. I'll make sure you know I could have helped but didn't, because you didn't use that pea-sized brain of yours."

Bile burned my throat, my stomach threatening to eject my dinner.

I wouldn't make this mistake again.

Chapter Twenty-One

The sound of scraping against the floor jerked me from my sleep. I shot upright, fear racing through my veins as I willed my eyes to adjust to the dark. Something thudded against my cot. I scrambled back, terror gripping my throat.

Before I fell asleep, I shoved my bed lengthwise against the entrance. It pressed against the door, acting as a barricade, allowing only enough space for a mouse to get through.

My eyes adjusted enough to realize my door was cracked open. A hand reached around the edge, trying to force its way in. I dove off the bed, pulling my blanket with me as I tucked into the corner.

"They can't get in," I whispered to myself.

The door slammed into the cot, followed by a muffled curse.

"They can't get in."

Hushed whispers reached my ears, and the door was shoved harder, as if multiple people were on the other side. My heart stopped, then took off at a frantic pace. I curled into a ball on the hard floor, never taking my eyes off the door.

"They can't get in."

They tried, though. Several hands reached through the crack, trying to wrap around the cot and push it out of the way. They rammed the door over and over. Surely the noise had woken the other men. Someone would come to my aid.

No. They wouldn't.

Horror pricked my skin.

They wouldn't come because they didn't care.

I was an intruder. I forced my way into their fold, but I was not one of them. They wouldn't protect me.

I took a shuddering breath. "They can't get in."

No one was going to help me. I was alone.

"They can't get in."

***

The bugle call had me throwing my hair up in a knot and dressing quickly, as it beckoned me from my room. I had gotten no sleep. Whoever attempted to get to me last night didn't give up. They tried multiple times, and I wouldn't let myself drift off. At one point, I had to nudge my cot back into place when they managed to shove it to the side.

I pushed my bed aside and exited the room, standing just outside the door. The other recruits stood at attention near their bunks. I didn't want to face them after last night. Even if those closest to the storage closet were not the offenders, they did nothing, knowing very well why men tried to get in.

"Recruits!" A bellowing voice drew out the word. The big, burly Sergeant Briggs stormed through the bunkhouse. "Bunks made in thirty seconds!"

I darted into the room at his orders and folded the blanket on my cot. Slipping back outside, I stood at attention at the door. Sergeant Briggs stomped to the far wall and screamed at those that hadn't finished, and inspected the ones that had. He tossed a few bunks to the floor with demands to fix them, then neared my room.

He stood in front of me and looked down, scowling. "No bunk for you?" he barked.

"Storage closet, sir!" I said, sidestepping, so he had access to the door.

"Did I tell you to move, recruit?!"

"No, sir!" I instantly regretted my actions.

His lip curled as he glanced at my thin arms. "Can you even do a pushup?!"

"Yes, sir!"

"Then give me twenty!" he roared, then leaned past the threshold to inspect the space.

I dropped to the floor and heaved out twenty agonizing push-ups, panting with exhaustion by the time I finished.

He watched me complete the set, a vein on his temple popping out under his dark skin. "You will eat twice your rations today. You will lick your plate clean or you'll be eating that as well, you hear me?!"

"Yes, sir!"

There went sharing my first meal with the bounty hunter.

With a brisk nod, he spun on his heel and moved down the line.

Sergeant Briggs dismissed us and gave orders to report to the training fields at the sixth chime. The sun hadn't risen yet, and the chilled air nipped at my cheeks. As I walked to the dining hall, I noted the bounty hunter beside me.

"Rough night?" he asked.

I grunted in response, and he chuckled. I sent a vicious glare his way.

"You're talking like us now," he explained.

"Hmmph." That was the best response he would get.

"From upstairs, it sounded like you had visitors. Take any to bed?"

White-hot rage blurred my vision as I turned on him. Clenching and unclenching my fists, my vision went red. I couldn't hit him. I couldn't alienate the only ally I had. "That *bed* kept them *from* my room," I growled.

He took a step back and eyed me, mirth disappearing from his eyes. "That kind of visitor, huh?"

My teeth ground together as I pushed past him. My foul mood had me more jaded than ever. Last night's events jerked me into reality, somehow making me feel older and more experienced—in a bad way.

I stalked to the dining hall and requested two portions of first meal, as Sergeant Briggs ordered. Sausages, eggs, toast, and an apple... times two. I couldn't eat this much. I took my seat at the corner table, back to the wall.

The bounty hunter came to sit by me, eyeing my meal curiously.

"Two rations," I grumbled. "Sergeant's orders."

"Switch."

I stabbed my fork into a sausage, frowning. "And be whipped for the trouble? No, thank you."

A sharp burst of laughter came out of his mouth. "They wouldn't whip you for that. Besides, the staff avoid me. It's the Corporals that have their eye on me, and none are here to witness your lapse in judgment."

My eyes narrowed before I scanned the hall. Sergeant Briggs was not present. "Eat it quickly?" I mumbled.

"I'm a bounty hunter, remember? I excel at subtlety," he whispered with a dramatic flare.

We switched plates, and he practically inhaled his extra portion, before taking the single ration at a normal speed. I ate my food, barely tasting it, but knowing I needed the energy for today.

When he finished, he leaned back against the wall. "You've really never held a weapon?" he asked.

"Never. Not even a bow."

"Hmmph."

I studied him from the corner of my eye. He crossed his arms over his chest, watching everyone in the room. I would learn to fight. I would learn like a soldier. Soon, I'd handle a blade just as well as Niehm.

"You carry your coin on you?"

My brows snapped together. I was irritable this morning. He seemed friendly enough—he wouldn't try to rob me... would he?

I formed my words with care. "I keep it in a safe place."

"Don't we all?" He snorted.

He grabbed his crotch, and my cheeks burned at the vulgar action.

He caught my offended look. "Girl, don't you know where a soldier keeps his coin?"

"In his pocket."

He scoffed and leaned back further, pushing up his hips. "Hardly. Pockets cost a pretty penny."

He shoved a hand into the front of his trousers and fished out a pouch that jangled with coins. It was looped around his belt but slipped inside his pants instead of outside. He offered me a smile before tucking it back in.

"So, do you carry your coin on you? Somewhere under that dress?"

I frowned as he looked me up and down. His tone was teasing, but after last night, I was in no mood for such jokes. "No. Why would I need to?" I snapped, pushing my empty plate forward.

"To buy a blade."

My scowl faded, replaced with open curiosity. "Buy a blade? I can buy a blade?" Hope flickered in my chest.

"Sure. You can't take them on the school grounds, or so I hear, but soldiers are allowed their own weapons."

I could buy a sword.

I could defend myself.

"Mind you, you're not allowed to use them against other soldiers—"

His words trailed off, and misery trampled whatever hopeful feelings I'd managed. What good was buying a blade if I couldn't use it to protect myself?

"Unless they're doing something equally unlawful," he added.

I bit my lip. General Rafe paid me well for the mendings. I didn't know the average cost of a weapon, but I could afford something. I would take *anything* at this point.

"I'll take you later," he said as he stood, grabbing his plate.

I followed suit, knowing that he, out of anyone, knew his blades well.

I still hadn't figured out exactly why a bounty hunter joined the ranks, or why he chose this barracks, but I was glad he did. I didn't completely trust him like I did Niehm or Elenor, or even Willhelm, but I was glad he was on my side.

At the training fields, they split us into groups of fifty. Commander Dewal claimed smaller numbers were easier to manage concerning weapon inspections. My group started with Sword Master Elon. He stood with several assistants who all held armfuls of wooden swords.

For the first time this morning, a thrill of excitement chased away some of my irritation. I didn't care what it took—I would learn to use a sword and use it well. I would sleep with it if possible.

"Two lines. Face each other!" Master Elon shouted.

We formed into lines of twenty-five. The bounty hunter moved to stand opposite of me. If we had to fight, I wouldn't stand a chance, but I'd give it all I had.

"Firstly, hold the sword like it's a sword. It might be wooden, but it will still hurt if you hit someone hard enough."

The assistants headed down the rows, handing each recruit a sword. I took mine, surprised by its weight. The weapon was nearly two-thirds of my height. Across from me, the bounty hunter held his sword with two hands, point raised in the air, away from people. I mimicked his stance, and his eyes caught mine before moving back to Master Elon, who walked down the middle path.

A recruit laid his practice sword on the ground, kneeling to lace his boot. Master Elon stopped in front of him, seething. "Recruit! Hold that sword! If I ever see you lay it on the ground again, I'll dismiss you!"

Master Elon neared the bounty hunter, inspecting his form before turning to me. Eyes wide, he smothered his surprise and examined my hold. "Loosen that grip a bit, recruit. It's a sword, not a club."

He waited till I released my death grip on the handle before moving on. Once he finished inspecting the line, he raised his voice once more. "Hold that sword out. Directly in front of you, now. Shoulder height. Keep it there, don't let it drop."

I held the heavy weapon out. Both hands gripped the pommel tight as I braced my feet and lifted it.

"On the frontline, you will live and breathe your weapons. That sword, ax, or whatever you choose will be the only thing between you and the Shadows. You will wield your sword, fighting for hours on end without reprieve." He walked up and down the row. "There will be no water breaks, no rest. You will hold your weapon until it fuses to your hand. I have seen men that had their swords pried away from their fists, unable to release them."

My arms burned and shook. Sweat beaded on my brow and I looked ahead, meeting the bounty hunter's challenging gaze, as if daring me to keep my sword straight. I breathed through my nose and focused. I could do this.

A few men grunted, their swords teetering. In answer, Master Elon turned on his heel.

"Hold those swords steady! I'm not finished!" He eyed the lines, and continued, "You will care for your weapon as though it were a newborn babe. You will never, ever sheath a dirty blade. If I catch a recruit sheathing a dirty blade, I will stick you with it myself. You will oil and sharpen your weapon after every use. You will care for it, and on the front, it will care for you."

Wincing, I couldn't control the trembling of my arms and the point of the sword wavered. The bounty hunter trained his gaze on me, his weapon steady. His gray eyes bore into mine, as if trying to tell me something.

I wasn't a mind reader. I had no idea what he tried to convey.

"Once you drop your sword, step back. You've been killed. Dead. Nothing more than a corpse."

Master Elon droned on.

Sweat trickled down my temple as I fought to keep mine up. Slowly, it drooped. I bit my lip, picking the point back up and raising it high. The bounty hunter appeared as if this was a cup of tea, not even breaking a sweat.

A moment ticked by, then another. My arms ached worse than they ever had before. The muscles burned, screaming for release. It felt as if they were being sheared from my body. My vision blurred, but I held on for dear life.

"Recruit. Lower your weapon."

I gasped as the sword fell. I managed to keep it from hitting the ground. It hung low, just above the dirt. Stars flickered as my sight cleared.

Master Elon stood beside me. "If you pass out on the field, you're still dead," he said simply before moving on.

Only two other recruits held their swords. The bounty hunter and another middle-aged man further down the line. I caught a few glares from the younger men, but the bounty hunter gave the slightest jerk of his chin in acknowledgment.

I did it. I held out as long as I could.

I heaved a tired breath and focused on the Sword Master.

We did several exercises, practice lunges, and deflections. He watched our every move, correcting our stance and technique.

Swords were the most common weapon used. However, soldiers could choose different arms based on their fighting style or physique.

There had to be something more suitable for me. Handling a blade two-thirds my size didn't seem the best option. Though I'd never witnessed someone fight with anything other than a sword.

"Here we go! Ready yourselves! I want to see you take on your partner!" Master Elon ordered. "First recruit hit, kneels. Ready stance!"

I was doomed. Eyes wide, I looked at the bounty hunter and braced myself. I was smaller than him, but doubted I was any faster. I had no advantage over him at all. Perhaps if I swiped his leg... I only had to land a hit, not a death blow.

I trained my focus on his arms, knowing he watched my eyes. He was far more experienced. He could likely tell by the mere shift of my foot where I'd strike. Maybe if I let him charge first...

"Go!"

Recruits around us clashed. My gaze flicked up to the bounty hunter's as we stood completely still. He gave me an open smile. Clearly, we had the same idea of letting the other person approach first.

I took a fractional step forward, and he stood rooted in place, utterly at ease. He hadn't even lifted his sword point from the ground. If I dove now, he would parry. I had to get his weapon up.

I raised my sword, keeping it close to my body, prepared for anything. He watched my movements, a look of curiosity coming over his face. With another shuffling step forward, I feigned a strike for his flank. He lifted his sword to his waist, calling my bluff. I dropped low, swiping at his leg.

When he realized what I was doing, he leapt back. I let go mid-swing, and my sword flew from my grasp. It barely brushed his ankle, but he sank to a knee with a snort.

"Creative." Master Elon stood behind me. He took a practice sword from another recruit. "But now you are without a weapon, and you've hardly scratched him." He pressed the point of the sword against my neck.

"But the goal was only to land the first blow," I replied tightly.

"The goal is to win the war, recruit. Always think ahead. You're dead," he said, tapping the sword on my neck before moving on.

I sighed and stood, brushing off my skirts.

I was exhausted. The day passed in a blur. We were up for shield inspection next, though it was far easier than weapons inspection. I only had to block strikes, not think about my own. Master Damon faltered when he spotted me, but like Master Elon, he acted every bit the Master and took it in stride.

After we broke for midday meal, and I ate quickly after switching plates with the bounty hunter. I tried to lay my head on the table for a moment of rest, but the bugle sounded, and I followed the stream of recruits.

Outside the training building was a row of tables, with a secretary stationed behind each. Piles of folded uniforms littered one table and on another, boots and belts. I stepped into line, frowning.

General Rafe took up his usual position, leaning against a wall. His intent gaze settled on me. The memory of what happened in the forest yesterday burned in my mind. Part of me wanted to ask him what happened to the man who attacked me, but the other part didn't want to speak of it at all. Acting like it never happened was easier. I shivered, focusing on the first table with the tunics and trousers. Surely they had something for me to wear.

The Corporal's words echoed in my mind—he would be sure I wore a uniform. I'd never worn a pair of trousers in my life. I imagined the sensation would be just as foreign as straddling a horse. For a brief moment, I wondered if I should object, but a glance at the General told me I shouldn't press my luck.

The line moved, and I found myself in front of the first desk.

The secretary didn't look up from his list. "Name?"

"Avyanna of Gareth."

His blue eyes shot to mine, frowning. He frowned down at my dress before looking back at his paper. He made a strangled sound and scoured the area, as if he wanted confirmation that I was really a recruit.

General Rafe pushed his large body off the wall and stalked toward us.

Why him? I held in my sigh and tried to look as pleasant as possible.

"Problem?" he grunted.

"Ah, yes General. This—Well–" he stammered. "Her name is on the roster as approved for a uniform—but, ah, sir–"

"She's a girl." General Rafe finished for him, not taking his eyes off mine.

"Well, yes, sir."

I met the General's stare, not backing down. What would he do? Let me remain in my dresses? Force me to take a uniform? For all his insolence, I wouldn't be surprised if he told me to strip here and change.

"Her name is on the roster. Give her a uniform."

"But ah, sir, we don't have–"

"Dresses? Skirts? Frilly things with lace? No. No, we don't. We're soldiers." It was probably my sleep deprived mind that made me respond—at least I blamed it on that. "Begging your pardon, General Rafe, but I'm not wearing anything frilly or anything with lace," I bit out. "My dresses are practical."

"Now look here–"

The secretary's words cut short as the General braced his hands on the table. He pinned me in place with his dark eye, and I clenched my fists.

"Girls are partial to pretty things, impractical things. Are you sure you're not wearing any?" His gaze traveled down my body, as if he saw straight through the fabric.

I fought the urge to punch his smug face right there in front of everyone. "Do you often question the recruits about their choice of undergarment? What I wear under my clothes is none of your concern," I snapped. I *so* wanted to slap that smirk off his face.

"Give her a uniform." He pushed off the table, still smirking at me. He had riled me and he knew it.

"But, sir–"

"Give her one. She's a soldier first, girl second. Soldiers wear uniforms."

The secretary snapped his mouth shut before glaring at me. General Rafe stalked back to the shadows, content to have resolved the issue.

"What size?" He spoke through gritted teeth.

"Pardon?"

"What size tunic and trousers?!"

I studied the piles and frowned. I didn't know what size I wore in men's clothing. How would I?

"Smallest." A hushed whisper off to the side drew my notice.

I glanced over. But the bounty hunter acted as if he was enthralled with the recruit beside him.

"I'll take the smallest you have, please."

The secretary grumbled and shifted through the piles. He snatched a tunic and a pair of trousers and stacked them in front of me.

"Fetch your belt and boots." He jerked his chin to the side as he checked something off his paper.

I took my uniform and headed to the next secretary. Having seen what transpired, he gave the General a forlorn frown before looking up at me.

"Avyanna of Gareth."

"Yes, yes."

He shuffled through the belts. He took his time, eyeing my waist as if it was a puzzle he couldn't solve. Finally, he grabbed the shortest length of leather and held it out.

"This is the smallest I have, though I don't think it's quite your size." He frowned, then leaned over the table to peer at my feet.

I pulled my dress up a fraction and stuck my boot out so he could better see it.

"For the love of all that is–" he muttered, heading to the mess of boots.

I followed, my cheeks burning as I held up the line of recruits. He rifled through the piles, searching for a pair that might fit my small feet.

Finally, General Rafe prowled over, interrupting once again. "Recruit, go get dressed." I looked at him wide eyed. Was I to go barefoot?

"You want me to wear my own boots?"

They were soft, tanned, calfskin leather, nothing like the thick black ones everyone else was receiving.

He leveled his glare on me. "Did I stutter?"

"No, sir," I bit out, glaring right back for all I was worth.

"Ah," the secretary let out a relieved sigh. "From here on out, you are required to wear only the uniform and no other personal accessories. Please dispose of your belongings, as you are no longer a civilian, but a soldier in the ranks of the King's army. The changing area is around the corner. Please proceed."

I sucked in a sharp breath.

So that was it? Once I changed into this uniform, I was a soldier?

"Go!"

I jumped at General Rafe's barked command and rushed to the side of the building. Sheets hung from a series of ropes as makeshift curtains, providing separate changing stalls. The breeze tugged at the sheets, showing glimpses of men in various states of undress.

My gaze hit the ground at record speed as fire nipped at my ears.

They were naked.

I was supposed to change behind that flimsy curtain?

Someone ran into my shoulder, and I looked up to see the bounty hunter walking away. I picked up my feet, following him. I knew I probably seemed like a lost puppy, but I had no idea what to do.

He went to the furthest set of curtains, ducking inside. I dodged into the makeshift stall beside his and stood there, frozen. The curtain blew in the breeze, offering a clear view of all the men milling about.

"Trousers on under your dress."

I stared at the sheet separating me from the bounty hunter. His silhouette shifted on the other side, but the fabric concealed him enough. Swallowing past the lump in my throat, I placed the belt and tunic on the ground and stepped into the trousers. I mentally cursed myself when I realized the tie was in the back. Switching legs, I faced the fly in the front and yanked them up.

They were so large they slipped off under my dress. I gathered them in my fist and glanced up. No one outside attempted to peer in at me. Safe for now.

"Turn around and get the tunic on." The bounty hunter's raspy voice guided me. As I reached for the tunic, he moved in front of the opening to my stall with his back to me, blocking me from view.

"Hurry, now," he said, adjusting his belt.

I turned around and yanked my dress over my head and scrambled to pull the tunic on. My movements were frantic as I punched my arms through the sleeves. Dropping my dress, I cursed aloud.

"Hmm?"

I ignored his question and spread my legs wide as the trousers fell to my knees. The tunic reached past my thighs. It had an open neck with a set of laces that dipped low on my chest. I rushed to tighten them as much as I could, then stuffed the tunic into the trousers. The legs were far too long. They covered my boots and flapped as I shook my leg. I shuffled my feet, pushing them through as I yanked the trousers high against my ribs.

Muttering about having to tailor my uniform, I plucked up the belt and shoved it through the loops on the trousers. I ran my fingers along the leather strip, searching for the smallest hole.

The smallest hole was a handspan too large.

"Got it?"

"No!" I snapped.

I bent down to roll the hem of my trousers to my ankles. When I straightened, I clutched my belt with one hand and held my dress in the other.

"This is as good as it's going to get," I groaned.

The bounty hunter turned around and broke into a laugh.

The tan tunic billowed around me, four times too big. Laces were drawn up to my neck, finished with a bow. The trousers swallowed my frame, and one hem threatened to unroll. I had a death grip on my belt because if I let go, my trousers would puddle around my boots. I blew a stray hair out of my face and glared.

He flashed a comical grin. "That's the funniest thing I've seen in some time."

"Thanks," I grumbled, pushing past him.

The rest of the recruits headed for a field lined with benches. I spotted Commander Dewal talking to another man and started toward them.

The bounty hunter cleared his throat, and I glanced back to find out what he was drawing my attention to.

General Rafe stared down at me, laughter dancing in his eye.

Don't say anything. Not a word.

He smirked, holding out a small but wicked-looking knife. I squinted at it and blinked, confused.

"Put a hole in the belt, so it will hold up your trousers, soldier." He definitely found this amusing.

I fumbled with my belt, unfastening it and pulling it tight against me. I gingerly took the knife, its silver edge glinting in the sun, and pressed it into the leather.

"Dung heaps, girl!" The General cursed, snatching the knife. "Never cut with the blade toward you."

He yanked on my belt, pulling it tighter. I cringed, leaning as far away as I could from his huge frame as he sank the point into the leather, creating another hole. He pulled back and nodded in satisfaction. I threaded the belt and fastened it in the new hole, bracing myself as I released the trousers. They stayed on my hips, though I didn't know if I trusted them enough to be crawling in.

The General reached for me, and I flinched. He frowned and grabbed the hanging excess of my belt and cut it off with a quick slice of his knife.

"Go," he growled, all amusement gone.

I spun and headed to the benches, scanning the rows for the bounty hunter. He sat alone in the back, and I took my seat next to him.

"Friend of yours?"

"Definitely not."

Chapter Twenty-Two

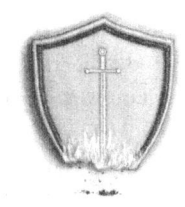

I shifted in my seat to study the patch sewn to my sleeve near my shoulder. The single sword indicated the lowest rank of soldier. I fingered the tight black threads. It amused me that wearing a rough tunic suddenly made me a soldier. I wasn't simply a woman trying to join the ranks anymore. It was real now.

My hands brushed over my legs, still not used to the sensation. The trousers were dark brown, almost black. Either someone had done a poor dye job, or they had been bleached lighter by the sun.

I wiggled my toes in my tan boots, the only thing that set me apart from the men. On the outside, anyway. Thanks to my days working in the laundry rooms, I learned my under-breeches differed from the men's, but no one could see those. I was blessed to be so thin that I did not have to bind my chest like some women. I could forgo that undergarment, at least.

The warm sun beat on me and I struggled to keep my eyes open as I waited for Commander Dewal's next orders. Earlier, I overheard that tomorrow we would be split into divisions and companies. I wouldn't mind serving under Commander Dewal's charge. He didn't let me get by with anything, but treated me the same as any soldier. He didn't even acknowledge that I was different. I appreciated that.

A figure caught my attention as they lifted their leg over the bench to sit next to me. I turned and smiled.

"Willhelm," I greeted.

His gaze flicked to the bounty hunter, then to me. A frown creased his brow, but he settled himself. "Avyanna."

The bounty hunter simply acted as if he didn't know me—it was a mere chance we sat together.

With a mental shrug, I turned back to Willhelm.

"How did the weapons inspection go?" he asked.

"It went well." I rubbed my sore arms. "Swords are heavier than I thought they would be."

Willhelm chuckled, leaning forward to place his elbows on his knees. "They are. You held a longsword today. They'll have you practice with every weapon to find what you fight best with. I doubt a longsword would be what suits you."

"I'll train with every weapon?"

"Every single one. You'll be taught the basics of how to handle them. That way, if an enemy attacks you with one, you will know what to expect. It's rudimentary training. You won't be required to handle them perfectly."

I rubbed my tired eyes and placed my head on my knees.

"Rough night?" The barest hint of concern lingered in his voice.

"You could say that."

I was too tired to go into the details. What point would it serve to tell him, anyway? He would feel worse about me being a soldier, and there was nothing he could do to help. He was tucked away in the officers' quarters, not anywhere near the recruits' bunkhouse.

He made a humming sound, but I didn't bother to look up. Exhaustion pooled in my bones, and as the warm sun beat down, I wanted nothing more than to close my eyes and sleep.

"Recruits!"

I forced myself to sit up at Commander Dewal's bellow. The recruits had all changed into their uniforms and made their way to the benches. In a chair pulled off to the side of the Commander, sat General Rafe.

I say he sat in it, but in all honesty, he dominated it. With his legs spread and his back relaxed against the chair, he openly surveyed the recruits. His hands rested on his muscular thighs—both feet planted firmly on the ground. He looked relaxed, yet ready to pounce at a moment's notice.

His eye found mine, and I turned away from the intensity to focus on the Commander.

"Those of you that sit here have passed inspections. Congratulations, recruits. You're now at the bottom of the food chain," Commander Dewal started. "Until you see next Recruitment Day, you are labeled as first year cadets. *If* you make it to next year, you will be free to gain rank and will have proven that you can obey orders. I expect nothing less.

"We are the King's soldiers. We are the force that fights the Shadows and keeps them at bay. Dragon Riders alone cannot hold back the tide. We are needed. You are needed. Some of you will be fodder. Some will make it to the front—and die." He paused, letting that last bit sink in. "And some of you will survive. We require complete and immediate obedience. When we give a command, you will reply 'Yes, sir!' and obey.

"Know that your survival depends on your Captain. Your Captain will be loyal to you, and expects your loyalty in return. You will be divided into companies of thirty. Those companies will be your new families.

"Cadets, understand that this will not be easy... but you are soldiers now. Yesterday is past, tomorrow is unknown, and today—you live. You obey."

He droned on about the difficulties that lie ahead and how loyalty and honor were valued above all else. I tried to listen, but I found myself nodding off, cursing my lack of sleep. At one point Wilhelm's boot nudged mine, and I startled back to awareness. I flashed him an apologetic smile and attempted to pay attention.

"There's much to train for. When you will leave these barracks, it will be as an elite fighting force. You have given your word and sworn your oaths. You will protect your home, your families, and face the Shadows, forcing them back from whence they came.

"I would advise that you take this opportunity to write home or find someone who knows their letters to write home for you. You may not have another chance for some time. Dismissed!"

The recruits, now soldiers, stood and took their belongings with them as they walked in different directions. I blinked wearily and pushed to my feet. I threw my leg over the bench. Fabric chafed against my skin. The trousers were somehow constricting and freeing at the same time. I felt as though I was confined, yet more exposed than ever.

We were free until the fifth chime signaled our evening meal. I muffled a yawn and rubbed my eyes.

"Did you not sleep well?" Willhelm asked.

The bounty hunter walked off without a word, and I turned to Willhelm with a frown. "I had visitors all night," I muttered.

His brows came down as his gaze cut through me. "Unwelcome visitors?" His tone pitched low.

"Do you think I would welcome anyone in my room in the dead of night? Of course not." I sighed after snapping at him. He didn't deserve that.

He hesitated, and his features softened. "Did you get hurt?"

"No, I pushed the cot in front of the door before I went down for the night. It kept them out at least."

He paused again, lost in his thoughts, before tilting his head and studying me. His eyes danced over the dark circles that were surely under my own, then over my frazzled hair.

"Come," he said, and started off.

"Where?" I grumbled, but followed.

"You have three chimes before the evening meal. You'll get some rest. I'll talk to someone tonight concerning your *visitors*."

"Please don't." I jogged to his side. "I want to do this on my own—I'll figure out something."

"Avyanna." Determination clenched his jaw. "This is unacceptable for any soldier. Had a Corporal found a soldier 'visiting' another in the barracks, you'd never find the offender's body."

"I know! But I've already been granted an exclusion by having a room. I don't want to cause more of an upheaval. Let me handle this, I beg of you." I put every ounce of pleading into my gaze.

His dark brown eyes flashed angrily. "One night. You have tonight and that's it. Then I'm informing a Corporal."

I sighed as he started walking again, and I took two strides for his one, trying to keep up.

We traveled the short distance to the recruit bunkhouse, now home to the first year cadets like me. He led me in and nodded to the secretary before crossing the space to my storage closet. He stopped, surveying the larger bunk room. I mimicked his movements, wondering what exactly he was searching for.

Just as I was about to ask, he grunted and walked to a bunk along the far wall. He grabbed a chair and dragged it over to me. I stood there as he frowned at the floor, still upset, and firmly set the chair in front of the door.

"Go on then," he said, taking a seat and crossing his arms. He spread his legs wide, settling in, and glared off into the distance.

"Go where?"

Was he telling me to go to my room? Was I grounded? This would be one of the first times he treated me like a child, and I wouldn't let him get away with it.

"Avyanna," exasperation drew out my name as he peered up at me, "sleep, lass. You're no good to anyone, especially yourself, if you don't get some shut-eye."

"Oh." I looked at the door to the storage closet, and back to him.

"I've nothing to occupy my time right now. Go, sleep."

All my fight melted away. If there was one man on this side of the wall I could trust, it was him.

"Thank you." I gave him a tired smile and stepped into my room.

I was thankful the uniform was clean, because as I fell onto my cot, I drifted into sleep faster than I ever had.

Willhelm woke me at the fifth chime with a sharp rap on my door. I rose, rubbing the sleep from my eyes, and followed him to the dining hall. He had sent word to Niehm and Elenor that I would wash after eating, allowing me precious moments to sleep.

I stood in line as the servers piled food onto my plate and glanced at the corner table where the bounty hunter sat. As I scanned the room, I spotted Victyr, who stared at me with a harsh glower.

"You know him?" Willhelm asked, nodding to the bounty hunter, pulling my attention off of Victyr.

"He's... an acquaintance." I clutched my plate as my stomach rumbled. I was starving, and for once, felt like I could finish my ration.

I turned to take a step, following Willhelm, and nearly ran into Sergeant Briggs.

"Double rations, soldier."

Taking a deep breath, I dipped my head. "Yes, sir."

I faced the server who looked between me and Sergeant Briggs before ladling more stew over my potato. I flashed an annoyed smile at the Sergeant before stepping around him to find Willhelm. As I neared, I noted Rory, Corporal Bane, and Sergeant Greyson. I placed my plate on the table and took a seat, listening to their conversation.

"–I don't like it, but we cannot impede him," Sergeant Greyson was saying.

I settled beside Willhelm and was taken aback to see Corporal Bane staring at me. His face was expressionless and I couldn't tell if he was annoyed, curious, or angry that I sat with them.

"Ah, I see our girl has taken to the uniform!" Sergeant Greyson stated, changing the subject. He gave me an appraising nod.

I was glad my trouser-clad legs were under the table, out of sight. "Am I allowed to tailor it?" I asked, glancing at Willhelm.

"Nothing wrong with that," he replied, deferring to Corporal Bane.

The Corporal grunted in reply. He steepled his hands in front of him and tapped his lip with his index fingers. I avoided his intense stare and took a bite of food.

Rory leaned around Willhelm, face beaming with pride. "A full soldier now! First year cadet! My, how she's grown!"

Greyson huffed, arching a brow. "It's barely been a day."

"But she made it a day!" Rory boomed.

"But I would like to know how her *night* went." Corporal Bane finally spoke, not taking his eyes off me.

His intense stare set me on edge. He was a law enforcer on this side of the barracks and I had the nagging feeling he somehow had it out for me.

Willhelm hesitated, his spoon freezing between his plate and his mouth. I glanced at him, catching his knowing expression.

I cleared my throat. "Fine."

One-word answers were probably best. It was fine. I hadn't been assaulted and, to my knowledge, no laws were broken. To him, that would equate to fine.

Corporal Bane struck me as cold and heartless. Bound by the law, and the law only. He would be a perfect Marshal. Marshals were the King's law enforcers. They wandered from hamlets to cities, visiting everything in between. They often traveled in groups of three, with two knights. It added protection and a measure of intimidation when they rode in to settle disputes and check on the citizens.

Marshals were trained to be devoid of emotion, empty of opinions, knowing only the law and how to enforce it. They were respected by the people but also feared. They had no empathy, only justice.

Sergeant Greyson gave the Corporal the side eye and glanced back at me, raising an eyebrow. "Nothing interesting happened?"

"Nothing worth mentioning."

I forced myself to refocus on my plate and take another bite. I didn't want to get on the Corporal's bad side by challenging him. It would be better if I acted like the submissive, docile girl I was... or used to be. Where was this challenging side of me coming from?

The Corporal grunted in response and leaned back to study me.

Willhelm changed the subject to an exercise his company was planning the following day, and Rory and Greyson chimed in.

I ignored them as I devoured my ration. My back was to the bounty hunter, but his plate had been empty when I arrived. I wanted to find out when he could take me to purchase a blade. Niehm would hopefully bring my coin with her when she came.

I considered asking the Corporal if I was permitted a blade on the barracks' grounds but thought better of it. He would want to know *why* I wanted a weapon and then keep a closer eye on me. Enough people monitored my actions. Stuffing every bit of food in my mouth, I felt sick. Sergeant Briggs kept glancing between me and my plate. I wouldn't dare an attempt to share any with the bounty hunter tonight.

"He's not punishing you." Willhelm's words brought my attention back to him. He tilted his head toward Sergeant Briggs. "He only wants you to put on muscle. You'll need the food to do that."

"I can't eat this much," I mumbled, pushing my plate aside. "I feel sick."

"You'll need to if you have any hope of keeping up with the others," Sergeant Greyson commented.

I grunted in reply and stood, grabbing my dish. Willhelm watched me rise and glanced behind me to the bounty hunter, as if knowing where I was headed.

"Be careful who you get close to, Avyanna," he stated, giving me a dark frown.

"Do you know him?" I asked as I threw my leg over the bench.

"Not personally, though I know of him."

"Do you know his name?"

"You'd have to get that from him."

I sighed, leaving Willhelm and placing my plate in the bin of dirty dishes, then headed to the man in question. He sat at the corner table all by himself, arms crossed, simply watching the men mill about. He didn't make a sound or acknowledge my presence as I took a seat beside him. I waited a moment, but nothing came as we watched the men.

"Will you still take me to buy a blade tonight?" I asked.

He turned to glance at me. "Bring the redhead and I'll buy you one myself."

"Niehm?" I couldn't help but let out a choked laugh.

"Now she has a name," he said. The first hint of a smile lifted the corner of his mouth.

"That she does. I'll see if she can come, though I'm sure I can afford my own sword."

He turned to fully face me. "Sword?"

"Isn't that what we're going to buy?" I asked.

He let out a sharp bark of laughter and stood. "You don't need a sword. Come find me when you're ready."

He took off toward the door, dropping his metal plate into the dirty bin. I stared after him, wondering how Niehm would take his interest. She'd probably attempt to remove his head from his body.

I sat there observing the dining hall from the corner. The men at Willhelm's table were engaged in some deep conversation, with Willhelm glancing in my direction now and then to check on me.

Corporal Bane scanned the room periodically. His eyes landed on mine and held my gaze until Sergeant Greyson nudged him, drawing his attention. He and Sergeant Greyson seemed closer than the others. They were near in age, so perhaps they had served together.

There were a few groups of younger men eating with one another. Some were louder and more obnoxious than others, but I didn't spot many loners. Most of the officers ate alongside each other as well.

Victyr and his lot were quiet at their table. He sent me a withering glare, which I promptly ignored. I wouldn't rise to his bullying antics.

Elenor appeared at the door, shoulders squared as she surveyed the crowd. I stood and cut across the room, offering a small smile when she spotted me. She dipped her head in acknowledgment and waited for me to exit before speaking.

"Avyanna."

"Master Elenor."

Niehm was waiting outside, arms crossed over her chest, sword at her side, glaring at the men whose gaze dared step too close to her.

"Niehm!" I called with a grin.

She turned and looked me up and down with a frown. I dropped into my best curtsy, pulling at the sides of my trousers as if they were a dress.

"You look hideous." Her face twisted into a grimace.

"Come along." Elenor gestured ahead and led us through the throng of men. Niehm and I followed, walking side by side.

"I thought I looked quite pretty."

Trousers were so odd. I felt exposed, yet the brush of fabric rubbed against my thighs as I walked, reassuring me I was completely covered. It was strange to have so much fabric wrapped around me and still feel so naked.

"I've seen cows prettier than you in that getup."

"You've seen cows dressed in clothes?!" I mocked, holding a hand to my chest in shock.

Niehm gave me the side eye and cracked a smile. "Even naked, they look better."

I scoffed. I had enough self-respect to know I was prettier than a cow.

I thought.

"I'm going to tailor them a bit." I shrugged.

With her head held high, Elenor cut through the men like a knife through butter as she led us toward the path for the hidden spring.

"I'm glad to hear that. You look like a feed sack draped on a stick. Do you only have one set?"

"She'll receive another now that her sizes have been recorded," Elenor commented. I stared at the back of her head—her black and silver bun as tidy as ever.

"That's good to know. At least I'll have a spare for when I wash them."

"Speaking of which," Willhelm strode up from behind. Clearly, he'd heard a bit of our conversation. "You'll not be allowed to wear dresses in the barracks, and only off grounds if you have orders to wear civilian garb."

He shrugged at my sour expression as he fell into step beside me. "I spoke to Bane concerning it. You're a soldier now. You belong to the King for the next five years and will wear what he demands."

I frowned, staring at the dirt path. The weight of my decision pressed on me. I had given up my liberty. There was much that I could no longer choose for myself—dresses were only the beginning.

Wilhelm made a strange sound. When I glanced up, distaste smothered his face. "It really doesn't suit you," he said.

"Drat, I was hoping to compete in the most beautiful soldier contest," I replied with a smirk.

He laughed, and we walked in peace, first heading back to the bunkhouse for me to grab my toiletries, and then to the spring.

The spring struck an emotional chord with me today. It was so peaceful. The deep, clear water with the sandy bottom was warm and comforting. The walls were a soft gray that reflected the light, making it feel brighter than it should have in a cave.

There were a few larger stones littered about on the sandy floor, on which Elenor perched facing the entrance. Niehm took her place at the mouth of the cave, leaning against the wall with her hand on the pommel of her weapon.

"Where did you learn to use a sword?" I asked her as I stripped, placing my uniform on a stone next to the pool.

"When I was a girl, and saw the first refugee women arrive at Northwing, I realized they did not know the way of the sword. They would always be mere prey to the Shadows. A man–" Her breath hitched as she stared out at the lake. "A man showed me how to use a blade. I know enough to protect myself."

I hesitated before slipping into the pool, realizing she must be referencing Valden. She was still hurting for him, even after all these years. I dipped completely under the water before standing back up to undo my wet hair from its braid.

"Women rarely need to use a sword. That's for the men," Elenor said.

"What if a woman needs to defend herself?" I asked.

Surely she was not opposed to me learning to use a sword. Not only was I a soldier now, but it seemed a fundamental liberty I could learn at the very least.

"There are other ways."

I bristled, ready to state my opinion when I caught her small, knowing smile. She stared out at the water with a cynical grin.

"Like?" I prompted.

"A woman does not have to wear a blade so large as a sword. There are more... subtle ways to carry a weapon."

Ah, that I understood.

"I have a–" Well, he wasn't a friend exactly. I started again, "There's a man who offered to take me to buy a blade tonight. He also mentioned I wouldn't want a sword."

"Oh, what is his name?" Elenor asked as I retrieved my soap to wash up.

"He hasn't told me, but he seems somewhat trustworthy."

"You don't know his name, but you're willing to trust him?" Niehm asked in a mocking tone.

"I don't trust him like Willhelm. I think he sees me as useful—as I see him. He is an ally that few men will venture to offend," I explained. "If I stay close to him, I'm safe from the younger cadets."

"What use could you serve to him?" Elenor's tone revealed exactly what 'use' she implied.

"I'm not sure at this moment, though he doesn't seem interested in my *womanly* attributes," I replied sarcastically, climbing out of the pool.

"I'll go with you. Just to check out this ally you have," Niehm offered.

I smiled, realizing I wouldn't even have to ask her to come along. I momentarily wondered if I should tell her that the bounty hunter would also check her out, but I omitted that.

I dried off as best I could with the small sheet from my toiletry pack, then dressed. Elenor eyed me up and down critically.

"I plan on sewing the lacing tonight," I said, tugging at the neckline that gaped to my ribs.

I pulled the laces tight and tied them securely. Tonight I would sew it closed, only allowing room for me to get in and out of the tunic. One less thing to worry about with the uniform. I didn't exactly have a buxom chest, but I was still woman enough to worry about the lacing coming loose at inopportune times.

"I don't know if it's *possible* to tailor it to yourself. Those trousers will be a nightmare," Elenor mused, circling me.

"They're uncomfortable." I shrugged.

"They're different. You'll get used to them."

Niehm turned, tilting her head as I laced on my boots. "I have to say they're far more immodest, in my opinion."

"I feel more exposed and I don't understand why. I'm more covered than before."

"Your skin is concealed. Even if they're much too big, they expose your outline. It's more suggestive, in a way, than a dress."

I stood and looked down at my baggy trousers. I could see Niehm's point. One knew a woman's shape, but it was shrouded in mystery when hidden by skirts. Trousers revealed every curve, even if they covered more flesh.

We returned to the clearing, where Willhelm stood watch. I braided my hair as we went, offering him a smile. Off in the distance, I heard the seventh chime ring. Curfew being at the eighth chime, I had to hurry.

Willhelm and Elenor settled into a conversation concerning the couples that snuck between the barracks and women's dorms. Soldiers could join the women in marriage, though, once they were joined, the woman had to move out of the dorms. They were allowed to purchase a cabin or room in one of the surrounding hamlets or villages. However, the man still had to live in the barracks.

It was not an ideal situation, and more than one couple had to be separated and moved. Elenor was adamant that no soldier should marry while in the service. Willhelm favored the idea of establishing an apartment or village close by where the couples could live while the man served his years.

I listened to the conversation idly as we walked. Glancing around for the bounty hunter, I didn't have to search long. He leaned against a building, head tilted and ankles crossed, watching a group play a game of dice on the ground beside him. His face was sober, and he was set apart from the others gathered to watch, clearly disinterested.

"I so dislike gambling," Elenor said in a sour tone.

"It's frowned upon, though not against the law," Willhelm replied with a shrug.

"That one?" Niehm asked me, jerking her chin at the bounty hunter.

"Aye."

"What about him?" Willhelm slowed, watching me with sharp eyes.

"He's helping me buy a blade. Niehm offered to go with us," I said.

Willhelm frowned and studied the bounty hunter again.

"Ready Niehm?"

I avoided Willhelm's gaze, not because I was trying to be rude, but because I didn't want to see the disappointment in his eyes. He disapproved of my closeness with the stranger, yet Willhelm could not always be there to watch out for me. The bounty hunter could be there when he was not.

"I hope you know I'm only doing this for you," she replied, glaring at him.

I grinned at her before starting his way. The bounty hunter lifted his gaze and pushed off the wall, heading toward us.

He flashed Niehm a sly smile, tilting his head as he eyed her up and down. "Avyanna, would you introduce this fine lady?"

I raised a single eyebrow in skepticism, looking at Niehm and waving my hand at him.

"Master Niehm of Fenor," she bit out, raising her chin to meet his gaze. Her red hair whipped around dramatically, and she gripped the pommel of her sword.

"Ah, a Master. It's a pleasure, Lady Niehm," the bounty hunter said with a slight bow.

"And what is your name, soldier?" she asked.

I searched his gray eyes as he smirked at her curious question.

"Darrak."

A small ping of jealousy resonated inside. He had no qualms telling a fair lady his name, but not me, his fellow soldier.

Niehm tilted her head and raised her eyebrows, waiting for his traditional longer title.

"My apologies, but it's only Darrak. Nothing more." Something in his eyes flickered, but he kept his face schooled to a smile.

It was rare to denounce any heritage by refusing to announce their father's name when prompted. To do so was to forfeit any inheritance or land that might be attached to that name. Apparently, he was either so well off that he needed no inheritance, or he had a feud with his bloodline.

That, or he was simply being secretive, at risk of offending any of his line, and therefore denounced his heritage outright.

Niehm made a noise of interest, and I looked past her to see Elenor and Willhelm continue walking. He cast a thoughtful glance back at me before replying to something Elenor said.

"Shall we then?" the bounty hunter, Darrak, asked.

He moved to Niehm's side. He should have known he would get nowhere with her, but she carried my coin and didn't trust him to be alone with me. Little did she know I was with him most of my day.

As we made our way to the arms market, the easy smile Darrak used on Niehm faded as he took in his surroundings. He was never quite at ease, never fully letting down his guard. He had a talent for observing his surroundings while looking as though he was oblivious, but I knew him better. If I asked, he could probably tell me the exact number of men we walked by, their topic of conversation, and give explicit descriptions of each one.

At the market near the gate to the school grounds, we ignored all the fancier merchants with their sparkling, jewel-laden blades, and heavy swords. We passed bright, colorful shields and intricately carved bows to a small vendor tucked up against the wall.

An old man sat in a wicker chair, clothed in a brown cloak with a thin cane to his side. The few wisps of white hair still attached to his scalp whipped in the light breeze, seeming to have a life of their own. His eyes were shut in slumber, and he breathed deeply, lost in his dreams.

"Gerald," Darrak called lowly.

I tilted my head as the old man stayed seated with no sign he heard us. His breathing remained the same and his eyes remained closed, his few hairs dancing wildly about. I shifted my feet and glanced at Darrak, who crossed his arms.

"Old man, are you going to sell me some steel or will I have to take my coin to another?"

The old man's face split into an eerie grin and he peered up with cloudy blue eyes. "You... I know you. You would not trust the steel of another," he said, staring down Darrak.

His smile unnerved me, sending a chill down my spine as his gaze landed on me and Niehm.

"Ah, you bring guests!" He leaned forward in his chair and squinted at me, looking me up and down. "So you must be the one they're all in a tizzy about."

"Begging your pardon, sir?" I rubbed my arms against a chill.

"The girl soldier. The child warrior. Do you think you're so special?"

That smile stayed plastered on his face, but his eyes told another story. I saw venom behind them—and malice.

"Gerald. A blade if you will," Darrak demanded, bringing the old man's gaze back to him.

"Ah yes, yes. Well, give an old man a chance to get up. I have one foot in the grave and my other is none so steady." He complained as he rose. I would have offered to help had I not seen the danger in his eyes.

"Ah—hmmph. Yes, now. What is it you need? A blade laced with poison? Blow dar–"

"A simple blade." Darrak cut him off, grinding his jaw.

He was irritated at the older man, though I didn't understand why. He brought us here, after all.

The old man turned a weary eye on us, dropping his smile. "I do not deal in simple blades."

"A discreet blade," Darrak clarified. "One that could be carried on a person without notice."

The old man's eyes darted to Niehm, her sword, then to me. "Mm-hmm. I see. I have a few."

He walked into his stall and moved a few boxes, leaning heavily on his cane, muttering to himself. Rifling from one box to another, he grunted with the strain of moving the crates.

"Ah, here's one." He pulled out a small triangular sheath with a leather thong attached. He tossed it to Darrak and continued his rummaging.

He turned it over in his hands, and I peered at it curiously. It was a petite knife, no longer than the width of my palm. It didn't have a handle, but rather two rings to thread one's fingers through to pull it out of the sheath. I realized it was a necklace and hung point-up so that I could grasp it and draw down to wield it.

Darrak drew the blade, and it glinted with the sun's last rays. With a curt nod, he tossed it to me. I caught it and Niehm peered over my shoulder to examine it.

"Then there's this." Gerald flung another item at Darrak.

This knife was larger, concealed in a sheath attached to a leather belt. The belt was tiny, narrower than even my waist. I frowned, noting the thin handle and the straight needle-like blade. It was slender and sleek.

He looked at my trousers and shook his head. "If someone gets that far, she wouldn't have a chance to use it. This isn't useful if she's wearing trousers."

I lifted my chin as understanding dawned. It was meant to be worn on my thigh. Perhaps under a dress. A small smile lit my face. Elenor would have appreciated the discreetness of the weapon. I would have felt much more confident with that on under my skirts.

Darrak placed it on a crate and waited as the older man continued to rummage and mutter to himself.

"Try it on." Darrack gestured to the first piece he'd tossed to me.

I moved to tie the leather thongs, and he stopped me, frowning.

"I don't know if this will work, either," he said.

He stepped up to me and secured the ties tight about my neck. My heart beat faster with him so close. I wasn't quite afraid of him, especially with Niehm there, but I also wasn't used to people pressing into my space.

"Tie it up here, and you'll be able to grasp it, but everyone could see it." The blade lay against my sternum above my tightly laced shirt. "Tie it lower," he loosened the ties to let it drop on my chest, "and you won't be able to reach it unless you have your tunic untucked."

"I have to tuck it in." It was large enough for three of me. It would be too cumbersome to train with it loose.

"Mm-hmm." He frowned thoughtfully before pulling the necklace off and placing it in my hand.

Gerald hobbled toward us with a sheathed blade. "This is the only other piece I have that might suit her."

It had a loop to be placed on a belt, but horizontally, not vertically.

"A bandit breaker?" Darrak asked.

"Hmm... is that what they're calling it these days?" Gerald sank heavily in his chair and regarded Darrak with eager eyes.

He drew the weapon, and I watched in awe as he flipped it around his hand. It had a straight hilt with a ring on the end. He had his thumb through the hole and gripped it tightly. The blade itself was curved, far more than any I'd seen before. Almost like a bird's talon.

"Try it," he said, handing it to me.

My fingers wrapped around the smooth grip and I slid my thumb through the hole as he had. My hand was much smaller than his, yet it rested in my palm securely. It didn't feel too big in the slightest.

"You'll need training with that, but it's one of the best self-defense blades," he said, watching me handle it.

"I know nothing of those blades. You'll be the one to train her?" Niehm asked, squinting at him. She clearly didn't approve of the idea of me spending more time with him.

"Perhaps," he replied, looking past us.

I followed his gaze and saw General Rafe perched against a vendor's stall, watching us. Gerald's stall was tucked away from the rest, but not exactly private.

"How much?" Niehm asked.

She reached for my purse. I had plenty of coin by my standards, feeling as though after my bout of mending for General Rafe, I had coin to spend for leisure for the first time. I had never bought a knife, however, and couldn't begin to guess what they would cost.

"For both," Darrak said, handing me the sheath for the bandit breaker.

I slid it in, and it held securely, the circle sticking out of the end for ease of drawing.

"Ah, I think they're worth twenty gold. It's not every arms vendor that would carry such goods," Gerald mused, relaxing in his chair.

All the blood rushed from my face. I had twenty-three gold, and thirteen silver. Not that I needed the coin, but I would have liked to buy my mother something for the winter solstice. And have spare coin to cover any costs that might come up.

"Gerald. Must we?" Darrak sighed.

"It's all part of the game, son," he said, offering a sly smile.

"They're decent blades, I'll give you that, but small. They're worth three apiece, at best."

The old man held a hand over his heart, acting mortally wounded. "Three gold in simply the materials, perhaps! The amount of work that goes into such small blades—think of the weapon smiths you're robbing with those words! I'll take eighteen for the pair."

"Weapon smiths could have these done in a day. Small, but crude. They have no flair or beauty. I'll offer ten gold for the pair."

"Crude? No beauty? The first time that girl sheds the blood of her attackers, she will think differently. She will see the beauty then. Fifteen. No less." He leaned back, clearly satisfied he had won.

Darrak looked at me and Niehm in question. I gave her a brief nod. It would leave enough to buy my mother a new blanket, or cloak. I earned two gold a month from my service in the ranks. There would be enough left over to cover any costs that might arise.

She counted out the coins, careful to not allow the old man see how much was still left. She reached over to give the coins to him.

"Thank you, fine lady."

I bristled at the way he looked at her. She stepped back and gave him a brisk nod.

"Fare thee well! Let me know when you break them in!" he called, laughing to himself as we turned away.

I handed the bandit breaker to Niehm and bowed my head to tie the necklace around my neck. I walked, watching the hem of her dress as I tied the knot securely. The blade dropped to my chest, and she came to an abrupt stop as I tucked it into my shirt.

General Rafe blocked our path. I stepped to Niehm's side as he jerked his chin at Darrak.

The bounty hunter simply walked away.

I stared at Darrak's retreating back as he took off without a parting word. He didn't question General Rafe, or act offended. That simple jerk of a chin dismissed him and he accepted it.

Interesting.

I looked up at General Rafe, who held out his hand expectantly.

"Begging your pardon, sir. We'll be on our way," I said, attempting to step around him.

He sidestepped, reaching up to grip my chin. He lifted my face, forcing me to meet his dark gaze. I heard the whisper of steel and gritted my teeth in annoyance.

"Don't Master Niehm. This is not your affair." He didn't even bother looking at her. His eye was locked on mine and I fought the urge to jerk away.

Niehm bristled. "This is my—"

"Your what?" he snapped.

His hand fell from my chin. He stepped close to her, crowding her, and I clenched my fists at my side, helpless. I couldn't touch him.

"She's what to you? A friend? You're a schoolteacher. She's no longer a schoolgirl," he sneered. "She's a soldier now. My soldier. She obeys me, not you."

Rage radiated from her. She straightened to her full height, still head and shoulders shorter than him, but I saw fire in her eyes.

"You dare to—"

"Yes. I dare."

He snatched the bandit breaker out of her hand and turned his back to her. She flushed red and glared at his broad shoulders, a mere breath away from her face. Her mouth opened, then snapped shut with a click. An amused smirk crossed his face.

"A bandit breaker. So he thought this would be a good bet," he murmured to himself.

"That's mine," I said flatly, knowing I sounded like a child, but having no other recourse.

"So it is. Here."

He tossed it at me, and I caught it, gripping it tight.

"Put it on, then."

I glared, glancing at Niehm as she crossed her arms, fuming. I unfastened my belt and held up my trousers with one hand while trying to thread the sheath onto my right side.

"No. You want it on your less dominant side," he growled.

He batted my hand away and tugged the sheath to my left side. My breath slid out in a hiss as his arm bumped me. My heart sped up, and this overwhelming desire to jerk away and run as fast as I could overcame me.

"General Rafe, I have to say–"

"You have nothing to say." He cut Niehm off as he let go of my belt.

I jerked it through the loops on my trousers a second time. When his hand sought my chin again, I sidestepped out of his reach, shying away from his touch.

Niehm's blade sang as she unsheathed it. Shocked, I forced my jaw to stay shut. She stood, sword drawn, glaring at General Rafe with all the righteous indignation in the world.

"Don't touch her."

Her shortsword was pointed to the ground and, in technical terms, she had not drawn *on* him yet. The few people milling about the vendors paid us no mind. I wasn't sure exactly how Generals ranked against Masters but I doubted she had the authority to challenge him.

"*School* Master... put it away."

General Rafe's dark eye bore into mine, but his attention was on the sword behind him. I saw it in the way he angled his body—if he had to fight her, he could turn quickly.

"Soldier or not, she is a woman. *Men* do not touch us unless we invite it." Niehm spoke through bared teeth.

If she only knew how many touches he had taken already.

"Niehm it's alright–"

"No, it's not." Niehm's voice raised with outrage. "It's not alright at all. You cannot let him walk over you–"

General Rafe spun and grabbed Niehm's arm as she attempted to snap her sword up in defense. He pried the weapon from her hands and tossed it to the side. She backed away, and he advanced on her like a cat cornering a mouse.

"General Rafe!" I called quietly, trying not to attract attention. This was unseemly. Masters and Generals did not fight like this. I didn't want anyone to get into trouble because of me.

"I will. I will walk all over her if I wish," he ground out. He crowded her against the barracks' wall. "I will order her, I will touch her, I will discipline her. She is mine. If I want her to kiss my boot, she will. She no longer belongs to you."

He slammed his fists on either side of her head, boxing her in. She trembled, but not with terror—she was livid. Her green eyes blazed as her lip curled up in a silent snarl.

"She gave up any right she had as a woman when she signed the contract to be a soldier. She has the rights of a soldier, and that's it. Nothing else."

He leaned in to whisper something in her ear, and her hand shot up. He snatched her wrist before she could land her slap. A small, arrogant smile slipped over his lips before he shoved her hand away and backed up a step.

"Stay on your side, Master. Get between me and my soldiers again, and we're going to have a problem."

Niehm held her chin high and retrieved her sword, sheathing it.

"Avyanna. Good day," she said.

She turned her back on us to walk along the wall toward the gate. I watched her fiery red hair blow in the wind as she went. She had a fierce temper, but even I understood she couldn't afford to go up against the General.

I looked back at him, puzzled to see that he was frowning after her. His black clothes were dusty and the cloth covering his eye seemed worse for the wear. He turned on me and I braced myself.

"You're *mine*, got it?" He glared, crossing his arms.

"I belong to the King, General Rafe," I bit out. My heart slammed into my ribs, but I lifted my chin. I could defend myself.

"No," he said, closing the distance between us, "you belong to me. You joined the King's army, and I'm the head."

"One of four," I replied, speaking of the three other Generals that led the King's army. My insides trembled as he took a step closer. I craned my head to peer up at him.

"There's only one General here. You obey *me*."

His deep voice sent shivers down my spine, and I tried to steel myself against his presence. As long as I didn't disobey him, he had no reason to hurt me. I opened my mouth, and he shook his head.

"Defend yourself!" he snapped, lunging for my arm.

I jumped back, thrashing against his hold as he latched onto me. With a squeak of protest, I dropped my weight, struggling to pull my arms out of his grasp. He chuckled, swinging a leg behind my knees, and released me. I grunted as my back slammed onto the dirt path and glared up at him.

"Those blades are useless without training. When you're ready, seek me out and I'll teach you," he said, his eye glinting with mischief as he stalked off.

I mentally cursed him and stood, brushing off my trousers. I checked my blades to be sure they were still sheathed and glared at the few men that chuckled at me.

"I'll never have you teach me anything," I muttered as I headed to the bunkhouse.

Chapter Twenty-Three

That night, I made use of my new blades.

The door rattled not long after 'lights out'. Even though I was ready for them, my stomach roiled with dread. Faint light trickled in from the crack as the door rammed into the cot.

Pale fingers curled around the wood.

"Go away!" I hissed.

Someone shoved against the door with a grunt. Their hushed whispers drifted from the other side, but I couldn't make them out.

"This is your last warning!" I growled through a tight throat, but somehow managed to keep my voice steady.

I gripped my bandit breaker. The handle felt warm and snug in my grasp, almost as if it was made for me—for this task.

"Come now, kitten."

Victyr.

Bile crept up my throat. He reached inside, far enough that his wrist breached the door, grasping for the cot's frame. My heart raced, thumping hard enough to bruise my ribs. Darkness spun around me as fear flooded my veins. I slid closer to that exploring hand, with its long fingers groping the air. I took a deep, steadying breath, clutching the blade's hilt.

His reach hovered right above the frame. If he moved the cot, they would storm into my room. They would attack me—hurt me.

I had to hurt them first.

I slashed the bandit breaker in a sloppy arc, catching his palm. His shrill cry cut short as he jerked his hand from the doorway. I leapt forward, slamming it closed. Crawling to press my ear against the door, I heard quiet curses and hurried footsteps receding from my room.

"Oi! Keep it down, or it will be latrine duty for the lot of us!" Another soldier growled from nearby.

I forced my heaving breaths to slow, listening for anyone else. I pressed my lips together, hoping that was the only slicing I'd need to do to deter them. Victyr had it out for me, and that he would be so bold to attack me in a crowded bunkhouse made me anxious.

I eased away from the door and wiped my blade on the corner of my blanket, mindful of the sharp edge. Only a few chimes had passed, and it had already been worth the gold I paid. Sheathing it, I laid back on my cot, clutching it to my chest. I dozed in and out of sleep throughout the night. It wasn't a good sleep, but it was far better than the night before.

The days passed, and they placed Darrak and I in a company under Commander Dewal. Every morning we rose to Sergeant Briggs' bellowing and followed an easy routine throughout the day. Well, the routine was easy to remember—the training itself was brutal.

Every day left me feeling more inadequate. I was so small and weak. No matter how hard I tried, I simply couldn't compete. The men were all bigger and, by the principle of gender, stronger than I was. Even the gangly young men, barely old enough to grow facial hair, seemed stronger than I. Even Victyr, with his bandaged hand, fared better than me. I applied myself nonetheless. This wasn't meant to be easy. The Shadows wouldn't grant me leniency simply because I was a woman.

As the days grew shorter and the cold of autumn set in, my body grew and developed. I tailored my uniform at night by the light of my lantern and noticed the gradual changes. Muscles, however faint, filled out along my limbs. It pleased me to see that I was getting stronger, even if I felt as though I couldn't keep up with my male counterparts.

What I did not appreciate, however, was the weight I put on in other areas—thanks to the appetite I worked up with the rigorous training, I was determined to prove myself as worthy as a male soldier, yet my body rebelled, proving that I was undeniably female.

For the first time in my seventeen-winters, I had to bind my chest. One recent stint of running triggered lewd laughter from the soldiers. The pain from the pulled muscles, combined with the fact that the ever-looming General Rafe was there to see, had me asking Niehm and Elenor for guidance.

I slept and worked with my chest bound, which helped me hide those changes, but alas, there was nothing to do about my backside. My trousers actually fit me. Yet, from the comments I overheard, that wasn't a good thing. Now, instead of resembling a lanky child, I bore the curves of a woman, and that unnerved me.

As winter approached, we had a bit more free time. I asked Darrak once to teach me to use the bandit breaker, and he simply said there were others more suited to the task. At first, I was angered that he wouldn't teach me, but General Rafe's constant presence reminded me that even a bounty hunter wouldn't want to cross him.

As the days went on, Darrak took to disappearing after the evening meal. I settled into a steady routine, seeing Elenor and Niehm for our walk to the springs, and then spent the rest of my evenings with Willhelm.

Willhelm's friends grew on me, though Corporal Bane still put me on edge. He dealt with the fallout from the night I cut Victyr's hand. I was sure he knew what happened, but with nobody coming forward, he made no move to correct anyone.

Commander Rory was a fine fellow, always ready to have a good laugh. Sergeant Greyson was a man of balance who sought to understand everything. He seemed to be closer to Corporal Bane than the others and acted as the mediator when things got heated between friends.

Willhelm often sat with me until curfew, and we talked about everything. We grew close, and he counseled me on many topics concerning life in the barracks—how to act, who to talk to, how to approach different tasks with my limited strength.

He was the one to advise me to try a crossbow in archery instead of the standard recurve bow. I was a fair shot, but lacked the strength to draw a heavy enough weight to wound anything further than fifty paces.

The Master Archer, Elias, offered me a crossbow with a winch and pulley system to make the draw easier. It was heavier, but far more effective at mortally wounding the target. I figured on the battlefield I could always rest the bow on the ground or a rock.

With the shorter days and first snowfall, I found myself in the dining hall, hands wrapped around a mug of hot cider, listening to Willhelm and his friends talk. Glancing back at the table in the corner, I noted with a frown that Darrak had been missing all day.

"So, have you heard?" Rory said, dropping his heavy frame to the bench beside me.

I glanced at him, raising my eyebrows in curiosity.

"Heard...?" Greyson prompted.

"About Master Brann's assistant? What was his name... Wevtyn?" Rory took a sip of his hot cider, peering over the rim of his mug.

"Yes," Bane grumbled, a slow blink crossing his bored features.

"No." Willhelm and Greyson spoke in unison.

"Ah, well, it seems your friend was more than met the eye!" Rory said, giving me a smile.

"My friend?"

"Mm-hmm. That tall, broody one whose company you're always in?"

"Darrak?"

"Aye! That's his name! Darrak of Nightfell... King's bounty hunter!"

Warmth spread over my cheeks and I diverted my attention to my half-full mug.

"What does he have to do with Master Brann's assistant?" Willhelm asked, casting me a worried look.

"Well, it appears he's been scouting for a bounty. It's all very hush-hush–"

"For a reason," Bane interjected.

"Yes, well, gossip will spread with or without me, Bane." Rory feigned offense, though we all knew it was in jest. Bane was Bane.

"Master Brann's assistant had a bounty on his head?" Greyson asked, looking from Bane to Rory.

"Not him exactly, but someone's been leaking information out of Northwing—to the Shadows. Have you noticed how many hits Southwing has taken since last year? He was sneaking information about the new school."

"Really?" I couldn't keep the shock from my voice.

It was hard to believe that anyone residing in Northwing would be on the enemy's side. How could anyone witness the suffering these people went through, then help the ones inflicting that hurt? What could drive someone to ally themselves with the Shadows? What did they have to offer?

"Aye, and it seems your bounty hunter found him by digging around."

"He's not *my* bounty hunter," I muttered.

Bane glowered from across the way. "You were simply a source of information to him."

I glared right back. Sure, I spoke with Darrack, and would have named him my friend if anyone asked, but I never noticed him pumping me for details. He was always intrigued with things on the school grounds–

A twinge of unease curled deep in my stomach. Perhaps he *had* used me...

I finished my cider in silence as the men chatted about the day's events. It appeared the man, Wevtyn, was due for an immediate escort to the King's Palace. Paperwork was being sorted concerning the King's bounty hunter—Darrak Nightfell.

So it was true then—that gossip almost six months ago. He really was a bounty hunter. Perhaps he had used me, but that didn't bother me nearly as much as the notion of him leaving. I had an ally with him, and I would lose that when he left.

I stood, feeling selfish that I only thought of myself when Northwing was probably in an uproar over this news.

"Avyanna?" Rory looked up at me as I stepped over the bench.

"Just going to turn in early tonight, is all." I shrugged.

I ignored Bane's intense gaze. He always scrutinized me as though I would cause trouble—or be the reason others did so.

"I'll walk you to the bunkhouse," Willhelm said, standing.

"No. No, that's all right."

Confusion crossed his features, and I offered him a smile. I didn't want to tell him I wanted space, but he seemed to understand without me stating it.

"See you tomorrow then?"

"As always."

I wrapped my cloak around me as I dropped my mug off in the bin, then left the hall.

The night was cold. Stray snowflakes fell here and there, lonely and solitary things. A puff of breath curled past my lips as I glanced up. It didn't surprise me to see the heavy clouds threatening the first real snowfall of the season.

The night sky was empty of dragons. The older beasts retreated to the warm underground caverns. This year's hatchlings—now strong and more than doubled in size—joined the others in the journey to Southwing for the winter.

I had to be honest with myself... I missed them and their constant racket in the background of everyday life. The squealing and trumpets of the young ones playing, the growls and bellows of the older ones reaching maturity. It was something that was always there–until it wasn't. It made the night feel so much quieter.

"There you are."

I jumped at the sound of Darrak's voice and squinted into the dark for the source. A silhouette snared my attention, moving away from a building nearby.

"Darrak?" I asked, as one hand went to the bandit breaker on my belt.

The shadowed form laughed quietly and stepped into the torchlight, revealing his familiar face.

His face might have been familiar, but his clothes were not. I couldn't discern many details of his red leather armor, aside from the gryphon embedded onto his chest piece. The King's Gryphon.

"So it's true then?" I asked. I released the hilt of my blade and clutched my cloak tight against the cold.

"Afraid so." He shrugged with an easy grin. He paused, noting my expression, and frowned. "Tell me you're more disappointed that I'm leaving, rather than for dear Wevtyn."

My eyes widened at his implication. "You don't believe I would sympathize with one of his kind, do you?"

"No, no." He chuckled again, then jerked his head, encouraging me to walk beside him. "I was afraid you wouldn't miss me."

I tried to offer him a smile, but I knew it wasn't convincing. My gaze dropped to the frozen path.

"Is it petty that I am saddened because I'll be alone?" I pushed out a breath, hating the emotion building up in my throat. "Is it selfish that my first thought was simply that you'd be gone? I'm not strong enough to hold my own yet."

He stopped, waiting to speak until I looked up at him. "Dear Avyanna, you've always held your own. You chose this path because you're strong. And you're strong enough to finish, too. I know you won't let me down—will you?"

I closed my eyes and shook my head.

"My job is here, you know? Looking over the homelands–"

"The King's own bounty hunter," I finished for him.

"That's my title. One day, I'll hear about the fierce Avyanna that has slain thousands on the battlefield. You'll come home a hero!"

When I opened my eyes to look at him, he wore a sad smile. "Thousands?" I teased.

He laughed. "Absolutely. You might even win the war single-handedly."

I scoffed, falling into step beside him.

After a span of silence, I gathered the courage to form the question that nagged at my mind the moment I heard the news.

"Did you use me?" My question was barely more than a whisper. I worried he would turn on me, telling me I was worth nothing more than the information I'd given him.

He didn't falter as he responded, "I don't use anyone, exactly. I use what they say." He paused for a moment, regarding me. "If you're asking if the only reason

I got close to you was for your intelligence concerning the school grounds, that would be false. I had no intention of befriending you. You sought me out, remember?"

A soft hum was the only reply I could muster.

"I have a job to do, you understand? I make it a point not to create enemies while in the field, and I do my best to respect individuals. No one is simply a means to an end." He nudged me with his shoulder. "You're worth more than that to me."

We stopped a few paces from the bunkhouse, looking up at it in silence.

"I'm not playing soldier anymore, Avyanna."

His voice was sorrowful and distant. He wouldn't sleep here tonight. He would probably bunk down somewhere in the officers' quarters.

"I'll be leaving in the morning." He rubbed the back of his neck. "I wanted to say farewell."

I held his gaze, feeling a little lost. I would miss him, but I didn't know exactly how to say goodbye. Was I supposed to hug him? That would be unseemly for us. A salute?

He chuckled to himself and rested his hand on top of my head. "Go Avyanna. Prove them all wrong. Show them what you're made of. Give them a reason to fear you." Something flickered behind those gray eyes. "I'll be hearing of you." He slipped his hand down to my back and gave me a gentle push before stepping aside and disappearing into the shadows.

So now, I was alone.

Winter of Year 896

The next few weeks flew by in a blur. I concentrated on my training and steadily ignored all the lewd comments of the other soldiers. Commander Dewal didn't allow me to be treated as anything less than the others and held me to the same standards. That helped me focus on my training and not on my comrades.

It was a few days shy of the Winter Solstice and I had written my mother, telling her not to visit. I claimed I was holed up in a job that wouldn't allow visitors... which, to be honest, was true. Soldiers were not allowed visitors. If requested, we were permitted a pass to visit the nearby villages, though.

I didn't bother with the pass, but rather had Elenor pick out a heavy winter blanket and send it to my mother with the letter. I wasn't quite ready for her to see what I had done, for her to judge my actions.

I walked along the path from the officers' quarters to the dining hall, where Willhelm and his friends waited for me. The snow crunched beneath my boots, and I pulled my cloak tighter around me to ward off the cold.

Tomorrow, I would be eighteen-winters. That seemed like a benchmark for some reason. Two more—and I would be old enough to be called a Lady. I would be a lady soldier. I scoffed, smiling at the snow. What a ridiculous concept. There was nothing ladylike about the way I trained or how I lived. There was no privacy, no illusion of femininity. I was a soldier through and through.

"Hail!"

My head jerked up as I searched for who had called out.

"Hail! Avyanna!" A young man stood beside a building, waving at me.

"Hail," I replied warily.

He was one of the men always clinging to Victyr's coattails. Not a bully himself, but one easily influenced by them.

"Well," he gestured between us, "I was wondering if we might talk."

I stopped in my tracks and turned to face him head on. I stood in the middle of the road. He was near the edge of a building backed up against woods. Tilting my head, I frowned at his position. I wasn't so naïve anymore.

"Then talk."

"In private?"

He sounded so pitiful. He didn't strike me as mature, but rather a child—not a leader, but a follower that took no initiative of his own.

"Begging your pardon, but my friends are waiting for me," I replied, turning back to continue on my way. Something didn't feel right.

"Wait! I—I understand being guarded. I just," he stumbled over his words, "I just wanted to apologize."

I stopped again, peering over with a brow raised. He hadn't moved from his spot at the back of the building. Prints littered the snow near him. None led behind the structure—perhaps he was alone.

"Could you just come a little closer so I don't have to shout?" he asked with a small, nervous laugh.

"Why won't you come onto the path?" Suspicion colored my voice.

He glanced off to the side, as if afraid to be seen. "What do you think Victyr would do if he saw me talking with you?"

He had a point there. He would be yet-another victim of Victyr's harassment. With a weary sigh, I peered over at the dining hall further down the way. I couldn't hear the voices from this distance, but I could see the lantern light through the hide-covered windows. Biting my tongue, I started toward the corner of the building. I took a few steps to the side, out of direct view of the road, but I could always backpedal quickly to be in plain sight of anyone passing by. Not that there were many left in the barracks with the Solstice so near.

"This is as far as I'll go. Don't try anything," I warned.

I could hold my own now. My fingers curled around the bandit breaker's hilt. I would not be easy prey.

He offered me a small, timid smile and shrugged his shoulders. "I just wanted to say I'm sorry."

"Sorry for what?" I wanted to hear him say it, admit to the part he played in Victyr's constant torment.

There were plenty of other weaker soldiers that his group preyed upon, but–

Someone slammed into me, knocking me off balance. I threw my hands out to break my fall. A heavy weight crashed against my back and I crumpled face-first into the cold snow. Frantic—I scrambled to reach my bandit breaker or necklace blade, but the weight pinned me in place, crushing my ribs. My hips crushed into the unforgiving ground. A sound wrenched from my lungs, a tight guttural scream–

Something hard smacked the back of my head and everything went dark for a breath. I blinked, struggling to clear the haze. I needed to get off my stomach—to draw my blade. My attacker shoved my face into the snow, muffling my cries. The frozen powder scraped against my cheeks as I thrashed.

"Stop squirming, whore!" A voice spat in my ear.

They snared a fistful of my hair, jerking my head back. I stilled as cold steel pressed against my throat. A sharp prick jabbed into my shoulder.

"That's better." Pure dread filled me as I recognized Victyr's voice. "Get her up."

The weight lifted off me. Every instinct screamed to run, to fight. My body wouldn't respond. Bile burned my throat. He pricked me with something. Poison? Master Elon mentioned such things, but how had Victyr gotten a hold of something like that?

Two burly men jerked me up by my arms and dragged my limp body to the backside of the building. My feet dangled in the air as they pinned me to the wall, level with Victyr's seething gaze. He slammed my head against the wooden planks. Fury burned his face an angry red against the dim night. The man who lured me off the road stood behind him with two others. Six. *Six* men.

I wouldn't have stood a chance even if I wasn't paralyzed.

Willhelm would come looking for me.

"You little whore. You made me wait this long? Six months?! Six long months?"

Victyr spat in my face and backhanded me, wrenching my head to the side. He grabbed my hair and slammed my head back again. As the stars burst, dimming my vision, panic seared my thoughts.

"You just walked around, taunting me. You wore your men's trousers, teasing me." His lip curled as his sharp gaze traveled over my body. "You wanted me to come for you. Didn't she?" He smiled over his shoulder for support and his goons jeered as expected.

"I knew you'd put up a fight, too. Deep down, a pretty thing like you just wants to be dominated." His fingers dug into my cheeks. "You'd fight me and demand I take control. So I am."

He leaned in and smashed his lips to mine. A whimper squeezed from my throat as I used every ounce of willpower to move—just a fraction, anything—but it was no use. Terror pried my eyes wide open as he moved his lips on mine. When he pulled back, blood stained his lip. Had he bitten me? Or was that from the blow he landed moments ago?

My pulse raced—this wasn't happening. Someone had to come. If no one found me soon, they'd do things that would scar me forever. I tried with all my might to scream, to wail for help, but all that escaped was a strangled moan.

"See boys? What did I tell you? She likes it!" Victyr said triumphantly.

Would Willhelm spot my tracks in the darkening night? How long would it take before worry prompted him to come looking?

Victyr stepped closer, bracing a small knife against the neckline of my tunic. I clamped my eyes shut, and my breaths came in terrified gasps.

"Look at me!"

He gripped my hair, slamming my head against the wall again. The world faded for a moment before he came back to light.

"This is your fault! You *watch* what you made me do!"

This was my fault? Hadn't I heard that before? My fault?

How? How was this my fault?

General Rafe's words echoed in my mind.

'*This was your fault!*'

'*I won't save you.*'

A rogue tear slipped out of my eye and trailed down my cheek.

"Oh look! She wants it so bad, she's crying." Laughter followed Victyr's claim. He jerked the knife through my tunic. "Just to get it started," he said with a wink, before tearing the tunic wide open.

Physically, I felt nothing as I was bared to the men. My chest was still bound, but the lust in their eyes cut deep. My thoughts screamed, *begged* for help that I couldn't voice.

He snickered, yanking my necklace free. "Oh look, our kitten has claws. Too bad she can't use them," he jeered, tossing it into the snow.

Victyr cupped my breast over the fabric and I envisioned a thousand ways I wanted to hurt him.

"I knew it." His tone lowered with a husky edge. "I knew you started to bind them. Hiding them from us. Shame."

Another flick of the knife and the pressure of my chest-wrap fell away, exposing me for everyone to see.

Acid scorched the back of my mouth. I couldn't puke, could barely breathe. I was stranded there—helpless.

No one was coming for me.

Someone whistled low—all eyes plastered to my chest.

"More!" the man holding my right arm grunted.

"Only a little." Victyr sneered. "Then I'm playing. You'll have your turn."

I reeled with panic. This was not just Victyr's attack. He planned to share. My body would be spread amongst six men. My eyes rolled back as consciousness threatened to slip from my grasp.

No—no. *Please*, no!

"Hey!" His fingers dug into my jaw, keeping my head upright. "Hey! Look at me!"

My gaze snapped forward, locking onto Victyr's hot and ravenous glare.

"You'll stay with us. You *wanted* this. Why else would you have surrounded yourself with men?"

He twisted his little knife in the air with a wicked grin and jerked at something near my waist. My belt. He tugged it free, and I focused on the forest.

I could handle this. I could survive this.

I watched the trees and the dark woods. Tears flowed down my cheeks as I pleaded for anyone—anything. I would take a rogue wolf pack. I would prefer my own death to this.

Trees. Trees. Brush. Trees...

Wait.

I tried to focus my spinning vision.

Was that a tree? Or someone?

Please be someone!

The shadow crept closer as Victyr tore at my trousers.

It was someone—someone big. I could see their mountains of shoulders and thick build. They stuck to the trees. What were they waiting for?! They needed to get help! I needed *help!*

Victyr cursed. My head lurched to the side as he landed another blow to my cheek. "Why are these so hard to cut through?!" he snarled.

"Just yank them down, Vic." A man scoffed, followed by amused snickers from the others.

Victyr forced me to face him, holding the blade to my chin. "She's done playing soldier." He spit, then looked down in concentration. "I'm going to cut these blasted things off. She won't be wearing them again."

When he pulled the knife away, my head rolled forward, and I watched as he sawed through my waistband. Small cuts seeped crimson from the places his blade nicked my skin in his efforts. I whimpered again, and the man on my left jerked me back against the wall. The goon on my left side pulled my head back up so I could see the woods.

I frantically scanned the woods for my last shred of hope...

My heart sank.

It sank so far, past my boots and into the depths of the earth.

There, near the trees at the edge of the woods, a single eye surveyed the scene. His immense body sat dropped into a crouch, the fur vest being one I had seen about—though the man had kept his distance from me. He wore no coat, no cloak, and no sleeves to cover his tattoo.

General Rafe watched.

'I will stand by and watch. I won't make a single move to help. You will see me and know that I could have helped but didn't—'

My eyes drooped closed as Victyr grunted and gave a small cheer. My body lurched with the sound of tearing fabric.

"I said *look* at me!"

My head was jerked forward and slammed back. My eyes blinked open, but wouldn't focus. I don't know why I bothered. I didn't want to see any of this.

Helplessness crashed over me in waves, drowning me. Defeat overwhelmed my heart like never before. It squeezed so tight—as if it refused to beat.

My sight focused, and I stared behind Victyr as a mountain of shadow tore itself from a tree. Shocked grunts sounded from the men holding me, and they released me.

I collapsed face-first into the snow. The icy powder filled my mouth and nose. I couldn't breathe. I gasped, only to have the stuff suck into my lungs. Unable to cough, to move, I choked in silence. Garbled shrieks surrounded me, oblivious to my struggle.

Footsteps crunched toward me, bringing someone closer. They rolled me over and I gulped for air, too desperate to register which man crouched beside me. After a few mad lungfuls, I focused on his face.

A single dark eye glittered dangerously as General Rafe tugged my cloak over my chest. He rose and walked over to a body on the ground. I couldn't see who it was, but the man whined as General Rafe stood over him.

"Don't look."

It took a moment for me to realize General Rafe directed the comment to me. I watched as he braced his feet on both sides of the man's body.

"Don't—" He eyed me, his lip curled in a snarl. "Curse it all," he growled and stomped back over.

Questions warred with my terror. I stared at my savior as he gently turned my head away to face the quiet building. Whimpers only came from one man. What happened to the others? Had they run? Were they unconscious? Were they dead?

"No! No, please!"

Victyr's voice distorted into one I'd never heard. I wasn't accustomed to that shrill, pleading tone. General Rafe gave no reply as Victyr begged and screamed and shrieked.

Why was no one coming? Did no one hear his screams? It seemed to go on for ages before it settled into tortured sobs.

"You'll have the rest of your penance served in the morning."

General Rafe's words rumbled across to me—placid and still. He didn't shout. He didn't need to raise his voice to convey his rage.

Weightlessness embraced me, and his hand cradled my head as he held me to his chest. He struggled for a moment, trying to pull my cloak to cover my body. After a few fumbled attempts, he cursed aloud and threw me over his shoulder. My head bounced against his back as he walked, taking us away from the carnage. Red splatters caught my gaze.

Blood in the snow.

I wanted to ask him where he was taking me. I wanted to ask him why he stepped in after swearing he wouldn't.

I wanted to thank him.

I wanted to thank him from the bottom of my heart. How could I? There weren't enough words to convey what he'd done for me—what it meant to me. This was the second time he rescued me from such a situation.

Limply, I hung over his shoulder and wondered if anyone saw us. Did they see my boots? Did they think I was nothing more than a kill from his hunt? I sighed and took a deep breath. He smelled of woods. Earth. Leather. Some kind of spice. A warm spice, perhaps cinnamon, or cardamom... maybe nutmeg.

My head had surely taken a hard hit if I was trying to dissect a man's scent.

He slowed, and a drawn out creak signaled a door opening. The lighting changed as we entered some building and he walked me to a corner. Pulling me over his shoulder, he laid me down on a bed.

It was dark, though an eager fire burned and crackled in the hearth. I glanced around the room as much as my immobility allowed. He'd brought me to someone's private quarters.

The area was sparsely furnished. A desk tucked off to the side was littered with parchments. Weapons hung on the wall, and animal pelts were draped over a bench.

General Rafe tucked my cloak around me and peered at my face. I blinked up at him—helpless. Why did he bring me here? Shouldn't he have taken me to the Healers' quarters?

"You can blink, aye? Blink once for yes."

I clamped my eyes shut, then held them open, staring at him.

"Do you feel the cold? The heat? Once for yes, twice for no."

I blinked twice.

"Do you feel pain? Once for yes, twice for no."

I blinked twice.

"Small mercy," he grunted. He sat on the edge of the bed and rubbed his chin before he rose and crossed the space to his desk. "Do you have any sensation coming back?"

I blinked twice.

"There's only one that he would have access to... but to be sure–" He returned to the bedside, looking down at me.

His stare was absent of all hatred—all malice or bitter irritation. Instead, only concern.

He *cared*.

"I'm going to check you over." His tone lowered. "I need to be sure that flaming son of a dung heap didn't leave a needle in you."

He rolled me to my side. I would have preferred a female Healer for this, but he moved with quick efficiency, not slowing, or fondling. He returned me to my back and went to the desk.

"Jewelweed," he said, shaking the liquid contents of a glass vial. It gleamed an amber color in the firelight. "It will bring you back."

He adjusted my face toward the ceiling. Gentle fingers gripped my jaw, easing my mouth open, and two drops of earthy, bitter liquid hit my tongue. He pulled away and laid my head on its side.

"You'll start to feel like you're being stung by a thousand hot needles, but that's a good sign." He shoved a cork in the bottle and returned it to his desk. "I have some business to attend to. I'll be back shortly."

With that, I was left alone in General Rafe's room.

Chapter Twenty-Four

The pain started in my hip. Just as General Rafe said—hot needles stabbed me—as if someone stitched me up without applying numbing ointment. I tried to wiggle to find some relief, but I remained achingly still, unable to escape it. The excruciating sensation spread through my pelvis and abdomen. It shot through my legs and up to my neck. Shivers jerked my frame as a cold sweat beaded over my skin. It stung and burned all at once. Tears leaked down my cheeks. I wanted to grind my teeth, to curl up and hide... When would it stop?

Minutes passed, though it felt like hours of torment.

Shouts were muffled from outside, and the windows rattled as the door jerked open and slammed shut. My chest rose and fell in rapid, stuttered breaths. I forced my eyes open to see General Rafe staring down at me, his face void of emotion. Someone banged on the door, though he didn't flinch or make any effort to answer.

"Breathe. There's no remedy for this." He pulled a stool away from the desk and took a seat, blocking the doorway.

Wave after wave of searing pain wracked my body. My teeth chattered together, and I bit down hard, forcing a slow breath in through my nose. A choking sob cut my attempt short, and I lurched onto my side, thrashing on the bed like a madwoman.

He appeared above me and wrapped my cloak around me again, before resuming his vigil on his stool. As my mobility crept back, the pain only worsened. I pressed my lips tight, but whimpers and gasps tore from my throat, refusing to be stifled.

I'm not sure how much time passed before the anguish finally ebbed. I laid on my side, gasping for air, sweat soaking my torn clothes. Though the sensation slowed, hot needles still pricked, sporadic and unrelenting. With each torturous stab, I winced, bracing myself for more.

"Drink."

He offered me a cup, but I had no strength to lift it, or even move, for that matter. My head throbbed, my face and lips stung, and I ached from the roots of my hair to my toenails.

He lifted my head, ignoring my cloak that fell far too low for modesty's sake, and tipped the cup to my mouth. Sweet, cool liquid coated my tongue. It soothed some of the havoc raging in my throat. He took the cup away and eased me down.

"Sleep," he rasped as he headed back to his stool.

Surely he would take me to the Healers now?

"Why–" I tried to form the words past my swollen, cracked lips and he leveled a glare at me.

"Are you sleep talking? No?" he growled. "I gave you an order, soldier. Sleep."

I had no more fight left in me, but I needed to know. Why was he helping me? Where was Willhelm? Why did he bring me here?

I wanted to thank him.

Alas, I wanted to sleep more.

I drifted off into the black oblivion that kept the pain at bay.

"I won't tell you again, Sergeant. Back off."

"Your presence is required at the sentencing! Let me take her to the Healers!"

"No. *Leave.*"

The slamming of a door roused me. A heavy sigh greeted my ears as I blinked away the haze of sleep. Throbbing pulses pounded through my head without mercy. Warm blood seeped through the cracks on my sore lips as I attempted to move my mouth. I touched the tender skin around my eyes. It was so swollen I could barely open them. A small groan squeezed through my aching throat as I tried to roll onto my side.

"Drink."

General Rafe lifted my head, placing the cup against my lips. I winced, but drank, ignoring the sting. Water never tasted so good. When I finished, he took the cup to a small table and placed it beside a pitcher and washbasin.

"Tha–" I tried to speak, but it came out airy and frail.

He turned toward the fire, keeping his back to me. "Quiet. If your watchdog hears, he'll start banging down the door again," he grumbled.

My lips twitched in agony and amusement. Willhelm.

General Rafe came to the bed and tucked my cloak around me.

"Too hot," I whispered, though it sounded more like a moan. Sweat still drenched me. I wanted nothing to do with the heavy fabric.

A frown pulled the corners of his lips down. "You're not exactly modest," he warned.

His tactic worked, and I stilled, even though it felt like I was on fire. He placed a hand on my forehead and muttered a curse. Rising, he moved to the door, prying it open. Stark daylight reflected off the white snow, threatening to blind me, and I clamped my eyes shut.

"Fetch a Healer–" he started.

"*Now* you want me to get a Healer?!" Willhelm's words were hot with anger. He would never raise his voice at a superior officer. Why would he yell at the General?

"Shut it. Go. Get Healer Rashel. Tell her to bring a spare uniform," General Rafe ground out before shutting the door on Willhelm's muttered response.

With the space dim again, I braved opening my eyes and watched as he shuffled some papers around on his desk. He moved quickly, grabbing several bottles, then shoving them in a drawer. He scanned the room, then crossed to the fireplace mantle and snagged a few books, cramming them in the same drawer. Shutting it, he retrieved a sleeveless tunic hanging on a rack near the hearth.

He glanced at me, his eye meeting mine, and started loosening the stays on his fur vest. I turned away, allowing him modesty, and the slight movement sent a fresh wave of pain cascading through my head. He probably wouldn't care the slightest if I watched. The man didn't have a modest bone in his body.

He rummaged about until the door flung open. I whined and flinched away from the light. It was far too bright for my poor head to take.

"Curse you, General. I curse you with all manner of irritating rashes on your man parts." A woman swore, and the door slammed shut to the outside world.

I sighed and relaxed as a cold but gentle hand pressed against my cheek.

"She's on fire." Her words were followed by a curse.

I opened my eyes to see a familiar black-haired Healer—the same who warned me about such horrible things months ago... Rashel? She set down a bag and rifled through it. General Rafe ran a hand over his head before he crossed his arms and propped himself against the door.

"Why didn't you bring her to me sooner? Is she the one everyone is whispering about this morning? Why did you bring her here?" Her green eyes flashed. She held a bottle of something up to the firelight, studying its contents.

"Don't. Not that."

"Pardon me? Are you the Healer?" she snapped. "No?"

General Rafe pushed off the door and stalked over to her. "Not that. Hear me?" His voice dropped an octave.

She straightened to her full height, which was only slightly shorter than him, and fumbled with the cork. "I am the Healer. I make the calls–"

He cut her off by snatching the bottle and tossing it into the flames. It hissed and shattered, sizzling against the crackling logs.

"Wha—you! Of all the–"

"They poisoned her with cloud flower. Do you know what that is?" His voice lashed at her like a whip.

She snapped her mouth closed and stood there, seething in silence.

"It's native to the Shadowlands. Ever been poisoned with it? Ever seen someone scream as their organs melted inside them?" He clenched his fists. "No? I have. Right after some *Healer* gave this to one of my men."

Their arguing caused another wave of pain to assail my head. I moaned and tried to curl into a ball, failing miserably. My muscles didn't want to obey.

There was a pause before she spoke, "Can I give her hesh seed powder?"

"Yes." General Rafe seemed eerily calm.

She prepared a tonic, without a word. He helped hold me up while I drank it, as foul as it was. They laid me back down, and Rashel peeked under my cloak.

"Did they finish with her?" she whispered.

"No. The worst is her face," he answered. "There are some minor cuts near her abdomen–"

She whirled on him. "*You* examined her?!"

He leaned against the door in silence, his face a mask of boredom.

"Please leave," she said, turning to me.

"No."

"Leave."

He stared at her, waiting for her next move.

"I want to give her a chance to relieve herself. Allow her that privacy," she huffed.

I watched through a haze as he grunted and opened the door. I blocked out the flash of daylight as my head throbbed, and sighed when the door clicked shut.

"Avyanna, tell me quickly. Was he involved? Did he hurt you?"

I met her demanding eyes, pleading with me to respond. Him? Hurt me? Only my feelings. I weakly shook my head, and she breathed a sigh of relief.

"Thank the sun, moon, and stars," she muttered as she unwrapped the cloak.

With quick, gentle hands, she peeled off my ruined clothes. She helped me relieve myself without getting up. Dressing me in fresh under-breeches, she bound my chest and covered me with the General's blanket.

"I know you're looming," she called, rolling her eyes. "You can come back in."

General Rafe entered, and I closed my eyes against the glare. They said some people went blind in the north, where there was always snow. I could believe them.

"She has a fever. Is that normal with—what was it? 'Cloud flower' poisoning?" she asked, setting out some fresh rags.

"No. Fatigue, muscle soreness, yes." He dragged the stool near the fire and took a seat.

"How is it administered?"

"Breaking the skin."

"Perhaps a dirty blade?" Rashel mused.

"Usually by needle. There's a small prick on her right shoulder." He reached for a knife and whetstone and set to sharpen his blade.

She shifted me to my side and examined my back. "I take it the red veining is also uncommon."

"Nothing I know of." He took a moment to cast her a weary glance. "That's why I called for you."

She heaved a sigh and placed her hands on her hips. "Where would he have gotten a poison from the Shadowlands?"

"That Master's apprentice."

"Hmm."

Fatigue clawed at the edges of my mind and I surrendered to it, falling into a dreamless sleep.

I drifted in and out of consciousness as days passed. I caught snippets of conversation at times. Sometimes Healer Rashel was there, and other times General

Rafe. If he was alone, he was usually reading, sharpening a blade, or hunched over his desk, examining dried plants.

I woke feeling as though my body finally fought off the fever. Sitting up, I found him nose-deep in a book.

"I didn't peg you as the bookish type," I rasped.

"You pegged me as a witless barbarian," he ground out, setting the book aside to fetch me a cup of water.

I gulped it down.

He placed the cup on a table. "Better?" he asked.

"Yes, much better."

Good enough that I pulled the blanket up around my neck, trying to hide my state of undress. He ignored my actions and placed a calloused hand on my forehead. Grunting in approval, he walked the few paces to the door and opened it, growling at someone before shutting it again.

"Thank you," I whispered.

He squinted at me, and I dropped my gaze to the blanket.

"Thank you so much," I repeated, braving a glance up. He stood there, frowning, arms crossed over his chest. He seemed upset—angry or disappointed, I couldn't tell.

"I beg your pardon for taking your bed and inconveniencing you. I don't know how I'll repay you, but–"

"Stop," he barked.

I flinched and pressed my lips together.

He moved to the stool and took a seat. "You stubborn girl. You foolish, stubborn girl." He reached under his eye covering, rubbing at the wound. "You acted like a child."

Blood rushed to my cheeks, and I glared at my hands. How was I acting like a child? Was he going to blame this on me again?

"You didn't seek me out to train you—either because you were too proud, or too scared. I highly doubt the latter. You've a penchant for being too brave for your size."

I peered up into his dark gaze. "A bit of both, to be honest."

He sat back and eyed me, brows raised in surprise at my admission.

"I don't like you," I started. "I should say, I didn't like you–"

"I haven't changed," he growled.

"My perspective has. I didn't like you, and to be fair, you *are* intimidating." I offered him a small smile in my defense.

"I aim to be."

"You succeed." I assured him.

With a scoff, he rubbed at his injured eye again.

"Why did you help me?"

He hesitated, glancing over at me as I went on.

"You told me you wouldn't. You said you'd make sure I knew you were there, and watch." My voice broke and tears welled in my eyes, but I blinked them back, refusing to let them spill. I would not cry in front of him. I was not a child.

"You were foolish, but not reckless. You took precautions, petty as they were."

I frowned and held the blanket higher to ward off any barbs he might send my way. "I tried–" I stared at the wall, unwilling to meet his gaze.

"Don't make excuses," he barked, standing to stretch.

I bit my lip and winced. The wounds were still tender. A shudder wracked my body as I remembered Victyr and his men. "Where are they?" I asked quietly.

"Dead."

My head snapped up, and I gaped at him in shock. They were dead? Dead? "All of them?"

I should be grateful, even pleased, with the news that they were all beyond the Veil, but for some reason, it was simply... *horrifying*. Six lives, gone. Their actions toward me were unjustifiable, yet I did not expect death to be their punishment.

General Rafe stalked to the edge of the bed and towered over me. I shrank away, pressing my back against the cold wooden wall, and he leaned closer, boxing me in with his massive arms. His gaze glittered dangerously as he brought his nose a mere breath from mine.

"I killed the five in the snow. The leader, I maimed and cut off his–" he stopped and his eye danced over my face as I held my breath in horror, "his offending member. I left him in the snow for Corporal Bane to find. He was executed the following morning."

A shiver ran through me. His voice was barely above a whisper and calm as a lake on a warm summer day. How could he speak of something so grim with such detachment?

"Because I am a woman?" I whispered.

He was so close, and my eyes flitted over his strong features. His face was that of a man, not some maturing youth. He was strong and sure. My gaze landed on the cloth wound around his face, hiding his battle wound.

"Because you're a soldier." His gaze landed on my lips, which had to look worse for wear after the beating I took. "My soldier."

He withdrew and turned his back on me. I shivered against the sudden chill, huddled against the wall. Tucking the blanket under my chin like a child hiding from a monster, I swallowed past the lump in my throat. My breaths were shallow and my heart raced. Was it because I was afraid? I didn't think so. I wasn't frightened of him anymore, though his actions unnerved me.

The door swung open. I caught a glimpse of muddy snow before Rashel stepped in, rousing me from my thoughts.

"So, ragwort extract, not hesh seed," she muttered. She hurried over, pressing her cold hand to my forehead. Satisfied my fever had broken, she held my wrist and closed her eyes for a moment before giving a firm nod. "I believe you're through the thick of it, dear."

"Thank you." I smiled.

"You may leave now, General," she stated, retrieving her satchel.

He grunted, grabbing his fur vest, and stepped out of the room.

"I swear, by the love of all things good and right, that man tries my patience." I chuckled, and she looked back up at me.

"You're feeling better?"

"Yes, ma'am. Sore, but better. I feel... more awake." I didn't know how to explain it. My body was aching and weak, but it felt as if I had woken from a deep sleep.

"Good... that's good to hear. I expect you will be uncomfortable for some time. You took quite the beating."

Expression dropped from my face as I looked at the blanket. "Are they—is it true?" I tried to form more words, but couldn't get them out.

"Avyanna, look at me."

I searched her green eyes as she reached for my shoulder, grasping me tight.

"You will not suffer a measure of guilt. I forbid it."

"I just—I didn't think they would die," I whispered.

"You amaze me. They assaulted you. I haven't the slightest clue why you'd feel remorse for them. Let me make this clear. You are a soldier. The General and Corporal dealt with your assailants as though they attacked a soldier. Had you simply been a civilian, the outcome might have been different.

"You belong to the King, and any crime against you, in essence, is a crime against him. You were not given special treatment because you're a woman. They sealed their fate the moment they attacked a soldier.

"It is brutal, but necessary. Those who would prey on the weak would thrive in this environment if given the opportunity. Such actions must be judged immediately and without mercy. The General's witness was all that was needed to seal the verdict. People who act as they did, as Victyr did—their mind is warped. There is no place for them here, and they're a danger to everyone. We're better off without them. Everyone is.

"So don't feel guilty or sad for a single moment over their loss. Had it not been you, it would have been someone else who tipped them over that sick ledge."

I sat still, listening to her words and seeking comfort in her fierce gaze.

"Now, moving on to more pleasant things."

She helped me dress, my muscles weak from lying in bed for three days, and took care to wash the cuts on my face. The swelling had gone down, though she said the bruises were still distinct. She braided my hair to make me appear somewhat in order.

The door opened, and General Rafe stepped in, holding a steaming bowl and spoon.

"My, my, aren't you the attentive nursemaid?" Rashel mocked with a hand on her hip.

He stopped in his tracks and blinked at her, then at me. He banged the bowl down on the small table and stormed back out, slamming the door.

Healer Rashel laughed outright and wiped away mirthful tears. "I daresay he has a soft spot for you."

"He has an odd way of showing it," I murmured.

He, more often than naught, treated me worse than the scum beneath his boots.

She made a thoughtful noise before handing me the bowl. I shoveled bites into my mouth under her careful scrutiny.

"I'd like you to rest for a few more days. However, your brute of a General will probably run you out the door tomorrow morning. Please try to take it easy. Don't be afraid to request a break if you need it. Commander Dewal is aware of the situation."

I frowned. There was no way I'd ask for a break. I'd push myself to the point of passing out before I sought any special privileges.

"A certain Sergeant has been asking after you, as well. I'll be happy to report that you're doing well."

"Sergeant Willhelm?" I asked hopefully.

"That's the one. He was... at odds with the General concerning your treatment. If it hadn't been for Commander Dewal, I'm sure that he would have ended up in the barracks' prison."

"Oh," I muttered. Willhelm didn't deserve to be punished because of me. He had a respected reputation, and I didn't want to tarnish it.

"Nothing happened, but he seems to have a protective streak."

"I'm sure he didn't mean to offend," I offered.

"You didn't see him. I've never seen that Sergeant so riled before. He definitely has a weakness for you. Speaking of which, while I'm here," she sat on the edge of the bed with a serious expression, "are you seeing anyone?"

"Begging your pardon?" I asked, confused. Seeing anyone? I saw many people.

"Are you sneaking around with any boys?"

My mouth dropped open, and I gave her a look of utter shock. "No—No, ma'am. I would never. It's against the law concerning soldiers," I stammered.

"Not even the dear, Sergeant Willhelm? I just want to be sure. You're the age where girls do silly things in the name of *love*." She squinted at me, and I blushed.

"My age means nothing. I have no love interest. Sergeant Willhelm is a friend." I kept my tone firm.

How could anyone think I would swoon over him? He was charming enough. I admit he was handsome in a dignified way, but I was not attracted to him. He was a counselor, a guide, and a friend. I couldn't bring myself to imagine being with him.

"That's good to hear. Keep it that way, dear. At least until you return from the front." She patted my hand and stood, grabbing her satchel. "I'll be off. I will come to check on you later tonight. Once you're up and moving, I want you to visit my quarters daily for the next fortnight."

I nodded and watched her leave. Falling back on the bed, my body was tired, but my mind was wide awake. I lay there counting the days and realized yesterday was the Winter Solstice. I hoped my mother had taken my letter to heart and didn't come. To think of what she would say if she saw me in such a place! If she knew of what had happened!

I rubbed my face vigorously. It all seemed like a bad dream. Was Victyr really gone? Was he really *dead*?

Against my wishes, guilt crept into my heart. He was someone's son. Someone would mourn him. The men General Rafe killed were all sons, maybe brothers. Some mother, some father out there would grieve their loss. How would the army send back word?

'*To whom it may concern: Your son was executed with a record of dishonorable conduct concerning a female soldier.*'

Female soldier.

They'd blame me for it. They would hold me accountable. To them, their blood would be on my hands, regardless of who struck the killing blow.

I groaned. Here I was, being selfish again, only thinking of myself and how this would affect me. They would blame me. Me. Me. Me.

General Rafe stormed in and I shot upright in the bed. He glared at my surprised face.

"This *is* my cabin," he grunted, and removed his fur vest, revealing a sleeveless tunic that clung to his sweaty skin.

I averted my eyes, as the fabric left little to be imagined. "I beg your pardon, General." It suddenly felt as though I was imposing. I was in his cabin. In his bed. A blush crept up my cheeks at that thought. This was so wrong. "I will sleep on the floor tonight, sir. I did not mean to impose."

His lack of movement drew my attention, and I looked up to see him frozen. He was halfway into a fresh tunic, it over his head and chest, leaving his thick abs shining in the firelight. I swallowed audibly and tore my eyes off him as he resumed motion, pulling it on completely.

"What did she say?" he demanded, crossing his arms over his chest.

"Pardon?"

"Why the change?"

"I'm in my right mind, sir." I offered a nervous smile.

"And you think I'm not?"

"I don't believe you would do this for just any soldier, sir."

"Enough with the 'sir'," he snapped, turning to his desk. "You *are* just any soldier."

I held my tongue at his tone. I was making him angry, but I wanted to stress the point that if it had been any other soldier, he would have relinquished them to the Healers.

"Did you think I was coddling you?" He whirled on me, sneering, with a book in hand. "Did you believe I'd fallen for your girlish charm?"

I flinched at his words. The world flashed white with snow and I saw Victyr's face. I shook my head hard and brought myself back to the present.

"No, sir. I just–"

"You're a soldier, that's all. The poison set you apart."

He tossed a book at me. It fell to the bed, and I picked it up, prying it open. The first several pages were filled in with the names of plants and herbs, with reactions, symptoms, and remedies listed beside them—almost like a guide. I skimmed it, realizing he was cataloging plants. Poisonous plants, and their antidotes. The book was only a third full, the rest of the pages blank. I looked up at him, holding the book gingerly.

"You're not so special. The poison is worth more to me than you."

I flushed and held the book out to him. "I think I'll move to the bunkhouse, sir. If you don't mind," I said, struggling to get my feet over the side of the raised bed.

"Now I've offended the child," he muttered, snatching the book from me. He dropped it haphazardly on the desk and pushed my legs onto the bed. "Tonight is your last night here. Tomorrow you resume training. You're weak and you've fallen behind. Don't be so eager. Dewal will push you."

"Where will you sleep?" I asked slowly, laying back down. I'd been here for days now. Surely, he was ready for his own space.

This man was maddening. One moment I thought him gentle and caring, then the next he was cold and cruel.

He didn't reply. He simply pulled the stool near the fireplace and sat. It was opposite of the bed, and laying on my side gave me a clear view of the brooding General.

"That looks terribly uncomfortable," I murmured.

He glared and leaned against the wall, stretching his feet out in front of him. He didn't take his eye off me, and I soon closed my eyes to shield myself from the heat of his gaze.

He was so intense. Everything about him was so... hard. Even when he showed sympathy, he went on to prove he had no tenderness.

After days of sleep, I wasn't tired in the slightest. I wanted to talk to him, ask him why he helped me months ago in the Dragon Canyon. But I thought better of it. I wouldn't risk losing my tongue for that. Still, I needed to make sense of what I saw. Did he somehow bribe Elispeth?

Where was his family? Did he have a mate? Where did he come from?

Those were all such private questions. A simple cadet such as I could not ask their General such things.

"General Rafe?" I opened my eyes to catch him staring straight at me. I swallowed and clutched my tunic under the blanket. "Will you teach me how to use my bandit breaker?"

My heart stuck in my throat. Asking for his training gave me a strange sense of vulnerability. It didn't help that it felt improper for a cadet to ask a favor of a General.

After a pause, he tilted his head. "Is that all you want to learn?"

I frowned, thinking. Wasn't that enough? No. I wanted to learn how to use any weapon. I needed to know how to protect myself, even without one.

"Could you teach me how to defend myself... against any odds?" I reworded my question and was rewarded with a low chuckle.

"Any odds?" he scoffed. "I'll do my best."

"Thank you," I replied quietly.

"Avyanna, you won't like it."

The sound of my name on his lips was so foreign. At least, without him barking it across a field of soldiers.

"Are you warning me?" I asked, holding back a laugh. I was under no illusion his training would be anything less than grueling.

"It would only be fair."

"Since when are you fair?" I teased.

He grunted in response, though I swore the corner of his mouth turned up. It must have been a trick of the firelight.

I laid there, listening to the crackle of flames and the wind howling outside. I was almost sleepy... but my mind crawled with questions.

"General?" I ventured again, and my answer was his eyebrows meeting in a frown as he glared. "How did you injure your eye? Is that why they sent you here?"

He continued his glower, and after a moment I realized he would not respond. I closed my eyes, hiding from that accusing gaze.

It took me a long time, but eventually, I drifted off into a fitful slumber.

Chapter Twenty-Five

I tore through the woods. The snow bit at my feet. I wrapped my arms around my naked chest. My lungs burned with need, but I kept running. Fear raced through my veins, demanding I go faster. Low branches whipped at my face as my legs pumped harder, stumbling into a tree. I yelped and whirled in terror. The snow was cold and harsh against my bare legs. A fist gripped my heart, and I panted, searching the trees for whatever sought me.

'*Run!*'

I didn't question the voice urging me on. My fingers clawed at the snow as I scrambled to stand. I spun, bolting through the cold forest.

Where was I going? What was I running from?

It didn't matter. I had to get away—had to find a way out.

'*Pretty little thing.*'

Panic chilled my veins, seeing a man just ahead. But the silhouette was... *wrong*. Bile rose in my throat. He held his head under his arm—the whites of his eyes stared at me, void of life.

'It's your fault. You wanted this.'
That voice. That face.
"You're not real!" Terror squeezed my heart.
Victyr was dead. He wasn't here. I looked down at my bare body, and a fresh wave of hysteria consumed me.
'It's your fault. It's all your fault.'
He came closer, repeating the words over and over, echoing through the empty woods. His jaw fell open, revealing rows of white teeth. It gaped wider and wider, growing until the mouth blocked out the head and body.

I stumbled back. My feet slipped on the icy ground and I scrambled to escape the monstrous mouth, threatening to swallow me up. I opened my own mouth to scream, but the sound was airy, suppressed. I crawled as fast as I could, but the snow got deeper, closing in around me. The gaping cavity lunged forward and–

"Thrice curse it all!"

The rough voice tore through the echoes of the dream as I spluttered and choked. Liquid burned down my throat and I jerked upright, coughing and holding my nose. I rubbed my wet face on the blanket and whined against the burn.

I jerked toward the sound of a cup slamming down and gasped as reality came crashing back to me. General Rafe stood with his back to me and his fists clenched at his sides.

He glanced over his shoulder, his eye dark and angry. "Are you with me?" His voice was rough with sleep.

Pulling the blanket up to my chin, I sniffed and nodded. He didn't respond. He grabbed his fur vest and stormed out into the dark night. I flinched as the door slammed shut.

Had I woken him? Shame warmed my cheeks. Had I woken others?

I groaned and dried my face and hair as best I could. Pushing my legs over the edge of the bed, I stared into the fire. Low flames flickered, warding off winter's cold.

Time crawled by, and I waited for him to come back, but as the sixth chime sounded, I realized he wouldn't. I sighed, guilt nagging at me. Not only had I stolen his bed for several nights, I proceeded to have such a terrible nightmare that woke him and scared him off.

I smiled to myself at that thought. My nightmare scared him off. If he had been in it, he probably would have simply glared at the... the...

A tremor ran through me.

Victyr was dead because of me.

Tears pricked my eyes, but I blinked them back and tentatively pushed myself to stand. My legs held, though they trembled, weak from disuse. I tried to smooth out the wrinkles of the uniform Rashel had brought. To sleep in a night shift would have been terribly inappropriate in mixed company.

I searched the space for my blades and found them lying atop his desk. I laced the necklace around my neck, tying the leather cord where Victyr tore it before he tossed it into the snow.

My bandit breaker slid into place on my belt, secured to my left side. General Rafe told me to put it on my less dominant side, though I couldn't see why. It was harder to reach there, and I had limited coordination with my left hand. Still, I trusted him.

I buckled my belt and mourned the loss of my tailored uniform. This one fit me so poorly. The shirt was far too large, and my trousers were rolled up three times just to keep them from dragging on the floor.

Sighing, I pulled the blanket smooth on the bed and fluffed the pillow. Frowning at the little I could do for him, I grabbed my winter cloak and put it on. After securing it in place, I looked around the room one last time. There was nothing else that I might clean or see to without invading his privacy. Taking a deep breath that my ribs smarted against, I walked over to the door with slow, careful steps.

My muscles complained at the movements, and I had the nagging feeling training would be slow going.

I ate my first meal alone. Every set of eyes in the hall felt like daggers. The men maintained a wide berth—no one approached or spoke to me. When I looked at my fellow cadets, they avoided my gaze and turned away. Their whispers got to me, tugging at my resolve. I finished my meal, then left for the training center that my company used.

When I saw my Commander's sober face as he spoke with another officer, some of the tension relaxed from my shoulders. The small sense of normalcy built up some of my confidence. Inside, spears, and shields lay against the wall and I smiled, happy to be back in the swing of training.

"Cadet Avyanna."

Commander Dewal's voice drew my attention away from the arms and I spun on my heel to salute him.

"Commander Dewal!" I called out. I hoped my enthusiasm would banish any concerns he might have.

He looked me over. "All is well, cadet? The Healer has cleared you?"

I wiped the smile off my face and slapped my hands to my sides. "Yes, sir!" I barked.

His only response was a half-hearted grunt.

The day passed smooth enough after that. It was quiet. The obscene comments that normally followed my exercises—nonexistent. I was thankful for that, though their cold shoulders got under my skin. Their ridicule I could handle. However, their silence and exclusion ate away at me bit by bit.

I leaned against a wall, lightheaded, when I noted Niehm's fiery hair through the throng of men. I smiled to myself and pushed off the building, heading toward her.

"Niehm!" I called, and she spun to face me, her dress flaring out.

"You little–" She grabbed me in a tight hug and squeezed so hard I squeaked in protest. When she pulled back, she eyed my bruises and her expression shifted from sorrow to anger. "Come."

She led me in silence to the bunkhouse. My room appeared untouched. Nothing had been disturbed during my absence. I checked over my things as I grabbed my toiletries and spare uniform. My new tunic laid on the table, where it rested in the process of my mending. My cot was still made—everything was where I had left it.

As we started for the springs, Niehm strode with her head held high. I had a nagging suspicion she would either give me an earful in private or grab me in another hug. I knew her well enough that I could tell she kept a tight hold on her emotions.

"Where's Elenor?" I asked.

"She wants to see you, but needs to wrap up something with the cook. She'll be along shortly." Her features softened as she spoke, and I realized just how worried she'd been.

This feeling in my heart was foreign. I focused on my toiletries and spare uniform to distract myself from the tightness in my chest. They cared about me. They really did. I had friends who I actually meant something to, and I didn't know why. I didn't benefit them, yet they'd always been there for me—trying to protect me. But why?

I chose Darrak as an ally for selfish reasons. I grew close to him, and could almost call him a friend, but we had an arrangement. We looked out for each other. I shared what I had with him and his presence kept the bullies away.

My breath caught, thinking of Victyr.

I stopped, searching the faces of the surrounding soldiers. Most everyone avoided my gaze. The ones who caught my eye turned their backs on me, whispering to their friends.

I was chilled and not simply because of the snow on the ground. My heart iced over. The men regarded me as a traitor. I'd been involved with their comrades' deaths. Regardless of whether I was to blame, that's how they saw it.

An older man made eye contact with me before making a rude gesture and turning away. At that moment, I felt utterly alone. Why had I believed these men would accept me? What had overcome me to entertain the idea that they would ever willingly fight beside me?

"Avyanna."

Niehm's voice cut through my thoughts and brought me back to the present. I shook my head and fell into step with her.

"Feeling well?"

"Well enough," I muttered.

Anxiety curled low in my stomach. I needed to get away from this crowd. I could almost feel their menace, their disgust.

As we made our way along the road, reaching the far buildings, I attempted to silence my thoughts and focused on taking one step after another.

"Cadet."

My head snapped up, locking my gaze on a single glittering eye. Niehm muttered darkly, but moved to my right. She must have remembered what General Rafe told her about getting between himself and his soldiers.

"General, sir!" I mustered as enthusiastically as I could, giving him a one-handed salute.

"Where do you think you're going?" His tone grated on my spine.

Did I have a previous engagement? Was there somewhere else I was supposed to be? This was free time for the soldiers and cadets. As long as we stayed in the barracks, we were allowed to do as we pleased. Yet, his expression implied I was out of line.

"To wash up... sir?" I said, trying to gauge his temperament. He left this morning in a foul mood, and it seemed as though it hadn't improved.

"Later," he growled, stalking past us.

His boots crunched on the packed snow before he stopped a few paces away, watching me from over his shoulder. He kept his back to me, watching me from the corner of his eye.

He wanted me to follow him? I clutched my things to my chest and took a tentative step in his direction. He grunted in approval and looked ahead, walking on. I cast a wary glance at Niehm. She reluctantly nodded, glaring at his back. I shrugged and followed the giant of a man through the barracks.

We walked for a good quarter of a chime to the training center. The structures stood empty, most with their giant rolling doors closed, though a few were open to the cold. I spied cadets in one, cleaning shields that were in a pile. I wondered what they had done to get the punishment when General Rafe stalked to an empty building.

General Rafe rolled open a door. The inside was sparsely furnished with a dirt floor and a single table off to the side.

"Master Niehm, do us all a favor and stay outside."

I squinted at the General as he took off his fur vest and faced me. Niehm muttered curses, but strode over to the wide entrance and leaned against the frame. General Rafe waved at the table, and I placed my belongings down.

"Blades," he demanded, holding out his palm.

I reached under my winter cloak and pulled out the bandit breaker. I still wasn't comfortable with it. It was far different from any of the weapons I trained with.

I placed it in his palm, and he examined it, testing the edge. The bandit breaker was a small weapon. Its curved handle fit in my hand with ease. The blade arched out at one end like a bird's talon, sharpened on both sides. A hole punched through the steel on the opposite end. It was meant to put my smallest finger or thumb through. It was wicked sharp, and honestly, I was a little frightened of it.

He slipped his smallest finger through the loop and snapped his arm out, giving the knife a spin. With a jerk of his wrist, he caught it with perfect precision. His movements were brisk and intricate. Somehow, he re-positioned his hand so that his thumb was through the loop. He gave a swift punch through the air and studied it again. Satisfied, he laid it on the table and looked at me expectantly.

I stared at him for a moment, wondering what else he wanted, wishing he'd talk more for once.

My other blade. Moving quickly, I pulled at the leather thong around my neck, lifting it high enough to tug at the two rings for a grip. I drew it from the sheath and handed it to him.

He tested the sharp edge against his thumb. "A push dagger," he mused.

I tilted my head as he gave an approving grunt and set it down. His gaze sought me again, and he leaned a hip against the table, waiting.

"That's it. I don't have any others."

I wasn't even comfortable with those. Why would I carry more? What else *could* I carry?

His sharp eye traveled down the length of my body to my boots and back up to my eyes. I shivered against both the cold and his intense gaze.

"These blades are made to be extensions of you."

He closed the distance between us and placed his heavy hand on my shoulder. I forced myself to be still even though every nerve in my body demanded I pull away. He trailed his hand down my arm, through my cloak, and pulled my arm straight. His touch was oddly warm for how cold it was. His calloused hand engulfed my own as he curled my fingers into a fist.

"How do you fare in hand-to-hand combat?" he asked.

I had to crane my head back to look at him. My heart raced, and I felt... odd. Lightheaded. Warm. Terrified. I tugged at my hand and frowned.

"Poorly," I stated, and he released my hand.

In hand-to-hand combat, I had several disadvantages compared to my male counterparts. I was weaker, smaller, and had far less stamina. I lost every time.

"Figured."

I glared, hearing his low comment. Of course, he figured I would be weak. He took a step into the middle of the building, giving himself space to move.

"Show me what you've learned."

I swallowed past the lump in my throat, studying him. Surely, this wouldn't be the moment he would beat me senseless. Perhaps he just wanted to see what I was capable of.

I took a few steps away from the table and relaxed my knees, bringing my fists to my chin. Watching his feet and muscles, I stepped closer and threw a punch at his stomach, pulling back so that my fist met nothing but air. I drove another fist at his chest, doing the same thing. In all honesty, with the height difference between us, I wouldn't be able to strike at his face without giving him a huge opening.

If there was one thing I had learned well in hand-to-hand thus far, it was how to block. I dropped my hands to my sides and waited for his criticism that was sure to follow.

He blinked and tilted his head, frowning. "Do they teach all my soldiers to fight the air?" Amusement colored his tone, and I blushed in embarrassment.

"Surely, you don't mean for me to hit you, sir."

I begged the sun, moon, and stars that he didn't mean for me to fight him. I didn't stand a chance against the average soldier. To General Rafe, I was as dangerous as a gnat.

A wicked smile crossed his face. "Don't pull your punches."

He threaded his fingers behind his head, giving me a huge target. I frowned, watching his muscles pull taut as he stood there, waiting.

I didn't know which was worse. The idea of him actually fighting me, or him asking me to hit him with no danger of retaliation. "It would be unseemly for me to strike a General, sir," I choked out.

"It's an order, then." The taunting smile dropped from his face, his patience fading.

I brought my fists back up to my chin and tucked my head down. I could do this. He wanted me to show him what I had learned. I could do this. I snapped a fist out to graze his stomach. My knuckles barely pressed into the layer of muscle under his tunic before jerking back. Again, I threw a quick punch at his chest, doing the same thing.

As I readied for another strike, I struggled with my heavy winter cloak, threatening to wrap up my arm. Fixing it, I glanced up and fear settled in my stomach like a stone. He glared at me with the fury of the sun, and I took a step back, trying to put distance between us.

He lowered his hands and took a ground eating step toward me, snatching my cloak. He gripped the front, closing it over my arms and torso, trapping me.

"First, never fight with a cloak over your shoulders," he growled, giving me a shake before throwing it back over my shoulders. "Second, don't pull your punches."

I shivered from the sudden cold and the fear that his burning gaze instilled. I tried to swallow, but my throat wouldn't work. He stood in front of me, his top lip curled in disgust, and I felt like a paralyzed rabbit.

"Fight," he ordered, taking another step toward me, crowding my space.

I opened my mouth and backpedaled, away from his anger, away from the dangerous mountain of a man.

"Fight!"

He snatched the neck of my tunic and charged, shoving me back against the wall. He glared, pinning me against it. I clutched his right forearm where he held me and looked up, eyes wide with terror. He was so much bigger than me—so much stronger. I was nothing to him. I might have put on a brave face when I thought we were on somewhat equal terms, but there was nothing equal about this. There was nothing fair about this, no way I stood a chance. I couldn't get the upper hand, even if I had proper training. The odds were stacked too high in his favor.

His left hand moved fast. My head lashed to the side with the force of his open-handed blow. I blinked as stars danced across my vision. The sting dug deep into my cheek and I straightened to gape at him. The hand he slapped me with slammed against the wall next to my head.

"FIGHT!" he yelled in my face.

Something snapped—a dam let loose all my rage. The world tinted red, and I curled my fingers around his forearm, digging my nails into his skin. He grunted and warmth ran over my fingers as he jerked away.

My vision cleared, and I reached up to slap his cheek. I knew it was a futile move, but I had to do *something*. He whipped his head back, and I took that moment to slip out. He spun, grabbing my cloak. I twisted in his grasp as he jerked me close and tucked up against his left side.

Knowing it was his blind side, I clawed at his back, trying to grab onto anything I could. His muscled arm rammed into my face, and I turned and acted, not thinking for a moment.

I bit his exposed tricep.

He cursed and threw me away from him. I stumbled for footing, hauling in a gasping breath. Cursing, he rubbed at the bite, and I charged again. I leveled my shoulder with his stomach.

I expected to push him back a few steps at least, but I misjudged how heavy he was.

I hit the wall of muscle that was General Rafe and tumbled backward, landing hard on my rear. The force of my momentum continued my fall, and my head slammed against the dirt. He braced his feet on both sides of me and he smirked down at me.

He *smirked*.

I pressed my body flat to the ground and launched a foot up, aiming between his legs. He snapped his thighs together with a grunt, trapping my foot between them. I growled and fought as he reached down to seize my ankle. He hauled me up. Blood rushed to my head as I squirmed and kicked with my free foot till he caught it as well. He dangled me in the air, and I grappled, fighting like a wild animal before realizing he had me.

I lost.

His body shook with a chuckle. I sighed and dropped my hands to the dirt as he lowered me back to the ground. I blinked up at the wooden ceiling, wondering what I had ever done to deserve this beast of a man in my life.

He crouched beside me. "Good girl."

Irritation welled within me, and I clamped my eyes shut. He knew how to get me to fight, he just wanted to see it.

"Good to know you're not afraid to fight dirty," he snorted.

I squinted, examining his body. I was torn. Part of me was proud of the red streaks left by my nails. The other part was horrified that I had drawn blood from a General. I was sure if Corporal Bane ever heard about this, I would be jailed for a month.

His eye sparkled with mirth, and I frowned. Why was he so happy?

"You didn't throw a punch. You fought with your claws and fangs." He tilted his head, looking me over. "You're like a feral kitten. Cute and fluffy, but wild and dangerous when cornered."

I glared at him. He was comparing me to a kitten? I shuddered—Victyr called me kitten, too. I bristled, chasing away the intrusive thought. For a man who barely spoke three words in a row while in public, after a fight, he was positively talkative.

"But you'll teach me to fight like a man?" I asked as he stood and held out a hand. I frowned, but took it and allowed him to pull me to my feet.

"No. I won't." He gave me a dangerous smile. "I'll teach you to fight like a dragon."

Chapter Twenty-Six

By the time General Rafe was done with me, I was sweating, trembling from exhaustion, and gasping for breath. He dismissed me by telling me to go wash up. I stumbled after Niehm with my belongings tucked under my arm.

"That man... there's something wrong with him," she sighed, tapping at her temple with a raised brow.

I threw a glance over my shoulder, making sure he was out of earshot, and shrugged. She was probably right—he was a bit messed up in the head. And honestly, it was quite terrifying at times, but now I knew how to throw a proper punch. He taught me what the Weaponless Combat Master had not taken the time to—how to step in and punch with not only my fist but my hips as well.

General Rafe claimed it would be more effective for me to practice with the heels of my hands instead of a fist for now. He'd flicked my knuckles, saying they were small and fragile, that I'd easily break one if I landed a punch wrong.

He had me throw punches against his palms and wouldn't ease up until I gave it everything I had. At one point, I tried tricking him by making faces and grunting with effort. Somehow, he read me well enough to know I wasn't giving it every ounce I had. If he had to taunt or humiliate me to entice me to give my all, he did.

I was dragging my feet when a set of boots joined mine.

"Avyanna."

I gave Willhelm a small, tired smile.

"You look terrible," he said, pulling back and making a face.

"Thank you," I groaned and focused on putting one foot in front of the other.

His brows pulled together with worry. "Honestly, are you alright? Shouldn't you be resting?"

"I did fine in training. I just want to get cleaned up and eat."

One foot, then another. Energy drained out of me with every step. My hands trembled uncontrollably, and I tried to hide them under my cloak. We were almost to the clearing, walking through the small patch of woods.

"She took quite the beating," Niehm offered.

Willhelm's steps faltered before accompanying my slower ones. "Begging your pardon?" he choked out—clearly confused.

"Apparently, our resident General has decided to take it upon himself to teach Avyanna how to defend herself," she explained.

"With a blade?" Distrust thickened his voice.

"Perhaps—though today it was more or less hand-to-hand combat."

I blinked rapidly as spots danced before my eyes. We were stepping into the clearing. Almost there.

Willhelm grunted. I knew he wanted to say that it was not the General's place, but he didn't work that way. He was far too principled to speak ill of a General, even if he disapproved.

Cold sweat broke out along my back and temples. "I think I should sit," I muttered.

My vision went black.

"Wha-"

Niehm's question was cut short as I collapsed. Someone caught me and I could only assume it was Willhelm. I closed my eyes and focused on breathing.

"Avyanna?"

I couldn't muster the strength to talk.

"Is it an effect of the poison?" Niehm asked.

"The Healer said that it was out of her system now."

He seemed worried. I remembered him lingering outside General Rafe's room. He cared enough to seek me out, then stand out in the cold, waiting for answers.

Niehm muttered a curse. "When did she eat last?"

"I would assume midday meal, but my company takes their meal an hour before hers. I don't know."

I moaned and shifted. Someone held me upright, but I wanted to be closer to the ground. The world spun, distorting the haze clouding my vision.

Cold fingers brushed against my cheek. "Should we send for the Healer?"

"I could carry her." Willhelm shifted. "It would be better if we simply took her."

"Just give—give me a minute," I moaned, my words slurring together.

"Avyanna, are you well?" he asked.

A soft smacking sound followed the question, and Willhelm flinched.

"Of course she's not well, you dumb oaf. She collapsed." A moment of silence followed Niehm's correction.

"Master Niehm, I'm going to have to ask you not to lay hands on Sergeant Willhelm."

Elenor's voice cut through my haze, and I opened my eyes against the setting sun to see her walking toward us. Willhelm held me in his arms, and Niehm crouched beside us.

"Good day, Avyanna," Elenor greeted with a tight smile. "Willhelm, be a dear and carry her to the spring, please."

"The Healer told them she wasn't ready," he muttered as he stood with me in his arms.

I bit my lip in embarrassment. I couldn't even get to the spring. This was mortifying. What weakling couldn't even walk? Yet, I knew if I attempted again, I would end up on the ground.

"Has she ever listened to anyone who told her not to do something?" Niehm questioned.

"She used to," Elenor said. I opened my eyes to find her looking at me with gentle concern. "She used to be such a good girl."

"Then she staked everything on those blasted dragons," Niehm spat.

"I'm right here," I breathed.

They could at least talk *to* me and not about me.

Niehm's features softened with an apologetic smile, and the lighting changed as Willhelm carried me into the cave. He set me down against one of the small stones and rubbed his neck nervously.

"I should—I," he stammered.

I blushed, realizing he thought he would have to stay.

"She'll be fine. Please stand watch outside. We may have company," Elenor urged him.

He needed no more convincing and ducked out of the cave with a shrug.

"Someone else is using this spring? Who else would need to?" Niehm asked with confusion.

"Are you well enough to bathe yourself?" Elenor asked, unfastening my cloak.

"I think so. I'll try to hurry."

She nodded and motioned Niehm to a stone and took a seat beside her with their backs to me. "I've heard another has been seen regularly heading this way at night."

"Who?" Niehm pressed.

I pulled off my clothes and quickly slipped into the spring. It felt as though my body pulled from every reserve it had to operate. I washed as quickly as my sluggish motions allowed, taking no time for luxury.

"Our dear General."

"No–" Niehm breathed in disbelief.

My hands stilled in my soapy hair, and I dropped my gaze to the water.

"He's never bathed with the other men. The women used to gossip about him bathing in the lake, but with it frozen over, that theory is no longer valid."

I could've died of humiliation—keeled over right then and there. "So he uses this water?"

"Pray tell why you would be appalled, Avyanna," Elenor called over her shoulder.

"This spring empties like the rest, and you've shared spring water often enough that I wouldn't think you would be that horrified," Niehm added.

"No, but—during my moon cycle," I choked out.

Since joining the army, my cycle had remained consistent. Though with the rigorous training and physical exertion, it had been much heavier. Dealing with a moon cycle in a barracks of men was mortifying.

I learned to keep a small bucket with a lid and wash my used sanitary cloths with my clothes each night when I washed my uniform. During that time, I took a risk and tried to find the most secluded spot and wash the cloths first before anyone found me. Then I would move to a more public location to wash my uniform.

I hated my moon cycle in the barracks. Living in the women's wing of the dorm, it was a common occurrence. No one said anything, and everyone treated it like it was nothing special. It was simply something that women dealt with.

In a barracks full of men, however, it was a different story. Men could see blood gushing from a severed artery, see intestines spilled in front of them, see someone's bone cleaved clean in two and not even flinch. Yet, if they caught sight of moon blood, or heard someone discussing a moon cycle, it was the most horrifying thing.

I looked down at the clear water that at times had run pink from moon blood and closed my eyes in utter humiliation.

"Avyanna?" Niehm's voice carried a hint of amusement.

I opened my eyes to find her smiling at me. She laughed and turned her back to me again.

"It's not that horrifying," she laughed. "You've been using it longer than him, I'd wager. If he came in and the water did not run clear, he is free to bathe with the rest of the men!"

"As ignorant as men often wish to act, they are not ignorant of our moon flows. During that week, I'm sure he can find somewhere else to bathe if he craves his privacy so," Elenor added.

I lowered my chin into the water. Why couldn't I get away from this man? Why did he haunt me wherever I turned? For the past few months, I had barely heard from him. He was always there, yes, but he was never mentioned. No one spoke of him.

Now it seemed as though I couldn't escape the madman.

I sighed and hauled myself out of the water, drying and dressing with shaking fingers. Steam kept the room somewhat warm, but the cold of winter still bit at me as I dressed.

Niehm came to my side and wrapped my cloak around me, leading me to sit on the stone beside Elenor. She settled in, taking a comb to my hair.

"Avyanna," Elenor started.

I tensed up. I knew by her tone, she was going to ask about the attack.

"You don't have to tell us anything. We know what happened, but you should know we are here for you."

Elenor laid her thin, warm hand on mine. Her eyes conveyed so much more than her words. They were normally a fierce, icy blue. Yet now, they were tender—caring, sorrowful. My heart constricted with her concern and it resonated through me. She cared about me more than anyone ever had, save my mother.

My mother and I grew apart over the years. It was difficult to maintain closeness with someone who only visited two times a year. Yet Elenor and I had grown close these past six months. I never knew just how much she cared. I saw her as a dutiful Master with a job she did well.

She was more than that, though.

In a way, Elenor was a mother to every girl in that dorm. Every girl who came in without a mother, every girl whose mother could no longer feed them, Elenor was there for them. She looked after them and made sure they were fed and clothed. She listened to their gossip and learned about their dreams and desires. Elenor was the leader of the women and the mother that too many girls simply didn't have.

I grasped her hand between mine and gave a gentle squeeze.

"I'm well—I swear it." I assured her.

She gave me a faint nod and looked out of the cave to the frozen lake beyond.

"One thing, then I'll not mention it," Niehm started and reached around me to pull my chin to face her. "Swear to me you'll take whatever training this General is giving you, and learn it. Swear to me you'll learn to fight, that there will not be a next time."

I bit my lip and gently shook my head. "I can't swear there will not be a next time."

Her features slipped into a dark frown.

"But I can swear, next time, I'll be ready."

I barely made it back to the bunkhouse under my own power. Willhelm retrieved dinner for me and stayed with me after Elenor and Niehm left. He remained in a chair outside the door, and I perched on my cot eating my food. We sat in companionable silence.

I was comfortable with Willhelm. He was a steady rock amidst all that had gone wrong. He was one who tried his hardest never to react to situations, and simply do what he was expected to do, yet I had changed that.

With me, he wanted to protect me, but did his best not to overstep his bounds. I knew that was not only because I was a woman, but also because I was young. He looked out for all the younger cadets, knowing barracks life was not easy. He was respected by not only me, but his fellow soldiers.

I, however, had lost all respect from my fellow soldiers.

"What is it?"

I peered up at Willhelm from my empty bowl and studied his firm shoulders and stern face. He was not only strong in character, but in body and mind as well. Perhaps that was why men followed him without question.

A dragon roared in the distance and I looked around, oblivious to the fact that I had no windows. Why would a dragon be roaring at night in the winter? Willhelm leaned in his chair, balancing on two legs to crane his head to look at the doors.

"Odd," he muttered and settled back to study me.

Clearly, it was nothing for him to worry about. He pinned me with his questioning gaze, not allowing the dragon to distract him from my questioning gaze.

"I–" I spun the spoon around the wooden bowl, avoiding his eyes. His pity was the last thing I wanted. "I feel as though the soldiers... distrust me now."

I knew the men would always avoid me—always choose each other over me. Yet, I had felt so close to earning their respect before. I never shirked away from a task or demand, even if I failed miserably. I gave my best in everything. Somehow, Victyr's actions robbed me of that respect.

Willhelm made a thoughtful noise and sat back in his chair. He tugged at his hair and looked up at the ceiling as if it held all the answers. "Soldiers are... Well, they're like wolves. They run in a pack. As they grow, develop, and train, they form bonds like family. No matter if you don't like someone, they're still family. We are all serving the same King, for the same purpose. We're aligned, and that draws us closer.

"When one of their own is killed, they want someone to blame. If they're unable to fight who they choose to blame—they fear them." He dropped his steady gaze to mine. "They are not angry, Avyanna. They're afraid."

"I don't understand," I scoffed and set my bowl aside. "Why would they fear me? I'm nothing compared to them."

"Perhaps Victyr was not the only one who entertained such fantasies concerning you." Willhelm spoke the words with care, weighing my reaction.

I held his gaze, anger crawling under my skin. Surely that wasn't true.

"Say, if another considered it, they might have been shocked when punishment was dealt," he continued. "Perhaps they realized that could have been them. The soldiers fear you now because they know they cannot touch you, and if anyone made a move on such thoughts, they would be dealt with accordingly."

"So you're telling me that all the men out there think of me... like that?" I growled, waving my hand at the bunkhouse.

"Not all of them," Willhelm corrected, shaking his head, "but enough that the fear spread. Those that could be easily influenced will now shy away simply because the majority of the pack thinks you're a danger to them."

"What can I do to regain that trust?"

I felt like such a child. I cared what they thought of me—how they treated me. Why? What changed from a few years ago? In the girls' dorm, I couldn't care less about what my peers thought of me. Why were the soldiers so much more important?

Was it because I believed myself stronger than the other girls? Was it because I figured myself destined to be a Dragon Rider, and now that I knew fate didn't have that in store for me, I was humbled?

"Nothing more than what you're doing. It will fade in time." Willhelm stood and stretched. "You've shaken things up since you came onto the barracks' side. They've gotten over it before."

He walked over to my bed and I looked up at him. The light in the bunkhouse silhouetted his frame. He towered over me and I waited for the fear that would accompany a large man looming over me. Nothing came. I studied his face as he bent low to retrieve my bowl. He was stern, strong, and friendly—but in a firm way. With Elenor and Niehm, he was more relaxed, but I always sensed a slight wall between us.

Emotion built in my throat and I fumbled with the wick on my lantern, coaxing a soft glow to the space. "Willhelm?"

He froze and tilted his head at my small voice. His eyes sought mine, silently inviting me to ask my question.

I didn't let myself consider the impact of my words—or how his answer might affect me. "Do you think of me... like that?" I stared into those warm coffee-brown eyes, trying to ignore the dread twisting through me.

He frowned and settled on his knees in front of me. His hands rested on the cot on either side of me, and his demeanor grew stern. "Avyanna, I have a confession, one that will never leave this room—swear to me it will never leave this room."

A tremble ran through me, and my dinner knotted in my stomach. "I swear," I whispered.

"Avyanna," he sighed and offered me a small smile, "I don't see you as another soldier. I should, but I do not. I see you as a lamb among wolves. You are the smallest woman I've ever seen. You were a tiny fragile girl when you first came to the barracks' side. I wanted to protect you, to keep you safe from the wolves that would swallow you whole.

"I don't see you as a soldier, but you have nothing to fear from me. You understand?" He took a moment and worked a muscle in his jaw, his gaze searching mine. "I simply want to protect you, keep you safe. I think what you're doing is brave and commendable, to be honest. Why it had to be the smallest female to be the first to join the army—I haven't the slightest idea, but here you are.

"If anything, I see you as–" he stopped and grimaced, "as a daughter—if I were to ever have one. Which I never will. But perhaps this is the universe telling me that since I won't, and you're here, I can treat you as one."

My heart thumped painfully at his words, and a strange emotion clogged my throat. I had wanted a father for so long. I resented the fact that the Shadow tore mine from me, and here fate was, handing me a man who had done everything to treat me as his own.

He scoffed before continuing, "You're special to me, and not only because you're the first female to join the army, but because you're *you*. You've grown on me, girl. You've got backbone, though you pretend you don't. You try to hide your anger more than your fear. You are a kind soul, yet you choose the most difficult tasks. I don't understand you, but I like you." He frowned and reached over to pat my hand awkwardly.

I laughed and grabbed his hand as he tried to pull away. He was so caught up in the formalities of life, he still never touched me unless I invited it.

"Thank you, Willhelm." I gave his hand a squeeze before letting go. "Thank you."

He cleared his throat as he stood, pulling the chair from the room. "You should be sleeping. Good night, Avyanna," he called as he started to shut the door.

"Good night, Willhelm."

The door closed with the click of the latch, and I rose to push my cot to its place in front of the door. I sighed, feeling a bit more at peace, and changed into my night shift and settled into bed. I leaned over to blow out the lantern and was asleep before my head hit the pillow.

Chapter Twenty-Seven

I woke to heated shouts and my door slamming into my cot. I shot up in bed and stared in horror at the sliver of light shining through the crack.

"Cadet Avyanna, if you don't move this bed in the next three seconds, you're not going to have a door!"

I flew out of bed at the sound of Sergeant Briggs' voice and scrambled for my trousers, jerking them on and shoving the cot to the side. Just as it hit the wall, the door crashed open and Sergeant Briggs stormed into my storage closet. His huge body took up the small space as he glowered. I struggled to stand at attention as he crowded close.

"Roll call was five minutes ago!" he roared, inches from my face.

I didn't dare move—didn't speak. I stared straight ahead as my mind tried to catch up with my body.

"Cadet Avyanna! What are you *wearing*?!" The force of his breath blew my hair away from my face as he yelled again.

"A night shift, sir!"

My cheeks burned with embarrassment. It's not like I had time to throw my tunic on and lace it up. Most night shifts were thin, comfortable, thigh-length garments with lace or beading at the neckline... the very low neckline.

"Is this part of a new uniform?!"

"I—eh. No, sir!"

Soldiers were not allowed to wear civilian clothing, but I hadn't thought of my sleepwear. I never intended anyone to see me in them. I was always up before roll call.

"Burn it!"

I flinched.

"Don't let me catch you in such... flimsy clothing again! Shameful!" He turned on his heel and marched the single step out of my room. "You'll run the obstacle course three times today because of that!"

I mentally groaned and saluted his back as he stalked through the bunkhouse, shouting at cadets who dared to meet his eyes. The cadet outside my room cast me a sidelong glance, and I glared at him before shutting my door.

Cursing under my breath, I changed into my uniform after binding my chest and pulled on my winter cloak and boots. Slipping my bandit breaker in place, I tugged on the push dagger around my neck, double-checking it was still secure. I never took it off.

I rushed from the bunkhouse and skidded to a stop, spotting Sergeant Briggs at a fire pit to the side, warming his hands. He pointed to the bunkhouse, then back to the fire. I gave a stiff salute and retrieved my night shift.

Sergeant Briggs turned and raised a single brow, making a show of holding his hands over the fire. "Well, cadet?" he prompted.

I kept my glare in check as I tossed the night shift into the fire and saluted him, refusing to watch months of savings go up in flames... literally.

The skin crinkled at the corners of his eyes as he gave me a broad smile. "Three laps around the obstacle course! Now!"

I opened my mouth to object, then snapped it shut. If I complained about running the course before the first meal, he would add at least one more lap to it.

"Yes, sir!"

I marched off toward the training fields with his laughter following me. Why they put such a man over the first year cadets—I didn't know. He had far too much joy in punishing us.

The bite of winter urged me on, my breaths fogging in the frigid air. I threw my cloak over the fence that framed the course and shivered. It would only slow me down. I leapt over the first hurdle, then charged at the rope netting, frozen with snow and ice.

The first lap was a struggle. My hands rested on my knees as I heaved for breath. I worked up a sweat even with the freezing temperatures. My lungs burned as I huffed and pushed myself to start again.

A dragon's roar tore my eyes to the sky. An enormous, red dragon arrowed toward the barracks. I should have kept going and ignored it, but something in my heart demanded I stop and watch.

The Dragon Rider sat atop his great beast, lying low against its neck. He was covered in the common black-leather armor of the Dragon Riders, but I couldn't make out any more details. On his back hung a large crossbow, as was typical for most Riders.

The dragon was a large red male. I only knew of one that immense. Ge'org was close to sixty paces long, from snout to rump. His tail flung out behind him as he cut through the overcast sky. His crimson scales shined like rubies in the dim sunlight. The only one who would ride Ge'org would be his bonded Lord Ruveel—the Dragon Lord. He commanded the Dragon Fleet on the front lines.

What was he doing here?

"What lap are you on?"

I jumped at the rough voice and noticed General Rafe resting against the fence. Taking a deep breath, I threw myself into the course again.

"The second," I called.

The snow and ice bit at my hands and I slipped on an obstacle more than once. My height already put me at a disadvantage. Adding the bitter elements definitely didn't help.

He waited till I doubled-over, panting after my second round, before he questioned me again. "How many?"

"One more, sir," I said between gasping breaths.

He grunted and settled in to watch.

The third took the longest. I was tired, cold, and my body was already exhausted. I was sure there would be nothing left from first meal even if I made it there a few moments before my roll call with Commander Dewal.

I tried for the sixth time to scramble up the rope to slap the wood beam at the top. My numb hands refused to hold my weight. I slid to the ground and laid there on my back, panting up at the gray sky.

How did I sleep in?

I guess that didn't matter. It wouldn't happen again.

I forced myself up as snow melted through my tunic and threw myself at the rope again.

"Enough." General Rafe came up from behind, glowering at me. The passing breeze tugged at the long fur of his winter vest.

"I was ordered to complete three rounds, sir." I turned back to the rope and wrapped it around my leg, attempting to climb like I normally did.

He cursed, and I yelped as large hands grabbed my sides. I squirmed and reached for my bandit breaker as he hauled me up.

"Don't," he ground out.

He heaved me up, and I reached my fingers high above my head to slap at the wood. I glanced down at him and annoyance pinched his features. He dropped me too quickly, and when my feet hit the ground, I stumbled. My backside collided with the snow.

"Let's go." General Rafe's deep voice had an almost sing-song note to it as he droned the words.

I struggled up and headed for the next obstacle, a set of three hurdles chest height. I started over them and noted Sergeant Briggs headed this way. He gave General Rafe a quick salute and a beaming smile toward me before marching on.

General Rafe helped me through the rest of the course, only stepping in when my numb fingers rendered me incapable of completing the task. He kept his distance and watched more than anything.

When I finished, I sat on a bench near the fence and wrapped my cloak around myself, trying to catch my breath. A man walked, or rather sauntered, down the path. He was lean, shorter than General Rafe by a few inches—perhaps a third his size. As he came closer, I noticed his windblown hair and Dragon Rider leathers. Black, with a red dragon sigil embedded on the front. He wore no cloak, only the fur-lined leathers. My eyes widened in shock as I noted the dragon patch on his shoulders.

Dragon Lord Ruveel.

My heart raced and my mouth went dry. This man was perhaps the strongest in the Kingdom, besides the King himself. Why was *he* here?

"Rafe."

My head whipped back at the degradation in that tone.

I went from an almost girlish crush on the man to instantaneous distrust. He had the cadence of a man who got his way, no matter how wrong it was. The tone from that single word, my General's name, was enough to snap me out of whatever had been going on in my head while he approached.

General Rafe took a deep breath and turned toward him. Crossing his large arms over his chest, he didn't bother to grace him with a reply. I realized that in title and formality, these two were ranked the same. The only difference was... well, the Dragon Lord had a dragon.

"Well, hello there."

The stranger's sickly sweet voice was aimed at me, and I forced myself to stand and salute. It was difficult, not only because I was tired, but also because of the impression he gave.

He drew closer, stopping a few paces away, and looked me up and down, his eyes belittling me. My soldier's cloak fell over my uniform as I dropped the salute. I forced myself to be still during his appraisal, but I wanted to run. Part of me wished that General Rafe would step in and do whatever General-like business they needed to attend to.

He ran a gloved hand through his black, tousled hair and smiled down at me, his blue eyes dancing. "Who might you be?" he asked.

"Cadet Av-" I started, but General Rafe stepped in front of me and cut me off.

"*Mine.*"

My heart jumped in my chest, and I blinked, staring at General Rafe's back. Did he... protect me? Was he possessive of me? That sounded... odd. Almost damning.

"Go, Ruveel."

General Rafe's tone was grating. This was a new side of the General I hadn't seen before. He appeared possessive of me before, simply because I was a soldier to command and order about. This was a different kind of possession—as if he wanted to hide me from an equal.

"Oh? What's this?" the Dragon Lord peeked around at me, smiling with glee. "What's this? Hold up... she—that's a girl!" Shock and confusion distorted his features as he glanced at General Rafe. "Is there a female infantry wing now? Are they providing services to the men? Wait, is she providing services to *you?* I'd like to-"

General Rafe's fist snapped out. His huge body followed it as he advanced. The Dragon Lord, in turn, laughed like a young boy and danced away, skillfully avoiding each blow.

"Oh, you'll simply have to tell me now!" he jeered, glancing at me before avoiding a grab from my General. "This is gold, pure gold!"

"Go," General Rafe bit out the word, so low I almost didn't hear it.

The Dragon Lord giggled like a schoolboy and leapt over the fence to the course.

General Rafe's eye snapped to mine, demanding obedience. "Go!"

I was moving before I knew it. I marched away from the scene, heading toward the dining hall. It wasn't like the Dragon Lord wouldn't be able to find out who I was. At the moment, I was quite popular for unfortunate reasons.

I missed first meal but made it through my day. Sergeant Briggs shared the error of my ways with Commander Dewal. Because I 'slighted the reputation of our company,' he, in turn, gave me more strenuous duties. I was ordered to clean up after every exercise, fetch all the equipment, and retrieve all the arrows during archery.

When the fifth chime sounded, I sighed with relief and leaned my forehead against the wall of the training building. The soldiers filed out, leaving to wash up or go straight to the dining hall, when someone patted my back.

I whirled at the unexpected sensation. Touch on the barracks' side never led to anything good.

Commander Dewal peered down at me and nodded. "You did good today. Just don't let it happen again."

The Commander had proven himself to be fair. He was firm, and he pushed everyone as hard as they could go, but he was fair to me, all things considered.

"Yes sir," I replied. He started to leave, and I rushed to stop him. "Commander?"

He turned around, waiting for me to continue.

"May I ask why the Dragon Lord is here?"

The inquisitive side of me needed to know. Had he been sent to retrieve something? Was there a respite at the front to allow a leisurely trip? Was he fetching someone? Did he have any new information concerning the Shadows?

"That's not your business, cadet."

I frowned and stared at the ground. Of course. I was a lowly cadet and wasn't worthy of that knowledge. I didn't need to know critical information to fight.

"Though, if I were to guess," he started, "I'd say he was here to see a certain General during the winter respite."

"There's a respite? Why?" I blurted before thinking better of it.

"You'll learn more about it soon enough. Don't be so eager to get to the front, cadet. You likely won't come back."

His words took me aback. With a somber face, he turned and melded into the flow of soldiers freed from duty.

Everyone knew the chances of returning from the front were slim, but people rarely acknowledged it. Most soldiers were young men seeking adventure. Others were avenging their families or loved ones. There were a few who had nothing better to do with their lives, along with a spattering of men the King ordered here as a punishment for crimes committed. Few that joined the ranks genuinely expected to return. Though some were that arrogant.

I rested my shoulder against the wall, lost in my thoughts. Usually, this was when I retrieved my toiletries and waited for Niehm and Elenor. Now, with General Rafe's training, I was unsure if he would come get me, or if the Dragon Lord had him preoccupied.

"Cadet."

I frowned at the rough voice and tilted my head as I turned. General Rafe stood behind me with a cloak and deep hood concealing his features. I blinked, confused, seeing his arms crossed over his chest. He was in a tunic—a *long-sleeved* tunic.

"Sir?" I choked out.

He never dressed like this. I'd never seen him wear anything with sleeves, even in the dead of winter. Was he trying to blend in? To hide? From who or what? The Dragon Lord?

"Move it." He jerked his head toward the door.

"Where to?" I asked, still in shock from his attire.

"Same place as yesterday. Move."

He seemed to be in a rush. I spun on my heel and hurried off. We made quick time, and yet again, the training building was empty. I stopped at the table, watching as the General glanced up at the sky. He let out a vicious curse and ducked into the building.

"If—if you don't want to train today–" I started, but his glare silenced me.

He was on edge and I didn't know why. Sure, the Dragon Lord showing up caused a bit of commotion, but nothing appeared to rile him before. He always acted as if he was at the top of the food chain and he couldn't be bothered to care about anyone. Now he seemed, at the very least, agitated.

"We're about to have a visitor." He tore off his cloak, then stalked to the table and threw it down in a heap.

I opened my mouth to speak, but the light from the sky was suddenly blocked out. A dragon landed directly in front of the door. I stared, mouth agape, as it settled in the middle of the road. Its huge tail curled in close, careful not to hit any of the nearby structures. Ge'org looked like a child in a glass shop, terrified to move lest he break something. I had always expected the great dragon to act as a ferocious beast—not a hatchling.

I snapped my jaw shut as the Dragon Lord himself slid down to walk in front of his bonded.

"Ha!" He pointed at General Rafe and gave a knowing smile before turning his finger on me. "I knew it! You and this girl!"

I blanched. Two feelings warred inside me. First—anger that he dare point his finger at me. Sure, he was the Dragon Lord, but I was no Rider and he had no authority over me as my General was present. And second... guilt, as if the General and I were caught in a compromising situation. Nothing we were doing was wrong or even frowned upon, yet I felt embarrassed. I frowned and blamed that on the simple fact that I was a woman. Had I been a man, it wouldn't be unseemly at all.

"You! You're the girl child I've heard of."

He sneered, and I bit my cheek to keep from snapping at him. He struck me as a bully, and the only way I learned to be rid of bullies was to offer no reaction. I ignored him and turned to my General. He stood with his arms crossed and glared at the Dragon Lord. For only having one eye, the man had a fierce glare.

"At least send your oversized pet away. He's done his job, sniffing me out like a dog," he said.

"Mm-hmm… had you brought the girl to me, I wouldn't have had to follow you," the Dragon Lord retorted.

He returned to his dragon. Ge'org lowered his massive horned head and made a whining sound. The Dragon Lord caressed his scaled cheek and stood there in silence, his gaze roaming over the dragon's head. I turned away as he smiled, feeling as though I intruded on a private scene.

With a huff, Ge'org strode onto the main road where soldiers scattered, making room. He stretched out his giant blood-red wings and crouched low. With a mighty leap, he pushed hard, launching himself into the air and taking flight.

I cursed the sense of longing that rose within me. I was done with that. It didn't matter anymore. I was not a Dragon Rider, nor would I ever be.

I was a soldier.

As I shrugged out of my cloak, I brushed off the Dragon Lord's exaggerated study of me.

"So denied twice, and this is what you choose?" His laughter filled the space. "Such a tiny girl and you want to be a soldier?"

"Ruveel, shut your mouth or I'll shut it for you," General Rafe growled, facing me.

"Oh. Touchy with this one, are we?"

He pinned the Dragon Lord with a fiery gaze before returning his attention to me. "Blades off."

I obeyed and laid my weapons on the table next to my cloak. The Dragon Lord came over to toy with them. I took a deep breath and settled my focus on my General.

"Fists up."

Throughout the first half-chime I led the attack, then General Rafe told me what I did wrong or right. He showed me how to attack without leaving myself open. For the remaining half-chime, he attacked me in various ways and taught me to defend myself.

His massive arm wrapped around my neck. My heart raced even though we had been training for nearly a whole chime. His arm pinning me in place sent my nerves skittering and my brain blanking.

"Fight." His voice rumbled low in my ear.

I clawed at his arm and backed against him. Feeling his solid body behind me did nothing to calm my fear.

I was trapped and helpless. General Rafe was as solid as the wall I had been pinned to. His arm held me as securely as Victyr's goons. Panic surged through me and I dug my nails into his skin, feeling a vise close around my heart. My breaths came fast and I couldn't calm them. I writhed and squirmed, but he held me fast. His steadiness didn't rub off on me and the longer he held me, the faster my breaths came and the more frantic I fought.

"Stop," the Dragon Lord spoke up from his place against the wall. "Stop and think. Your poor General has simply taught you to fight. You need to *think*. Dear Rafe, will you actually teach her or only allow her to make all the mistakes she possibly can, first?" He pushed off the wall and approached us.

General Rafe released me and I took a few steps, gasping for air, trying to calm my frayed nerves. I struggled with the urge to distance myself from the men. General Rafe would never attack me like Victyr and his lot. He was doing this for my benefit, not to torture me.

"Care to show the little lady how it's done?" the Dragon Lord asked, rolling his shoulders to loosen up his limbs.

A grunt was my General's only reply. The Dragon Lord turned his back on General Rafe, offering me a wink. I glared and hoped that my General hurt him... just a little.

General Rafe was larger than the Dragon Lord in both height and girth. He wrapped his arm around his neck and hauled back. The Dragon Lord lifted his legs high and threw them down, resulting in his body weight dropping hard and fast. General Rafe was yanked into a doubled-over position. The Dragon Lord rolled in his grasp, jerking to the side, and squirmed out of the hold, freeing himself.

He looked at me and beamed, but that smile was short-lived. General Rafe tackled him, pinning him to the cold ground. I watched as he tried to free himself, to no avail.

"Rafe, *really*?" he sighed. He stopped his struggle, relaxing as he peered up at the General with an exasperated glower.

"Don't tell me how to teach my soldiers," he warned. "You order your little flies around all you want, but don't think for one minute you can order my soldier around while I'm here."

I crossed my arms against the sudden chill. Watching these two was a bit like witnessing boys fight in the barracks. I expected the bickering out of the young men who had not yet grown into themselves, but I didn't expect it out of my General and the Dragon Lord.

"Yes, yes. The men are yours." The Dragon Lord's tone was that of an appeasing child to their irate mother.

"The soldiers, Ru. The soldiers are mine."

The Dragon Lord squinted at him, noting the difference. "She's not a soldier, Rafe. She never will be."

"She's mine."

I shivered. That tone had my stomach twisting nervously. I told myself that the only claim that General Rafe had on me was that I was a soldier. He didn't own my soul.

"Fine. Fine! She's yours. Get off, you oaf."

General Rafe slowly stood, followed by the Dragon Lord. He brushed off his backside and smirked at me. I held my glare but didn't speak.

"Don't think I won't be asking after her, though."

General Rafe stopped in his tracks while walking to the table.

"I think I could find something for her to do in the Dragon Corps. After all, she does have an aptitude concerning them."

General Rafe didn't turn to him like I expected. Instead, his dark gaze settled on me. I blinked, confused. Could the Dragon Lord get me transferred? I'd work with the dragons on the front lines? Did I want that? Would I be hauling dragon dung, or would I truly work *with* them?

As if he read my mind, a disapproving frown darkened his features. I took a deep breath and silenced my thoughts. He was right. For now, I was a soldier.

I was his.

Chapter Twenty-Eight

Summer of Year 897

Time seemed to fly by, the seasons changing before I knew it. I heard nothing more concerning the Dragon Lord or why he'd come. Even Willhelm had no information to offer.

As the months passed, I grew more confident with my training, getting stronger and growing more capable. I wasn't bulky like the men, but I built muscle in the right places. I could draw both long and short bows now, though I had to release my draw quickly to be somewhat accurate. Repetitive firing was my weakness in archery. When I handled a crossbow, my marksmanship was excellent. Otherwise, my ability was lacking.

In armed combat, I fared much worse. With a shortsword, I was a decent fighter, but if you added a shield, I simply didn't know what to do with myself. I fought well in a group if we held a shield wall or advanced in unison. However, fighting solo, I barely held my own.

Horseback riding was one of my favorite tasks. I loved the beasts—riding was as close as I'd get to flying. As long as the horse wasn't a giant, I could mount it myself using a fence post, hay bale, or even a bucket. I forced myself to do things alone. On the war front, there would be no one to help me. My horsemanship was exemplary, but I lacked the strength to carry a lance or spear and juggle it from side to side as needed on horseback. I couldn't hold them in place long enough to damage whatever target I charged.

In endurance training, I also failed miserably. They packed us up with chainmail, plate armor, shield, sword, and a heavy pack filled with stones or whatever else they found to weigh us down. Then they sent us off to run the track. I never lasted as long as the others, even when I gave it my all. I dropped from a run to a walk, and then eventually my knees would buckle under the weight and I couldn't rise.

Strength training... another disappointment. My body contorted in ways my fellow soldiers' could not, but I was no match for their strength. I grew to love the obstacle course—I ran it faster than the others. My small stature and lighter weight gave me the advantage of agility. Alas, the obstacle course was not the only test of strength.

Failing in almost all my training, only one thing kept me somewhat motivated—I improved in hand-to-hand combat. General Rafe's lessons paid off, and I began to look forward to my sessions with him.

I ached with exhaustion afterwards, and he offered no praise, yet I felt as though I accomplished something. My body began to act with its own reflexes. When he attacked, defending myself was pure instinct. I didn't have to think about it. I couldn't best him, and I doubted I ever would, but I still gave it my all.

Other than Niehm, Elenor, and Willhelm, we kept my training with General Rafe secret. For some reason, I didn't like the idea of others finding out I trained with him. Perhaps I simply didn't want to lose any advantage I'd have over any would-be attackers.

I don't know how it happened, but it was my secret, and I liked it.

Night terrors often plagued my sleep. Images of men banging on the door, or slamming it into my cot. The theme was always the same—Victyr and his lot trying to get me.

Among the other soldiers, I developed a reputation for being distant but present. I was cold and withdrawn, telling myself that I didn't need their friendship and no longer cared what they thought. I joined to be a soldier, and I could do that on my own... if I improved at fighting alone.

I applied myself completely to every task, though more often than naught, I failed. The Masters were unsure of what to do with me. Commander Dewal admired my determination, but I knew he considered me the weakest link. I never got close to any of my company, always maintaining a mental distance. They saw me as a leech, one who was strung along by *their* strength no matter how hard I tried to stand on my own.

This was the path I chose, and yet again, I felt like a failure. A constant sensation of worry lingered. What if I'd made the wrong choice? When I considered it, I didn't see another option left to me. Even if it were possible, I was too old to switch occupations. I was contracted to the army for another four years. If I tried to get out now, I would be labeled a coward, a traitor, and hung.

Definitely not the way I wanted to die.

Hatching Day came, and I barely had time to reflect on its importance. A day of freedom was welcome, even if I didn't have plans.

A few weeks prior, I wrote to my mother, telling her yet again not to come, but was vague in my reasoning. I needed to admit to her what I had done before autumn. I could only put it off for so long. My mother brought me into this world and raised me as best as she could. She cared for me and loved me on a level I could not comprehend. She didn't deserve to be left in the dark. I kept my recruitment from her for my own selfish reasons. I didn't want her to know until I had a solid standing with the Masters. If I proved I was good at this, perhaps she would not be so against it. She would surely be against it, but maybe not so adamantly.

The commotion of dragons and their Riders sounded across the King's grounds, but I continued about my day, ignoring the excited din. I didn't have any training, but I busied myself in the bunkhouse, tailoring my uniform.

Willhelm left with his fellow officers to visit a nearby village. He invited me, but as time moved on, I felt more and more out of place at the table with his friends. Commander Rory was a great sport, but Corporal Bane and Sergeant Greyson seemed guarded around me. Honestly, I was glad that Willhelm got away. I didn't want him to always feel like my nursemaid.

I sat on my cot and sighed at my pile of mending. I finished the last bit and had nothing to do. It was a little after midday, and the Chosen were already forming their bonds with the hatchlings.

I shook my head, trying to banish those thoughts, and stood. I straightened the few items in my room and set off. Perhaps I'd find out where General Rafe was and see if we were training today.

Pushing my rolled sleeves up further against the summer heat, I bared my forearms to the scorching sun. Its glaring rays beat down on me as I walked through the barren streets of the barracks.

I glanced around at the empty buildings. During the Summer Solstice, the school grounds were packed with people bustling about, enjoying life. Here, it was quiet, except for the distant noise of the crowds and the intermittent roar or bellow of a dragon.

I walked around to the officers' quarters but saw no sign of the General. Moving on, I checked the training fields where he sometimes exercised. Not finding him there, I checked the stables to see if he was perhaps working his horse.

Sighing when I didn't find him, I stopped and sat on a bench outside the stables. I looked down at my legs wrapped in trousers and boots. The uniform no longer unnerved me, as it once did. It kept me far warmer in the winter, being covered head to toe in clothing. In the summer, however, it was a pain. The ankle-length trousers were hot and stifling in the heat. The boots were also a nuisance. I was accustomed to wearing sandals in the hotter months.

I shaded my eyes and peered up to see a brilliant green dragon barreling through the cloudless sky. It was a young beast, perhaps three-winters old. Likely enjoying the last few days of freedom before it left for the front. The Rider gripped its shoulders with their legs and threw their arms out. The sun glinted off the beast's vibrant scales as it bellowed and ducked into a dive.

I felt my smile falter, knowing I would never experience that, and watched them drop out of sight. Pushing myself to my feet, I headed for the King's Lake. I wouldn't allow myself to wallow in pity or the jealousy of others. This was the life I was given, and the path I chose. I would learn to accept it and move on.

My feet took me toward the place I ran to last Hatching Day. I walked for a good chime or two, following a different path than before. I looked up at the trees and the sky as I distanced myself from the main core of Northwing. This place was peaceful—quiet.

I took my time enjoying the sights and cadence of nature. Being away from people and the buildings, the sounds of civilization, did something to my heart. It was like waking from a dream and seeing the world for the first time.

Everything brimmed with life. Cities were alive too, but in a different way. Being alone in nature made the present more distinct. Animals bustled about on their way, eating or building homes. Perhaps the squirrels were already thinking of winter, or the birds glorying in the empty nest that the summer brought.

The forest was busy, yet calm. Every animal, every plant, had a focus and a purpose to fulfill. Wanderlust flared in me like it often had when I was younger.

I smiled, trying to pull from the faint recollections of my childhood. Studying the thick trees, I remembered climbing with the village children, racing to the tops.

The distant gurgle of a stream reminded me of when I tried to catch fish with my bare hands. I was so sure I could catch one if I just moved fast enough...

I spotted a wild hare in the underbrush and had a faint memory of chasing rabbits away from my mother's garden. My smile slowly fell, remembering my mother. I was living as independently as possible, and she likely missed me. I had not only lost a father in the war, but also my mother.

That was selfish and vain thinking, however. She had lost not only her husband but her child. She'd been unable to care for me on her own, and the village had too many widows as it was. I had been torn away from her as much as she had been torn away from me. Here I was, trying to further my life, and ignoring the one who cared for me. It was awful of me to tell her to stay away. I wasn't thinking of her, only of myself.

I resolved to write to her soon and tell her I missed her and needed her to come in the autumn. Hopefully, she'd be able to. I could even try to find jobs to help cover the cost of travel. I wasn't very good at sharpening or polishing blades like the rest of the soldiers, but I was far better than them when it came to mending.

Every soldier knew how to do a rough mend, but I took classes, and thanks to dear General Rafe and my uniform, I had some experience mending men's clothing. Maybe I'd hire out my services as a tailor.

I couldn't stop the small smile that came with thinking of the 'alteration' I had done for General Rafe. I snickered to myself as I cleared the thick of the forest and the dirt gave way to sand. Looking up, I expected the beach to be empty. This section of the King's Lake was the furthest point from the barracks and school. Though technically still on the school grounds, it was rarely traveled to.

However, someone else sought solitude here.

Chapter Twenty-Nine

I blinked, and my feet grew invisible roots, grounding me in place. I stood frozen as I gawked at the large man in the lake.

He was a fair hundred paces away, far enough that I didn't think he heard my steps over the low crash of waves. He faced away from shore with his muscular, barren back to me. Not a stitch of fabric covered those rugged shoulders, nor the valley that ran down the center.

My mouth went dry and my heart raced.

I knew that back.

Not only because I'd seen it bare once before, but because I was so familiar with it clothed in a sleeveless tunic.

He ducked his shaven head down and plunged into the water, coming up a few paces deeper. That movement startled me and a blush heated my cheeks. Here I was, a grown woman, ogling a man like some love-struck puppy.

He turned, now chest deep, and I noted something different. His broad stature was familiar, but so was the cloth over his eye... *that* was missing.

I couldn't see it clearly enough to make it out, but it appeared as though his eye survived the injury. Perhaps he was blinded and kept it covered. However, he didn't seem like the type to shy away from any shock factor he might cause.

Curiosity drew me in and bolstered my resolve.

I was not just a woman—but a soldier. I'd been looking for him anyway and simply found him in a place I hadn't expected. If I were a man, I wouldn't have thought a thing of it. Only my gender made me think twice.

Boldly, I struck out a foot and continued, all the while my heart raced. The butterflies in my belly refused to let me ignore the fact that I *was* a woman, regardless of occupation, walking upon a man in a state of undress. Ignoring the flutters, I made as much noise as possible while approaching. I didn't walk straight toward him, but rather angled myself to a stone's throw away. I watched him out of the corner of my eye and waited for him to notice.

A deep chuckle reached me, and I turned to give him my full attention. His shoulders and head were above water, but the rest was hidden under the blue waves.

Thankfully.

"Cadet," he greeted with a dark smile. He kept his damaged eye closed, but his right eye sparkled with a glint of danger.

"General Rafe," I replied, taking a seat on the warm sand.

He grinned and started for the shore. I glanced at his pile of clothing as his chest rose out of the water. Diverting my gaze, I focused on the water, the clouds—anything else. He was messing with me. He found pleasure in pushing people over the edge. To be honest, it was growing on me, and I knew to expect it. He didn't push too far, just enough to rouse me. He did certain things to make me fight and better myself. Other times, I got the feeling he was rude or brash simply to push me away. As if he wouldn't allow people to get close to him.

I thought back on our first meeting and granted him some leniency. He was a soldier, rough and rugged. He was bristly and hard. Anyone on the front would have to be to watch their friends and fellow soldiers die.

I heard more about the horrors on the front and wondered how I would react to it. Some became softer, kinder. Some didn't seem to be affected. Others, like General Rafe, hardened, cut deep by the cruelty they lived through. Almost as if they had to be sharp and cut back to avoid getting hurt. If they kept people away, they wouldn't get hurt when something inevitably happened to the people they knew.

Being a General, he not only saw men killed, but led them to their slaughter. That level of responsibility and guilt would weigh on anyone, no matter how strong they were.

I learned to brush off his barbs and taunts. It took some time, but I was beginning to understand how to read him and what he wanted without him using words. The world would be a much simpler place if he decided to use more of his vocabulary, with the exception of curses.

His feet sloshed through the lake, and I kept my eyes forward. The sun was still high in the sky, casting a glare on the water, which I squinted against. Low waves lapped at the shore, bringing stringy bits of plant life and driftwood with them.

I focused on a particularly interesting twig when he lowered himself beside me.

I glanced at his bare feet and smiled as his toes dug into the warm sand. He was human, after all. Even the tops of his feet were scarred, and I followed his ankle to his trouser-covered leg. Braving my gaze higher, I held in my breath of relief that he had his tunic on. It wasn't fastened, but at least it was on.

I had to be thankful for the little things.

The butterflies in my belly opposed this thought.

My gaze traveled to his face, which was directed toward the lake, ignoring my study of him. He had wrapped the cloth around his wound again, covering his left eye.

"I—ah," I cleared the tightness from my throat. "I came because I couldn't find you, sir."

His head turned, so he could take me in with his good eye, and he smirked. "Enjoy the show?"

"I wouldn't know. I only caught the end act."

He laughed outright at my reply and shook his head at the water.

"I came here to be alone." For some reason, I felt the need to explain myself. The warmth in my cheeks deepened. "So, are we training today?"

He made a thoughtful noise and looked me up and down, as if judging something. After a pause, he pushed himself to his feet. "New game," he stated.

"I was unaware that these were games, sir," I said in a guarded tone.

He chuckled and tilted his head, watching as I stood to face him. "Drop the 'sir'. Stop the pretense that you see me as your leader."

"Well, today *is* the Solstice. If you wish, *sir*." I beamed at him.

I felt far more comfortable and familiar with him than I should have. He was in a good mood, and I was pushing him back. The butterflies urged me on.

Cursed excitable critters.

He scoffed, stepping further onto the beach. Stopping a few paces from the water, he waved a beckoning hand toward me. I followed, but flashed him a wary frown, stopping a healthy distance away. When he was in a cheerful mood, I had to be on my toes. He would teach me some lesson, usually a painful one.

"Up the ante, shall we?" His voice rumbled.

"Play for reward?" I asked, unable to curb the grin that spread across my face. This could be fun. I wanted to know so much about him, about the war front.

"Whoever wins gets the reward."

My smile fell. I likely wouldn't win against him, motivated or not. The more important question was, what would he ask of me as a reward?

The butterflies roared with excitement.

"What kind of reward?" I squeaked, watching him drop into a fighting pose.

He grinned dangerously, and my heart answered his dare with a frantic beat. When had I begun to find him attractive? His dark eye danced above a strong nose and jaw. The cloth over his left eye made him appear roguish, dangerous, and exciting. My eyes traveled down his frame, noting his firm muscled chest. His abs weren't chiseled like a pretty boy's, but deep and thick, like a man who had grown into his body.

"Whatever we want," he chuckled.

I swear his reply left me a little lightheaded. Flushing, I realized he caught me staring. I dropped into my fighting stance and tucked my fists close to my chin.

"Anything?" I clarified.

"Anything."

I blew out a breath to calm myself. I would win—at least *once* I would win. And I already knew what I'd ask. A year ago, in the Dragon Canyon with Elispeth... I wanted to know what happened. Or perhaps I'd ask him to show me his wound—to prove I wasn't afraid of it, that I wouldn't find it ugly.

Lost in my thoughts, I failed to notice the shift in his weight and the sudden movement of his feet. He lunged, and I spun to the side.

Blast it! I knew better!

I cursed myself as he snatched me from behind as I spun, and wrapped an arm around my neck. I threw my feet high in the air and slammed them into the sand, bringing all of my petty weight down. He followed me, not willing to let go. I struggled to get to his side like the Dragon Lord had shown me, but he shoved me forward and sent me sprawling—and dove on top of me.

He crushed me into the ground, and I turned my face away from the sand, coughing. He released his grip and simply laid on me, letting his weight pin me to the sand.

"One. Two–"

"Three!" I finished for him, gasping and choking on sand, struggling to push his weight off.

His deep chuckle sent shivers down my spine as he rolled off. I rolled onto my back and sat up.

He lay on his side, watching me. "Question."

I raised an eyebrow. Easy enough.

"Why did you join?"

I frowned and tilted my head. "Because my father was—"

"No. The truth, Avyanna." All mirth fell from his features, his expression growing serious.

I opened my mouth, then closed it, pressing my lips together. My gaze dropped to the sand, and I crossed my legs. I had been about to tell him I was avenging my father. If he didn't accept that, perhaps I would have told him something along the lines of joining because I didn't want my life to be a waste... but was that the truth?

"I—bear with me." Shame built, muddling my thoughts. Something about this moment lowered my guard. He was playing a *game* with me. He wouldn't rush me as I worked out my reasoning.

He propped his head up on his hand and waited—a model of patience.

"I am vain—selfish, really. I figured if I worked hard and minded what I was told, I believed myself destined for greatness. To be selected as a female First Chosen was a difficult task to achieve, let alone being offered the opportunity twice. I thought I was special, that I could defy the odds and become a great Rider. I would live a life filled with miraculous deeds, and my dragon and I would be renowned.

"When I was refused the second time, I hoped I could still carve out greatness another way. Perhaps I could still make something of my name and bring myself glory. I could be the first female warrior. So I joined." I bit my lip and shrugged to myself.

He studied me for a moment, before asking, "Do you still feel you're destined for greatness?"

I smirked, rising to my feet. "You'll have to win again to get that answer."

He grunted, but smiled as he rose, dropping into his fighting stance. I exhaled and drew my fists up near my chin. This time, I wouldn't lower my guard for anything. I wouldn't let him grab me like that.

He charged me again, and I stepped to the side, not giving him my back. He moved with far more speed than a man of his size should have, and I swung at his head as he doubled-over and barreled his shoulder into my chest.

The air was knocked out of me, but I still attempted to bring a knee up to his face. He wrapped an arm around me and lifted me into the air. He caught the back of my leg with a thick, corded arm. His shoulder dug into my stomach, and I froze, clueless as to what I could do. I hung over his shoulder like a rag doll. I tried to squirm free, but he just gripped my legs tighter. Frustrated, I lurched in a sudden movement that my abs would hate me for later, and brought myself straight up, body parallel with his, before falling back.

I realized my mistake as soon as he let go. My plan was, as my body weight fell, it would bring him forward with me.

I didn't expect him to let go.

I fell to the ground with a yelp. The sand was soft, but not that soft.

Moaning, I squinted up at him. He moved in line with the sun and placed his bare foot on my chest.

"Surrender."

"I yield," I groaned.

My back protested any movement. I needed a moment to gather my strength. Now would be a good time to grab his leg and make a move, but knowing him, I would just receive more pain for my effort.

He grinned and removed his foot, dropping into a crouch beside me. "What would you think of joining a team?"

"Pardon?" I narrowed my eyes. "A team?"

He nodded, face sober.

"What kind of team?"

"My team."

As if that clarified anything. Memories flashed of him and the Dragon Lord, Ruveel. I rolled to my side and mimicked his pose from earlier. Propping my head up with my hand, I offered him my brightest smile.

"My dear General, that might clarify things for you, but I am but a lowly soldier. I need more of an explanation," I said sweetly.

He grunted and sat back on the sand, watching me. "You're not good at anything."

All traces of amusement left my face. "Thank you," I replied dryly.

"You know it. I'm offering you a chance to be on a team, separate from the companies."

"Separate from the companies? If I'm not good at anything, why would you want me?"

His logic made no sense. Were his insults supposed to convince me?

"I'm returning to the front next year. I'm taking my team with me," he said.

My eyes went as wide as saucers, even as the butterflies in my belly died at the mention of him leaving. "You make no sense! You tell me I'm no good at anything, offer me a position on some secret team, and then tell me that you're heading out next year? Even for the soldiers who are somewhat decent at training, they wouldn't be ready in two years!"

"I'd be your Commander," he said. "You'd be ready."

"Pah!"

His arrogance could only get him so far. I eyed him, trying to piece together his logic.

"Up, again." He shoved himself to his feet, his good mood fading fast.

I stood and brushed the sand off my clothes. What was this about a team? To be honest, the only thing I felt adequate at was what he trained me in—hand-to-hand combat.

Perhaps it wouldn't be bad to have him as a teacher in everything.

I readied myself and watched him. He stood as still as a statue, waiting for me to attack. I danced closer and made a kick at his shin. He snapped his leg out of the way and around mine, bringing me in. I growled and fought for my leg as he pushed me to the ground.

The more I thought I advanced with my training, the more he proved I still had a lot to learn.

I tried to scramble up, but he dropped his weight to sit on my stomach, bracing his feet at my sides. All the air rushed out of me as the whale of a man pulverized my internal organs. My eyes bugged out of my sockets as I pushed at him. He crossed his arms and stayed right where he was. Like a boulder—an immovable, heavy boulder.

"Give up?"

I hissed and rocked my hips, attempting to unsettle him, but he weighed too much.

"Yes," I wheezed.

He stood, and I gasped for air, holding my chest.

"You could... lose a little... weight," I said between gasping breaths.

He made an amused sound, more of a scoff than a laugh.

"Fatty."

His eyebrows rose at the insult. I rolled away and put some distance between us, wary of how he would respond to a friendly jest. He peered down and patted his abs. Looking back at me, he winked. Or that could have been a blink. I wouldn't know, as I couldn't see his other eye.

"Cut your hair."

I blanched and gaped at him. "Excuse me?"

"Your hair. Cut it," he said slowly, as if spelling it out for me.

"My hair?" My voice came out in a squeak.

He stalked closer, and I shirked from his grasp. I struck at his jaw, and he took the blow, rolling his head with it. His hand whipped around at the same time and snatched my hair.

Tears sprung to my eyes as he manhandled me, hauling my back to his chest. My hair was always braided up on my head. I wasn't dumb enough to leave it down, but I had never thought of it as a weakness.

"Cut it. I won't have anyone on my team with such an obvious weakness." His deep voice rumbled in my ear.

My breath came fast as the butterflies woke with a vengeance. My head was tucked against his chest, the height difference between us glaringly obvious. His warm body pressed against mine and I struggled to form rational thoughts.

He tugged my hair again, and I snapped back to reality. General Rafe wasn't a man I could let my womanly feelings impede. How could I feel like this toward a man like him?

I hissed and rammed an elbow at his core. For once, it landed with solid impact, and he huffed in response. Alas, that was the only sign I hit him. He reached his left arm around and pinned mine against my sides, tucking me against his body.

"Cut it, Avyanna."

"Who said I'm joining your 'team'?" I snarled and squirmed against him. "I didn't!"

He growled and tightened his hold. "I won. That's my reward."

I screamed between clenched teeth and fought with everything I had. I sunk my nails into his thighs like claws and tried stomping on his toes. He took all the abuse, grunting with each blow, but didn't move.

"You stubborn mule! Let go!" I snapped, trying to bite at his arm.

His grip on my hair tightened, and he pulled my head back, a safe distance from his arm. "Cut your hair. I've given you long enough to do it yourself."

I stilled at his words. Had he been taking it easy on me in training? Had he seen a weakness and not exploited it? That was unlike him. Why would he do that? It didn't make sense... unless... unless he was being gentle with me before.

General Rafe? Being gentle?

Absurd.

"No," I whispered.

He sighed and yanked my head back further, craning it back at an odd angle to look up at him. Tears sprang to my eyes as my scalp stung from his tugging.

"I'm not asking." His eye was dark, all traces of humor and amusement gone.

"No, you don't under–"

"I do," he said as he tugged again.

I yelped and blinked to clear my vision.

His voice lowered. "It's pretty."

My breath hitched in my chest. My mind reeled with confusion. He was hurting me, perhaps trying to help me, and calling me pretty? My brain spun, grasping at what was going on.

"You're a woman, and you think it's pretty." His eye left mine and traveled to my hair, and he rubbed it between his fingers. "Pretty, but illogical. It's a weakness your enemies will exploit. It's something else to care for on the front lines when you won't even have enough water to drink, let alone wash with.

"You think it's precious, you consider it dear. It's a beautiful part of you, but will it be beautiful caked in mud and blood? Will it be beautiful when you won't have the time and leisure to put it up? The Shadows will snatch it and use it as a bridle to have their way with you." His gaze returned to my watering eyes. "Cut it, Avyanna."

I snarled and tore myself from his embrace, and he relinquished me, content he had made his point.

"Fine!"

I didn't want to. A few soldiers wore their hair long, though not the length of mine. I fought for it because he was right—I thought it was pretty. If there was one thing about myself I considered beautiful, or that made me stand out, it was my hair. Without it, there would be nothing feminine about me. My physique would remain female, but all my femininity would be hidden. I would wear men's clothes, have a man's haircut, and train like a man.

I blinked away rebel tears and glared at General Rafe. He had a weakness, too. One I had never exploited.

"Again," I demanded, raising my fists to my chin.

He shrugged a large shoulder and dropped into a fighting stance.

This time, I threw a punch and positioned myself with care. He grabbed my hand, and I swung out with my leg, knowing what he would do. He rushed forward, pinning me to the ground. I thought it through as I moved, trapping his arm with mine. I pulled it to my chest, gripping with the joint of my elbow. He grunted, and I braved a glance at his face, seeing recognition—he knew I was doing something.

He braced his legs on either side of me, and I snapped my right leg over his. He dropped his weight at the same time I heaved with my left leg, pushing against his body and somehow managing to roll his massive frame.

I panted and sat on top of him, and for good measure, placed my hand on his thick neck.

He smirked up at me. "Good girl."

I took a moment to catch my breath, and the reality of this position hit me. For once I had bettered him. I sat back on his hips, grinning down at him.

"Look what happens when you get riled up." Dark amusement colored his voice.

"Tell me I don't have to cut my hair," I demanded.

"No."

"Take it back–" I started, but was cut off as he bucked his hips, lurched out from beneath me, and pinned me again.

"No. That's not part of the game."

I rocked my hips as I struggled to flip him again, and failed. I couldn't roll him when he expected it. He kept my elbows tucked in, protecting himself from my attempts to grab him.

I stilled and studied him. He was partially keeping his weight off me by putting it on his arms, but his legs were free to fight me as I tried to roll. Looking up at him, something flared to life inside me. A dark side of my mind whispered a terrible idea, and I felt a thrill run through me.

I sighed in mock defeat, watching him, not missing a thing. When I sighed, his gaze traveled to my lips for a split second.

The dark part of me whispered with more urgency. Butterflies wreaked havoc in my stomach. I reached up, slow enough for him to take notice. As soon as I touched his jaw, his eye flashed. I had just crossed some invisible line. His eye twitched. My hands crept up to cup his cheeks, rough with stubble too fine to see.

"What are you–" His voice was darker, raspier.

My thumb traced over his lips, cutting him off, and he relaxed a fraction. For once, being a woman was a glorious thing. I felt powerful, silencing my General with a mere finger against his lips. I moved my touch higher, caressing his face and his eye sought mine, questioning. His gaze was intense, as it always was, but now it was almost as if he warred with himself.

I snatched the cloth over his eye and threw it.

There was a moment when time seemed to move faster than I could comprehend.

A flash of gray.

A bit out curse.

He dropped his forehead onto my chest. I used the distraction to roll him again and drew my bandit breaker, placing it at his neck. He clenched his bad eye shut and glared with the other.

"It seems I'm not the only one with a weakness."

He reached for the hand holding the bandit breaker, but I pressed in, drawing a drop of blood.

"Open your eye."

"No." His tone took on a lethal pitch.

I walked a dangerous path. "That's not how the game works, Rafe." Smiling down at him sweetly, I dared the use of his name, taunting him.

"What would someone think to find you in such a position?" he rumbled, not taking his angry gaze off me.

I gave his chest a pat like a mother would a child. "You're grasping at straws, darling. Open your eye."

He stared at me and I wondered how long this would go on. Would the sun fall, and the moon rise to find me still sitting on my General with a blade to his throat? Would someone else find us?

He lay there under me, glaring for all he was worth. I flashed him a grin and settled on his hips. I would wait all day. My curiosity was insatiable, and I likely wouldn't get another chance. What could be so horrible he refused to show me for the simple sake of scaring me?

What was so awful that he would hide it?

He lurched up, ignoring the press of my knife to his throat. Blood trickled down as I jerked the blade back, shocked. He propped himself up on his elbows and glowered, putting every ounce of hatred he could muster into his gaze.

"If you so much as *think* of telling another soul, I will rip out your tongue." His tone was deathly calm.

I swallowed past the lump in my throat, all traces of playing gone.

"I mean it—I will find you. I will reach into your pretty mouth, grab that quick tongue of yours, and rip it from your throat."

I shivered at the coldness in his tone. This wasn't a game anymore. I won a reward, but he wasn't playing.

"Will I ever be in a position where I would be obligated to tell anyone about it?" My voice cracked as I asked.

If he was hiding this, there was a reason—a reason others might like to know. Perhaps it was the way his eye was damaged. Maybe it was injured by a special weapon and the wound held secrets somehow. If someone found out that I knew, would I be endangered?

"That's not how the game works, Vy."

His angry smirk, combined with his use of a nickname, made every nerve in my body scream for me to run away.

"I won't tell," I breathed.

His mouth twisted in a sardonic smile and he opened his left eye.

Chapter Thirty

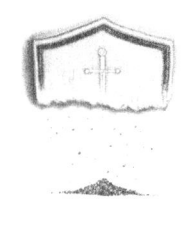

Scars veined out from his eye socket as if it exploded. His eye, however, was fully intact, albeit different from any I'd seen before. It was gray with a blue tint, but had no pupil. The entire iris, and where the black pupil should be, was a pool of swirling, almost reflective, color.

I frowned and leaned closer, completely forgetting what a precarious position I was in. I moved from side to side, watching as he tracked the motion. He could see out of it, which puzzled me. Why would he cover it? Why would he hide it and willingly handicap himself? He received it on the front, battling the Shadows. I tilted my head in thought. Shadow Men had eyes described as mirrors. Did magic cause it? Did it change him somehow?

I traced the scars surrounding it. It was beautiful—in a harsh, brutal sort of way. It reminded me of a sunburst, with his reflective iris at the center. The white of his eye remained untouched, as if unaffected.

"What happened?" I breathed, entranced, as I stroked my thumb from the corner of his eye to his temple.

"Vy-" he rasped.

My attention slammed back to him—and the position we were in. Awareness came crashing down. My face was less than a handspan from his. I could feel his breath against my lips. I startled and jerked up. He snorted, but didn't shift under me.

"Was it magic?" I asked.

He bucked his hips and I scrambled off him, sheathing my blade. We stood and brushed the sand off our clothes.

"Why do you hide it?" I tried again.

The chance of any explanation was slim, yet I had to try. I'd never seen anything like it. Surely the Healers treated him. After all, wasn't that the injury he suffered to be sent back to the homelands?

He walked up to me, and I stood still, letting him approach. His steady gaze was soft, not angry. I knew him well enough that he wouldn't hurt me unless provoked. He brought a hand up and held my cheek, looking down on me with... was that tenderness? It felt peculiar to see both his eyes upon me, one dark and familiar and the other frigid and strange.

"Avyanna. Not a word. No one—I don't care who they are to you." A cold hardness crept into his voice. "I don't care how they torture you. I will do far worse."

My eyebrows dropped into a frown as I glared up at him. "Do you think so little of me? I don't understand it, but I understand you, Rafe. At least a little. I will take your secret to my grave."

His features softened again, and his gaze traveled down my face to rest on my lips. The butterflies in my stomach took flight, and heat burned beneath my skin as he looked at me. Something flickered in his eyes, a hot, wild thing that sent my heart racing.

"I'll cut your hair."

Just like that, the butterflies died.

"No. I can." I spun away from him.

He went from soft to cruel in the blink of an eye. My cheek seemed cold from the absence of his warm hand. He had never touched me in an affectionate way before. Come to think of it, I'd never been touched with affection by any man. This was all unfamiliar territory for me—new and dangerous. I shouldn't have these feelings toward any man, let alone my General. This was why they didn't want me in the barracks.

"Avyanna."

I turned to face him, after putting space between us. The growl of his voice affected me in foreign ways—distance made me feel safer.

"You've never cut men's hair," he said simply, sitting to pull on his boots and lace them up.

"I don't need it to be pretty."

"No, but you need it to be functional."

I glared at his back and put my hands on my hips. "I don't want a shaved head."

He chuckled as he stood and secured the cloth covering his silver eye in place. "You wouldn't look nearly as pretty." He strode past, patting my head, and I shirked away from his touch.

I mentally threw curses at his back as I watched him leave. Sighing, I picked up my pace to follow him back to the barracks.

I sat on a stool just outside General Rafe's room, watching him warily. He held a pair of shears and a comb.

"Is that what you use for your hair, sir?" I asked quietly, poking fun at him, but also trying to stifle my nerves.

He smirked and stood behind me. Finding the pins in my braid, he let it down. It slapped against my back, falling below the seat of the stool. His large, calloused hand came into view, offering me the shears.

"Make the first cut," he ordered.

I twisted in my seat, pleading with him to take it back, to not make me do this. Yes, it was logical. Long hair had its disadvantages... yet it was *mine*. Seeing no change in his resolve, I snatched the thrice-cursed shears and faced away from him. Holding my braid at the nape of my neck, I braced the shears, ready to cut.

One cut, then I was done. That was it.

I took a deep breath and closed the shears, expecting the braid to fall. They barely closed around the length and caught. Closing my eyes, I realized it was too thick to be lopped off in one go. I sat there in silence, working the shears—open and closed, open and closed, sawing through my white hair.

It took for what felt like an eternity, and when the braid finally fell free, tears streaked my face. I had nothing else to show for my femininity. There was no going back. Sure, one day it would grow long, but until then, I would look like an outcast. If I ever walked the school grounds again, I'd stand out more than ever.

My hair sprang free, the loose ends tickling my neck and chin. I held the shears out for General Rafe and pulled the thick braid into my lap. Perhaps I would keep it—a memento of who I once was.

He combed and made rough cuts, white hair falling to the ground. More tears pricked my eyes, and I blinked them away. I was stronger than this. It was just hair, it would grow back. I was doing the smart thing.

"Where did you learn to cut hair?" I asked, clearing my throat.

"Every soldier learns on the front. It's cleaner, and keeps your vision clear," he rumbled behind me.

I smiled at the thought of the General behind me. If I had ever seen him cutting someone's hair, I would have laughed. He would probably shave it all off like he did with his hair. Yet, with mine, he took his time.

My eyes fluttered closed, blocking out the hair drifting around us like snow on the Summer Solstice. I rubbed my fingers against my braid, noting the smoothness, the intricacy of my design. I prided myself on my braids—practiced every day, even after I joined the army. My heart twisted as I bit my cheek. It was done now.

General Rafe stilled, then gave a satisfied grunt. I opened my eyes and watched as he walked into his room, then returned with a small bronze mirror. He offered it to me and I took it, braving my reflection.

The person who stared back looked nothing like me. I ran my fingers through the short mop on the top of my head. It hung loose and choppy. Some length laid over my forehead, giving the illusion of bangs. My fingers trailed up the nape of my neck over the tapered hair. I frowned, finding a small lock he hadn't cut. It was barely as long as my middle finger, but it was there. I glanced up at him in question.

"Braid it." He shrugged, leaning against the door.

I looked back at my reflection. Sun-kissed freckles speckled a young girl's small face. Her short hair made her seem even younger than her naïve eyes did.

I would never be a fierce warrior.

Sighing, I handed the mirror back and stood, shaking out my clothes. I pulled my shirt free from my trousers and aired it out, trying to be rid of all the hair flying about. He set the mirror off to the side, and leaned against the door frame again, studying me.

"Did you do that to prep me for your team?" I asked, not bothering to hide the sharp edge in my voice.

He scoffed. "You'll join regardless of your hair. I simply wouldn't have given you a choice then."

"You didn't give me much of a *choice*." I straightened and scowled. "Besides, what makes you so sure I'll join?"

"You will. And you did. You played the game."

"I didn't know you were going to tell me to join your little club," I growled.

He pushed off the door frame and closed the distance between us, forcing me to look up at him. "What did you think I would ask?" His voice dropped to a dangerous level.

Something flared in his gaze—the same heated spark that told me to run away as fast as I could.

"Not that," I huffed, turning to give him my shoulder.

I glanced across the empty barracks. There wasn't a soul in sight. A few stayed, but most had left. We were only given two holidays as cadets. Most didn't want to waste it.

I looked back at him to find a confident, knowing smile on his face. I cursed the idea of him realizing what he did to me. If he knew he made me flustered or that I was attracted to him, he would use it to his advantage and unnerve me more often.

An ugly thought reared itself. I had seen his reactions to me on the beach. He didn't have a mate, at least not one that anyone had mentioned. Perhaps I could push him as well.

I shook my head, ridding myself of that terrible idea.

And a terrible idea it was. To think that I would win in any battle against him, let alone attempt to taunt him because I was off limits, was foolish.

"Tell me about this team you're putting together," I sighed.

He pointed to the stool and walked into his room. I tilted my head and noted the setting sun, but picked up the stool and followed. Once inside, he took it from me and gestured to the bed. I sat, remembering almost six months ago when I laid here suffering from fever after my attack.

He perched on his seat and folded his hands behind his head. "You know why I was sent back?" he asked.

"Because of your injury," I said, motioning to his eye.

He scoffed with a bitter smile. "That's what they want people to think."

I tilted my head in puzzlement. Why would they send him back if he wasn't injured? Why would they remove a valuable asset from the front?

"Why then?" I asked when he made no further comment.

"I'm reckless." He lifted his chin with a cocky smile, as if it was something to be proud of.

As if I didn't know that already. I blinked to avoid the urge to roll my eyes.

"They claimed I needed time in the homelands or I would get killed."

I nodded. I could see that happening with how stubborn he was.

He took a deep breath and reached under the cloth, rubbing at his eye. "I'm not going to give you details, cadet." He pinned me with his dark gaze. "I got men killed. A lot of men. I was reckless with the lives of others. So, they sent me back to the homelands to cool off."

He leaned forward and there was a gleam in his gaze—a wicked, bloodthirsty gleam. "I've been thinking... I need a special team. If I led a group of unique soldiers who fought how I told them to, they might not die so easily."

I winced at his words. These were men, human beings, and he just referenced them dying as if it were nothing.

"But soldiers are trained to fight in a company on the front lines. Why would you need a special team to fight with everyone else?" I asked.

He leaned back again, and his dark eye judged me. I raised my eyebrow in question. Finally, he offered me a shrug.

"I won't fight on the front lines."

My mouth fell open. He wouldn't fight on the front? Then where? He couldn't fight in the sky with the dragons. That had to mean he was going to–

"You want to take me, a first year recruit, behind enemy lines?" I waited for him to squint, acknowledging he might have misjudged me before going on. "As you so graciously put it, I'm not good at anything. What makes you think I'll last more than the span of a breath in their territory?"

He smirked and crossed his arms over his chest. "Decided you're not destined for greatness, eh?"

I glared. I hadn't answered before and I wouldn't answer now.

He shifted his feet and gave me a bored look. "They're training you wrong."

"How so?"

He waved a hand as if shooing a fly. "Like a soldier."

I hung my head. Was he disillusioned? Was *this* his attempt at convincing me I needed to join his special team and die that much sooner?

"Like a man."

I snapped my head up and narrowed my eyes at him. Of course, they trained me like a soldier, like a man. That's what I fought for since I arrived. I didn't want special treatment, and I didn't get any here.

"Don't be a fool, cadet. You're nothing like a man. You can't fight like them. It's that simple. You need different weapons, different training. Given the right tools and the right teacher, you'd be a force to be reckoned with."

A chime rang, echoing the hour chime, and I had never been so thankful for the toll of the bell. I stood and leveled my gaze with his. "I would be a fool to think that I'll ever be ready for the front lines, with or without exceptions being made. Have a good evening, General."

With that, I left, his dark chuckle chasing me as I practically ran away.

As to be expected, the haircut came as a surprise to my friends. Niehm was adamantly against it, telling me I could fight just as well with long hair. Elenor judged me in silence but did not condemn it, and Willhelm disapproved but seemed to understand when I gave my reasoning.

A few days later, we made our way to the 'washing cavern' as we came to call it, when Willhelm brought up that General Rafe had removed a soldier from a company.

"Why?" I asked, as subtly as I could.

They didn't know of my conversation with Rafe, and no one needed to. What happened during the Summer Solstice didn't need to be spoken of... any of it. Including my apparent lapses in sanity where I thought the General was a nice man.

"It's said that he's forming a Tennan." Willhelm frowned.

Niehm wrinkled her nose. "Tennan? What exactly is that?"

"It's an old term from before we formed the army," he explained. "Ten fighters joined in league with each other and fought to the same end."

"Is he permitted to do that? Would that not disrupt the companies?" Elenor asked, walking primly beside me.

"He's more than permitted. There's no higher authority at Northwing. It's being reported to the other Generals and the King, but I'm certain he would be allowed to form his own company if he so wished. The companies will deal with it. They're just wondering who he'll take next."

"Who did he take?" I asked. Perhaps I knew the man.

"Jamlin. He's out of the Fifty-Seventh. You probably haven't met him." Willhelm shrugged.

The Fifty-Seventh was a company of third year cadets. They would be shipped out to the front lines next year, anyway. But the fact that General Rafe singled him out meant something.

"What makes him so special that our resident General has taken him under his wing?" I asked as we neared the clearing.

"He's a fair soldier, all things considered, but outpaces his company quickly. His skill and initiative challenged the authority of his old Commander. The man is a fiend in the night. His stealth is unmatched, and he's known to play tricks on other companies that can't see him coming," he replied with a grin.

I smiled back, knowing of the friendly antics between companies. Sometimes one would find a burr under their horse's saddle, or some other trick to be played in the name of good humor.

It meant Rafe was recruiting, and I simply had to wait till he had ten soldiers. Then his little *Tennan* would be on their merry way. I could wait that long.

I picked up my pace with a bright smile on my face. Soon, I would be rid of this General that I so disliked.

The butterflies in my belly objected.

Chapter Thirty-One

Autumn of Year 897

As the months passed, I continued to struggle with my training. I felt as though I did worse, even when I worked harder. In the back of my mind, General Rafe's offer to join his 'Tennan' nagged at me, a constant shadow over my thoughts. I ignored him at all costs and tried to prove myself as a soldier at the same time.

I didn't need him.

His Tennan was often the topic of discussion in the dining hall. He collected six soldiers from the companies and, with winter fast approaching, everyone was making bets on the next soldier he'd recruit.

"My money's on Collins," Rory said one night while devouring a meat pie.

"The skinny kid?" Sergeant Greyson asked, puzzled.

Willhelm tilted his head as he ate, watching his friends. I picked at my food, sick of hearing about the great General and his new team.

"Aye. He's a terrible soldier, but quick as a rabbit. He's a smart lad," Rory said between bites.

Corporal Bane's cold eyes surveyed the soldiers in the dining hall, watching their movements, keeping an idle ear on everything around him. He was ever the silent, judging type.

"He's in Fredrick's company. He won't like that," Willhelm commented.

"Not like anyone has a choice. Eh, Bane?" Sergeant Greyson sighed, resting his chin on his hand.

"None at all," Bane droned.

His hawkish gaze settled on someone, and I fought the urge to turn and look.

"To be fair, we might have to thank him in the end. The soldiers he's taking are bodies, but they all seem to do poorly in training." Rory shrugged.

Willhelm glanced at me, and a blush warmed my cheeks. He knew as well as anyone how awful I was. I was just as they expected—a weak woman who couldn't hold her own. My company seemed to feel as though they had to double their efforts to make up for my lack of skill.

I stabbed a knife into my pie.

"He's not taking the weak ones," Corporal Bane added.

I looked up and met his cold stare. His icy blue eyes cut through me, condemning me as if I was too weak to be considered. I frowned and stood, pushing my uneaten pie to the side.

"Avyanna?" Willhelm looked at me curiously.

"I'm turning in early. I'll see you on the morrow," I said with a wave, heading out of the hall.

The nights were growing cold once again, and I shivered, plunging into the chilled evening air. I rolled my shoulders and rested my hand on my bandit breaker. The sun's setting rays lit the sky, but I learned never to be caught off guard.

General Rafe still trained me, though he grew rougher and colder during our sessions. That wasn't new, as he'd always been distant and hard, but I found myself pulling away. He never mentioned joining his Tennan again, but at the end of our bouts, he'd stare, as if waiting for something. Every time I sensed the question in his silence.

I always left with no reply.

I was grateful to General Rafe for so many things. He was brash and boorish, but was willing to teach me—though he was a terrible teacher. Even so, I did learn from him. He treated me as fairly as he did anyone. Even I had to admit—he was a good man, in a way.

I scoffed to myself as I walked to the bunkhouse. If he ever heard me mention that I thought him a good man, he'd put me on the ground and strut away with his signature smirk.

Inside, I crossed the space to my room with a nod to the secretary. A few soldiers laid in their bunks or stripped out of their uniforms. I ignored them as steadfastly as they ignored me.

That was fine with me.

I entered my glorified storage closet and lit my lantern before shutting the door. I changed into a clean tunic and stepped out of my trousers. It was not as comfortable as my night shifts of old, but it fell to my thighs and if I loosened the lacing at the top, it was comfortable enough to sleep in. Then the next morning, I only had to pull on my trousers to be ready for my day.

I shoved my cot in front of my door, as I always did, and climbed in. It's not that I had any reason to be afraid. I was confident in my self-defense abilities now. Nobody attempted to get in after the incident with Victyr, but I refused to let down my guard.

Not even for one night.

After putting out the lantern, I settled on the thin mattress. I still needed to write to my mother and tell her not to come in the autumn. I wouldn't have any time off, aside from the Winter Solstice, but I wasn't sure if she could make it in the snow. She wasn't as young as she used to be, and getting around was difficult. I wanted to see her terribly, and let her know I truly was grateful for her. Through the past few months, I learned to appreciate her and her sacrifices more than ever.

Not every parent made an effort with their children once they were sent to the King's schools. Some were forgotten about and were related in name only. Any familial ties faded away over the years. My mother's visits were something I took for granted, and I wanted to express my thanks.

I thought of everyone I had to be thankful for, those who I hadn't expressed my gratitude for. Niehm and Elenor were irreplaceable. Without them, I would have never made it through my transition from the rejected Chosen to a soldier.

Then there was Meredith. I smiled, thinking of the older woman. She would probably just pat my hand and tell me to do my best. She was so kind and sweet and had always been there for me.

In a way, I was thankful for Vivian, too. Her sass and barbs toughened me, made me more resilient to the crude remarks in the barracks. I snorted, amused, as I imagined the expression on her face if I were to tell her 'thank you'. Had she settled with a life mate and made his life miserable? What if she was genuinely happy? What if I thought all these cruel things about her, and yet she was the one living a joyous life?

I rolled over and my hip dug into the wooden cot. Who was I to judge others? Look at the life I lived. I dared to be different. Yet I'd become a living example of why one shouldn't. I wanted to make my own way and force the issue. I did, and now regretted it.

There was a roof over my head and food to eat, but I wasn't happy. I had friends, but I wasn't thriving. I hated failure, and it seemed as though there was nothing I could do to reduce my limitations. Being short and weak was a defect I couldn't overcome. No matter how much I trained or practiced, I wouldn't grow taller. No matter how much I exercised and tried to eat, I wouldn't get much stronger.

General Rafe claimed he could teach me and said I was just being taught wrong. What if I was allowing myself to be hindered? I growled and rolled to my other side, mentally cursing. I would not take a way out. Besides, I didn't like him.

My belly clenched as I pictured him—tall, strong, rugged. He was a man that didn't take no for an answer. A man that didn't let people push him around. He was proud and cocky because he had earned that right. He was–

Ugh! I slapped my palm to my forehead.

He was rude, mean, and a bull-headed pile of dragon dung.

Why was I thinking like this? I had no interest in joining his Tennan. If anything, I had made it so clear now that if I gave in, it would almost be wrong by virtue of holding out for so long.

I needed to calm my thoughts and think about nothing. Lack of sleep would do me no favors with training tomorrow. Thrashing on the cot, I heaved a sigh, trying to get more comfortable. I just needed to sleep it off. I would feel better in the morning.

My cot shifted, and I woke in a flash. I spun into a crouch, drawing my push dagger from its sheath. My brain scrambled to make sense of the faint light coming through the crack of my door.

A hesitant voice stammered on the other side. "Ah, er, Lady—I mean Cadet Avyanna?"

He sounded young, very young. Perhaps he was put up to this by older soldiers?

"What do you want?" I hissed.

"I was ordered, I mean, well, I was sent to—I mean, if you're busy–"

"What is it?!" I growled. This boy needed to snap out of it.

"Well, you see, I was sent to retrieve you."

I squinted at the door, trying to see if there was a hand or any sign of him inside my room. It looked as though he simply opened the door and jostled my cot to wake me.

"I do not wish to be retrieved. Go away."

I kicked the blanket off my feet and balanced my weight on the cot more evenly. If I had to lash at something that came through that crack, I didn't want to fall in the process.

"I—er, well, I can't. You see, I am supposed to—I mean I am–"

I lurched forward and slammed my palm against the door, closing it and cutting the voice off. I pressed against it, waiting for him to try to open it again.

Two soft knocks rapped against the wood.

"Did you just knock on my door?" I whispered in disbelief. How polite was he?

"Well, yes," came the hushed reply.

"Go away."

"I can't!" Exasperation lingered in his tone.

He obviously felt obligated to fulfill his duty. "Who sent you?" I asked.

"General Rafe!"

I recoiled, glaring at the door.

No.

There was no way.

General Rafe sent some boy to retrieve me in the middle of the night—in the bunkhouse, where soldiers slept not five paces from my door? The whole barracks would know! Just how would that look?

I bared my teeth and growled like a wild animal. "You go tell General Rafe if he wants me, he's going to have to come get me. There's not a snowflake's chance in a plume of dragon fire that I'll be meeting him in the dead of night." I raised my voice, hoping the men beyond would hear it.

"But–"

"No! You hear me? No!" I snapped. "Now go, or I'll come out there and gut you."

After his discouraged groan, light footsteps sounded his retreat.

I glared at the door, anger boiling in my veins, too hot to let me sleep. If it was indeed General Rafe who sent him, I could expect a visit from him shortly. Perhaps he would explain things, and not make it seem so inappropriate.

I stepped off the cot and pulled my trousers on. At least when he came and busted down the door, I would be fully clothed.

Sheathing my push dagger, I shoved my belt through the loops and drew my bandit breaker. Sitting back down, I waited. I wasn't past the point of doing physical harm to General Rafe. He'd be asking for it if he came to my room. The law would be on my side if he tried to assault me.

I frowned at that thought.

He wouldn't assault me. Sun, moon, and stars knew that he had plenty of opportunities to. That brought me back to why he sent for me. In my opinion, the 'why' didn't matter. It was the dead of night, in a barracks full of men who would think me an army whore after this. He had to know that.

Creak.

I tilted my head, straining at the sound. A wooden plank groaned nearby. Someone was silent enough for me not to hear their footsteps, but unfamiliar with this side of the bunkhouse to know which floorboards were loose. The latch of my door whispered as it was freed. I gripped my bandit breaker. I widened my eyes as far as they could go, trying to see in the darkness.

I made out a thin patch of gray where my door cracked open, and I tensed, creeping into a crouch.

The door slammed into the cot, and I collided with the floor, my knife tumbling from my grasp. I growled, righting myself, and pulled my fists to my chin, knowing I had no time to search the dark space to retrieve it. I kicked my leg out, feeling for my cot, finding it pushed against the wall. The room wasn't big, but without it blocking the way, anyone could get in. I cursed the darkness. I couldn't see a thing.

There was a whisper and a flash. It could have been a candle or a match for all I knew, but the transition from complete darkness to instant light burned my eyes. I clenched them instinctively before forcing them open in a squint. I threw my fist out, making contact. The surprised grunt chilled me to my core.

It wasn't Rafe.

That moment of fear, of hesitation, was all my attacker needed before he snared my hands and shoved a cloth over my mouth.

The light died, and I struggled against their hold as they fastened the cloth tight around my head. I kicked and flailed, to no avail. They threw me over their shoulders like a felled deer and stepped over the cot, leaving the room. I tried to scream, but my muffled moans and yelps were either unheard or ignored by the sleeping soldiers.

I bucked and pulled at my pinned arms and legs. His head snapped back and collided with my stomach, ripping the air from my lungs. I craned my neck, hoping to see the secretary at the desk, but no one was there. The man's shoulders dug into my hips and ribs as he descended the stairs, walking around the bunkhouse to the alley that led behind the buildings.

He held me and walked calmly, as if taking a midnight stroll. The moon peeked out from the clouds, and I grappled to take in any details I could from my abductor. He was dark-skinned. Intricate braids plaited his hair down the center, though the sides of his head were shaven. In his right ear hung earrings made of bone and metal.

I fiddled with the cloth around my face, pushing at it with my tongue, trying to get it off my mouth. It wouldn't budge.

He moved further and further away from the established barracks. I stilled, letting him think I was exhausted before thrashing again. He chuckled and held me tightly. I was sure I'd be sporting bruises for the next few days.

If I lived.

Who was this man, and why did he abduct me? Was this part of General Rafe's plan? Did the boy send for the big brute?

I sighed and waited. There was nothing else I could do.

He kept a steady pace, and we soon crossed the training fields and entered the copse of trees. Beyond it, fires burned low in pits. It was almost impossible to see through the foliage. As we neared, men came into view, milling about as though this was a common occurrence. They simply found themselves awake in the middle of the night and wandered out here to enjoy a chat by a secret fire.

The man carrying me walked past the others, drawing stares and outright laughs. Fury lit my soul ablaze. These men were laughing at me? At what sport would come? As soon as I had a chance, I would show them sport. I would ask if they were laughing when I buried my dagger in their throat.

"Calm down, little one," my abductor said, humor coloring his voice.

I growled, and he chuckled, continuing his trek.

He aimed toward a spot where a young boy, perhaps still near his fifteenth-winter, stood with three other men. One of which was the tallest I had ever seen, bigger than General Rafe. He had to stand at least eight paces high. He had short, light-colored hair cropped close to his skull and bore a smile that seemed too friendly for his intimidating stature.

The other two were odd. They were both lean and wiry, standing tall but thin. I squinted at their features, puzzled that they wore the same face. They had dark hair and neatly trimmed beards cut short to their chins. They both wore amused expressions aimed at the man carrying me.

"Ah, so you snagged her. You keep surprising us, Jamlin," one of them said.

The one carrying me laughed deep and loud. "I keep telling you, there's nothing I can't do in the dark."

The boy fidgeted and kept sneaking glances at me, though never looked at me directly.

"Are you going to take her to Rafe like that?" the other that shared a face asked.

They had odd accents with clipped words, as if the common tongue was not their first language. It unnerved me how identical they were.

"I wouldn't let her go as she is. She's a wild one," Jamlin said.

The biggest man stomped over and peered down at me. He smiled and lifted a finger to tap my nose. "Cute little thing," he rumbled.

"Korzak, hands off the goods." Jamlin jested, turning to pull me away from the giant's curious touch. "Come on, then." He started off toward a brighter section of the clearing.

The surrounding men snickered and a few more laughed and pointed. As we got closer to the main clearing, I spied a group gathered near a large pit. It was so deep that I couldn't see the bottom. Fear flooded my veins, but I lifted my eyes and glared around, finding a familiar figure.

General Rafe leaned against a tree, watching us with a dark eye. The corner of his mouth was lifted in an amused smile as he watched us approach. "Thought I sent Collins to fetch her," he stated, pushing off the tree and crossing his arms.

Jamlin shrugged, jostling me with the motion. "Seems as though she was too much for the little one to handle."

"I tried, General. I really did, but–" the boy started.

"She's cute. Can we keep her?" The giant, Korzak, came into view again as he peered at my face.

"Korzak, back off." General Rafe's order was followed by a retreat of the giant's head. He turned to Collins and frowned. "You need to be able to handle things like this. Grow up, boy."

"Yes, sir." The lad looked down at his boots, clearly disheartened.

"Jamlin, you going to keep her up there?" General Rafe asked.

"I think she has a better vantage point. She might like it up here," he replied, lifting his left shoulder, then his right, jostling me.

General Rafe grunted in amusement, and I glared at him for all I was worth.

"Are you sure she's the right one, General? She's rather unimpressive." One of the dark-haired men with a shared face came into view.

"Do you think there's a single other woman in our barracks?" Collins asked.

"Jam, set her down," General Rafe ordered as a cheer echoed from the group near the massive pit.

"Aye, aye. I hear you," he replied, easing me off his shoulders.

As soon as he let go, I tore away from him and grabbed at the cloth, yanking it from my mouth. I spat and reached under my shirt to draw my push dagger.

"Aw!" Korzak stepped toward me and bent close to the blade. "It's tiny! And pointy!"

"Korzak." General Rafe's tone carried an unspoken warning.

I whirled on him. "You better have a thrice-cursed explanation!" I hissed, keeping every one of them in my sight. I backed against a tree and pulled myself into a fighting stance.

"Cadet, meet my Tennan," he said, nodding toward the men.

Jamlin snickered, putting his hands on his hips. "The better half of it."

"Why am I here?!" I growled.

This wasn't fun and games. I trusted the General, but not these other men. I didn't know them and it unnerved me to be paraded around like some prize stag.

"Tonight, you'll watch," he said.

I blinked in confusion but maintained my frown. "Watch what?" I asked, not letting my guard down for a moment.

"Hmm?" One of the men that shared a face tilted his head.

"What year is she?" the other asked.

"She doesn't know about the pits?" Korzak stood to his full height and hit his head on a tree branch. He cried out and rubbed his head, moving a safe distance away.

"General Rafe," I said slowly, locking eyes with him.

He held my gaze as he replied. "She's never attended."

"Oi! She's a second year! Never seen the pits?!" Jamlin laughed.

"Go, all of you."

General Rafe spoke quietly, but his tone conveyed his message well. His men walked off with shocked conversation and laughter. I relaxed a fraction as they melded in with the others gathered.

"Come," he said, turning his back to me.

"Rafe–" My voice was tight and strained.

He turned and I think at that moment he truly saw me.

I was terrified.

I had just been abducted from my room, humiliated, and treated like I was nothing more than a toy. My hands shook in fear as memories swelled. Memories of being helpless and weak. Memories of not being able to stop a group of men and their laughter aimed at me.

He closed the space and stood in front of me, blocking me off from the crowd. "You're safe." His voice was low and calm.

Even though I wanted to beat the man senseless, I dropped my gaze as my breaths came fast and panicked.

He was so much taller than me, bigger than me, bigger than my fears. I trusted him, no matter how he went about things, or how much I wished he would simply ask me for things. I knew he wouldn't let me get hurt.

He reached out slowly, giving me plenty of time to pull away. Placing his hand under my chin, he tilted my head back to look up at him. "You're safe," he said again.

His dark eye didn't move from mine. He stayed like that, taking deep, steady breaths as I collected myself. Realization hit me that we were not quite in a private setting. I inhaled, stilling my nerves, before jerking away from his touch and scanning the clearing. No one watched us. They were all focused on the pit.

"Come." General Rafe beckoned me with a nod of his head and started toward them.

The crowd jostled together and cheered. I pressed close to his side as he pressed into the mass of bodies. Men snapped and lashed out at him till they caught sight of his face or tattoo, then let him pass.

We made our way to the edge, where a small hill of earth was heaped up around the perimeter of the pit. The hole itself was a good twenty paces long and half as wide. It was perhaps ten deep. The only way out was a rope on each side held by men. They peered below with eager expressions.

Down in the pit, two men fought.

Chapter Thirty-Two

The two were well-matched in size, but not in skill. One was far more beaten than the other. I glanced up at General Rafe, who stared at the men with a bored expression.

"You want me to watch a fight?" I shouted over the cheers.

He glanced at me and shook his head, then pointed to the far side of the pit where Korzak's towering figure loomed. The behemoth pulled off his tunic and rolled his shoulders. He was a giant, and though he wasn't weak, he didn't have the well-defined muscles I'd seen on General Rafe.

Nor did any other man.

Not like I made a study of General Rafe's muscles.

I blinked away from the mountain of a man and studied the victor in the pit. He stood with his arms raised and the loser collapsed on the ground, passed out cold and covered in blood. I grimaced, disgusted, as others jumped in and hauled his body up. The winner climbed out of the pit and took a bag of coins from a man standing to the side with a piece of parchment.

"I don't want to–"

General Rafe ignored my protest. "Watch," he growled, nodding back to the pit.

I followed his gaze and sighed as Korzak leapt into the hole. Landing in a crouch, he stood and trotted over. He jumped up, his head lifting above the ground level, flashing me the goofiest smile. I scoffed as he did it again, thinking he resembled a gopher sticking its head out of a hole. He turned away as another fighter dropped opposite of him. His opponent seemed average, with nothing much to note concerning his physique.

"Watch." General Rafe was close, his mouth next to my ear as he spoke over the roar of the crowd. "Korzak used to be a poor fighter. He's too big to fight alongside other men."

Korzak lumbered toward his opponent.

"He is strong and big, but he doesn't use that to his advantage. He failed at the simplest tasks."

In a few moves, Korzak caught a well-timed kick and hefted his opponent in the air. A count was sounded, and the crowd cheered as he set the man back down.

"I taught him to harness his strength and use his head, not just his body. I chose him for my Tennan because he's different."

I frowned at General Rafe, and his dark eye met mine. I wondered if this was all a ploy to get me to join.

"Watch."

Next came one of the men who shared a face. "That's Blain. He and Dane are inseparable. They're a pair that can't be matched. They know what the other is thinking, even while separated."

"What are they?" I called back over the roars as a much larger man climbed into the pit.

"Twins. Theirs is a kind that shares the soul. They'll do poorly on a battlefield where they're used as fodder. They're more valuable than that."

"Is that why they look alike?" I asked, watching Dane at the top of the pit, looking bored.

"Aye. Watch."

Blain and the other man fought. It seemed an even match, but oftentimes Blain deflected a blow from behind when he had no way of seeing it. I peered over at Dane, who had his eyes tracking every movement of his twin's opponent.

In a few moments, Blain won as well.

"Are you just going to show me how good your men are?" I asked, folding my arms over my chest.

He smirked. "Watch." He motioned toward the far side again and I saw the thin boy, Collins, strip off his tunic.

"Oh, no," I moaned.

He was as frail as a twig—even smaller than me, I'd assume. He had no muscle and was barely taller than me.

"Just wait," General Rafe murmured.

Collins dropped into the pit and rubbed his ankle. The crowd laughed and spat jokes at him. He searched the crowd, locking eyes on General Rafe. He nodded once and straightened. An older, muscular man jumped in. He was far larger and more intimidating. His biceps were as thick as Collins' waist. He lunged, and Collins dodged.

"I don't need to tell you about Collins. He was a lot like you."

I glanced up at General Rafe for a quick moment before looking back at the fight. "But I'm far prettier," I muttered.

A deep chuckle came from him, and I smiled to myself.

It was entertaining to see the different fighting styles. No one was getting pulverized like the first man, and it seemed fair enough. The hum and excitement in the air was tangible as men cheered for their favored competitor. I was sure that bets were recorded and probably far outweighed Collins' favor.

He moved like a rabbit, quick and deft, avoiding each strike. Soon his rival was drenched in sweat, and heaving for breath. Collins waited for the right moment. Finally, his opponent reached for him and Collins ducked under his arm, spun around him, and leapt onto his back. Wrapping his thin arms around the man's neck, he held on for all he was worth. His opponent stumbled back and slammed Collins into the wall, trying to be rid of him, to no avail. In mere breaths, Collins was declared the victor.

Men parted into smaller groups, and it was obvious that Collins was the last fighter. General Rafe led me to a tree, far enough to be out of earshot.

"You're failing, cadet."

I ground my teeth together. "We've been over this."

"You're miserable."

My gaze snapped to his. He couldn't know that. I told no one.

"Your eyes tell all."

"Do they now?" I asked with a mocking sneer.

He chuckled and crowded me in, backing me against the tree. "They do, Vy."

I shivered. His tone sent warmth flooding through me. I leaned back against the rough bark and gazed up at him. "I'm not so eager to die," I huffed.

His eye shone in victory. "You won't be so easily killed if you join me."

"Why don't you just force me? You seemed to have no issue forcing your hand concerning other matters," I asked, waving a hand at my hair.

"Some things I can push you toward, others you have to choose."

"So, I have to choose to be in your Tennan?"

He smirked at me and waited, not giving me an answer.

"If I join you, I'll be on the front—as in front of the army, behind enemy lines—in a year," I clarified.

"Less."

I deadpanned. He could at least make it seem as though I had a chance.

"If I stay, I will go to the war front in two to three years. Seems like I'll have a better fighting chance with my company."

Something snapped, and his eye flared with anger. He snarled and slammed his fist against the tree beside my head. "You'll be fodder. A human shield. Nothing more than a body waiting to be taken," he growled, leaning closer.

"At least I'll be with a larger group! My chances of survival will be higher than tagging along with you. I'm a burden, Rafe! I can't do anything right! There's no point. I'll just slow you down as you do—whatever it is that you do," I said, the words rushing out of me like a dam had broken.

"You're not a burden. Curse it all, Avyanna. You're not like the others. Korzak isn't like the others. He would simply be a larger target. Collins—how long do you think he'd last on the front lines? A day? I'd give him two if he ran like a coward." He let out a slow breath. "You're special. You're unique. Blast it all." He pushed off the tree and paced like a wild animal.

"Is it because I'm a girl?" I ventured.

"A girl?" He scoffed, looking me up and down in a way that made me very aware of my maturing body. "You chose this path. You chose to be a soldier. Now choose: Join me and live, or stay where you are and die a miserable death with your company."

He walked over, all traces of gentleness gone. His eye flashed like a fierce dragon. "I'd wager three days. Three days—and some Shadow man would have your head on a pike. He might even take a finger as a souvenir. All the training you received at the Masters' hands would give you three days. Think about that."

"Why me?" I bit back, not caring who saw. "You say I'm special? What makes me special? That I'm a woman? Is it that, General Rafe? Is that all you would have me for? To warm your bed?"

I wasn't anything special, and from his flinch, I hit a nerve.

"Girl, if you think I intend to bed you, you're sorely mistaken," he hissed in my face.

"Then what?!" I demanded through clenched teeth, pushing at his chest.

His lip twitched in a sneer and he boxed me in with his hands. "Gareth."

I blinked.

I stared at his mouth, confused by the word that came out. "Gareth?" I breathed. My father?

He nodded and leaned in, lowering his voice. "I served with him. Little did I know I'd serve with his brat girl."

"I—what," I stammered. "What was he like?"

I had no clear memories of him. Only vague feelings attached to my childhood. I wanted to know my father. Something hungry unfurled inside me, demanding to know more.

"Stubborn. Foolhardy. Like someone I know."

"How did he die?" I whispered.

He looked away. I recognized that look in his eye. He was shutting down. He didn't deem me worthy of this, of the information concerning my father?

I reached up and held his face, pulling it down. We had crossed so many boundaries tonight. What was one more?

"Rafe. How did he die?"

The General stared at me and something I never expected to see welled in his eye. Sorrow. Remorse.

Regret.

"He was killed by the Shadows."

There was more. It was written all over his face. "How?"

He closed his eye and tore away. I stumbled after him a few steps as if an invisible cord connected us. He cast a cold look over his shoulder.

"Join me and find out."

The following day, I was in a terrible mood. I had an awful day training, weaker than ever before as I struggled to keep up with the men. Whenever the soldiers looked at me and raised a judgmental brow, I wanted to scream.

I was doing my best. I shook with effort during strength training. Endurance training had me on the edge of passing out. I moved as fast as I could in swordsmanship, but it was never enough. Still, I came short. I simply couldn't compete.

It wasn't even that I couldn't keep up with the other soldiers that bothered me. It was the fact that they treated me as though I was a burden. I was leeching off of their strength and talent, riding on my company's back. Commander Dewal shouted at me several times, bringing my shame to the forefront. He only raised his voice to refocus me, but it still hurt.

My foul mood didn't magically disappear when I joined General Rafe for our training session. He was as cocky and cold as ever, and my fiery mood didn't help matters.

"Temper, temper," he muttered, slamming me onto the ground.

I shoved against him, struggling to complete a move to get him off. He watched me with his lip curled up in amusement, and I thought about cursing him aloud for the first time.

We were in the training field, tucked away on the far end where few would see us. We stayed formal during our sessions. Well, I stayed formal. He was Rafe, as always. Still, I tried to maintain some mental distance from him.

I pushed at his broad chest, and he let me roll his massive body and shifted into a crouch before he stood. He put his hands on his hips and stared down at me.

"Enough."

"Again, sir," I growled, sitting up.

"Enough." His level tone simply stoked the fire.

I rose, brushing off my trousers. "Again, if you please, sir."

His hand shot out and clenched the front of my tunic. I thrashed like a mad animal, twisting away from him and freeing myself at the cost of ripping the fabric. I danced around him, ignoring my torn top, and brought my fists to my chin.

"Enough, Vy."

"Don't call me that!" I shrieked, stepping toward him and launching a fist up at his face. "Sir!" I added for good measure.

He jerked away from my strike and watched me with open amusement, crossing his arms over his thick chest. He braced his feet, and I stepped close and slammed a fist into his core. His abs flexed against it, taking the blow.

I growled, frustrated, and darted back a few paces. Even in hand-to-hand combat, I had a fair chance at defending myself, but my offense was almost laughable. Especially against someone so large and thick as General Rafe. It was as if he had no weakness. Every part of him was solid and covered with muscle. His experience in fighting gave him an edge over me as well, and nothing I did seemed to take him by surprise.

I refused to go for his eye, no matter how mad I was. He trusted me with that secret, and I wouldn't exploit that weakness in a mock fight.

He chuckled and rocked back on his heels. "You're an open book."

I sighed and stepped back. Rubbing the heels of my hands against my eyes, I tugged at my short hair. "I'm done," I groaned, turning away.

"About time," he said in approval.

I trudged off, knowing I looked like a whipped puppy, but unable to help it. It seemed as if General Rafe held all the answers. If I wanted to learn to actually fight? He would teach me. Who had information concerning my father, answers to questions I hadn't given thought to in many years? General Rafe. I kicked at a loose stone on my way to the bunkhouse. Who would get me killed in a year? General Rafe. Who was I also stupidly attracted to? General Rafe.

I didn't keep a mental distance from him only because he was a crude ox. I did it to protect myself. Too many times I found my thoughts wandering to the moments he had me pinned to the ground, his heavy weight pressing against me. My mind replayed that moment on the beach, when something clicked between us. His glances at my lips made me realize I had some effect on him.

My body betrayed me. I shook off those feelings and didn't let myself dwell on them. Those womanly desires had no place on the battlefield—or the barracks.

He was a handsome man, in a rugged, brutish way. Any woman would appreciate his muscular physique, but what about his attitude? He was harsh, sometimes cruel. How could I find a man like that attractive? Sure, he'd proven he had a small conscience—he'd rescued me more than once. He offered to train me and did so. I could hold my own now, thanks to him. That day on the beach, he showed me he had the tiniest streak of caring under that rough exterior.

Yet, of all people, I couldn't be attracted to him. He was my bloody General.

He was *the* bloody General.

Niehm met me at the bunkhouse, but sensing my mood left me alone. She walked with me to and from the washing cave, and I was grateful for her company. She read my moods well-enough to know that trying to talk at the moment would get her nowhere.

I wanted to ask someone for advice. I couldn't decide what I should do. Everyone always seemed to know exactly what they should do, but I didn't. In the past, I chose the option that made the most sense, and it never turned out well.

Niehm was hot-headed, and though she was intelligent, I knew her loathing of General Rafe would color her opinion.

She said her goodbyes and left for the school grounds, casting me a concerned look. I nodded to her and returned my toiletries to my room before setting off to the dining hall. If there was one person I could trust on the barracks' side, it was Willhelm.

I rubbed my arms against the autumn chill and looked up at the clouds. Perhaps we would have an early snow. The dragons were more lethargic than normal. Some of the older ones were already entering brumation.

In the dining hall, I picked up a plate. The line was short, as most soldiers went straight for their meal after dismissal. I offered a small smile to the cook's assistant, who slapped a potato on my plate and ladled a thick chowder over it.

I grabbed a spoon and headed to the table where Willhelm sat with his friends. Sergeant Greyson and Corporal Bane sat beside each other, and Rory sat by Willhelm as always. I took a seat by Willhelm and dug into my meal.

"So I was explaining it to Briggs, and he had a laughing fit over it," Greyson was saying.

Corporal Bane gave his friend a tired look. "A Corporal should have handled it," he droned.

"And ruin the fun? I think not. I'd pay to see Briggs' retaliation," he replied with a grin.

"Speaking of fun," Rory stood and moved to sit at my side.

I paused with my spoon halfway to my mouth, watching him warily.

He leaned his heavy arms on the table with a cheesy, knowing grin. "I heard you had some fun last night, too."

My heart dropped, and I stuffed the bite into my mouth, buying myself time. I glanced around the table. Greyson observed his nails, uninterested. Willhelm seemed intrigued, but Corporal Bane pinned me with his cold eyes.

"Don't worry about him. He's all bark and no bite," Rory assured, noting my anxious glance.

"I don't want to talk about it," I mumbled.

Sergeant Greyson looked up, interested now. "Fun? Last night?" he asked.

I frowned and took another bite. Once I was done, I could take my leave.

"Mmm, at what hour, pray tell?" Corporal Bane pried.

"Now, now Bane. Calm down. She's a good girl, you know that. She would never break curfew," Rory taunted. "Not on her own."

"On your own? Were you with someone else?" Willhelm straightened, and my cheeks burned.

"Rory, enough," I said with a warning glare.

"So there's truth to it." Sergeant Greyson leaned forward, excitement lighting his features.

"Who else broke curfew?" Corporal Bane asked.

I scraped my plate and stood. "Willhelm, may I have a word?" I asked, stepping away from the table.

He made a noise of interest and nodded. His friends watched us like kittens spying a ball of yarn. They were sure at any moment I would make a move that would give them something juicy to gossip over.

Willhelm joined me with a wave to the others and followed me out. "Does it have to do with last night?" he asked as he fell into step beside me.

"A little," I sighed. I rubbed at my arms, defending against both the chill and my insecurities.

"Hmm."

We walked in silence as we headed for the obstacle course. I didn't want to risk any soldiers eavesdropping and gossiping like school girls.

I sat on the rough bench near the fence and dropped my elbows to my knees, placing my head in my hands. "I need advice, Willhelm," I groaned, tugging my short hair.

"You look like you could use it." He sat beside me, stretching out his arms behind me.

I looked up and gave him a small smile. He was one of the calmest, steadiest men I knew. He took everything in stride and was respectful to everyone.

"I was out past curfew last night." I admitted. "Mind you, it wasn't under my own power. I was taken from my room."

"Why wouldn't you tell Bane?" he asked.

I noted the way his fists clenched, like he wanted to say more, but kept quiet.

"Because I'm not necessarily mad about it," I said, dropping my head to my hands again.

There was an awkward pause, and I realized he had the wrong idea.

"I didn't spend the night with a boy!"

He blew out a sigh of relief, and I laughed.

"You should know me better than that," I grumbled in jest.

"Well, you're a woman. You might have... needs." He grimaced.

His obvious discomfort with the topic brought a smile to my face, and I leaned back against his arm. "I assure you, I do not." I looked off into the distance and pulled my knees up to my chin. "General Rafe sent for me. He sent his Tennan. I haven't been completely forthcoming with you concerning him."

I bit my lip and snuck a glance at him. He was frowning, but staring down the darkening road, content to let me finish.

"Willhelm, I need your advice. You're the only one I trust to give me sound counsel. I don't see a clear path ahead of me, and I need your wisdom."

His frown disappeared as a sly grin tugged at his mouth. He watched me out of the corner of his eye. "You need sage counsel from a wizened old man?" he asked playfully.

"Something like that."

"Well, I shall do my best. Though tell no one that the 'wizened old' part pertains to me."

I took a deep breath and settled in. "A few months ago, General Rafe approached me with a proposal. He asked me to join a special team, and I said no. He told me he would take his team, his Tennan, when he left for the front again.

"He said they'd leave by next Hatching Day, which would cut my training in half. Two years isn't enough to keep me alive on the front, let alone enough for me to thrive."

"You'd be right," he agreed.

"Aye, that's what I thought, too. He made the argument though, that I'm being taught incorrectly. As if there was a way that I could match the other soldier's abilities, if only I was trained properly. He offered me personalized instruction if I joined him.

"I still told him no. I thought I would get better on my own if I simply tried harder, if I fully applied myself. Well, I've given it almost six months and I'm not doing any better. I'm still failing. My company carries me like dead weight. I'm a burden. I'm miserable and can't keep up."

My eyes burned, and I brushed at them angrily. This killed me inside—admitting this all out loud to a person who sat and listened with a caring heart. Vulnerable didn't seem a strong enough way to describe the emotion that threatened to suffocate me.

"Last night, he took me to the pits." I turned to gauge his response.

"Mm-hmm... I've been there a time or two," he said, nodding.

"You?" I choked out a laugh. I hadn't expected that.

"I have anger issues. I need to vent sometimes, especially when a certain General showed up. It's easier to take my temper out on someone when it's looked at as a game."

"You've fought Rafe?" I blurted. Somehow that was more surprising than him admitting he had an issue with his temper. I'd never seen him angry.

"Rafe?" His brown eyes found mine, and he searched my gaze, noting my lack of a formal title. "Yes, I've fought him. Even won a time or two."

I smiled and returned my head to my knees.

"Well, he wanted to show me how he's changed the men in his Tennan. How they were misfits before he took them in and they have to fight differently. He tried to make the case that he can do the same for me. Now, I have less than six months to train... before going to the front.

"And that's not all. He would have us go behind enemy lines, not fight in a company. That's a death sentence. I want to learn to fight, but I don't want to be led to my death if I'm unprepared."

I looked up as a dragon roared and flew through the air, aiming for the Dragon Canyon.

"He also knows about my father," I added, closing my eyes and laying my head back down. To get proper advice, Willhelm needed to have all the details. "He served with him and knows how he died. He knows what he was like.

"I'm a terrible daughter. I haven't given my father anything more than a fleeting thought, lying to myself and saying that he was the reason I wanted to be at the front. I'm selfish, Willhelm. I want to make a name for myself. That's all. I want to make a name for myself at the front lines, where I don't belong.

"Mentioning my father made me wonder again. What was he like? How did he die? General Rafe is withholding that information, unless I join his Tennan."

Tears burned my eyes as I let everything I admitted linger between us. My shame weighed heavy on my shoulders. I hadn't thought of the people who made the ultimate sacrifice for me, or who cared for me.

"Anything else?"

I cringed, not wanting to voice the rest, but if he was to give me sound counsel, he needed to know.

"Aye." I swallowed past the lump in my throat and bit my cheek. "I, well, Rafe is—I mean, I feel—"

"Avyanna," he leaned forward, "has he done anything with you?"

I peeked at him from under my lashes. "Well, I mean we train—"

"Avyanna, you know what I mean." His tone wasn't urgent or angry, but firm.

"No. We've not done anything. I don't think he sees me like that." I rested my chin back on my knees. "But you could say I might have a crush on him. I would never act on it, I swear. But to be honest, for the first time I feel... like a woman around him."

Willhelm leaned back and sighed. "I was concerned he would use that to coerce you into joining. If you choose to bed someone, that is none of my business," he said roughly, then cleared his throat. "You would like my advice?"

"Please. If I join, am I signing my death warrant? I will learn more about my father, and I might have a fighting chance. On the other hand, it might be a mistake. I might end up dead, paying the ultimate price, and for what?"

He stretched his arm behind me again and looked into the distance thoughtfully. "I want you to have the best fighting chance. Any soldier, yourself included, needs all the training they can get to make it even a week on the front. You should know, even with the training we put you through, we don't expect soldiers to last long.

"It's a cruel twist of fate, but the ones who last on the front are the veterans. The fresh soldiers we send every year either have a talent for war, or they don't.

"You don't seem to have the knack for it." He brought his warm gaze back to me and gave me a soft look. "I hoped your tenacity would make up for it, but I watch you struggle. I hear tales of your training. And I know, Avyanna, you've signed your life away, and there's no going back. There's no easy way out.

"That being said, going to the front in six months would seem like suicide to me. I wouldn't recommend any soldier face that fate with only two years of training. That's reckless. However," he turned thoughtful again, "if anyone were to know how to fight, or what you're going to face there, General Rafe would be that man. If I could handpick someone to train you, I would choose him.

"To be honest, I have a hard time believing this—but I would venture to say if he thinks he can train you in six months, it would be worth far more than what your company can offer in two more years. Truly," he grimaced as he spoke, "I don't trust the man as far as I could throw him, morally. Yet, as a General, I trust him explicitly. If he's saying you'd have a better chance if he were to train you, I would let him."

"So, you're saying I should join his Tennan?" I murmured.

"I'm not saying you should. I'm simply telling you what I think. You have to make that choice. That being said, I do have some sagely counsel concerning your heart if you would have it." He winked and smiled down at me.

I nodded, urging him on. He'd given me sound counsel thus far.

"Concerning your... feelings toward Rafe. Do not act on them."

Embarrassment burned my cheeks in the chilly air.

He continued, "Speaking of Rafe as a man and not my superior, he's the worst kind. He will have one of two responses toward your advance. He will either take you and ruin you, or he will toss you aside and mock you for it."

He moved his hand as if he wanted to pat my shoulder, but rather pulled his arm in to clasp his hands on his knees. "Don't give that man your heart. He's not deserving of it."

My head ducked lower. I wasn't in love with the General. I had no intention of giving him my heart. It was nothing like that. I was simply attracted to him. Perhaps Willhelm read me wrong.

"It's not like that," I muttered into my trousers.

"Whatever it's like, that is advice from a man concerning a man." He cleared his throat and eyed me. "May we never speak of this again."

I smiled at his uncomfortable tone. "If you find it so distasteful, I'll permit us to never speak of such matters again."

He sighed in mock relief. "By all that is right in this world, I do find it distasteful!"

I laughed and peered up at the darkening sky, watching the few yearlings swarm in the distance above the Dragon Canyon.

And with that, my choice was made.

Chapter Thirty-Three

The next day, I woke with anxiety wrapping around me like a web. I barely ate any of the first meal, which I regretted during training, though it had no effect on my already poor ability. My day rushed by in a blur, and besides getting kicked off a rather cantankerous old mare, there was nothing out of the ordinary.

Commander Dewal didn't treat me any differently, and I wondered if this would be the last time he would command me with his company. Likely, he would be glad to be rid of the odd one, the female, in his group.

After the fifth chime, I hurried from the training field to where General Rafe always waited for our sparring matches. I brushed past soldiers heading to the dining hall or to wash up, ignoring them as butterflies flew tight circles in my belly.

I slowed when I saw him, surveying the soldiers like nothing was different. He leaned against the giant door frame, arms crossed over his chest and feet crossed at the ankles, observing the world. When he saw me, he didn't move, but his dark eye trailed me as I came to a halt before him. He arched a brow in question, offering a smirk.

I saluted and stood with my hands clasped behind my back. "I'm here to inform you I've decided to join your Tennan, General."

He blinked and stared at me for a moment, digesting that. Straightening, he approached me, pressing so close I had to crane my head to see his face.

"Who's to say I haven't filled your spot?" His voice was deep but amused.

"You just said it's my spot, sir. Being mine, you wouldn't let another fill it," I stated, giving him a matching smirk.

"Ha!" he barked before giving me a rare, full smile. "Go get your things."

I blinked in confusion. "Get my things, sir?"

His features melted into a bored look, as if I knew exactly what he wanted. He would not deign me with a repeated order.

"Eh, all of them? Enough for a night?" I asked for clarification.

"Only what you can carry. Anything you leave behind—is left behind," he said, lifting his chin and peering down at me. He was testing me, seeing if I would obey.

"Yes, sir."

I wouldn't give up just moments into my new role. I turned and marched to the bunkhouse. Inside my storage closet, glancing around, I realized I didn't have that many things. My eyes landed on the small chest tucked under the tiny table in the corner. It held my dresses and night shifts, my sandals, comb, and hairpins, along with my collection of ribbons for my braids.

Running my hand through my short hair, I looked down at my trousers. None of those things would be useful on the front. I bit my lip and snatched my extra uniform off the table. Opening the tunic, I shoved the trousers inside. Then I grabbed my spare socks, bindings for my chest, clean menstrual rags, sewing kit, and my mirror, placing them inside as well. After securing a few other necessities, I tied up the shirt and hefted it over my shoulder. My thin blanket lay folded on my cot. I wondered if I should take that, too. If wherever I stayed had a cot, it would probably have one I could use.

I gazed about the room once more. This might be the last time I was in the bunkhouse. I heard that once General Rafe took a soldier, they no longer slept or ate with the others. Where he hid his Tennan, I had no idea, but it was safe to assume I would stay with them.

As I left, the secretary noted my belongings and frowned. I shrugged in reply and headed out the doors. A few curious looks and murmurs were aimed at me as I pushed against the flow of soldiers and made my way to the training hall.

General Rafe talked to an older man in the building's shadow. I say older only because he had silver streaked through his long black hair. I tried to keep my jealousy in check—this man was allowed long hair when I was not.

As I approached, General Rafe turned to me.

"Vy, follow Xzanth," he said, jerking his head toward the stranger.

I pursed my lips, taking in his fur vest and brilliant eyes. They were the brightest brown I'd ever seen, almost amber. Their brilliance did not dull his boredom, however, as if he didn't want to play nursemaid.

General Rafe slipped into the crowd, and I watched him go. Normally, he would train with me until the sixth chime. I wondered where he was going.

"Come, little one."

I turned back to the man and frowned with disapproval. "My name is Avyanna."

He ignored my reply, walking through the training hall and out the opposite door. I rushed after him. His long strides were a struggle to keep up with. I kept my head down and focused on making good speed with my belongings, not paying attention to where we were headed.

When he slowed, I braved a glance up. My breath caught in my throat as I admired the scene before me—ruins of a small fortress. We must be far on the barracks' side for me not to have stumbled upon it before. Regardless, I recognized my abductor from the other night, Jamlin. He split wood while the giant, Korzak, stacked it in neat piles.

The fortress was in a small clearing, and beyond that, the King's Lake sparkled in the distance. Collins ran around the building and jumped, scaling the walls with ease. He threw himself to land on a balcony at least fifteen paces in the air. He spun to face Jamlin and shouted with his hands on his hips. Korzak bellowed a laugh and Jamlin shook his head.

Collins spotted us and shaded his eyes against the glare of the autumn sun. He called something to his friends, and they turned, finding us at the edge of the woods. Xzanth started for the men and I followed suit, keeping my chin up and focusing on my surroundings.

"Hail! It's the girl!" Jamlin called as we neared. He wore his uniform tunic loose and unlaced, revealing strong muscles beneath.

I glared and trailed behind Xzanth as he approached the fortress.

"Oi, are we keeping her, then?" Korzak asked, coming to walk beside me. My two steps matched his one, and he reached out to pat my head.

Xzanth slapped his hand away. "General said we are." His voice was raspy and deep.

"Oooh!" Korzak cooed, following us.

Collins slid down the wall, then flashed me a shy smile, and I gave him a nervous one in return. He was probably closer to my age than any of the men. At this moment, I felt all of my eighteen-winters, as a child being led along.

Xzanth pulled the door open, and it creaked in complaint. I blinked, surveying the space—cold and barren of decorations. The wood lining the walls had rotted in places, leaving a musty stench. It might have been a grand room once, but now, it was simply a large, makeshift bunkhouse. Piles of belongings laid by each cot, of which I counted eleven. There were two doors leading out of the room, beside the main doors we had walked into. A staircase led to a loft of sorts along the far wall.

"Pick an empty one," Xzanth muttered, heading to his bunk.

I hefted my makeshift bag and surveyed the cots. Eight were taken, though two were pushed together to make one long bed. I assumed that was Korzak's attempt to make a space large enough for his tall frame.

The remaining three were near a pair of windows. Though the windows were high on the wall, meaning snow or rain could easily blow in. It made sense why they were unclaimed. I chose the cot beneath the southernmost window. It was pushed against the wall. A simple sheet lined the thin mattress, but no blanket. I frowned and set my belongings down. The space to my left had books piled beside it, and I stared in wonder. Who could afford their own book? And who chose books to take to the front, of all things?

I shook myself and sat down to take out my things. Every occupied cot had a pack of some kind, and a weapon or two against them. I felt barren, as if I should have grabbed more. I didn't know what I would have packed, though. My dresses? I snickered to myself at that thought.

"Find something amusing?"

I turned to see one of the twins enter through one of the interior doors. I tilted my head and flashed him a wary smile. He didn't need to know my thoughts.

"Hail," I said simply.

"Hail. I'm Blain." He quirked up an eyebrow. "Avyanna, correct?"

"Aye." I squinted at him. How was I to tell the difference between him and his twin? Was there a way?

"It's a pleasure." He crouched down and eyed me as if sharing a secret. "If I were you, I'd choose another bunk."

I frowned, looking at the spaces beside me. There was the one with books, and to my other side was the interior door.

"Zephath has taken residence there," he said, indicating the cot with books. "Have you met him?"

At the shake of my head, he proceeded, "Probably a blessing for you, though that will soon be remedied. He never sleeps. He lights a candle and reads all night until the General orders him to put it out. Quite a prickly character, too."

"Thank you for the warning," I said.

I wasn't sure if I wanted to befriend this twin. Besides, anyone who read would at least have something in common with me.

Noting my lack of initiative to gather my things and follow his advice, he chuckled to himself. "It's been a pleasure, dear. Also, Dane extends his greetings," he said with an easy smile, then walked away.

Did he speak for his brother? What exactly did sharing a soul mean? Was that magic? I sighed and stood, following Blain as he exited the fortress and headed into the clearing.

I righted a log and sat on it, watching the men interact. Blain was off speaking with Collins. Xzanth disappeared. Jamlin still split logs, with Korzak stacking them. He looked at me as if I was a puppy he wanted to hold. From my seat, I could see the path through the woods that we had come in on, though the fortress blocked my view of the King's Lake.

"Did you eat last meal?" Jamlin called.

I shook my head.

"Pity. You'll have to deal with Xzanth's cooking. He leaves much to be desired."

"Does he cook for the Tennan?" I asked, standing to hand him a log.

"He does. Dane does the hunting, but he would rather eat meat raw than cook. Xzanth took up the cause. None of us know more about cooking than he does, so the job goes to him." He shrugged and sank the ax into the log with a dull thud.

Korzak grabbed it and gave me a giddy smile before trotting away.

"Don't mind him. He's harmless," Jamlin said.

I didn't feel a sense of malice from the giant. His childlikeness simply unnerved me. I eyed him, but nodded with understanding. Some girls were like that in the dorm. There had been a handful that never quite matured mentally. They were still humans, and still valuable to society, just different.

I worked with the men, finding tasks to do, since no one gave me specific orders. As time went on, I wondered if Niehm was looking for me. Was I allowed to go back to the main barracks? When would I see her or Willhelm again?

General Rafe appeared on the path in the woods, headed for us. I hesitated and lifted my chin, watching him come. When the men noticed him, they nodded their heads, but didn't salute. He motioned to me and walked to the pile of logs to have a seat. I perched on a log next to him and he regarded me with a narrow eye.

"We're doing weapons training tomorrow."

I mentally cringed, but kept my face straight and nodded.

"Any weapon you're more comfortable with?"

"No, though I have the most practice with sword and shield," I replied.

Jamlin scoffed, and I glared in his direction as he brought the ax down to split a log.

"What about distance weapons? You're better with a crossbow?"

"Aye, but I'm rarely allowed to use one." I glanced at Jamlin and he nodded with a smile to himself.

"Avyanna," General Rafe snarled. "I'm talking to you."

I met his glower. "Yes, sir."

"Do you ride well?"

"Well enough."

"Circles around a paddock," he muttered, leaning back. "Jam, take her to the foot course. Have her run it twice." He stood and rubbed the nape of his neck, looking me up and down. "I want you to tail Jam or Xzanth. Don't let me catch you with anyone else."

I rose and brushed out my trousers. "Am I allowed to return to the main barracks?"

"Not without good reason."

"What is a good reason, sir?" I asked, frowning.

He stepped close, glaring down at me. "Why do you want to go?" His tone was almost accusing.

"I have friends."

He scoffed at my reply. "The Sergeant? That redhead? No. You won't be visiting friends on the battlefield. Learn to focus, girl, or you'll be dead before you know it."

I ground my teeth but nodded, turning to Jamlin and letting my shoulder hit Rafe's chest. Jamlin glanced between us with a sly smile before motioning to me and starting off.

"Come along then, little one," he said.

I held in my growl as I followed. He led me to a thin opening in the woods, tucked in the shadow of the fortress. He stopped and pointed to a dark green strand of yarn tied high in the branches.

"You'll be following the path marked with that," he said, grinning at me and relaxing against a tree.

"A thread?" My mouth twisted into a grimace.

"This is the easiest course. You have a quarter of a chime to run it or you'll be cleaning the chamber pot."

"You're joking," I breathed in disbelief.

The 'trail' was less than a game trail, with thick underbrush that would hinder my progress.

"Not in the slightest." He positively beamed.

"Where does it end?" I asked, tucking up my sleeves. If I could get above the underbrush, it might not be so bad.

"Ah, I won't be telling you that, but I'll be waiting for you." He tilted his head, listening as the quarter chime rang. "That's your cue."

I let out a curse and shot up the tree, climbing as fast as I could. I reached the level with the thread and held my breath, searching for the next thread tied down the path. The 'trail' completely disappeared five paces into the woods. I groaned and crouched on a branch, searching.

I sat there for a ridiculous amount of time, listening to Jamlin chuckle at my struggles, before the wind picked up, jostling the small string tied to a bush ten paces in. I jumped and launched myself at the tree closest to it and scrambled for purchase. My feet found a branch, and I steadied myself, climbing to the far side of the tree.

I waited for the wind to blow, frantically searching for the blasted thread.

I would not be emptying their chamber pot.

I gagged and muttered curses, dumping the chamber pot into the hole I dug in the woods. Jamlin hummed nearby, ignoring me. He was my escort while I carried out my punishment.

Trying to keep my hands clean, I shook out the feces, turning my face away. It had taken me almost a half and a quarter chime to finish the first run. The second went faster, only taking me half a chime.

I tossed the chamber pot to the side, then grabbed the small shovel and threw dirt in the hole. The course was a good idea. It would teach us to watch for the smallest things in the woods, but this was an awful punishment. I hadn't even used the chamber pot I emptied.

We returned to the fortress after washing the pot in a small run-off leading to the King's Lake. It was nearing dark and the smell of cooked meat had my stomach growling in anticipation. After I returned the chamber pot to its place, I headed to the cookfire.

There was nothing on it.

The men lounged about. Jamlin retrieved a plate set aside for him and sat, shoveling in bites. I didn't see another plate saved.

"You're late."

I turned to General Rafe, who sat on a log near the fire, just as the rest of his Tennan.

"Begging your pardon, sir?" Surely, he was not saying I was late to eat.

"You want to eat? Work faster."

I blinked at his calm tone. I hadn't eaten since midday meal. Surely they didn't expect me to run on nothing?

"I saved her a–" Korzak held up a leg... of rabbit?

"No. She doesn't eat tonight," Rafe stated. "Perhaps your hunger will hurry you along next time."

Clenching my fists, I leveled my glare at him as I found an empty log to rest on. So be it. I would eat first meal.

"Now, Avyanna," Rafe started, "what do you know of the Shadows?"

I glanced around. It was unacceptable to talk about the Shadows after dark—a silly superstition, but one most men respected. Korzak stared at his food rather sadly, but I caught Blain's—or Dane's—eyes and they gave me a small shrug.

"A little," I answered. "What do you want to know?"

"Everything," he replied darkly.

I rested my elbows on my knees and settled in. This would be awhile.

Chapter Thirty-Four

"The Masters told us very little. I learned more from my wanderings in the Records Room. I was told we would learn more when we were older—if we chose an occupation that warranted it."

Blain snorted, but I ignored him and pressed on.

"Regent came to know the Shadow Men years ago when they raided our villages to the west. Dragon Riders were ordered to dispatch them, but they proved to be a more worthy adversary.

"They pushed back against the dragons and seized our territory beyond the Sky Trees. The King launched a campaign against them, though it's said that we only have enough strength to hold them back, not advance on them."

"Vy," General Rafe interrupted, "I'm not here for a history lesson. What do you know of them?"

"Well... not much. Even the Records Room has very little on them," I started. "Some claim they can control men. They hunt us for our dragons, not for our land or resources. They attack our villages to draw out the Dragon Riders, not because they want anything in the villages themselves."

"And what do you know of how they attack?"

"They kill our men. They leave most of our women alive, though." I paused, rubbing at the nape of my neck, uncomfortable with the topic. "The refugee women that come tell stories of the Shadows and their... affinity toward our women.

"I've heard their seed cannot take with us—no children are born of their raids, which implies they are a separate species. Some say they're only skeletons, mismatched bones from other creatures. But I've also heard they're just men, so I'm uncertain. They are ruthless, murderous beings that want to steal dragon eggs.

"They come from the southwest, where the continent divides. I've been told they have magic and can use it without dragons. Our battleground used to only be the Sky Trees. But with their raids on the south, it's rumored that they've taken to the water and we're not safe on our shores. That's all I know," I said, trailing off. I wasn't anticipating this line of questioning and didn't quite know what answers he expected.

He heaved a heavy sigh and leaned back, rubbing underneath the cloth covering his eye. "This will take a while," he groaned.

"Have Zephath teach her," Korzak offered.

Collins choked on a laugh, blushing when I looked at him.

"I will teach her," General Rafe stated. "First, they're not skeletons. They're flesh and blood like you and me. You can gut them just the same. However, the way they fight is entirely different from us. You'll rarely find a blade on any of them, and if you do, you've lucked out and found a weak one."

I squinted in skepticism. If they didn't use weapons, then how did they fight?

"They use magic. They control people, animals—the more intelligent the prey, the bigger the trophy." He leaned forward and leveled a steady gaze at me. "That's why they wear the bones of their kills. It's a trophy to them. Some of the most dangerous carry human bones, which means their magic was strong enough to control a human. If you ever see one that wears a suit of bones that looks like a dragon, you're as good as dead."

"They wear dragon bones? Some have controlled a dragon?" I interrupted. I had never heard of such a thing. The idea that they could take freedom from such large and powerful beasts was horrifying.

"Aye. The ones with that level of power are known as Shamans. They can control a dragon, with or without its Rider. After the kill, they make a suit of bones, mimicking the dragon's shape, and wear it as bragging rights—and a warning."

"That's why it's so hard to fight them. They can control our men. No matter how many we throw at the front, they turn them on one another. That's also the reason that if you make it through a week of fighting, you can usually make it longer."

He paused, and I took the advantage to question him. "How do they control us? Is it just their magic? Is there no way to avoid it?"

"Little one," Jamlin chuckled. "She's like a child. Full of questions."

General Rafe turned a hard eye on him before returning his focus on me. "Their eyes."

My gaze immediately went to his concealed eye. He waited, judging me, daring me to say something. I frowned and studied his face. He waited in anticipation for my reaction. His gaze dipped down to my mouth, a silent reminder of his promise if I revealed his secret. Did he think I would mention it in front of his Tennan? Did he think so little of my promise to him?

"Avoid their gaze. Once you look into their eyes, they can steal your soul. Your eyes are the key, and if you meet their gaze, they unlock that door and control you however they wish. You'll be training with the men to fight without eye contact."

I ground my teeth together. That was what we were taught as soldiers, to watch the eyes. A person's gaze could hint as to how they would attack. Watching their eyes helped anticipate their movements. Not utilizing that ability would put me at a disadvantage.

"That being said, there are many who could control you, though most simply control beasts. Creatures roam the battlefield, preying on our men. They aren't like the animals you know here. They are creatures of nightmares, pieced together.

"There's one known to take to the battlefield that is half-sea monster, half-wolf. Another I killed was half-wild cat, half-horse. They stitch them together and keep them alive with their magic. We call them the Hunters, and you'll find yourself fighting them far more often than the Shadows. You need to remember you're always after the Shadow behind the Hunter. If you only slay the Hunter, another will rise in its place. Slay the Shadow, and its Hunters will die."

"How do you find the Shadow?" I asked.

"That's the hard part. The army is far too busy fighting Hunters and our own turned-soldiers to focus on the real threat. The Shadow Men hide deep in the Sky Trees, controlling their Hunters from the furthest distance possible.

"They know their weaknesses and strengths and fight accordingly. They're not fools, and you'll never have the upper hand with them. Never forget that. You're always going to be weaker than they are. They've been at this far longer than you've been alive. They know their trade." He sat back and rolled his shoulders to stretch his neck. His dark eye glittered as he watched me take this in.

"Why are they after dragons?" I asked.

"Dragon parts are important to their magic. The only sure way to draw them out is when they slay a dragon. Then they fight and squabble like vultures over carrion. They'll carry everything away in pieces if left to it. It's possible dragons have a magic they do not, or perhaps they bolster their own magic. It's not clear, and we cannot sacrifice a dragon to find out."

I thought about that. Was that really the only reason they fought us? They wanted our dragons? They were a weapon the King would not give up willingly. The dragons and their Riders helped us maintain peace throughout our lands. They were the biggest and most effective weapon for deterring invaders.

"Let's also clear up this 'their seed doesn't take' nonsense," Rafe added. "It would take—were it allowed."

My gaze sharpened on him, and Xzanth stood abruptly, stalking off into the darkness. I watched him go before returning my shocked stare to General Rafe.

"There are no records of children born out of their raids," I stated. It was true. I had never stumbled upon a record of a half-Shadow child.

"Having no records doesn't mean it hasn't happened. Women are forced to drink the purging tea after a raid. Don't think they started that to err on the side of caution."

My mouth dropped in horror. I lived in a women's dorm. How could I not hear of this? We always made a special tea for women who came after a raid, but it was a blend to calm and relax them. One that was made to ease their fears and help them settle into a normal life. Not a purging tea. Not a tea that forced their bodies to begin its moon cycle, emptying their womb.

My eyebrows met in a fierce frown. "How would you know this, sir?" I added the formality in anger.

"You are a soldier. I am a soldier. When the King orders us to see something through, we do." He leaned forward as I jumped to my feet, and he snatched my wrist in a painful hold. "You don't get to ask questions or debate morality as a soldier. Remember that, Vy."

So that was why he shared this with me. He wanted me to acknowledge that if he told me to do something, and I doubted it was the right thing to do, I would still be required to carry it out.

"Yes, sir," I hissed, pulling my hand away.

He let go, watching me as I stood there trembling in rage. How many children? How many babes had been sacrificed due to that method? Babes were innocent. It was not their fault that such a horror had taken place. What if a mother wanted to keep the babe? That choice should be left to her, and her alone. The idea of forcing women to drink the tea, without their consent, had my blood boiling. Was General Rafe hinting that he forced women to drink it? Perhaps he had.

At that moment, I no longer knew if I trusted him.

A wicked smile appeared on his face. I whirled and headed toward the fortress' large wooden doors, hidden in the dark of night. With the light of the fire behind me, it was difficult to see anything. I fumbled for the handle and pulled the door open.

A young man sat on the cot next to mine, reading a book by candlelight. I took a calming breath as he noticed me. All I could tell from my distance is that he had sand-colored hair. His focus returned to the pages, dismissing me.

Perhaps I'd get along with this one. He read books and wanted to ignore people. We at least had that in common.

Stepping in, I pulled the door shut behind me. At my bunk, I shuffled my things about. I realized I hadn't washed my uniform, even if there was a place. I also couldn't sleep in only my tunic while sharing a room with men.

I snuck a glance at the man next to my cot. He appeared young—perhaps close to my age, if not a few winters older. His high cheekbones, straight nose, and stiff posture made him a vision of... grace. He didn't quite fit in with the normal recruit kind. There was an air about him, as if he thought himself too good for it. Though how he managed to convey that while simply reading a book, I had no idea.

"Share your flame?" I asked, holding my small candle.

He eyed me with disgust, but shrugged. I lit the wick and grabbed my clean uniform, heading to the storage room to change. This would be a difficult situation with no door or walls to hide me from the others. Though, to be fair, I wouldn't have that luxury on the battlefield either.

I dressed and returned to my cot. With no blanket, I'd have to use my soiled tunic from today to ward off the chill.

"My name is Avyanna," I offered, blowing out my candle.

He ignored me.

I bit my cheek. Perhaps he was shy. "Zephath, correct? Blain mentioned that was your bunk." I didn't need conversation, just a simple 'hail' would be pleasant enough after the horrors of today.

"Then I'm sure he also informed you I'll not be needing your services." His words were crisp and held the sharp tone of nobility.

"Begging your pardon?"

My services? As a fellow soldier? Was he a lone wolf, preferring to fight alone? He looked up at me, and my lips fell into a frown at the malice in his eyes.

"Your whoring."

I recoiled as if he slapped me, going from shock to anger. I cleared the bed and drew my push dagger, pouncing on him. He fell back, letting his book fall to the floor, and glared up at me as I straddled him, giving me a look as if I inconvenienced him.

"I'm not a whore, you steaming pile of dragon dung," I snarled, pressing my blade to his throat.

Too many soldiers called me that, both to my face and behind my back. Too many comments were made in passing. I let them get away with it. But if I was to be an equal in this Tennan, I would have to stand my ground. I couldn't let them push me around.

"It looks like you're well-versed in the position," he sighed, waving a hand at my seat on his hips.

I growled and pressed the dagger deeper into his skin, looking up as the door swung open. General Rafe halted in the doorway, watching us. He surveyed the scene, judged it, then proceeded to ignore us, walking across the room to the stairwell.

"Call me that again, and it won't be your head I'll be removing," I hissed, sliding off him.

So much for trying to befriend him.

I returned to my cot and flopped down, pulling my soiled tunic over my chest. It would be a miserably bleak night, not only because the temperature was dropping, but because I felt even more alone than I had before.

Something chased me—something I couldn't see. Cold and numb, I stumbled, tearing through the woods. Underbrush ripped at my skin, trying to catch me, yank me down.

I shot into a clearing, gasping for breath. An eerie cry pierced the air. As I dared a glance back to glimpse what hunted me, a cold shadow blocked the sun, covering me in darkness. I looked up in horror. A dragon swooped into the clearing, claws extended. Terror squeezed my throat as my feet skidded to a stop. I backed away, petrified, as it opened its great maw.

'*Hold her! Thrice-curse it!*'

Branches and roots grew from the trees. Dirt, rocks, and leaves scattered as they snatched my arms, holding me fast. I tried to scream as footsteps pounded toward me from behind and I thrashed against the hold.

The dragon shrieked as its great wings pumped hard, throwing itself back into the sky. Breathy moans in place of screams wrenched from my throat as I jerked my right arm free and clawed at my left. Why couldn't I scream?! I sank my nails into the branch, shredding the bark. Warm sap spilled over my arm.

'*Let her go!*'

The branches fell away, and I charged further into the clearing. I would rather face an irate dragon than some monster I couldn't see. I looked up at the sky, not seeing the creature, and took off across the expanse.

A vine seized my ankle, and I stumbled. I kicked at it, trying to free myself. It held fast. I froze, looking up as a cold shadow enveloped me again. The dragon swooped down, its golden eyes burning like an all-consuming fire. It opened its maw, revealing rows of sharp teeth perfect for cleaving skin from bone. Its flammable oils shot out at me, and I screamed, dreading the flames to come.

I choked against the cold liquid, threatening to drown me. Jerking up, I coughed and tried to catch my breath as I scanned the room.

General Rafe stood beside me with a dripping bucket. Jamlin was at his side, watching me with curious eyes. He held his arm, which dripped blood. Korzak towered behind them, staring at me with pure horror in his wide, childlike eyes. And Collins lingered at the foot of my cot, watching me warily.

They were all in a state of undress—I'd woken them.

"You with us?"

I looked back at General Rafe. His voice was rough and groggy. But his eye was sharp, aware, and skeptical.

He wore nothing, save his under-breeches.

I peered down at my sopping wet clothes. Shame burned my cheeks. "Yes, sir," I whispered.

The men heaved a collective sigh of relief, and General Rafe threw the bucket. My eyes followed it as it clanged against the wood floor.

"Korzak, get her a spare blanket. Collins, lend her a clean uniform. Jam, take care of that arm." He rattled off orders, and the men moved to obey.

I looked to where Zephath laid on his side, under a fur-lined blanket, anger furrowing his brow. I pulled my knees up to my chest and held myself, shivering in my wet clothes.

"Avyanna–"

I swallowed past the lump in my throat and turned to General Rafe, carefully keeping my eyes above his neck.

"Will this be a common occurrence?" he asked. His tone carried a sense of understanding, but also dread.

"No, sir," I whispered.

He rubbed at his wounded eye. "Thank the dragons," he muttered.

"I—I apologize. I didn't mean–"

"Stop." His gruff order caused me to snap my mouth shut. He sighed and sat on the dry edge of my cot, watching as the men rummaged through their things by the meager light of a single candle. "The one place we have no dominion over is our dreams. Your night terror unnerved us—not because of your dream, but your struggles."

I held myself tighter and stared at my cot. My mind was fuzzy, and I didn't trust my eyes not to wander.

"Do you remember in my quarters, when I woke you the same way?" he asked wearily.

"Yes, sir."

"I was not angry because of your terror. I was angry because of what it reminded me of." He paused until my gaze lifted to his. "I've heard too many women scream to have slept well after I woke you."

"I'm sorry," I breathed.

Pain and unspoken horrors riddled his features. Sometimes, I forgot the things he must have seen at the front, the things he must have witnessed. The things he must have done.

"The others are disturbed for their own reasons. Korzak and Collins, because they've never witnessed a true night terror. The rest, because it triggered a memory." He blinked and became the teasing man he rarely let me see. "Or another reaction they'd rather hide."

"Begging your pardon?" I asked, confused, as Korzak approached with a thick blanket.

"Having a woman moaning, writhing on a bed in a room full of men–"

He trailed off with a wicked gleam in his eye and I had the strong urge to kick him off the bed.

"Perhaps we are simply terrified of her attacks." Jamlin called from his cot as he wound a bandage around his arm.

"She fights like a kitten," Korzak rumbled, handing me the blanket.

I couldn't hold back my small smile. "A kitten?" I choked out.

"One with the sharpest claws I've ever seen!" Collins said, handing me a spare tunic and pair of trousers.

Being the closest to my size, his uniform was the only one I'd fit into. I took the items with gratitude warming my heart. Perhaps General Rafe's Tennan wasn't so bad.

"Up. Change," Rafe said as he stood and stretched. "We have an early morning. Best try to get some sleep."

Chapter Thirty-Five

The distant ring of the fifth chime echoed through the fortress. It roused me from my sleep, but I shivered in my damp cot till the sixth chime when the others started rising. They seemed to have a routine down. They relieved themselves, shaved by candlelight as the sun rose, then dressed.

When I told Jamlin I wanted to wash my uniform, he grunted in reply, then moved his shaving supplies to the courtyard. He stayed within sight while I pulled cold water from the well to fill the small washbasin.

We worked in silence, and I hurried to lay my uniform out to dry. Jamlin finished shaving the sides of his head and tied his braids together with a leather thong.

"You come from the south?" I asked, concealing my under-breeches beneath my drying tunic. The Tennan didn't need to see my undergarments.

"Aye, from Jasiri. A village on the northern edge of the Sands," he replied, gathering his things.

"Do all men there wear their hair the same? I've never seen braids like that." I walked up to him and studied his intricate braids.

"Some. Our hair is different from yours. We either shave it or plait it to keep it out of our way," he said, holding up a single braid.

I reached out and touched the thick, coarse hair. "It is different," I agreed.

"Let me braid yours tonight," he offered, walking with me back into the fortress.

I pulled at the small braid at the nape of my neck. "You mean this?"

"No, I can braid the top."

"It's too short." I objected.

"Not the way we do it."

If he could find a way to braid the top, where my hair was starting to flop in my eyes, I would gladly take him up on his offer. "Perhaps. I would like to see it."

I tucked the tunic into my borrowed trousers, tightening my belt. Collins' uniform was too big, and trousers too long. I sat on the cot to roll the hem, looking up as General Rafe descended the stairs.

"Jamlin, fetch these from Elon," he said, handing him a small parchment. "Take Zephath with you."

"Yes, sir."

"Xzanth, get the bows and head to the range. Korzak, you and Collins run the foot course. Blain, work on the mounted course. You're getting sloppy with your seat."

I watched as General Rafe tossed out orders like... well, like it was his job. When his eye settled on me, I snapped to rigid attention and saluted.

Zephath snickered at my side before heading toward Jamlin.

"Jam, have Zeph carry the weapons back."

The snickering stopped, but I only had eyes for my General. I waited for orders. His stare lingered, scrutinizing me. My body itched to move, to squirm under his assessment, but I forced myself to stay still.

"Come."

My shoulders relaxed at his command, and I fell into step behind him. We walked through the courtyard, then the clearing toward the King's Lake. Only a few trees obscured the view. The clearing was hemmed in on all sides by woodland.

I waited till we were out of earshot before braving my question. "Where do you wash, sir?" I asked hesitantly, fidgeting with my belt. Surely we were close enough to the secluded spring that I could still make use of it.

"Wanting to join me?"

I turned to see a smirk on his face and blushed. "No, I–"

"The men wash in the lake. I, however, bathe the same place you do. With the exception of certain times of the month."

My blush heated, and I focused on the ground as we walked.

"Speaking of which, I'll send Zephath for tinge berry tea."

"Tinge berry?" I asked. I hadn't heard of it, though I didn't know my teas and herbs as well as he did.

"Aye. It's frowned upon by most women."

He stopped, and I looked up at him in question.

"Avyanna. You're a woman. Accept that. Accept your limitations, and move on. For the love of the sun, don't be ashamed of your womanhood."

I bit my tongue. He spoke of womanhood with such detachment, as if it didn't phase him in the least.

"Tinge berry tea will prevent your moon cycle."

I dipped my head, trying to hide my burning cheeks. I did not want to have this conversation.

"Eyes up, girl."

I looked up, meeting his sober gaze.

He continued, "It will serve two purposes. First, it's the best option on the front. Dealing with a moon cycle in a sanitary way will be near impossible. Second, if you choose a bed mate, it will prevent a child."

"I'm not choosing a bed mate!" I burst out.

I felt so vulnerable, so young and naïve with this man. Times like this, he acted as though he was much older and more wizened than I. Which I was sure he was. He was older than me and more worldly, but I didn't notice it half of the time. I simply saw him as a man.

"Of course." He arched a brow, clearly expecting a reaction from me. "Should you, I will know of it."

I bristled. "If I do, that would be my business!" I fired back. This was absolutely a conversation that I did not want to have, especially with him, but I had to defend my right as a woman.

"Wrong." He moved forward to crowd me. "You're my soldier, now exclusively in my Tennan. Who you bed is my business."

I glared and stepped forward, bumping my chest against his tunic. "How would it be your business, sir?"

"First, it would be on my time. Unless you choose to bed someone once on the Solstice before we head to the front. Second, if you bed someone from my Tennan, it would disrupt the balance. I can't have one of my men looking over their shoulder trying to protect a pretty face."

He grabbed hold of my chin, forcing me to keep his gaze. "You are mine. Remember that."

We met up with Xzanth near the King's Lake, on a long stretch of cleared land—at least two hundred paces long. Bags of sand lined the length of it.

An archery range.

Excitement flitted through me. Archery was the one thing I was somewhat skilled at. Even so, my elation warred with dread as I eyed the short bow Xzanth held. It was a powerful one. I could manage two, maybe three draws before my shots would get sloppy.

"Short bow," Rafe said, taking a seat on one of the feed sacks that littered the beginning of the course.

Xzanth handed me the weapon, and I tested its weight. It was light and would shoot light arrows. I wouldn't get much distance, but I'd have more accuracy with it. I eyed the crossbow with envy.

"Short bow first, Vy."

I sighed and took an arrow from Xzanth, nocking it but waiting to draw, and looked at Rafe.

"Second target. Thirty paces out," he said.

I squinted against the rising sun and focused on the target. It had the rough shape of a man drawn with charcoal.

"Head or body?" I asked, drawing the bow in one smooth motion.

"Body. Never aim for the head of a Shadow."

Right. Lowers the chance of catching their magicked gaze. I exhaled and let the arrow fly, watching it as it struck the left-center of the target's chest.

"Again."

I took another arrow, aimed, and loosed. It found its place in the center of the chest. General Rafe had me fire three more arrows. All hit the chest of the target, but grew less consistent with each shot.

"Enough. Xzanth, crossbow."

I held in my excitement as I traded bows. He handed it to me with care, and I admired the craftsmanship. It had a winch-assist draw, which meant even though it was a stronger bow, I could still draw it, being as weak as I was. I hefted it and loaded a bolt that Xzanth provided.

"Fourth target, sixty paces out."

After a deep breath, I lifted the heavy crossbow. I was jittery with excitement to show them what I could do with the right tool. Pressing the trigger, I reached for another bolt without question. One was placed in my hand and I drew and took aim. Rafe shaded his eyes against the sun, peering at where I hit the fourth target.

"Sixth target. Some ninety paces back," I called, then loosed the bolt.

There was a moment of silence as I rested the crossbow against my thigh.

"Zan?" Rafe questioned.

"Center chest," Xzanth replied without hesitation.

I beamed, looking from Rafe to Xzanth. Surely that proved my worth.

"Tenth," General Rafe called, standing. "Shoot the target, Vy, not me." He smirked before walking down the range toward the targets.

I reached for the bolt Xzanth held out. The tenth was nearly a hundred and fifty paces out. I could barely see that far, let alone make a good shot. I winched the drawstring back and nocked the bolt. Taking a deep breath, I hefted it to aim.

"Lie on the ground."

The crossbow dipped toward the ground as I looked at Xzanth, taken aback by the fact that the quiet man spoke to me.

"On the ground?" I asked, dropping into a crouch.

"On your belly. Like this," he said in his dry, raspy voice. He lay flat on the earth, hands propped up, holding an imaginary crossbow to his face.

I mimicked the position, squirming against a stone digging into my hip.

"Be still."

I sighed and tried to ignore the discomfort. Holding the crossbow up, I lined up the sights, taking care to make sure they were aligned perfectly.

"Aim high. As if he were raising his hands to the sky and you were shooting his palms instead."

I took a deep breath and held it, trying to still the trembling of my grip. My hands were far steadier when braced against the earth, but I wanted to impress Rafe. I wanted to prove my value to his Tennan.

"Breathe."

I let out a breath and pulled the trigger, letting the bolt fly. I held the crossbow steady, hoping it flew straight and true.

Xzanth made an approving sound, and I peered over at him. He gave me a reluctant nod and pushed himself to his feet. I looked one last time at the target. The bolts were smaller than arrows and had thin wooden fletching, making them harder to see.

I stood and waited while General Rafe studied and walked around all the targets I hit. He looked at the front and back. I assumed he was checking if they went through or how deep they were. After examining them, he removed each one, then headed our way. He had removed the bolt from the furthest target, so I knew I at least hit it.

"Xzanth, have her practice till the eleventh chime," he said, handing the bolts to me.

My smile fell from my face as I took them. I didn't expect praise, but the soldiers I trained with before never could have made those shots. I expected him to express some form of approval.

He turned his back on us and stalked off toward the fortress. I gripped the bolts tight and looked to Xzanth.

"Your stance is horrible," he said dryly.

I spent the next few chimes practicing with Xzanth. I was a decent shot, even at far distances, unless distracted. The first time he tickled my ear with a blade of grass while I was aiming, I nearly bit his hand off.

He helped me practice different stances and techniques to steady my hands and keep my aim more consistent. He taught me that I would rarely ever have a clean shot—something else would always vie for my attention.

He stood beside the targets and waved a branch in front of them, forcing me to time my shots. He had me practice in different positions, even told me to climb a tree at one point. Most of the time, my aim rang true, except when I was distracted. He made me run to get my bolts, not allowing me to walk. He claimed I needed the exercise and I wouldn't be out for a stroll when I retrieved my bolts on the battlefield.

We practiced until we heard the eleventh chime in the distance and I helped Xzanth carry the bows. As we walked back, the only sound was the dry grass and twigs crunching beneath our feet.

"Xzanth, how did you get so good with a bow?" I asked.

"I was a hunter."

"A game hunter? For furs?" Wild furs were a luxury item. It was a hard job, one that required patience and perseverance, but it paid well.

"Aye."

"Why did you join the ranks? That's a fair occupation." Why would someone give up a good life to fight in the most dangerous place?

After a long pause, he responded. "You remind me of my daughters," he rasped.

I tilted my head and studied him. His solemn attitude slipped. In its place, sorrow flooded his face. He took a deep breath and tucked it away, putting on his sober mask.

He lost them.

It was easy to tell. Most of the soldiers who lost loved ones had it written on their faces. Their haunted expressions screamed sorrowful rage at the losses they suffered. Xzanth hid it well, especially by being quiet, but it was there.

"I'm sorry," I murmured, focusing on my feet.

Silence fell like a blanket over us as we walked to the fortress.

"Hail!" Jamlin beckoned as we made our way into the courtyard.

Hunger ached in my belly as I eyed the bread and cheese he waved above his head.

"Ha! Come, Avyanna!" he roared, motioning me to join him in a small cleared area of the ruined courtyard.

Xzanth nodded his approval, and I handed him the short bow and arrows. Heading over to Jamlin, I saw General Rafe and Blain sitting on the ruins of a gate, eating bread and cheese.

"Hail," I greeted, coming to stand in front of Jamlin.

"Let's see how bad you are then, little one." He teased, holding the food above his head. "If you can get it, you can have it."

I narrowed my eyes. He wanted to play games? I could play games.

I was starving.

"Jamlin?" I said, dropping my voice.

Rafe snorted, already reading my tactic. A strategy I would never use on him again... for personal reasons.

"Call me Jam, everyone else does."

"Jam–" I brought my palms up to rest on his abs through his tunic.

His eyes narrowed, a playful grin growing on his face. "Now, now. Don't do anything improper in front of the General," he teased.

"I'm so hungry," I whined, sliding my hands up his chest. The man was a wall of muscle. I felt the tips of my ears burn in acknowledgment, but kept my eyes on the prize.

His smile didn't falter, but I noted the twitch in his jaw. Moving faster than a cat, I snapped my knee up and grabbed for his arm. His thighs slapped together a moment too late, and my strike barely landed.

It wasn't enough to drop him, but it was enough to lower his arm within my reach. I hooked my arm around his and stretched out, reaching for his wrist. He straightened, which freed my knee, and I hung from his arm in the air.

"Oi, little one." He winced, holding his crotch.

I intended to pull his wrist behind him but misjudged his strength. He held my weight in the air as if it was nothing. General Rafe chuckled in amusement. I growled and swung my legs up around Jam's shoulder, wrapped around his arm as if it were a branch.

I tried to pry the food from his hand, but he held it fast.

"I swear, you are not the woman I thought you were, Avyanna," Jam said, amusement coloring his tone.

I glared at his bandage, a reminder of the damage I'd done in my fit of a night terror. I was hungry. It had been an entire day since I last ate. I gripped the food around his hand and bit down. I bit hard. Cursing, Jamlin released his hold on me and my food, sending me tumbling to the ground with it.

"By all that is good and right in this world! You fight like a girl!" He cursed, rubbing at his arm.

I hadn't broken his skin, but deep indentations marred his flesh.

"She has a wicked bite," Rafe said with a deep laugh that spread goose flesh over my arms.

"You knew?" Jamlin demanded.

"She's bitten me more than once."

I crossed my legs, content to eat my bread and cheese on the ground, watching the exchange.

"Sounds like a story I'd like to hear," Blain commented from his seat.

Rafe grunted without reply, coming to stand in front of me. He offered me a hand, and I took it, allowing him to help me up. I ate as quickly as I could and eyed the weapons lined against the wall of the fortress.

"Pick one," he said, motioning to them.

I stuffed the last bit of bread in my mouth and walked over to the array. Short swords, shields, a staff, a spear, a mace, hatchets... all the weapons presented had a similar theme. They were small, aside from the spear and staff. The only training I had with a spear, however, was in formations with other soldiers. Also, how was a staff a weapon? It was something shepherds used.

I picked up a shortsword and shield. These were what I was most comfortable with, especially if not fighting in a group. Turning around, I tested the weight of the blade.

My mouth fell ajar when I lifted my eyes to Rafe. He held two arming swords. They had to have been custom smithed for him—they fit him well. Naked steel winked at me and black leather wrapped the hilts. Simple, yet menacing.

"I... er–" I stammered.

He brandished the blades as if they were extensions of his long, muscular arms. He towered above me, a mountain of thick muscle. His eye was alight, eager for a fight.

"You've smitten her, now," Blain teased.

"Give me your all," Rafe ordered.

His gaze might have been alight with joy, but his tone carried an order. If I didn't fight him with everything I had, he would humiliate me. Though part of me acknowledged that would happen, regardless. I looked down at the shortsword. It had a standard edge, blunt, but enough to draw blood.

I glanced at his blades and had to swallow past the lump in my throat. They were no mere practice swords. They were wicked sharp. One wrong move and he'd filet me like a fish.

Deep down, I knew Rafe would never hurt me, but I couldn't help fearing that steel.

"Now, Vy."

I brought my sword and shield into position and frowned. I was doomed.

"Don't look me in the eye. You'll pay for that."

I dropped my gaze to his thick neck and attacked. It was feeble, but with only a year and a half of training, it was the best I could do.

Blocking a blow, I stumbled, yelping against the force of it. I peeked around my shield to glance up at him, and he smacked the flat side of his sword against my ribs.

"Don't look me in the eye!" he snarled.

I whined from the sharp ache.

So that's how I would pay for it.

Within a few moments, and two smacks of his blade to my ribs, he backed off and lowered his swords.

"Enough," he groaned. He didn't bother to hide his disappointment.

"Two blades, Rafe," Jam called. "Let her use her speed."

"I'm not that fast." I quipped.

It was true. I hadn't mastered the art of parrying, and was much better at blocking with a shield.

"Go," Rafe ordered, jerking his head to the stack of weapons.

I held in my groan and dropped the shield against the wall, then picked up the second shortsword. Dread filled me as I returned to Rafe.

"Look at me like that, and you'll regret it," he said, glaring.

I wiped the frown off my face and pasted a toothy smile in its place.

Jamlin burst out laughing and I charged Rafe. Within seconds, he tore a sword out of my hand and had his hilt pressed against my throat. Pushing me away, he cursed.

"I didn't think she was this bad," Blain mused.

I ground my teeth together and kept my gaze on Rafe.

"Staff," he barked.

"You'll just cut it—"

"Staff! Now."

He was irritated.

His eye flashed in anger, and I wondered if he was angry at me or himself. He knew I failed at training. Perhaps I was worse than he anticipated. Or was he angry at himself because he took on a soldier who was terrible at fighting, with only six months before we went to the front lines?

I growled and stalked back to the wall, resisting the urge to throw the shortswords on the ground like a child, and picked up the staff. I had never used one. It was large and unwieldy, towering above me nearly two paces. It was light, but sturdy.

I eyed Rafe's swords. Not as strong as those, though.

"Now," he ordered, stepping into position.

I cringed and held the staff as comfortably as I could. No one showed me how to hold such a thing. I took a deep breath and relaxed. I could figure this out. If he wanted me to attack using a weapon I never tried, he had enough faith in me that I could do it. I gripped the staff and stepped up to him.

The first thing I noticed was that I didn't have to get as close to him to strike. I swung, which he parried easily, but it still kept him at a safe distance.

The wood was strong in my hands, and as he parried, there was a distinct difference in the blow's strength. It was heavier and more powerful than my strikes with a short sword. The momentum I built made up for my lack of strength.

Rafe let me attack again. He parried, then slipped in his own attack. He held back, but even so, he moved fast. I jerked the staff to block and was surprised at how easy it was.

I grinned, keeping my eyes from his, feeling my confidence build. I swung at his right shoulder, then up at his left flank as he spun. He blocked both with ease, but I moved quickly, pulling the staff back and thrusting it at his chest. He was forced to dance back, unable to bring his swords up in time.

He lowered his weapons and eyed me with approval. "Called it," he said, watching me with a small smile.

"Thrice-curse it. Dual wielding is still a good option," Jamlin grumbled from his seat.

"Is this the weapon I'll train with?" I asked, looking between the men.

"Train with, yes. Use—no," Jamlin answered, standing and tossing a coin to Rafe.

He clutched both swords in one hand and snatched the coin out of the air. "You'll get a spear when you learn enough of a staff that you won't skewer yourself." General Rafe clarified.

I studied the weapon in my hand. They didn't train the soldiers with staffs, or even to use spears in solo combat. Running my hands up and down the smooth wood, I felt more confident in that small test fight than I had in all my weapons' training. The weapon one used really made a difference.

Rafe stepped into position, rolling his shoulders.

"Again."

Chapter Thirty-Six

I clenched my legs around the gelding, urging him faster through the woods. He responded and picked up speed, hooves pounding over vegetation. I leaned low over his neck as he left the ground, leaping over the creek cutting through the course. I yanked on the right rein, dodging a tree and launching him through a thicket. He obeyed and plunged through, racing as sweat lathered his chest and shoulders. I kneaded his neck, urging him faster as he pushed through the thick undergrowth.

A felled tree blocked our path, and I didn't think. I squeezed my legs tighter. The gelding didn't falter. He breathed hard but kept going, launching us over the tree. My teeth clacked as we landed, and he stumbled one step before he righted himself and raced into the clearing.

My breaths came as fast as his, feeling like I had run the race with him. I eased him into a walk and patted his lathered neck. He snorted in response and pricked his ears forward, ready for another run.

"Easy," I murmured.

I pulled him to a stop in front of Xzanth, and he held the reins as I dismounted.

"Better," he called.

"He's a good horse. Fast," I replied, shaking out my legs.

The mounted course wasn't easy. General Rafe changed it constantly, making alterations before we got too familiar with it.

I settled into a routine within the first week at the fortress. Everyone else had their own routine as well, aside from Xzanth and Jamlin. Their job was to monitor my training when Rafe wasn't around.

Every morning at first light, Xzanth and I headed to the archery range and spent the next few chimes practicing. Some days, we focused on distance shooting. Others, he had me walk or run while shooting. Only once had he brought a horse, and had me ride while shooting. After a series of terrible shots, getting bucked, and nearly having a hoof to the head, he resigned to wait before training me in mounted archery.

Afterwards, we returned to the fortress where Rafe would be waiting. Jamlin always tried to buy me a moment to shove a piece of bread or hard cheese in my mouth before sparring. Rafe didn't take it easy on me, forcing me to learn by mistake more often than naught. He wasn't a good teacher—he didn't explain things verbally. He showed me... physically. Which often resulted in me getting a beating under the guise of training.

Following my session with Rafe, he passed me off to Xzanth who put me through my riding paces. I was a decent rider, but when I added weapons, I was terrible. I didn't have enough confidence to trust my horse as I made large maneuvers. These horses were bred and trained for their even temperaments. Even so, having a twelve-hundred pound beast thundering beneath me, and being asked to trust it with my hands free, was another thing entirely.

I took the reins from Xzanth as we walked back to the fortress.

"Come to the stable." He offered me the faintest of smiles.

He knew I had friends in the main barracks. This was his small way of giving me a chance to see them. I nodded, not pushing my luck, and lengthened my stride beside him.

The walk back to the barracks' stable cooled the horse down, and I stopped to let him drink at a trough outside a paddock. Passing soldiers eyed us curiously. I wasn't sure what reputation Xzanth had before he was recruited by Rafe, but I had been fairly well known. Which I'd rather not have been.

We walked the gelding to an open area and tied him. I loosened his girth and tugged the saddle off, taking it to the tack room. Wiping it down, I returned it to the rack and retrieved a comb to brush the horse out.

The army had stableboys to do this job, but General Rafe required his men to take care of their own mounts. There would be no stableboys running with his Tennan, and each soldier was required to care for their own belongings.

I returned to the gelding and started brushing the dried sweat out of his coat. "When will we know which horses we'll be traveling with?" I asked, rubbing at a dirty patch.

The beast blew through his lips and leaned into the comb. I chuckled and pushed back against him.

"General Rafe has his own stallion. Jamlin has a mare he favors. There is a horseflesh auction in a fortnight. I assume that is where we'll purchase them."

I smiled, thinking of what horse I would end up with. Rafe wouldn't choose a poor match for me. Whatever beast he assigned me would be calm and steady. I would have to learn to trust it with my life... and with letting go of the reins.

"Hail, Avyanna."

I dropped into a crouch, beaming as I peeked under the gelding's belly. Willhelm leaned against the fence, the slight breeze tousling his black hair.

"Willhelm!"

"Riding?" He gestured to the horse.

I stood and finished with that side. "Just getting back."

Xzanth and Willhelm nodded at each other in acknowledgment.

"How's your new training?" he asked.

I moved to the far side of the gelding, closer to him. "Great, truly great, to be honest," I replied, smiling.

"That knot on your head says otherwise." He jerked his chin to point out the large bruise at my temple.

"I'm a terrible rider. A horse threw me two days ago," I offered with a light laugh.

"You're a fine rider... for a lady," Xzanth spoke up. "Just not a mounted warrior... yet."

Willhelm regarded Xzanth. "She doesn't trust them." He jerked his head toward the gelding.

"Being so small in comparison, it will take time," Xzanth replied.

I climbed a rail on the fence to brush the gelding's back. "Maybe I need a smaller horse," I jested. "A fine little pony to ride into war."

Willhelm laughed, and even Xzanth cracked a smile.

"I've heard the ponies from the foothills of E'or are quite fierce," Willhelm mused. "Shaggy things, though."

"Riding an oversized dog would suit her," Xzanth agreed.

I squinted at Xzanth, intrigued that speaking with Willhelm was bringing him out of his shell.

"How's Niehm?" I asked, starting on the mane.

"She came once after you were transferred, but I haven't seen her since. She doesn't care for the barracks."

"I hope she's not worried." I frowned, tugging at a tangle.

"She's less worried about your training and more worried about... other matters."

I looked at him from the corner of my eye. "Other matters?"

"Another woman would be concerned for your virtue," Xzanth clarified.

"Oi," I sighed, dropping into a crouch to start on the gelding's tail. Brambles and large thorny seed pods were nestled in the coarse hair.

"You've been whisked off to a hidden location, isolated with a group of men. She was... upset," Willhelm said with a shrug.

"Well, tell her I'm learning to fight better and can hold my own."

"In armed combat?"

"Aye."

Willhelm looked to Xzanth. "Truth?"

"She's shown marked improvement," he replied, eyeing Willhelm through his long hair.

"That's good to hear." Willhelm's eyes sparkled with pride. So far, his advice had proved true... after a week, at least.

I finished cleaning the gelding's hooves and handed him off to a stableboy.

"Come, little one," Xzanth said quietly, heading in the direction of the fortress.

"Farewell, Willhelm," I called, waving to him as I followed.

Humming as I walked, a smile lit my face. I was thankful Xzanth allowed me to come and talk with Willhelm. Even the shortest conversation meant something when it came from a friend.

We returned to the fortress as the sun neared the treeline. Dane tended the fire, glancing up as we approached. A pile of hares lay next to him, ready to be cooked.

Dane preferred to keep to himself—a silent hunter, always observing and rarely speaking. He was the quietest of the Tennan and had never spoken to me. He didn't come across as rude, but rather withdrawn.

His twin, Blain, did the talking. That was the primary way I could tell them apart, That and which did any labor. Dane wasn't afraid to work, but Blain detested it. If he couldn't accomplish something with pure talent, he gave up. Unless, of course, General Rafe set him to it.

"It's the girl!"

I turned at the sound of an unfamiliar voice and searched the clearing. Two men stood with General Rafe. One newcomer had short red hair with a long fiery beard braided tight. His hair was a shade more orange than the deep ruby of Niehm's. He pointed at me, his pale face splitting in a smile.

The man beside him had simple brown hair and seemed fairly average. Nothing about him stood out from any other soldier. He eyed me before turning to General Rafe. I walked over with a nervous grin, wanting to be polite. They could have been the last to join our Tennan.

"–hands off." I caught the end of General Rafe's gruff words.

The redhead looked between me and Rafe with a knowing glint in his eye.

Rafe locked his gaze on mine, and my smile faltered. His eye was dark and held a hint of danger. I had given him no reason to be angry with me... so I closed the distance between us.

"Hail," I called. "I'm Avyanna."

"Hail. We know who you are, girl!" The redhead's voice boomed larger than life. "You've been the talk of the barracks! I'm Tegan, this is Garion. General Rafe plucked us from our companies to join his Tennan. He took you as well, eh?"

"Hail, Garion," I greeted. "He offered me a position, and I accepted," I clarified.

General Rafe grunted and pushed past me to head into the fortress.

"I'd heard he was a prickly one... but my, my! He really does have a twig up his arse, doesn't he?" Tegan muttered, watching Rafe disappear behind the doors.

"You'll get used to it. He's not too terrible." I shrugged.

"I bet he's not terrible to you," Garion retorted.

My eyes narrowed as I studied him, ready to defend my reputation, but he was looking elsewhere. He didn't seem to have meant the comment as rudely as I took it.

"He's gruff with everyone, myself included," I said. "Helpful hint—don't give half of your all to him. He'll sense it like the wild cat senses a weak deer. He'll push you harder."

"So we've heard." Tegan shrugged.

Garion huffed a sigh. "What a motley group."

I frowned, turning to see what he referenced. Korzak loomed above Xzanth who added rabbit meat to a stew pot. Collins drew in the dirt with a stick, and Zephath was tucked in the shadows reading a book. Dane had disappeared, but Blain and Jamlin were wrestling over a piece of bread.

"Perhaps... but we work well together," I explained.

The fortress door creaked open. Rafe came out with his sack of toiletries over his shoulder—my cue that it was time to wash up. I excused myself and rushed to gather my things before chasing after him.

I jogged, my sore muscles complaining, bringing myself into step next to him. "Garion and Tegan?" I prompted.

He glanced at me but didn't respond.

"What makes them different?"

"Are they different?" he countered roughly. His voice had an edge to it. He wasn't angry at me, but something unnerved him.

"You only choose unique soldiers."

"Do I?"

I wanted to pull him out of this mood. I enjoyed the teasing, playful Rafe much more. Determined, I spun and walked backward, facing him. "Yes, you do. Or did you not realize?" I teased.

He frowned at my antics and grunted in response.

"Perhaps you chose the oddest soldiers because you're an odd one," I offered.

He raised an eyebrow, daring me to continue.

"Don't tell me—no one told you how odd you are?" I gasped in mock horror, holding a hand to my chest.

"I've been called worse," he grumbled.

"Ah, but I simply think you're odd. Nothing worse," I said.

"Just odd, nothing more?" His questioning eye met mine, and I hesitated.

My heel caught on something, and I fell flat on my rear. My toiletries flew through the air, scattering over the ground. Rafe snorted in amusement and kept walking. I hurried to pick up my things with a smile and rushed after him.

We walked along in silence toward the lake. From there, we followed our small, well-worn trail through the woods and down the steep cliff that led to the spring. Rafe entered before me, and I took a seat on the sun-warmed sand, waiting for him to come out.

The lake sparkled in the autumn sun's warm rays. Looking out over the glittering waves, a sense of peace enveloped me. I finally felt settled. As peculiar as I was, I belonged to a company of soldiers. We each had our own strengths and weaknesses. We fit in like some haphazard family thrown together.

But we weren't thrown together.

Rafe brought us together. He was the one who saw our potential and chose us for one another. It was obvious he knew what he wanted far before he made his first move. He was calculating and prepared.

I had seen the way he interacted with his men. I felt it when he trained with me. He wanted to give us our best fighting chance. He chose us to serve together so that we wouldn't fall as easily as if we were left alone.

I admired that about him. He went after his wants without hesitation. When he wanted me for his Tennan, he went after me. He didn't give up. He said that he couldn't force my hand in that decision, but he was relentless.

Smiling, I thought of just how relentless he was. He was bold and aggressive with things. The man didn't have a demure bone in his body. He was hard as nails and as tough as rawhide. He didn't tolerate excuses. Nor did he accept anything but my best. He gave his all and demanded the same from his Tennan.

There was a grunt as he dropped his large frame to the sand beside me. His skin was scrubbed clean of the day's grime, and his tunic was tossed over a shoulder. I was always freezing when I left the spring—but this man was a furnace.

He looked at me with a drawn out blink.

I blushed, realizing I sat there ogling him, and stood. "I'll be quick."

He snorted in disbelief and turned back to watch the sun dip toward the lake.

I hurried to the spring and washed quickly. It was much faster now that my hair was so short. Longing rang through me at the memory of my long intricate braids. I bit my lip and scrubbed at my nails. When I returned from the front, I would let it grow out.

I slowed, thinking that through. Did I want to return? What would I do when my years were up? When I was a free woman again? Would I want to leave Rafe?

I frowned at that thought. I didn't want to leave him. He was irritating, but I was like a moth to a flame with him. Sometimes he pushed me away, and other times I couldn't help but want to be close to him. Whether he was at the front or not, shouldn't influence what I wanted to do after my years were up... yet it did.

Sighing, I hurried to finish washing and dress. The cavern was still somewhat warm, but the air outside took on the chill of nightfall.

With my soiled clothes and toiletries under my arm, I returned to where Rafe waited on the beach. He didn't look up, but I noted he had donned his tunic. His arms were bare to the cold, and I didn't understand how he wasn't chilled at all. I pulled my long sleeves lower around my hands and sat beside him, placing my belongings on the sand.

We sat in silence, content to watch the waves lap at the shore. I studied his face, knowing he could see me. He ignored my stare and looked on, lost in thought.

I pulled my knees up and rested my head on them, watching him. Lines creased the corners of his eye, surely from squinting in the sun for so many years, not from smiling. He had a faint scar on his cheek, small, and fine enough that most might not notice. He had a firm jaw that portrayed masculinity... and stubbornness.

My eyes trailed down to his neck where the scars became more common, smaller ones littering his neckline and traveling below his tunic. His shoulders were broad and solid. His arm was thick, almost as thick as my thigh, and corded in strong muscles. Over his shoulder he had the flying dragon tattooed, revealing his rank as General.

I reached out before I thought better of it and traced the ink staining his skin. He turned a fraction to glance at me before returning his gaze to the lake.

I blushed, afraid he would push me away, but he let me be. My heart skipped a beat as I traced the dragon's wing. It was a perfect replica of the General's patch. I wondered what would happen if he were ever demoted. Would he lose his arm? Would they carve it out of his skin?

My fingertips trailed down his arm to his elbow, then followed the thick vein down his forearm to his wrist. Something unfurled inside me, something my brain screamed was dangerous. I swallowed the nerves threatening to close off my throat and grasped his hand lying in his lap.

He turned to face me full on, and my heart faltered at the look in his eye.

Longing burned in his gaze. And such turmoil. I'd never seen him like that. He never let his guard down, never let people see the true Rafe. Whatever he had been thinking about tore down the mental barrier he always had up. Empathy surged within me, wanting to erase whatever hurt he had. He was the strong leader—the invincible one. He wasn't supposed to hurt.

I pushed myself to my knees and trailed my hands to his face. His dark gaze held mine, but he didn't move. He spoke with his eye, whether he realized it or not, pleading for help, for comfort. Something rose within me, a desire to protect. Perhaps it was a feminine impulse to safeguard what I deemed was mine. Either way, whatever hurt my General would pay.

I touched his jaw and slipped my fingers under the cloth covering his eye. He flinched, and a sharpness flashed in his right eye. He smothered his emotion as quickly as it came, and watched me, guarded and curious.

Gently, I tugged the cloth off. His eyebrows snapped together in a frown, but his left eye opened, squinting against the light. I cupped the back of his head and leaned forward. My pulse raced, excited, but I worried he would push me away.

What was I doing?

My heart threw that thought to the side, deeming it unimportant.

I pressed in close and placed a chaste kiss over his injured eye. I pulled back, terrified he would laugh or curse, but he sat motionless, regarding me. Seeing both his eyes open was disconcerting, simply because I was so accustomed to his patch.

"You don't need to wear this around me," I breathed, clutching the cloth at the nape of his neck.

"My fearless kitten, I don't wear it for you."

My breath rushed out in a quiet laugh at his deep voice. He smirked, but didn't pull away. I traced the scars near his eye, wondering what happened. I didn't want to ask—didn't want to break this spell, whatever it was.

At this moment, I was simply Avyanna, and he was Rafe. We were two broken mortals, each suffering in our own way, trying to make it by in life. Just trying to survive. For a few breaths, I let myself think he was just another man, and I, just a simple woman.

We sat there for what seemed like both an eternity and mere moments, looking at each other. There was such power in being as small and frail as I was, holding the biggest, strongest, fiercest man I knew. I felt empowered, simply by touching him, knowing for just a moment he needed it, and tolerated it from me.

"Stay like this much longer," he rumbled, "and someone will get the wrong idea."

His voice caused my belly to clench. I cleared my throat and pulled my hands away, a blush heating my cheeks. My heart instantly objected to the loss of warmth and closeness, while my brain heaved a sigh of relief. He stood and brushed the sand off his trousers, and I followed suit. Picking up our toiletries, I handed him his cloth covering. He grabbed it but paused when I didn't release it right away.

"I mean it. You don't have to wear it." I let go and studied the silver current in his left eye. I knew he could see me through it, even if it was damaged.

Damaged or not, it was part of him, and it was beautiful.

Chapter Thirty-Seven

Garion ended up having a gift with horses. He joined Xzanth and Rafe at a horse auction in a nearby village. I stayed and trained with Jamlin in the morning. After that, Rafe said I was free to do as I wanted as long as I was within sight of Jam.

It was my first free day since Hatching Day, and even though I wasn't allowed to go anywhere I pleased, I still enjoyed myself. I ended up racing Collins around, and he taught me how to scale the fortress walls, finding footholds as I went. It was far more exhilarating than I imagined, being able to fly up the walls and land on the balcony.

I sat down on a log, panting for breath, face flushed with the effort of keeping up with Collins. Looking over, I eyed Zephath. "Trees of E'or?" I read, squinting at the cover.

He looked up from his book, offering me a glare.

"Tell me, what about the trees of E'or? Are you reading about the foothills, or the mountains themselves?" I pressed. "The deciduous trees that change their colors with the seasons, or the evergreens? Or perhaps some rare species I've not heard of?"

Zeph had the temper of a snake. I could never read him and usually tried to keep my distance. He was cold and cruel in such a way that seemed intent on hurting people.

"Such a commoner wouldn't understand," he snapped, going back to his book.

"Oi, a commoner?" I exclaimed, perking up. "So that's it."

"What is?" He frowned, glowering at me above the pages of his book.

"You're a noble—or something of the sort. That's why you're different."

"I am different. I'm not a thing like you," he sneered.

"You're not. I'm fine with that." I shrugged a shoulder, watching him. "Are you?"

"Of course I am." His gaze narrowed on me. "Why wouldn't I be?"

I rested my elbows on my knees and watched as Blain and Dane wrestled Korzak in the distance.

"You're a noble then?"

"The son of one," he murmured, leery.

"And you joined the army," I mused. "So, you are either trying to be something you're not or you're on the run." His face flushed at the latter and I nodded. "Running then."

"You wouldn't understand," he snarled, standing.

"Try me."

He faltered, hurt flashing in his crystal blue eyes, then he snapped his book closed. Hatred and bitterness glimmered in that gaze, and he twisted his face into a grimace. "You're not worth it," he said before stalking off to the fortress.

I sighed and returned my attention to the others. Tegan joined the skirmish, fighting everyone and taking no sides. Jamlin stood aside and howled with laughter. I smiled at the sight.

"It's no use," Collins stated, coming to sit by me.

"Hmm?"

"Zephath. He won't let anyone close to him. I don't know how General Rafe got him to agree to anything. He's the only one he listens to."

I studied Collins. His sandy hair was always tousled. He sat awkwardly, as if he hadn't quite grown into his height.

"He's been hurt. He's scared. Rafe offered him safety. Whatever he's running from, the war front is the furthest thing from it, and that's where he wants to be."

"That's not what bothers me about him," he grumbled. "He lashes out at everyone. He doesn't mesh well with us."

"I would agree, but I didn't think that any of us would work well together," I said, gesturing between us and the others. "Rafe knows what he's doing. He recruited him for a reason."

"You sure have a lot of faith in the General."

"I wouldn't be here if I didn't trust him with my life."

A soft whinny caught my attention. At the edge of the clearing, Rafe rode a bay, sturdy and big-boned—a stallion but one that walked calmly. He led two horses. The first was massive—the second biggest I'd seen, the largest being the draft horse I rode during my recruitment. That one had to be for Korzak. The other Rafe led, a medium-sized black. It was slender but strong. Garion rode behind him on a chestnut, leading two bays.

As Xzanth entered the clearing, my attention flew straight to the beast trailing behind him. It was the smallest horse I had ever seen—something between a horse and a pony. Its ears were ridiculously long and its shaggy bay coat faded to a black mane and tail.

I gaped at it in amused horror.

That one was mine... I just knew it.

Everyone roused and gathered near the horses, but I remained on the log and stared. Xzanth looked around and motioned toward me with his head. Unable to move, my jaw fell open.

They really brought me an oversized puppy.

Rafe distributed the saddled horses, and the men wasted no time mounting and riding them about. He approached Xzanth and took the reins of the... shaggy, small horse and started my way.

"You bought me a pony." I scoffed when he came within earshot. We were far enough away from the men that they wouldn't hear my informal, accusing tone.

He smirked and held out the reins. "Garion assured me it's a horse... half of one, at least."

"You bought me a mule?" I slapped a palm to my forehead.

Rafe chuckled. "Get on him."

"Him?" I peered at the creature's underside as I stood. "Hard to tell under all that... hair."

With a sigh, I took the reins and regarded the thing's face. I pushed aside the unruly forelock to find two bright eyes. It blinked at me and snorted, offended that I revealed it to the world. I smiled and scratched its chin, walking to the side to get a good look at it. I studied his small head and the obscenely large ears. Its bushy mane stuck out at all sides.

My gaze traveled down his fuzzy body, and I reached out to feel along his legs. He stood still and calm, resting the tip of his hind hoof with ease. I felt his strong bones beneath the coat and patted his shaggy withers. They were level with my shoulders, which was far better than the other horses I had ridden. It seemed like a well-built creature, albeit a bit forlorn in appearance.

I took a deep breath and mounted, expecting to have to hold it steady. The beast didn't even bat an overgrown ear. I let out a relieved sigh.

Rafe chuckled again at my antics and patted its neck. "It's a pigou. They're bred in the plains between the foothills of E'or and the King's plains. Garion recognized it. I'd never seen one."

"I guess his size is more suited to me," I mumbled.

Honestly, I thought he looked ridiculous, but I gave his neck a fond scratch. As long as he didn't throw me, we would be fast friends.

"Go." Rafe slapped its rump.

The pigou craned its hairy head in his direction and snorted. I smiled, secretly charmed that it didn't bolt. Squeezing my legs, I prompted the animal forward. He took off at a slow walk, completely at ease with me and accepting my instructions. I gave his neck another pat, trying to convey I was pleased.

Pressing my heels into him, I clicked my tongue. He picked up his pace to a graceful trot. Pulling to the left, he responded immediately and turned. I urged him faster, away from the other horses. He sped into a gait that I had never ridden before. He glided over the ground with such grace it felt as if he flew through the air. I could have drank a cup of tea and not spilled a drop. Laughing, I coaxed him into a full gallop toward the King's Lake and he shot off like a bolt from a crossbow.

I lay close to his furry neck as he ran with all his might. Wind pried tears from my eyes and I gave a wild whoop. His giant ears flicked back in interest. He was a fast thing for being so little, and at that moment, as we flew across the ground, I fell in love.

With a pigou. Pitiful.

We returned to Rafe at a walk, and my smile was so big that my cheeks ached, but I couldn't help myself. I loved this creature. He was so eager to please and obedient—calm and not startled by anything. He was shaggy and had giant ears. What wasn't to love?

"I see you enjoyed your run," Rafe said, grasping the bridle while I dismounted.

"He's a dream. He has this gait that–"

"A waltz. It's a gait exclusive to the breed." He finished for me.

I sank my fingers into its thick coat. "It's so smooth! It felt like flying!"

"Zan thought it would suit you. With your sharp aim, shooting from horseback would be an invaluable asset."

I looked at the pigou and gave a little giggle. I knew it was childish, but the more I learned about this creature, the more I loved him.

"You know, I trusted you," I said, turning to Rafe. This creature was mine. He bought him for my use in the army.

"Hmm?" Rafe's mouth quirked in a small grin as he towered over me.

"I trusted you to bring a horse that suited me."

He grunted and twisted his lips as if he fought a full smile.

"But you did better than that," I continued. "You brought one that's perfect for me. Thank you."

Rafe took his eye off mine and looked at the other men, rubbing the back of his neck. "I did the same for all the Tennan."

"I'm not all the Tennan, but thank you, Rafe."

I reached out to place my hand on his arm, but thought better of it and dropped it to my thigh. Any of the others might be watching.

"He'll need his coat sheared at least once a year, if not twice," he said, changing the subject.

Genuine thanks made him uncomfortable. I tucked away this new information, smiling to myself.

My fingers trailed through the pigou's thick fur. "I've never cut a horse's hair."

"I'll have Garion show you." He gave me one last puzzling look before walking off toward the men.

"Now," I said, turning to peer under the creature's forelock. Alert brown eyes looked back at me. "What shall I name you?"

A few days later, I cut Thunderbolt's hair with Garion. He was normally serious and unfazed, but he laughed at my name for the pigou.

"I'm not sure one has ever had such a grand name," he jested.

"He's as quick as one," I said, cutting at the length of fur on his belly. "Besides, once people see me shooting from his back, they'll understand the name."

Thunderbolt's trim took the entire day. We had to use a comb and shears, and the poor thing had so much dirt caked beneath, I kept running into mats.

Finally, as the sun began to set, he was done. His coat shone with care, a burnished copper that melted into black on his legs and mane, and tail. We trimmed those up as well, and his bright eyes watched me. He stood still and was well mannered while we tended to him. He looked like a completely different animal.

I, however, now looked like an animal.

I picked at my tunic that was covered in hair, dirt, and other things that I'd rather not think of.

"I think I look like a pigou now," I said, stretching with a yawn.

Spluttering, I pulled a horse hair out of my mouth. Thunderbolt blew through his lips as if to laugh at me. I smirked at him and scratched his neck.

"Let's head back."

We cleaned up and had a stableboy put Thunderbolt away. The small boy laughed and mocked his ridiculous ears as they left.

We returned to the fortress, Garion as silent as ever. I headed straight for the cookfire, hoping that dinner was done. Who knew that cutting a horse's hair would take so much energy?

"Avyanna."

I faltered and spun on my heel at Rafe's barked call. He approached me with a heavy frown, looking me up and down. He plucked a piece of hay out of my hair and held it up accusingly.

"Did you think you were going to eat like that?" he asked. His tone was not teasing, but rather demanding.

"Well, I was just–" I trailed off at his blank expression.

"Get your things."

My stomach growled in protest, and Rafe dropped his gaze to my belly, arching a brow. I sighed in resignation and headed to the fortress. Food would simply have to wait.

I grabbed my toiletries and my winter cloak. It was getting colder—the first snow would come soon. I had been inside a stall all day with Thunderbolt and forgot how cold it got at night now.

I followed Rafe to the spring. The sun was touching the horizon, and he picked up his pace, forcing me into a jog to keep up with him.

"This is—I should bathe closer to—the fortress," I said between breaths.

His gaze flashed to mine, but he said nothing.

We arrived at the spring, and he bathed quickly. When he came out, steam rolled off him, giving him a comical look.

"Go."

He jerked his head to the cave entrance, and I rushed inside to bathe, disgusted at the amount of grime streaking off me. I dried and dressed quickly. I threw my winter cloak over my shoulders, hoping to hold in the warmth. On my way out, I almost ran into Rafe just outside the cave entrance.

"Oi!"

Normally, he waited on the beach. He looked at me and opened his mouth as if to say something, but his gaze traveled further down. I waited for him to speak, and after a moment, his eye darted back to mine.

"Your lacing is undone," he said. His tone was dark and raspy—full of... something.

I peered down and gasped, dropping my dirty clothes. I pulled at the lacing again and tied it more securely. After picking up my clothes, I braved a glance at him as a blush heated my cheeks. I was thankful for the darkness of dusk to hide my embarrassment. All he would have seen was my chest binding, but that was far too much.

"I must have been in a hurry. Someone was rushing me," I huffed.

The light in his eye changed, and he smirked.

I gave him a small smile.

Bathing with a man at dusk? Having my tunic lacing come undone? Standing far too close for societal standards? My heart raced in rebellion as my gaze traveled to his lips and I wondered, not for the first time, if they were as hard as the words that came out of them.

"There's news of unrest."

"Hmm?" I was jolted back to reality, and I snapped my attention up to his dark eye.

"Up north—rumors of a beast killing off livestock."

My brow furrowed. "Why would the army hear of a simple beast?"

Farmers dealt with their own predator issues. Oftentimes, if it was a pack of wolves or a bear, the entire village took up arms to take care of the problem. It wasn't a task that anyone would ever see fit to pass to the King's Army.

"They claim it's a dragon."

I frowned in deeper confusion. A dragon? Where was its Rider? Why didn't they control it? Why wouldn't it be passed to the Dragon Riders here?

"How could that be?" I asked.

His eye took on a dangerous light—one that I didn't like. One of hatred and anger.

"A Shaman."

My jaw dropped, and I gaped at Rafe in disbelief. Shadows never attacked from the north. They maintained their front to the west, with sporadic attacks in the south.

Rafe lifted a hand and cupped my cheek, placing his thumb over my lips. "Hush. We're not sent for... yet."

Winter of Year 897

A month passed, and the snows came. The first snow was always thrilling, but after that, no one found joy in it.

Except Collins.

We took up throwing balls of snow at each other whenever we were outside. Sometimes we hit others, much to their displeasure. Jamlin especially detested the snow. Being born in the deep south, he was acclimated to the hot summers, not freezing winters.

My training went better, and I was more confident than ever. I upgraded from a staff to a spear, and my skill improved with each passing day. I could hold my own against most of the Tennan, though I struggled against Jamlin. The man was wicked with his sword. Blain was infuriating, as well. He was cunning. He used deceit to his advantage, which I hated, but it gave me good experience. The Shadows weren't going to fight with honor.

Sparring with Rafe was another thing entirely. The man moved with more speed and power than a human should be capable of. He seemed to know my moves before I made them—always three moves ahead. He was a magician with his blades. I had no chance against him.

I grew to be proud of my archery. I was the best shot in the Tennan, with the exception of rapid-fire shooting with a short bow. That title belonged to Xzanth, who shot with impossible speed and accuracy. I was sure he could mow down the entire Shadow army if he simply had enough arrows.

Thunderbolt and I got along famously. I rode him without a bridle, forcing myself to give up my weakness—clinging to the reins. I learned to guide him with my legs, and not rely on my hands.

He was so steady, I could shoot with my crossbow at a good distance while he ran along, and never missed. He navigated the mounted courses without mishap. On the few occasions he slipped on a patch of ice, his deft recovery left me barely needing to steady myself.

With the snows came the Winter Solstice. I had sent word to my mother to meet me at the Dragons Beard Inn in Hamsforth. I was sure she would fear the worst... well, perhaps not the worst. After all, I don't think she would ever imagine that I would join the ranks.

I had won a free evening from Rafe by stitching patches on the Tennan's uniforms. Our new insignia depicted a dragon leading a lion with swords crossed behind. We were Rafe's lions then. I took pleasure in sewing during the dark, snowy days while Zephath read next to me. Jamlin often sang with Korzak humming along in that deep voice of his. The others would beg for a bawdy ballad, and oftentimes Tegan would join in and humor them.

I used my free evening to shop with Niehm and Elenor for the Winter Solstice. My mother deserved a special gift, and I wanted to spend time with my friends. I saw Willhelm now and then in the main barracks, but meeting the women was far harder.

As I matured, I grew to crave their company. Not that I didn't enjoy the Tennan, they were fantastic. We were like a big, obscene family. Tegan was a terrible prankster and always ready for a jest. He made every task, even cleaning the chamber pot, a laughable ordeal.

Being around men, however, had its drawbacks. Though perhaps it was one man in particular who was a drawback.

I grew bold—and foolish when we went off to bathe at night. Something about it felt as if we slipped away into our own world. Sensations like that whispered dangerous things to my heart.

Rafe treated me different when we were alone. I could tease him out of his shell, and he responded almost playfully. I'm unsure how it happened, but somewhere along the line, I realized we were friends. He was still the same rough, crude, brash General. That hadn't changed. Yet, when we were alone, I could fire back and pull him out of his rudeness. He would soften and allow me to push at his rough exterior.

Sometimes he would be lost in thought, looking out over the frozen lake. I would take those moments not to question him, but simply sit next to him and press my shoulder against his arm—just enough to let him know I was there.

When he praised me, my heart sang. But my mind screamed a warning. This was dangerous. I was feeding a part of me that shouldn't exist, let alone flourish, yet I was helpless against it.

The more I gave into the craving to be close to him, the greater it became. I had to admonish myself for thinking treasonous thoughts concerning him. Every time I watched for him when he left, I felt like a puppy waiting for its master to return. I hated it.

I loved it as well.

I understood why women snuck around to visit men from the barracks. If this attraction was what they felt, it didn't excuse it, but I could certainly relate. I was helpless against the yearnings of my heart.

***

Niehm left her sword at the dorms, thankfully. I walked with her and Elenor through the vendors set up at the gate to the King's grounds. Some sold fresh foods and baked treats, but many were gift stalls. With the Winter Solstice in two days, many were out shopping for loved ones.

"I don't know what to get her," I groaned, tugging against my belt.

My coin purse hung off a belt loop, not tucked in my pants as Darrak once showed me. I smiled at the memory of him and clutched the small bag. I had my cloak thrown over my shoulders. Rafe would have my hide if I hindered my fighting abilities by having it closed. My uniform screamed soldier, and my patch told others I was in an elite class. Yet my chest told people I was a woman, and some might think that made me an easy target.

"Perhaps something useful?" Niehm offered. She broke the sweetloaf she purchased into three pieces to share.

"I can't imagine what she would need," I said, taking a bite of the soft, sugary bread.

"Avyanna," Elenor's hesitant and serious tone brought my gaze to her. "Think of this. Perhaps you do not return from the front."

"Elenor, don't be such a downer," Niehm gasped.

I frowned, swallowing the pastry down a dry throat. "Aye. What if I don't?" I said, forcing as much cheerfulness as I could.

It was true, I might not. No matter my chances, I was heading behind enemy lines. I could die any day.

"What will she have to remember you by?" Elenor asked. Her icy blue eyes searched mine.

I shrugged, fighting my frown. "Not much."

"Perhaps that's something to consider," Elenor said.

"Yes," Niehm agreed. "For when you're far away, but alive and well on the front." Niehm eyed Elenor as if she had betrayed her.

I cracked a small smile. The cruel reminder of what the war front had in store for me loomed. My belongings were minimal, bare necessities. I had no heirlooms, nothing she could hold and think of me. I didn't even have my dresses anymore—I had passed them on, to be given to other girls.

I surveyed the vendors with fresh eyes. What could I purchase that my mother could look at and remember me?

"A knife?" I thought.

Niehm snorted and both Elenor and I looked at her in shock at such an unladylike sound. We burst into laughter together and headed around the vendors again.

I made my way toward a jeweler's stall, knowing most of it would be beyond my coin. I saved every bit I could and had quite a tally. Jewels were also impractical, and therefore relatively inexpensive... in a regular village. On the King's grounds, the vendors knew that people would be buying frivolous things, especially at this time of year. Therefore, they had no quarrel about raising their prices.

I glanced through the trinkets, slowing at the earrings. My mother, as well as I, never had our ears pierced. What was the point of carrying a jewel in your ear for all the bandits and robbers to see? As my gaze traveled over the rings, the same logic appealed to me. Why wear a jewel on your finger where it could easily slip off and be lost forever?

I was about to move on when I noticed the necklaces. I peered at the small medallions, some with jewels and others plain. Some were simple bronze designs and others were gold or precious silver. Hanging from a leather thong was a simple silver cabochon with a green stone inside. I waved at the vendor asking to see it. Elenor and Niehm pressed close to peer at it as the man showed it to us.

"It's the same color as your eyes, lass! What a wonderful gift for that special man in your life! With it, he would never forget your beauty."

"It's for my mother," I corrected dryly.

"And what a handy reminder of her lovely daughter—eyes as green as the forest in the height of spring!" he rattled on, unfazed.

"The gem matches quite well," Elenor agreed quietly.

"It would be a nice reminder... till you come home and she can see your beautiful eyes in person," Niehm added.

"How much?" I ventured.

"Five gold."

That was far less than I expected. "What is the stone?" I asked, reaching over to tap my nail against it.

"It's one of the rarest and most precious—"

"It's simple green quartz." A passerby spoke up from behind and shook his head. "Highway robbery," he murmured, walking on.

Looking back at the vendor, I raised my eyebrow in question.

He smiled, clearly accustomed to defending his wares. "Perhaps it is but simple quartz, but see how it's polished? How it sparkles in the candlelight? You could fool anyone!"

"Like me." I grimaced.

"Ah–"

"Two gold." I cut him off.

"No less than four!"

"Three."

He held his heart as if in pain. "You hurt me, lass."

"Three gold or I walk away," I said, straightening and shuffling my feet.

"Aye, aye!" He rushed his words. "Three gold it is!"

I paid as the vendor wrapped it in burlap and boxed it. My purse was lighter, but I was far more excited to see my mother. At least she would have something to remember me by.

In case I died.

"Oh, look at that hair comb!" Niehm exclaimed.

We shopped around for another chime, walking and chatting about life. We shied away from anything that hedged close to my departure in a few short months. Most topics surrounded the women's dorm and the drama and gossip that always ensued. We talked about the women who had taken lovers and been found out, during which I tried to hide my blush. Niehm teased me, claiming I was all grown up and understood what they spoke of.

If she only knew how right she was.

The sensation of longing—of being so close, but not close enough. The uncertainty of each move made, wondering if it would be the last before it all came crashing down.

Something caught my eye, and I stopped, pivoting to face a stall. The fur vendor grinned and waved to me, eager to tend to a new patron. I wasn't interested in the hides he had on display or how warm they were. My eyes were on something else.

"Avyanna?" Niehm called, rushing to my side.

"Furs? For sewing?" Elenor prompted.

Niehm huffed a small laugh. "Do you even have time to sew?"

I pointed to a jar, and the grizzled man retrieved it.

"Buttons?" Elenor asked.

I reached in and felt the smooth, worn sides and filed points.

"Tooth buttons? Really, Avyanna, are you that barbaric?" Niehm laughed.

"Not just any teeth, fine lady. These are wild cat teeth!"

Niehm groaned with distaste. "Lovely."

"How much for five?" I asked, picking out the best ones.

I wasn't thinking. I wasn't using my head. And that was all right—or so my heart told me.

"One gold."

"For buttons?" Elenor narrowed her eyes.

"They're made from the wild cats of–"

"Here." I handed him a gold coin. I didn't care what the cost was. I was getting them.

"Well, well! Thank you, fine lady. Is there anything else that might interest you? Perhaps–"

"No, thank you. Farewell," I said, walking off before he could rope me into talking. I slipped the teeth into my coin purse.

"Wild cat teeth, Avyanna?" Elenor asked hesitantly, as if I sprouted a second head.

"Who are those for? Your uniform doesn't have buttons," Niehm pressed, eyeing me from tunic to trousers.

A blush heated my skin, and I ducked my head.

"No," Niehm whispered in horror.

"It is a masculine gift," Elenor affirmed.

I cleared my throat, rushing my words. "It's not like that."

"That's what they all say, Avyanna." Niehm reached out, gripping my shoulder. "Don't do it! I'm telling you, whoever he is, he's not worth it. He's not worth you. He's not worth your future." The wind picked up, teasing strands of her hair.

"I swear, it's not like that!" I laughed, hoping it hid my nerves, and danced out of her hold.

Elenor sighed in resignation. "Well, who is the lucky boy?"

"There is no lucky boy!" I turned and headed away from them and their questions.

Niehm groaned and followed me. "There's definitely a boy."

I barely made it five paces before she darted to my side.

"Just tell us what they're for," Elenor urged. "Tell us, and that will be the end of it."

I swallowed past the lump in my throat. Would they understand? Could I spin it in a way they might not realize my deepest secret? I couldn't tell them how I truly felt. No one would understand. Not even my friends.

"Well, you see Rafe's winter—"

"You mean, General Rafe?"

Elenor cut in at the same time Niehm let out a howl like a madwoman in pain. People turned to peer at us with questioning gazes. I offered a tight smile and urged them on.

"Niehm!" I hissed, whirling on her and grabbing her cloak.

"That walking pile of dragon dung?! That's who you're sneaking around with?!" she shrieked.

"I'm not sneaking around with him!" I growled, looking to Elenor for help.

"Honestly, Niehm. He wouldn't let her get close to him. He's a General after all, and no General would be beyond the penalty of bedding a fellow soldier," Elenor said calmly.

I stared at her, shocked. Her words were spoken directly to me and not Niehm. She held my gaze until I dropped my head in shame, dejected.

"Nothing has happened," I muttered. "I swear."

"As nothing will," Elenor stated with a firm nod.

Her eyes were cold and demanding. She knew what would happen, as I did. Despite my brain's best efforts, my heart wanted what my heart wanted.

"He lost a button on his winter vest. I thought I could replace them for the Solstice—to show my gratitude for his training," I explained.

I released Niehm's cloak, and she turned a weary eye on me.

"But Rafe, of all people? You choose to be nice to General Rafe?!"

Chapter Thirty-Eight

The guards stationed at the gate had Jamlin caught up in a game of chance. Returning to the gate, I found him still playing and sipping ale. He sang a ballad I'd never heard as we trudged through the snow to the fortress. He wasn't drunk, but certainly tipsy.

When we arrived, Rafe's glare fell on us as soon as we entered. He sat on Korzak's spare cot that had been pulled next to the fireplace along one wall.

"Jamlin!"

He used his General's voice, and I knew better than to push at that. I snapped to attention.

"Aye?" Jam was all business. He snapped out of his tipsy haze, focusing his eyes on General Rafe.

"We've news."

I studied the somber faces of the Tennan, all of them gathered and sitting along their cots. Jamlin and I crossed the space, both of us curious.

Rafe's eye flashed to me, then spoke. "We're setting out in four days. We're heading north."

A thrum of panic resonated through me.

I wasn't ready—nowhere near ready. We were supposed to have another few months of training and preparation. Sure, my confidence had improved, but now faced with imminent danger, I felt like I was a pawn in some grand scheme.

A pawn that could easily be killed.

"Oh? What calls us there?" Jamlin asked.

"There's been unrest. This Solstice will be the last reprieve you get."

Jamlin took that news with a flinch and grunt. I studied Rafe, wondering why he didn't tell them what he told me. Perhaps he wanted to avoid frightening them? I looked around the room at the men, all bigger and stronger than I. If he didn't want to frighten them, why would he tell me?

Rafe's dark eye assessed me. "I hope you enjoyed yourself."

"I did, actually–" I started, pleased that he was talking to me.

"I'll be heading out with you tomorrow. No one travels alone," he said, cutting me off.

Jamlin shifted on his feet. "It's the Solstice, we're free to–"

"Soldiers are free to do as they will. My Tennan is not. You will pair up and accompany one another on your travels. That's all."

General Rafe rose and started toward the staircase. I watched him go, puzzled. He ripped off his tunic in a rough, aggravated motion, and I tore my gaze away from his broad back.

We'd travel in pairs? Was he afraid of losing one of his Tennan to the Shadows? Were they that close now? Was he afraid because we were his miniature army? Or because he had grown to care for us?

I returned to my cot while Jam gazed up at Rafe's loft. I took my time packing my gifts away, thinking of tomorrow. If Rafe was coming with me, that was going to make quite an impression on my mother.

'Hail, mother! Your little girl has joined the army! And I'm being sent off to my death in two days, thanks to this monster of a man. By the way, I also have feelings for him. Mother, what should I do about them?'

I bit my cheek. That would go over well.

I retrieved my clean uniform and stepped into the small room to change. I hadn't bathed today, but Rafe didn't seem like he was in the mood to go gallivanting through the night so I could clean up.

I left my tunic loose and slipped into my cot, pulling the blanket over my shoulders. I closed my eyes and felt dread wind through me. It would be a long night, thinking of all the ways I could die.

When I woke the next morning, most of the men were pairing up and heading out. I listened to their low voices and tucked my tunic in my trousers, tightening the belt. Garion was going with Tegan and Collins. Zephath and Xzanth were joining up. Jamlin was with Korzak and the twins were leaving for a nearby village. Thankfully, not Hamsforth, where Rafe and I would be headed.

I waved farewell as they all shuffled out the doors with glances back at the loft. Rafe leaned over the stone banister, peering down at me as the door shut behind them. His tunic was off, and I couldn't see his lower half.

"Good morn, Vy."

Oh, today was going to be tough. As soon as I heard that rough morning voice, I knew I was done for. I swallowed and looked down at my stockings.

"Morn," I squeaked.

He chuckled, and a blush heated my cheeks. He knew what he was doing—he had to. As I grabbed my boots, I sucked in a deep breath to calm my beating heart. I could do this—I could get through today. I wouldn't mess up now.

My cot creaked as I sat to lace up my boots, repeating the mantra in my head. I could do this. What was one more day of being close, yet unable to act on my attraction? This was the same as every other day.

Except we would be alone.

Except he would meet my mother.

Except I was giving him a Solstice gift.

"Rafe, I—"

When I looked up, my words abandoned me. He strode across the room, his bare feet silent on the wood floor. His tunic hung open, and I swear he looked like a man who was after something.

Someone.

Me.

I snapped my jaw shut with a click as he walked straight to me. I craned my head back, and he placed his hands on the cot on either side of me. Leaning in, he pressed his face to my neck. My pulse roared as my heart slammed a frantic beat, trying to process my emotions. I lifted a trembling hand to hold his neck and press him closer as he spoke.

"You stink."

I choked on a laugh and shoved at his chest. The tension broke, and he smirked as he pulled away.

"I do not!"

"Lift your arm. Have a sniff," he taunted.

"I will not—I do not!" I shrieked, laughing.

"Aye, a bath is first on our list this morn," he said, fastening the buttons of his tunic.

I watched his deft fingers as I tried to keep my nervous smile from wobbling. "Then where? Do you have a place to be?" I reached for my toiletries. Surely his errands would take priority.

"No. You were off to see family?" he asked, heading back up the stairs.

"Yes, my mother," I called, pulling on my cloak.

I heard his grunt and smiled. He probably disapproved of seeing family. Perhaps it distracted a soldier from their duty.

He came down carrying his boots and took a seat beside me on my cot, putting them on. I noted his bag of bathing supplies and wondered if he had not bathed yesterday either. Leaning toward him, I pressed my face to his neck. He stilled, and in that moment, I forgot what I was doing.

I froze like a terrified child with their hand caught in the honey jar.

"So, do I smell?" he rumbled. His voice was rough and thick with some unknown emotion.

I leaned closer, bracing my hand on his thigh. His leg twitched beneath my palm and I sniffed at his neck. Heat filled me and the room seemed far too small and stifling.

"Yes," I breathed against his skin.

"Hmm." He grunted and cleared his throat, still frozen in place.

"Like leather, wood smoke—sweat." I paused, bringing my lips to brush against the vein in his neck that thrummed with his quick pulse. "Like a man."

With a groan, he jerked to his feet, and I shrunk away from him, embarrassed. That was too much. Far too much. That was definitely crossing the line. I fidgeted with the drawstring of my bag. Surely, he would call me out now. Push me away or charge me with a crime.

"Coming, Vy?"

I looked up, and instead of a judging glower, I saw a man. Not my General, but simply a man. He had the smallest of smiles, but to me, that smile was the world. I flashed him a grin and stood, following him out the doors.

The walk to the spring was quiet, and I was thankful for the chill taking away some of the heat of the moment. I stumbled in a snowdrift and his strong hand gripped my arm, pulling me upright. I smiled my thanks and looked back at the deep snow as we headed on.

If this was what attraction—love, lust, whatever it was—felt like, I could see why women sought it. It was addictive. The risk behind the move, the bold play, the wait for a response, the rush of excitement. I now had far more understanding of the matters of love than I had ever wanted.

I didn't feel like this with any of the boys on the school grounds, or toward Willhelm. Why was General Rafe the one that made my blood boil... in a heated, delicious way that had me craving more?

Lost in thought, my foot slipped near the steep edge above the cliff that led to the spring. I yelped as Rafe grabbed my arms and pulled me to him. My momentum pulled us over the edge and he rolled with me as we tumbled down the cliff. We landed at the bottom in a snowdrift. I lay there for a moment, blinking up at the sky, wondering what just happened.

"Vy–" a muffled voice from beneath me urged.

I scrambled off Rafe and sat in the snow, looking at him. He was pressed into the snow, his arms, and legs askew. His dark clothes and positioning seemed almost comical, and I burst into laughter.

"What in all of Rinmoth," he said, struggling to stand, "is so important that you'd think about it and not watch your footing?"

My laughter died in a nervous giggle, and I pushed to my feet, trying to shake out the snow. "You don't want to know," I jested.

"I really think I do."

I looked up, and a strange pull warmed my belly. He raised his brows with a knowing smile. Slowly, he slid his hand under the cloth around his face and tugged it off, opening his left eye. He squinted against the snow, and I let my heart dictate my actions.

I reached up and held his face, rubbing my thumb across the scars at the corner of his eye.

"Beautiful," I breathed.

He placed his hand over mine, holding it in place. Turning his face, he watched me. He pressed my palm to his mouth, and I thought I would die in suspense. His lips parted, and he gently nipped at my palm, tugging the skin before dropping it and stepping away.

I struggled to breathe and took a moment to gather my wits.

Wits? What wits? Surely they had fled with the rest of the Tennan this morn. Turning, I followed Rafe to the spring. "My mother."

He glanced back, his silver eye shining with an unnatural light. "Hmm?"

"I was thinking of my mother." I lied.

He clung to the stone wall, walking to the cavern's entrance. I took up my position right outside as he ducked in. We waited for each other here in the winter months, staying out of sight, but close enough that the spring's heat offered warmth against the elements. I settled against the cold stone and looked out over the frozen lake.

"Liar."

I jumped at his deep voice, so close to my ear.

"Come here."

I turned and swallowed past the lump in my throat. He stood in the cavern.

Come here?

Come there?

In there?

With him?

"I—Rafe," I stammered.

He watched me with an amused smirk. "You're soaking wet. Bathe first. I'll shave, then wash."

My heart beat so hard I thought it might jump out of my chest. He was asking me to come in with him. It made logical sense. It was the sensible thing to do.

Then why did it seem like this was not the most sensible thing to do?

I jerked my head in a nod and entered, setting my bag next to the spring. He sat on the floor between the spring and the entrance with his back to me. He started pulling items out of his bag, and I stood there, frozen in terror.

He wanted me to strip.

In the same room as him.

Why had I thought this was logical?

"Vy–" He peeked over his shoulder, his silver eye watching me.

I brought my arms up, trying to cover my chest... which was still fully clothed.

He chuckled. "I swear, I will not look. You have my word."

I nodded, and he pulled out a mirror from his bag. I'd forgotten he shaved with one.

"A mirror? I don't like playing with fire," I choked out.

"I rather think you do," he replied. He didn't turn to me but put the mirror back. "If I miss a spot, that's on you."

"Then I'll help you shave it," I retorted, tugging my tunic free from my trousers.

I moved slowly. I trusted him implicitly, but he was just a man, after all. My General, I trusted with my life. Rafe? I wanted to trust him, but was terrified.

I unwound my chest binding and hurried out of my under-breeches as he lathered his cream for shaving. Rushing, I slipped into the water.

Literally.

Flailing, I spluttered, coming up coughing. Pushing my overgrown bangs off my face, I gasped for air.

"Vy–"

"Don't look!" I shouted, trying to cover myself.

He hadn't turned, but he sat tall and stiff as if he wanted to. "I'm regretting that promise," he groaned and continued lathering the cream.

I buried my hot face in my hands and threaded my fingers through my hair. Could I be any more of a fool? This was a terrible idea. Why did I let him talk me into this? Not like he talked me into anything. I'd gone willingly.

Far too willingly.

Lathering the soap, I watched him shave. He was methodical and went by touch. He started with his head and moved to his face. I stared in fascination as he swept the sharp blade against his skin, and wiped it, sweeping it again.

"Why are you worried about your mother?" he asked between strokes.

I startled out of my haze of watching him and worked on my hair. "She doesn't know I've joined the ranks." I dipped back to rinse my hair and ran my hands over my face.

"You never told her?"

"No. I—I haven't seen her since the Wild One rejected me."

He grunted in response, brushing his fingers along his neck for missed spots. I climbed out of the spring and dressed, taking care to be sure I was properly clothed.

I walked over and crouched by his side. "Finished," I said.

"I see."

Flecks of white stuck to his skin here and there. The domestication of the whole scene pressed in—he trusted me. He wouldn't let another soul see him in such a vulnerable state. He was the great General Rafe, stuck with bits of shaving cream on his face.

"Missed a spot." I smirked.

He held out the razor to me, and I stared at it.

"It's right there," I said, pointing at the small spot of stubble and shaving cream on his cheek.

"I believe you said you would help." He dared, raising his eyebrows.

"I'll probably cut you."

"Unintentionally, I'm sure."

"Of course."

I took the blade with a nervous but steady hand. He trusted me. The least I could do for the man was shave a small spot on his cheek. His warm fingers wrapped around my wrist, bringing my hand to his cheek. After a deep breath, I pressed the blade to his skin. I applied gentle pressure and pulled it across his face.

I inched away with a smile, admiring my work. "There, I—Oh no!" I winced as a spot of red appeared.

"You cut me."

"I didn't mean to! I—really! Do you have a rag?"

I looked around and back at the small drop of blood. Panicked, and obviously not thinking clearly, I leaned forward and pressed my mouth to the small cut.

Licking the blood away, I wrinkled my nose at the taste of the soap, then sat back. It's what I would have done if I had a cut.

If *I* had a cut.

Not on someone else.

He stared at me, and I slapped my hands over my face. I had done more than enough to hide today. Rafe gently pried my hands down. I looked at the spot where blood no longer stained his cheek.

"Thank you."

I stumbled back on my rear, at his words or losing my balance, I wasn't sure. He held my hands, bracing my weight against my fall. Once stable, he released me and stood, heading to the spring. I watched him, attempting to wrap my mind around the fact that this was happening.

He placed his pack on the ground and grabbed his belt. He pulled it through the buckle, one bit at a time. "I'm sure it's not modest to watch."

I cursed and spun, turning my back on him.

His chuckle taunted me. "Not that I'm a good judge of modesty."

"Do you have any family?" I asked quickly.

Anything to get us off this topic.

Anything.

There was silence, besides the rustling of garments, then the sound of water lapping against the stones, followed by a low groan. A groan that heated my skin and something deep in my belly clenched in response.

"No," he answered.

"Not even a brother or sister?" I pressed.

It was odd to be like me, an only child. Parents often had several children, as the chances of them surviving to adulthood were poor.

"No."

I sighed and crossed my legs, reaching back to redo the braid at the nape of my neck. The ripples and splashes of him moving about the water were far too familiar for my liking. I didn't feel like I had the right to this much of his trust.

"You've not told me of my father," I said, tying off the short braid.

The sounds of splashing eased, going still. "What do you wish to know?" His voice took on a guarded tone.

"How did he die?" I asked.

All heated sensations fizzled out and died with that question. I was beyond mourning my loss, but the sudden shift in tension made it seem like something between my father and Rafe was unresolved.

"I was seventeen-winters," Rafe started with a sigh. "I blew through training and they sent me to the front. I was young and foolhardy. I knew a blade, I knew of the enemy, but I lacked experience. I didn't know the enemy.

"Gareth looked out for me—as much as I resented it. He was always there to take the blame or catch my falls. He was a good man. I was sent to assist another company trapped by Hunters. Gareth was assigned to me.

"He told me not to charge in, that it looked like an ambush. My men were better trained, better equipped. I thought I could handle it. I charged and made it out alive." He paused, and silence reigned.

"But Gareth didn't," I finished.

"Aye." The word sounded like it was choked out of him.

I pulled my knees to my chest and sat there. "It would have been nice to know him," I thought aloud.

"Aye."

My eyes focused on the frozen lake in front of me. Did Rafe feel guilty for that? Did he feel responsible for my father's death?

"Everyone dies someday. We can't always be ready," I murmured.

There was a grunt and the sounds of water splashing. I frowned at the tension still lingering in the air. Did he think I thought differently of him? That was years ago, when he was young. I wasn't so cruel as to hold the sins of a young man over his head for the rest of his life.

"Finished."

I turned to look at him as he fastened his belt. His tunic hung open and his skin shone with water. I stood and boldly walked up to him.

"Rafe." I reached up to hold his face.

His dark gaze shined with anger and remorse—the silver in his eye radiated unnerving coldness. "Don't you dare tell me not to feel guilty, or some other dung, Vy," he growled.

He wanted to feel guilty? He wanted to retain that sense of sorrow? So, I would let him.

"Rafe, thank you." I tugged against him until he gave in and let me pull his temple to mine. "Thank you for telling me about my father."

He leaned back enough to search my face, looking for something. A trick? A lie?

Whatever it was, he didn't find it, and his anger melted away.

"At this pace, we'll never make it to the village," he whispered, voice rough.

We returned to the fortress, and I placed my toiletries alongside my cot as he retreated up the stairs.

"I assume your mother doesn't know of me?" he called.

"No. She knows nothing of the ranks." I shook off the melted snow from my boots.

There was a grunt, and moments later, he walked down the steps. I looked up and squinted at the cloak tossed over his arm.

"Where's your vest?"

"It's the Solstice. I'm wearing my patch," he said, turning to show me his tattooed shoulder.

"But I need it," I blurted.

He blinked in confusion. "You need my winter vest?"

"Yes, please." I winced before I could take it back.

He gave me a puzzled look, but returned to the loft to retrieve his fur-lined vest. Walking down, he handed it over, watching me carefully.

"I need this today," I muttered, holding it to my chest.

"Only today." He frowned.

I offered him a smile and retrieved my belongings. "Shall we?"

We rode for Hamsforth, which was only a chime's ride away. I urged Thunderbolt to a quick but steady pace to keep up with Rafe's stallion. His stallion was massive, a muscular creature that looked like he could eat me alive. He was a dark dappled gray with a black mane and tail. He was a fierce beast and Thunderbolt and I stayed out of his path.

We arrived in a timely manner and passed our horses off to the stableboy of the Dragons Beard Inn. I looked around at the strangers milling about and felt lost. I had never been outside Northwing beyond my early years. People walked and touched freely, perhaps because of the holiday...

"Vy, let's go." Rafe placed a palm between my shoulder blades. "Have you been outside the grounds?" he asked.

"No," I whispered back, anxiety thrumming beneath my skin.

"Let me handle it."

"No!" I grabbed his cloak when he moved to walk in front of me. "Please, I have to do this, Rafe." I needed to be mature—more worldly. I couldn't hide and allow myself to be locked behind the safety of the King's gate.

He must have recognized the need in my face, because he shrugged and let me go.

I headed for the door and opened it. The smell of hot food, warm cider, and wood smoke wafted out onto the breeze. Laughter spilled out onto the street. Shouted conversations overwhelmed me, and I stood there with wide eyes, gaping at the scene before me.

Women bustled about with trays laden with drinks and food, serving the patrons. Most of the people seated at the tables were men, with few women scattered about. The maids—barmaids, whatever they might be—weaved through the crowd, dodging and juggling dishes as if it was as easy as breathing.

"Shut that door!"

I jumped at the shout of a man at the table closest to me. His wizened old eyes peered at me as he shivered away from the draft. Rafe's heat pressed against my back and the old man lifted his gaze to Rafe, then dropped it with a curse.

I stepped in and wandered to the counter. Was this where I found the innkeeper?

"What will it be?" An older man with missing teeth shouted from further down the bar.

I shifted uncomfortably. "I'd like a room."

"I *said*, what can I get ye?" he yelled again.

"I'd like a room!" I called a little louder.

He glanced around me, found Rafe, then looked back at me. He paused in drying a mug and eyed Rafe again. "Yer daughter say something to me?" he asked.

I didn't hear Rafe respond, but the man took a step closer and held a hand to his ear.

"Speak up, little girl!"

I ground my teeth. "I'd like a room!!" I shouted as loudly as I could muster.

The people crowded around us stopped and gaped at me and Rafe. The other patrons went about their day, but it felt as if the whole world stared at me.

"Aye, lass. All right then, no need to shout." He laughed to himself and walked over. "It's fifty silver a night. Prices are high, 'tis a holiday, you know? We only have one room left," he said, holding out his hand.

I clenched my toes in my boots and counted out the coin carefully and handed them to the man.

"One night. First meal is at the seventh chime. Don't be late. We don't serve stragglers. Bits! Bitsy! A room!" he bellowed over the clamor.

A woman weaved through the crowd. Her dress was pulled low, revealing her generous cleavage, and her bodice was laced so tightly it left little to the imagination.

"Right this way!" she called, waving to us.

I followed her, trying to dodge all the spilling drinks and flailing arms of the rowdy crowd. She led us up a stairwell tucked in a corner to the second floor. It was quieter up here. She stopped at the end of the hall near a lone door.

"Name?" she asked, pursing her lips at Rafe.

"Avyanna of Gareth," I said firmly.

"Oh!" She glanced between us. "I'll write that down, sweetling. Now, you sir, if you need someone to watch your dau–"

"Go."

Rafe snarled at the woman, and she recoiled. Patting her chest, she eyed us both before offering a quick farewell and disappearing down the hall.

I took a deep breath and opened the door, revealing a tiny space. It was a smidgen larger than my storage room at the barracks. It had a cot, a table, and a potbelly stove in the corner with a small stack of wood. Rafe crowded in behind me and suddenly the room felt far smaller than my storage closet ever did.

I turned to object as Rafe shut the door and tore his cloak off, tossing it on the bed.

"I'm sorry. I forgot to ask for two rooms. I'll just—I'll be right back." I tried to get around him, but the cramped space allowed no way around him without pressing against him.

"Leave it, Vy."

"No. I—really. It will only take a moment–"

"Stop. Last room, remember?"

I looked up at him—shaken. I didn't know what I was doing. This was all wrong. Why hadn't I let him take the lead? Why did I have to do things by myself and mess them up?

He grunted and eased down to sit on the cot. He gave a small bounce before scooting up against the wall and resting his feet along the length. "Sit," he ordered.

I promptly obeyed. He shifted, giving me more room, and I just stared at him.

"This is worse," I muttered, feeling dazed.

"Hmm?"

"This is so much worse. What will my mother do when she comes to find I've a man in my room?" I whispered, horrified.

He shrugged. "Well, let's not be caught doing anything suspicious."

I slapped at his leg, and he chuckled, knitting his fingers behind his head and leaning back. His muscles bulged with his movements, rippling under his tunic.

"Keep looking at me like that, and we'll end up doing something suspicious."

I flushed and stood, taking off my cloak and laying it on the cot as well. I set Thunderbolt's saddlebag on the table and pulled Rafe's winter vest out. He watched me with keen interest as I grabbed my small sewing pouch and sat back down.

I crossed my legs and scooted back to get comfortable, pressing against his ankles. He lifted his right leg and placed it in front of me, positioning me to sit between his legs.

I glared at him from the corner of my eye.

"Think of my mother," I hissed.

He chuckled, but didn't move. Instead, he settled to watch whatever I was about to do. I flattened his vest on my lap and studied the five wooden buttons down it. They were well-worn and loved, but someone else could make use of them.

I reached into my shirt, glancing at Rafe, who watched with careful eyes. Pulling my push dagger out and tugging it from the sheath, I set to work. I pried the button away from the vest and started cutting at the threads.

"Vy—I trust you."

I glanced up to see a small smile on his face. "I'm glad you trust me with your garment. I've had lots of experience, you know."

"I was just helping. You seemed like a girl that needed to practice your mending."

"I hardly think you were helping. Do you remember that one vest I did?" I chuckled as I placed the buttons in my sewing bag and retrieved my needle and thread.

"I still have it. Hoping one day I'll fit it."

"I hope you don't," I said, glancing back with a smile.

"Like me fat?" he jested, reaching down to pat his abs.

"You're perfect just the way you are." I assured in a tone I would use on a child.

He snorted and settled in to watch. I threaded the needle and pulled a new button out of my sewing bag.

"Give it here."

"No," I said, twisting away from him. "Let me mend!"

He leaned around me, pressing his chest against my back, and snatched up my sewing bag. Placing it between his thighs, he rummaged through.

"That's mine, you know," I muttered, but made no effort to stop him.

"Soon to be mine," he said, pulling out a tooth button. He rubbed it and held it up, turning it over. "Wild cat?"

"Aye."

He let out a booming laugh, the force of it shaking the bed.

"Stop, I can't sew when you're moving like that," I chided.

Amusement colored his tone. "I'll have a bit of wild cat on my vest."

"It's better than wooden buttons."

"It will remind me of my wild cat."

"You have a wild cat?" I tied off the first button. "Where do you hide it?"

"Away from the world."

I looked up at his teasing tone and shuffled round to face him, snatching the button back.

"I hide her in a fortress in the woods. Where no one else can find her."

"How awful," I replied dryly.

"I don't think she thinks it's awful."

"And how would you know?" I threaded the needle through the second button.

"The way she looks at me."

I yelped and jerked my hand back. Blood beaded the tip of my finger. Rafe snatched my hand before I could stop him, and shot forward, taking my finger in his mouth. My heart slammed into my chest and I sat there frozen in shock.

He swirled his tongue around my finger and slowly drew it out. Heat spread through my body, flushing my face. Releasing it, he let me pull it away. A dark glint danced in his eye, screaming danger, demanding I run for my life.

"Payback," he growled.

I dropped my gaze to his lips, still wet, and I swallowed hard. He smirked and leaned back against the wall.

This day was not going at all how I planned.

Chapter Thirty-Nine

A knock jolted me upright. I blinked, taking in my surroundings, confused. It all came crashing back in a wave, and I whipped around to gape at Rafe. He was awake, leaning against the wall, watching me with hooded eyes. A drool mark dampened his tunic. A small smirk lifted the corner of his lips, and he jerked his chin toward the door.

I must have dozed off after finishing his vest. How I managed to end up on top of him, I couldn't guess. Wiping the drool from my face, I rose, placing Rafe's vest on the table. I brushed out my trousers and faced the door.

"Avyanna of Gareth?"

There was another knock. I took a deep breath and opened it as Rafe shifted on the cot.

"Annabelle of Vicoth is here to–"

"Avyanna?" My mother's expression morphed into one of pure horror and confusion.

"Mother, I–"

"What have you done to your hair?!" she shrieked, pushing into the room with a covered basket clutched in her arms.

The maid wasted no time escaping down the hall.

"I had to–"

"And what on earth are you wearing? For decency's sake, Avyanna!" she howled.

Rafe reached around her from his spot on the cot and shut the door to the hallway.

She jumped with a yelp and whirled, facing him. "A man! In your room! Avyanna! Explain this!" She whipped out a crusty loaf of bread from her basket and brandished it as if it were a weapon, waving it at Rafe.

"Mother, I have something to tell you–"

"Who is he? Why is he so big?! What are they feeding men these days?!"

He pulled his hulking body from the cot, rising to tower over both of us. I let out a groan and buried my face in my palms. It was all going so wrong.

"I am General Rafe Shadowslayer, formerly known as Rafe of Deomein. Avyanna of Gareth is part of my Tennan." His voice rumbled as he spoke.

My mother backed against me, wielding her bread. "Pray tell, what is a Tennan, dear sir?! She'll not be part of your harem!"

"Mother, I–"

Rafe burst into laughter and both my mother and I stopped and stared at him, jaws hanging open in shock. He roared with laughter, throwing his head back. I watched with horrified amusement as his muscles spasmed with each laugh.

"Is he mad?" she whispered, voice frantic.

"Sometimes I wonder," I mused.

Rafe calmed himself, blowing out a sigh. "I see where she gets it," he muttered.

He snatched the bread out of her hand. The door creaked as he opened it, crowding us with the movement, and stepped out. His teeth sank into the loaf, tearing off a hunk, and he snorted one last time before latching the door shut behind him. We stared for a solid moment in pure confusion. My mother's hand was still raised in the air, no longer wielding bread, with her back pressed against me.

I wrapped my arms around her and squeezed. "It's good to see you, mother."

It took a few moments to calm her down, but eventually she did. She rested her large frame on the cot, and I sat on the small table, letting my feet dangle in the air. I told her everything that had happened—about my depression, my sense of uselessness and mental struggles after the Wild One rejected me. I spoke of the refugees, about Ran, and how he was my turning point, the moment I snapped.

When I shared the details of the day I signed the recruitment papers, she wailed and dug into her basket of baked goods. I explained my hardships and how General Rafe helped me. I told her about the friendships I'd made and the Tennan I was now a part of.

I left out the parts with Victyr and when I was sick. The recent events involving Rafe were also avoided. She didn't take any of it well. I could hardly ask her advice on love at a time like this. She finished another sweetloaf as I gushed about Thunderbolt, trying to lighten the mood.

And she cried when I explained I was headed out in two days.

To see my mother cry was the most torturous thing I ever witnessed. The one who birthed me, cared for me as a babe, who tried her best when her husband was taken from her, who loved her child from afar for so many years, cry—because of me. Because after all these years, she might lose me the same way she lost her first love. This war would rob her of both the people she loved with all her heart.

I jumped down and sat on the cot with her, holding her as she sobbed. She cried, and I cried with her. Her tears soaked my tunic, and I expressed all I had realized. That I knew she cared for me, and how awful I'd been at reciprocating that love. I stroked her hair as I made it known how much I loved her, and how I'd never be able to repay her for everything she'd done for me. When I confessed how selfish I'd been, I stroked her back, and the words tore at my throat.

She sniffled and wrapped her arms around me, holding me tight. "Avyanna, you are your father's daughter, if nothing else." Her voice trembled. "You will carve your own path, regardless of what other people want. You're headstrong and always have been—it's a part of you." She pulled away from me and held my face. "I love all of you, even the broken pieces, darling."

Something in me shattered. I crumpled in her arms and sobbed. I let her hold me, knowing this could be the last time I'd ever drink in my mother's comfort.

I wept.

My mother departed that evening and I was stuck in the small room with a basket half full of sweet cakes. My eyes burned from crying. Exhaustion weighed them down. It was bittersweet. I was saddened by her loss, but pleased all was right between us.

When I gave her the necklace, she started crying again, knowing exactly why I gave it to her. I tied it around her neck and she left, believing her daughter would be dead in the next two days.

Night had fallen, and though the sun went down, the noise from the first floor grew. I tossed on the cot, finding Rafe's cloak. The warm fabric brushed against my cheek as I pulled it close. I buried my face, finding solace in his scent. I was alone. There was no one left to comfort me—I had to take care of myself. I inhaled deeply, trying to memorize his scent of masculinity. The smell of a man, not perfumed or spiced, simply Rafe.

The door crept open, and I stiffened. Rafe's head led in and his body followed, shutting the door behind him. I sat up as he lit a candle from the stove. He placed it on the table and looked at me.

"You said your goodbyes," he stated.

"Aye," I whispered. I thought my tears had run out, but a rebel drop trickled out of the corner of my eye.

He sat beside me and pressed his warm hand to my cheek. His thumb trailed across my skin, brushing away the tear. I reached up and pulled off the cloth around his face. His left eye flashed in the dark, reflecting the candlelight.

"I should get my own room," he rasped.

"That's what I said," I breathed, leaning forward.

He stood, clearing his throat, and I thought he would go demand a room. Instead, he took my cloak and sat on the floor.

"What are you–" I started.

He pulled off his boots and set them beside him, then laid back, flat on the ground with his feet at the door.

"No–"

"Hush, Vy. Get some rest." He settled in, using my cloak as a blanket. "Get the light."

"You're the blasted General, you shouldn't be on the–"

"I am the blasted General, Avyanna. Get the light."

"There's room enough for both of us."

"There's only one way there's room for both of us up there, and you know it," he growled. He sat up and glared. "Who do you want on top, Vy? Me or you?"

I shrunk into his cloak and reached for the candle.

"Good girl."

I blew out the flame and took my boot off, tossing it in his direction. There was a soft grunt, and I threw my other one.

"Vy–" he warned.

"I only have two boots," I grumbled in defense, flopping on the bed like a child.

"Stay on top of the cloak."

"I know," I snapped. "Bugs and such."

He chuckled, and silence lapsed. Rumbles of laughter howled from downstairs, and I wondered what all those people were doing. Perhaps, because of my sacrifice, they would have a future. I would fight the Shadows and save them—protect them.

The barmaid crossed my mind, Bitsy. She was one life I'd protect. My mind wandered to how she flaunted her beauty, how she wanted Rafe.

"Rafe?"

"Hmm?" He grunted in answer.

"Did you think Bitsy was pretty?"

"Who?"

"The barmaid, Bitsy?" I grimaced in the dark, hating the fact that I was bringing her back up to his memory. I didn't want him to think about her.

He heaved a sigh. "Why do you want to know, Vy?"

"Just curious."

"Liar."

I peeked down at him, his silhouette faintly illuminated by the coals from the stove in the corner. "Well?" I prompted.

"Tell me why you want to know."

"I'm curious."

"So you've said."

I laid back and stared at the ceiling. Perhaps, under cover of darkness, it wouldn't be as bad to be open with him. He was my Rafe today, not the gruff General of his Tennan.

"I want to know what you think is pretty," I choked out.

There was a pause.

"You want to know what I think is pretty? Me? Not men?" His tone took on a strange edge.

"Aye," I whispered, blinking against the darkness, hoping against hope that he wouldn't push me away.

There was a groan and a thump and I rolled over to see him put his hands behind his head. He stared up at the ceiling as well, his silver eye glinting in the weak light. Returning to my back, I waited.

"I think strength is... pretty—attractive," he paused. "Tenacity. Determination. Perseverance."

"What about women?"

"Hmm?"

"Do you think women are pretty?" Perhaps I had read him wrong this whole time.

"Aye, Vy. I think some women are pretty," he drawled.

"What are... pretty attributes of women you like?" I scrunched up my face at my question. I was acting like a total child.

Silence prevailed.

"You want to know what makes me want to bed a woman?" His voice was rough in the darkness.

"Aye," I breathed, still holding my eyes shut and clenching my fists.

He groaned, and there was a rustle of fabric. I peeked over the side of the cot to see that he had brought his knees up and was rubbing his face with his palms.

"You play a dangerous game, kitten," he warned, his voice muffled.

I laid back, cheeks flaming. "I know."

"I don't have a type. I haven't been back to the homelands since I was seventeen-winters. I hadn't had the chance to explore that realm," he sighed. "I think I would like someone who didn't run from me."

"Hmm?" I encouraged.

"Women always think they want some big strong man to care for them. They forget big strong men come with big strong attitudes. Every time I've told a woman to do something, they shrink away like a whipped puppy and run. If one ever dared to defy me, I'd find that attractive," he finished.

I wiggled my toes. I had defied him. More than once. That meant he found me attractive, right?

"Fair game, Vy. Your turn."

"For what?"

"What makes you want to bed a man?"

My pulse raced with excitement, and I curled my toes. This was dangerous territory. My head objected with all the logic in the world, but my heart ignored it. "I can't say for sure. I've never wanted to bed a man."

"A woman, then?"

I snorted. "You didn't even let me finish before you go guessing that I like girls."

"I've heard it's a thing."

"Not my thing," I retorted.

He scoffed, and I closed my eyes, hiding behind the false security of my eyelids. If I couldn't see him, he couldn't see me... right?

"I've never wanted to bed a man before. Not till... oh, about six months ago or so. Perhaps longer, without me realizing it."

"Who is he?"

Rafe's voice sharpened, and a smile tugged at my lips. Jealous?

"That's not the game," I quipped.

"Well, you didn't answer the question."

He seemed frustrated, and I grinned at the ceiling.

"Well, let me tell you about him."

"She's going to tell me about her crush," he moaned and made a gagging sound.

"Wait, wait!" I laughed. "I think you'll like him!"

"Doubtful. Probably a pansy."

I snickered at that thought and writhed on the bed in pure joy.

"What are you doing up there?"

"Thinking. Hush."

"She tells me to hush," he muttered, but remained quiet.

"He's big, strong—built like a beast. Muscles everywhere."

"Do you often admire men's bodies?"

"Hush!"

He snorted, and I continued.

"He is taller than me–"

"Everyone is taller than you."

I sat up and reached down for something to throw at the insolent man. Seizing one of his boots, I chucked it. His laughter rumbled, and he shifted as I reached for the other one. He grabbed my wrist and pulled me to the floor. Wrestling with him, we thumped and banged our heads and limbs on the floor, laughing and cursing each other.

A bang on the wall cut our laughter short. We froze. He was pinned to the ground, holding me with my back pressed to his chest. He held an arm around my waist and his legs were wrapped tightly around mine.

"Get it over with in there!"

The stranger's muffled shout made Rafe snort in amusement. He chuckled, bouncing me with the movement. "If they only knew," he rumbled.

I giggled and relaxed on top of him. My soft curves fit against him perfectly, like pieces of a puzzle. I shifted, something hard digging into my backside.

"You never finished," he whispered in my ear.

Heat coiled through me, making my heart race and face flush. My logical side reared its ugly head, screaming for me to run away.

"Where was I?" I teased.

"Big, tall, strong, ruggedly handsome, wears a cloth over his eye. Makes him seem more dangerous," he offered.

I laughed and squirmed in his arms. "I did not say all that!"

"You meant it," he said.

His legs lowered from around mine, and he cradled my hips inside his strong thighs. He nestled me against him, letting me feel every firm muscle and hard ridge of his body.

Letting me feel his need.

"I–" I started, but didn't know what to say.

I lay there against him, feeling like the game was up. I had lost. My heart raced, and the simmering heat beneath my skin convinced me I wanted to lose this game.

"Say it." His voice was rough.

I wanted to roll and face him. I wanted to see the emotion on his face. What was he going through? What was he feeling?

"It's true," I whispered.

"No, say it."

"Say what?"

"Say the name of who you'd bed."

His tone was dark and demanding. He needed me to say his name, as if it were permission for whatever acts would follow. It was as if saying his name was the dam holding back the reckless flood of need and want that was both pleasure and ruin.

I was tipping over the edge of the abyss, knowing if I made this choice, there would be no going back. I could never come back from the actions and consequences that followed.

"No."

As soon as I breathed the word, he released me, groaning as he pressed his limbs to the floor.

"Up."

"You don't like my game?" I rolled over to see him.

The light was too poor to make out anything, much less read his face. I maneuvered my legs to straddle his hips, settling back against his hard length. My cheeks burned with the tangible proof of his desire. He had the same all-consuming need that threw my good sense to the wind.

"Avyanna of Gareth, I warn you. If you don't get up right now, I'm not responsible for my actions," he growled between clenched teeth.

He held his arms to the floor and dropped his legs, freeing me from any restraint. His muscles were hard and taut beneath me, as if letting me go was the last thing he wanted to do.

I smiled sadly, too afraid to commit. Fear and insecurity had me biting my lip and rising off him. I knew when the game was called, but it wasn't a game for Rafe anymore. Something changed and rewrote the rules. I stood, knowing he could see my outline from the dim light, and unfastened my belt.

"Vy," he choked out in warning.

I dropped my trousers, and the hem of the tunic brushed the top of my knee. Stepping over Rafe, I laid them on the table. I climbed onto the cot and burrowed into his cloak. He let out a fierce growl and slammed his fist on the floor.

"You cruel witch," he hissed.

Smiling, I drifted off into a fitful sleep.

I stretched, sore and cold. Rolling over with a moan, I saw Rafe tending the small stove in the corner. His broad back was to me, and I pulled his cloak around me, content to lie there and admire him.

His muscles coiled and moved under his skin with every shift as he balanced on the balls of his feet, pushing more wood into the stove. He was a giant of a man, but graceful at the same time. Korzak was a true giant, but lacked the grace that came with Rafe.

He shifted, turning to reach for my cloak on the floor. He glanced up and froze, staring at me.

"Morn," I said, groggy with sleep.

He frowned, gaze traveling down my body. I was wrapped in his cloak, except for a leg that I had kicked out during the night. His eyes stopped at my exposed calf and he glanced back up at me.

"Cover yourself."

"Someone didn't sleep well." I teased, but obeyed and pulled my leg back under his cloak.

He stood, stretching his arms above his head. I watched as his tunic rose, exposing the thick muscles above his trousers.

"I slept on a wood floor," he groaned.

My shoulders lifted in a lazy shrug. "I offered the bed."

"I would have slept far less," he said, dropping his arms and eyeing me.

I smirked and kicked off the cloak. Closing my eyes, I stretched to my limit, waking my limbs up. When my eyes fluttered open, Rafe's hungry gaze was on me. His eyes were fastened to where the hem of my tunic had risen on my thighs. I threw my legs over the side of the cot and stood. He bit out a harsh curse and sat on the floor to jerk his boots on. I smiled sweetly and retrieved my trousers from the table. Stepping in, I watched Rafe from under my lashes. He tied the cloth over his injured eye, glaring at me. I pulled my trousers up and slowly pushed my tunic into the waist, but his dark eye never left my face.

"Careful how much you taunt me, girl," he growled.

He opened the door and stormed out, slamming it shut behind him. I stood there for a moment looking at the solid wood, hearing his heavy footsteps travel down the hall.

Throwing my hands in the air, I danced a jig with myself and fell onto the cot, flinging my arms wide. "He likes me," I whispered to the ceiling.

It was childish—inappropriate. I shouldn't feed my desire, but I was helpless against it. I didn't fully understand it, but the power to make him tick, to put him on edge was exhilarating, empowering—addictive.

I wanted more.

I took a deep breath, knowing it ended today. We would join the barracks again, surrounded by the Tennan. Part of me knew I would have to be careful, as well as Rafe, when we went to the spring from now on. The temptation would be great, because I had fed it and teased it.

I writhed on the bed, giggling.

I had never felt this before. Both this longing deep in my belly and the joy that came with having a terrible, glorious secret. This was between me and Rafe, and it would stay that way. We both knew we each desired each other and understood we couldn't act on it.

The risk was great, but I cherished the ride. I didn't feel like I had to fulfill my longing. Staring up at the ceiling, I wondered if Rafe felt the same. Last night, he clearly enjoyed himself. He acted in a manner I'd never seen, with his walls completely down. But this morning, he seemed angry.

Perhaps, because he was older, he didn't revel in it like I did. Maybe it was harder on him. I sighed happily and rose from the cot, gathering our things. Whether he enjoyed this as much as I did wasn't the question. As long as the feelings were mutual, it was fine.

I smiled, packing my saddlebag.

It was more than fine.

It was wonderful.

After gathering our belongings, I started for the main floor. I stopped at the bottom of the stairs and searched the room, spotting Rafe in the far corner. I walked to him and laid our things on the table. He reached into the basket and snatched a small loaf as a maid weaved over.

My heart warmed at his acceptance of my mother's cooking. He ate what he saw Xzanth prepare, but he hadn't seen my mother bake the loaves. He trusted her because he trusted me. I held back a smile at his confidence.

"First meal?" she asked, placing a steaming cup of cider in front of me.

"Please," I replied.

She smiled and tried to set out a mug for Rafe, but he brushed her away with his hand, shaking his head.

"Just one, please," I corrected.

She hummed in confusion, but nodded and bustled away.

Rafe ate the sweetloaf and eyed the few people in the room. I took a drink of the cider, moaning in pleasure as it warmed my hands and throat. Rafe's eye danced to me, then flitted away. I pushed the mug to him and he shoved it back.

"How long will it take before we know if it's poisoned?" I whispered.

The corner of his mouth twitched. "Depends on the poison."

I grinned, and he sighed. He dragged the mug to him, and I watched as his throat moved, pulling the burning liquid inside. When he licked his wet lips, I stared at his mouth and thought terrible things.

The maid rescued me from my thoughts as she placed a bowl of porridge in front of me. My nose wrinkled with distaste. The flavor would be bland, but it would be warm and fill my belly. I thanked her as she refilled my mug and whisked off.

Rafe waited until I ate half the portion before snatching it and finishing the rest. I pulled a loaf out of my mother's basket and nibbled on it. In public, he didn't let his guard down for a breath—constantly watching and listening. He might appear focused on his food, but I saw the darting glances at the door whenever it opened. The way he positioned his body to rise quickly without the table impeding the motion.

He was always on edge, always ready to fight.

After scraping the last remnants from the bowl, he stood and donned his cloak. I followed, wrapping mine around me but pushing it back over my shoulders as he did. A man nearby eyed our patches and whispered to his friends. They turned and eyed us with lewd smiles and bloodshot eyes.

"Enjoy the night of the Solstice?" One called with a grin, glancing between us.

Rafe turned his fierce glare on them, and another laughed.

"I don't think he did, lad. Looks like he didn't get what–"

The man's statement was cut short as Rafe moved. He closed the distance in three strides. He grasped the man's hair and slammed his head onto the table. The others shouted and leapt from their seats, grabbing for their friend.

Rafe turned to me and jerked his chin at the exit. I gaped, eyes darting between him and the men, before snatching our things and heading out the door. The cold winter air bit at me, tugging at my short hair. Rafe pushed against me, then disappeared around the corner. I followed him out of the wind and into the stables. We found and saddled our horses, then set off to the barracks.

We rode in silence with our hoods pulled up. Thick snow fell in sheets and the wind lashed at us, obscuring our view. Rafe led, and I followed, not knowing the way. By the time we made it back through the barracks' gate, Thunderbolt was covered in snow and ice. Rafe's stallion had its head bowed against the bitter elements.

At the stables, we brushed down our horses. Thunderbolt shook his wet hair like a dog, and I laughed at his antics. After bedding him down, I caught a stableboy and told him to feed him extra for his trek in the snow.

Rafe stood at the entrance to the stables, leaning against a wall. He watched the snowstorm, tracking the swirling white flakes with his eye. I came up beside him, peering at the hazy buildings.

"The others won't brave the storm," he murmured.

"Then they'll be late." I frowned.

The punishment for being off barracks' grounds without leave was a flogging at best, and execution at worst.

"Better late than buried in a snowdrift." He righted himself and pulled his hood up. "The Corporals will make an exception this once."

I nodded and wrapped my cloak tighter around myself. I followed Rafe's lead and hefted my basket of belongings closer to me, plunging into the snow.

We walked back to the fortress more by memory than any seen path. The snow piled quickly, obscuring everything. The wind howled in my ears and I kept my head low, watching Rafe's boots in front of me. We didn't see another soul on the roads. Everyone was sheltering in place.

I gasped when we entered the fortress, finally out of the bitter cold. Rafe closed the door behind us and headed straight to the hearth. I placed my belongings on my cot and shook out my cloak, hanging it to dry. After removing my boots, I approached Rafe as he tended the fire. There were still a few hot coals buried from the morning prior, and he nursed them to a flame.

Pulling Korzak's spare cot near the hearth, I sat, warming my cold limbs. Rafe climbed to the loft and shrugged out of his cloak. I boldly watched him. We were alone, after all. No one else had returned.

He bent over to pick something up, and I had a fleeting moment to appreciate the way his trousers clung to his thick thighs. Biting my lip as he stood, I tried to tamp down the desire that coiled low in my belly. Nothing would happen. We wouldn't let it. He descended the stairs with a long, slender item wrapped in a sheet. I eyed it curiously, wondering what it was. It looked like a staff, but why would he have a staff in his loft? He sat on the cot beside me and handed it over.

"Happy Solstice." His voice dropped to a low rumble.

My brows rose with surprise. He bought me something? Now, I was positive it was a staff. If he were to buy anyone anything, it would be a weapon.

It wasn't unbearably heavy, but had some healthy weight to it, versus a lighter training staff. I tore the sheet off, eagerness getting the better of me. The sheet fell to the floor, and I sucked in a breath at the item that Rafe deemed appropriate for a Solstice gift.

A spear—not a staff. Black metal wrapped the light wood handle and curved up the shaft in an intricate design. Delicate and feminine. I slipped the sheath from the head, and my mouth opened in silent awe.

The head was long with a tapered, double-edged blade. The steel was beautiful, polished to a shine. A strange hue shimmered with the gray, a blue tint, as if something more than plain steel had been forged into it. Wrapped around the socket where the blade met the shaft was a white braid finished with beautiful green beads. I traced my finger along the strands and looked at Rafe accusingly.

"Aye, it's yours." The corner of his mouth lifted in a small smile.

My breath caught. He saved my hair from when he cut it. Did he know from that time, I would join his Tennan—that a spear would suit me far better than any other weapon? Did he plan this that long ago?

"Up." He stood and jogged up the stairs two at a time. "Clear the center room," he called.

I grinned like a fool and sheathed the spear. I pushed the cots along the walls, clearing the space. It wasn't a huge area, but it was at least fifteen paces in diameter. Large enough.

Rafe hurried back, and I eyed his three blades as he approached. He carried his arming swords that he normally sparred with, as well as a longer blade. By longer, I mean it was as long as I was tall. Its hilt was the same as the others, wrapped in a simple black leather.

I readied my spear and tossed the sheath on a nearby cot. Rafe braced his twin blades and stepped into position. I smiled and planted my feet, lowering the tip of my spear.

"Let's go."

He didn't wait for me, but rather launched an offensive attack of his own. He twisted, lashing out, and I cringed, using the shaft of my spear to block. It was brand new! I mentally complained, but this was what it was designed for.

I spun with him, locked in a dance of blades. Firelight licked at our shadows, and I matched him blow for blow. I whirled, throwing in my own attacks, ones that he had to dance away from the force of. I warmed quickly, the movement and fire from the hearth heating me through. My skin grew damp from exertion. I noted the sweat beading on Rafe's upper chest, pleased that I was not the only one expending myself.

He finally parried a blow and dropped his sword, grabbing my spear shaft with his bare hand. In a quick movement, he jerked me to him and wrapped his arm around me, pinning me against him. I panted, breathing hard as I surrendered to his hold. He looked down at me, fire burning in his eye. His chest pumped as he sucked needed air into his lungs and I felt something dangerous draw tight between us.

"Now would have been a good time to use your bandit breaker," he whispered, his voice rough.

"Perhaps... if I wanted to escape," I gasped.

He bit out a curse and released me, spinning away. I grinned—I had gotten to him. Pulling myself back, I wiped the sweat from my temple. He sheathed his blades and drew his longsword. It was nearly as long as my spear, and I took a deep breath, letting it out in a sigh.

He moved into a new stance and nodded. "Again."

This time, my skill seemed less efficient. His reach matched mine, robbing me of any advantage. I danced with him, trying to call his bluffs and parry his strikes fast enough to get a hit in. Moving quickly, my arms shook, and I gasped for air, taking in his every move. I swung my spear, deflecting a blow, and charged into his opening. He held out a hand, but I swung the spearhead at it, and he snatched it back. I rammed my shaft to his neck and shoved him against the wall.

He dropped his sword, and I blinked up at him, gasping for breath. My arms were extended, keeping the shaft in place. I couldn't hold him for long because of the height difference. He looked down at me, relaxing against the wall, and smirked.

"Good girl," he said, throat jostling the spear with his words.

I quirked a smile and waited. "Now would be a good time to free yourself," I said, knowing I was wide open.

Something poked me under my ribs and I peered down to see a knife at my tunic.

"I am," he said with a wide grin.

I heaved a breathless laugh. He was good.

The door to the fortress crashed open, and we both whipped our heads as the howling wind shrieked in.

Jamlin stumbled inside, glancing up at us, and froze. He blinked, taking in the scene, and cleared his throat. "I'd hate to break up whatever this is, but Korzak is stuck in a drift and I can't get him out."

Chapter Forty

Korzak was a chime's distance from the barracks, buried in a snowdrift. Thankfully, he was still breathing, though blue and freezing. We managed to pull him onto a horse and made for the fortress. We made it back just as night settled in.

Rafe and Jamlin heaved Korzak's giant body onto a cot.

"I'll take the horses back. Jam, Avyanna, tend to him," Rafe ordered, starting for the doors.

I stepped after him. "I'll go."

"And get lost in the snow as well? Obey your orders," he growled, then stormed out of the fortress.

My brows met in a frown and I turned back to Jam and Korzak. Was he ashamed to be caught in such a situation with me?

"Help me move him closer to the fire," Jam instructed.

I hurried to help push the heavy cot. Jam's shaking hands fumbled as he attempted to remove Korzak's wet clothes.

I batted him away. "Tend to yourself," I insisted. "I'll ask for your help when I need it."

A silent question lit his eyes, and I shooed him off like a child. He shrugged out of his cloak, and I started on Korzak's tunic. I removed his clothes with no assistance. It was a struggle, but one I did willingly. His state of undress didn't faze me. There was something about caring for someone in need that took all immodesty from the situation.

Once Jamlin got dressed in dry clothes, he removed Korzak's under-breeches, and I turned away until he'd been covered with a warm blanket. I found a spare rag and dabbed at Korzak's wet face, drying his head and hair as much as I could.

Jamlin finished fussing over the giant and dropped beside me. His weight bowed the cot, and I shook my head as we studied Korzak's peaceful expression. While asleep, he was handsome, as if he were a mature man. It was when he opened his eyes or spoke that made his childlikeness apparent.

"What happened?" I asked.

"The fool wouldn't listen to me. He swore he would be put to death if he was left outside the walls," Jam said, rubbing his face. "I tried to tell him that no one expected us to travel in this weather, but he wouldn't listen.

"I followed him, leading him back to the path several times. His horse spooked halfway back and disappeared. My mare couldn't carry us both, so we walked. It's as if his size robs him of any endurance or stamina. He fell into the drift, and the blasted man is too heavy for me to lift."

I looked from Jam's thick arms to Korzak. Korzak was massive, putting on weight in the past few months. He was no longer the lanky giant I was first introduced to.

"I'm glad we found him," I whispered.

"Likewise." Jamlin faced me, jerking his chin at the door. "You and Rafe were practicing?"

"Aye, I have a new spear," I said, grinning as I nodded to the weapon tucked under my cot.

"Looked like maybe more."

"More what?"

"More than just practice." Jam spoke carefully, scrutinizing my face.

His dark brown eyes pinned me, and my heart stuttered with guilt. I ducked my head away from his gaze.

"It wasn't. I swear," I breathed.

"Not my business.".

I peeked up at him, cursing the heat in my cheeks.

He shrugged. "But there might be others that would object if you shared a bed."

"We're not." My face felt like it was on fire, but I spoke the truth.

He stared at me for a moment longer before nodding, his expression sober. The fortress door opened and Rafe hurried in, shutting it behind him.

"Will we still head north in the morn?" Jamlin called.

Rafe joined us by the hearth and warmed his hands, casting a glance at Korzak. "We take our leave at midday, as long as the storm breaks."

Jam nodded and stared down at his lap. Tonight was unexpected, but we had a mission. One that, at this point, could no longer be ignored. Rafe glanced at me and pressed his lips together. His dark gaze assured me. Sighing, my lips pulled down into a frown as I watched Korzak, knowing he would not be coming with us.

The next day, our Tennan slowly filtered in. Zephath and Xzanth came in at first light. They traveled as soon as the storm broke in the middle of the night. They were cold and hungry, but otherwise well. Garion, Tegan, and Collins returned a few chimes later, with Blain and Dane returning last, closer to the midday chime. All cursed the sudden storm but accepted the fact that we were still moving on with the plan.

I readied my saddlebags with my sparse belongings and supplies. We packed for a short journey, but one for the road with no inns.

Glancing at Rafe, who was in the loft, I studied him as he strapped his weapons on. He wore his arming swords on his back, hilts protruding from each shoulder over his thick winter vest. He looked down at us as we gathered our things. When his eye found mine, he turned away.

I finished packing and set my saddlebag on my cot. Garion, Blain, and Collins were ordered to stay behind with Korzak. The rest were riding out with us. Rafe didn't want to leave Blain behind, but he would need word as soon as Korzak was well and they could join us.

As the others finished their tasks, the neighing of horses drew us outside. I took Thunderbolt from Garion's offered hand, and loaded my belongings onto the pigou. My spear looked comically large strapped to his saddle, as if nature itself mocked me for taking this small creature into battle.

I'd just finished double checking all the straps when Rafe emerged, heading to his stallion. He greeted the beast, rubbing his muzzle, and muttered words too quiet for me to hear. Rafe stepped to his side and threw his pack over his saddle to tie it down.

He strapped his longsword to his saddle as well. With his arming swords secured to his back, and a few daggers sheathed along his frame—the man was armed to the teeth. It was obvious he didn't take this mission lightly.

Xzanth approached, handing me the crossbow. I took it and a large wrap of bolts. Nodding my thanks, I fastened them to my saddle. Thunderbolt seemed even more comical. He turned his shaggy head to peek back at me as if accusing me of thinking him unworthy.

"I know you're the bravest of them all," I whispered, rubbing between his ears.

"Mount!"

I jumped and swung my leg over Thunderbolt at Rafe's order. The others mounted as one. Blain spoke a few words to Dane, slapping his twin's thigh. Rafe spoke to Garion, and the rest of us waited for orders.

Garion saluted and stepped back, and Rafe rode to the front.

"Move out," he called.

His stallion snorted and pranced in the fresh snow, lifting his hooves high. Thunderbolt huffed and pulled his ears back, unimpressed with the stallion's antics. We fell into formation and slowly rode out.

A mix of anticipation, excitement, and dread rushed through me as we neared the barracks' gate. The knowledge that I was riding out with the Tennan for the first time, and for perhaps the last time, didn't hit me until we passed under the King's gate. As Thunderbolt stepped over the threshold of the wall, fear struck my heart, its barbs sinking deep.

I wasn't ready for this.

"Easy."

I glanced over to Xzanth, who looked at me, but patted his gelding as if he spoke to it.

Swallowing past the lump in my throat, I tried to relax my muscles. I could do this. Rafe wouldn't bring me along unless he knew I could handle myself.

I picked my chin up and studied my surroundings as we headed north. Snow covered the landscape in a thick white blanket, glittering with the sun's rays. There was not a cloud in the sky, as if the weather itself denied the storm last night.

Settling deeper into my saddle, I determined I would enjoy this bit. It was freedom like I had never known. I would accept it and enjoy it.

We made camp while it was still light. Xzanth found a small copse of trees that would offer shelter, and we cared for our horses and set to our tasks. Dane went off to scout and hunt. Zephath gathered firewood. Jamlin and Tegan strung the horses on a line after we all rubbed them down. Rafe studied some parchments in the light of the setting sun.

I organized the cooking supplies as Xzanth started a fire. We readied our dried food but held out hope that Dane would bring back fresh meat.

"Avyanna."

I looked up from the pot I set near the fire.

Rafe was focused on his papers, but glanced up at me. "Forage."

I nodded and retrieved my crossbow. I hefted it up on my shoulder and headed out. The snow was deep, almost coming to my knees, but I pressed beyond the camp.

I smiled, embracing this sense of freedom. At this moment, I could go where I wished and do as I pleased. I had a task, but I was free to do it how I chose.

Rafe was in General mode, barking out orders, and his mental walls were raised. I didn't mind it in the least. I knew in my heart how I felt about him and knew his reaction to me. Warmth spread through my body as I pondered our stolen moments. Knowing our secret was enough for me. I didn't need him to put aside his role as General to care for my feelings. I was his soldier first and foremost.

Pausing near an evergreen, I picked a few of the needled twigs. They would make a decent tea. I pushed them into my pocket and thought about the first time I foraged with Rafe.

I had brought him prickleberries. Now, knowing his prickly nature, I realized how ironic that was. I remembered him throwing them in a fit of rage. I didn't understand his behavior then, but now, I did.

The other Generals sent him to the homelands against his will, as a punishment. I'm sure he hated leaving his men on the front. Coming back and seeing all the soldiers being trained poorly must have weighed on him. He made it his responsibility to correct their training and prepare them for the war front.

Even I lashed out from time to time when I was overly stressed. Rafe seemed to be more balanced now, a sense of purpose grounding him.

I stopped near a creek bed and pushed the snow aside with my boot. Karven leaves poked through, stiff and green, holding onto their life regardless of the snow. I plucked a few. They were bitter, but if boiled in a stew, that bitterness left a savory flavor.

I stayed out for another quarter of a chime, watching the sun recede and measured the distance as Xzanth taught me. Not finding anything else under the thick snow, I headed back to the camp, closely monitoring my direction, and following my tracks when I could.

When I returned, I was pleased to see Dane carrying two hares. I worked with Xzanth, preparing the evening meal, and chatted with the men about the storm.

They were all in a good mood, surprisingly happy for being on the way to their probable deaths.

Rafe had disappeared, and I wondered if he slipped away to relieve himself or to think. The rest of the Tennan were here, enjoying the meal. I busied myself talking with the men, eating warm food, and drinking my tinge berry tea. The stuff was earthy, bitter—but not bad. I packed a few months' worth, in case we were out longer than expected. I wouldn't be caught off guard.

Zephath sat on his blanket, knees pulled up to his chest, lost in his own thoughts without a book to read. Tegan recounted a humorous tale about a bear that stormed into an inn, in his home village in the mountains of E'or, and terrified the people and itself. We laughed as he told of the female cook, who was the only one brave enough to charge the bear, armed with only a frying pan.

Rafe drew my attention as he drifted back into the camp with a deep frown. Dane rose to greet him and they spoke in low tones, a stone's toss away from the rest of us. My smile faltered. I didn't like that look. Even if I didn't know Rafe well, anyone could read that something had unnerved him.

We set our watches as night fell, and I curled into my blanket, exhausted.

Someone shook me awake, and I jolted upright, startled.

"Easy there, lass," Tegan huffed a quiet laugh. "You sleep like a stone!"

I gave him a small smile and rubbed my eyes, glancing around at the sleeping men. I stood and stretched. Winter's chill bit at me, and I reached down to snag my cloak and wrap it around me.

"Care for yer needs while I stoke the fire," he whispered.

I nodded and headed off into the night. The moon reflected against the snow, making the forest seem bright and alive. I relieved myself behind a shrub and returned to camp, fetching my crossbow.

After giving Tegan a small salute, I followed his tracks around the camp, watching and listening. I looked out along the snow-covered plains, at the patches of woods peppering the white expanse. There were no houses, no farms, nothing. We were only a day's ride from Northwing. I thought there would be more traffic, though it was possible the storm warned people off.

A dragon roared in the distance, and I turned southward. Though it was far, I presumed it had to have come from Northwing. Most of the dragons there were in brumation, but maybe one had woken and been distressed by the cold.

I resumed my walk and searched the northern skies. Perhaps it was the Shadow-controlled dragon that Rafe feared from the north. I still wasn't aware if he told any of the Tennan his concerns, or only shared them with me.

I shook my head, eager to finish my watch and return to sleep. I would deal with that Shadow and its Hunters when we came to it. There was no sense in creating evil where it might not exist.

The time passed, and I rushed back to camp, late to wake Jamlin. I knelt beside him and patted the big man's shoulder. His eyes snapped open, though awareness took a moment to come to them.

"It's your watch," I whispered.

He nodded, sat up, and squinted at the moon through the trees. Noticing the time, his gaze darted from me to where Rafe lay on his side, sleeping.

I slapped his shoulder and gave him a mocking glare. "I was enjoying the evening."

"Just making sure you weren't enjoying someone," he moaned as he rubbed at his shoulder.

"Pah!" I replied, smiling.

I stoked the fire as Jam walked off to answer nature's call. Returning, he picked up his sword and strapped it on. Giving me a salute as I removed my boots, he headed off into the night.

I slipped into my blanket, pulling my cloak over me and up to my chin. I sighed and studied General Rafe's sleeping form. After a few breaths, he rolled to his back and looked at me, firelight dancing in his eye. He gave me a smirk before facing the sky and closing his eyes.

I drifted off to sleep with the biggest grin on my face.

The next morning, we woke before the sun. We ate a quick meal and packed up camp. By the time the sun's first rays peeked over the horizon, we were mounted and ready to go.

We made our way north, Rafe urging us faster. Thunderbolt kept up with the longer legged horses easily, not even breathing hard when we would stop for small breaks.

Rafe grew more and more withdrawn, and I began to worry. I watched the others. They would look at him, frown, then avert their eyes. They seemed content to let him be the one that stressed and worried.

He sent Dane on endless scouting missions, having him trade horses with Zephath when his own mount tired. Rafe kept us in open territory, but as evening fell, he angled us toward a rocky outcropping.

We set up camp a little later, forced to eat dried rations as Dane was exhausted. He slipped under his blanket before the sun even went down, right after he filled his belly. I watched him with a frown, and my eyes darted to Rafe. He had climbed a boulder and stood on top of it, scanning the sky.

A somber blanket weighed on us all. Even Tegan didn't spare a joke. As the sun sank, we all retired to our blankets. As I laid there listening to the sounds of the night, more than just the cold tried to chill my bones. My watch was right after Rafe's tonight. I was determined to speak with him and, at the very least, try to offer him comfort or empathy.

It didn't take long before I drifted into a fitful sleep filled with night terrors. Black dragons snapping at me, things I couldn't see chasing me, headless Victyr. I fought and screamed, trying to be free of them.

I was jerked awake, my mouth smothered by a large, calloused palm. My eyes shot open to meet Rafe's dark glare. He glanced at the others and pulled his hand off, tapping my lips.

Groggy, I nodded and rose as he stalked away from the camp. I glanced at Jam, seeing his chest rise and fall with his sleeping breaths, and wondered if he was truly asleep. What if I had woken him and now he knew I was slipping off with Rafe? What would he assume?

My teeth chattered as I pulled my cloak about me. What he thought didn't matter. What mattered was that nothing was going to happen between us. I simply wanted to talk.

I headed in the direction Rafe had set off in and found him leaning against a boulder in a thin line of evergreens. He watched the night, alert for anything that might bespeak danger. I stopped beside him and leaned my cloak-covered shoulder against his bare one.

He heaved a sigh. "The purpose of a watch... is to watch."

"So watch." I shrugged, innocently staring out over the landscape.

He grunted in amusement. "It's impossible to focus with you around," he muttered, leaning forward to rest his corded arms against the boulder.

I stepped behind him and boldly ran my hands up his biceps and to his shoulders. He moaned and bowed his head. He wore his longsword at his side, and I took the opportunity to rub at his tense muscles.

"What is bothering you, General?" I asked quietly.

He hissed as I worked out a knot and looked up, surveying the land. "It's closer than we thought," he muttered.

"The Shadow?" My fingers continued kneading his shoulders. I refused to falter in the meager care I could give him.

"Perhaps. It's a dragon, and that's all we know for sure. It left fresh signs in the area."

I blinked in puzzlement. "If it were a Shadow's Hunter, would it not stay close to its master?" I questioned.

"Some can travel far, but to retain control of a dragon, they would need to be close. The connection fades over distance." He hung his head as my hand moved up his neck, massaging the base of his skull.

He spun and grabbed my wrists, tugging me against him. He looked down at me and I recognized that fire in his eye.

"I don't know what we're doing here," he rasped.

"Investigating a dragon." I hummed as he caressed my cheek.

He smirked. "Is that what you tell yourself?"

"No," I whispered, turning my head to nip at his fingers. "I've come to help my General."

"Oh?" He trailed his thumb over my lips.

Exhilaration coursed through me. This was addictive—this feeling that he caused. The heat that flooded my body, the knowledge that I had some amount of power over this man.

This was dangerous.

"Aye. I came to talk," I said, voice cracking.

His touch moved to the nape of my neck, tugging on my braid. "About?" he urged.

He let go of my wrist and wrapped his arm around me, pulling me flush against him. I closed my eyes as pleasure simmered beneath my skin. He was hard everywhere I was soft. I was so close to him that I could feel his heart beating against my chest.

This was what I craved.

I clutched at his vest, needing to hold on to something—to ground myself.

"Rafe, I–" I gasped as his hand traveled from my shoulders down my back to rest on the curve of my hip.

"Yes?"

"I don't know!" I said, frantically looking up at him.

He chuckled and slid his hand to my thighs. When he lifted me, I moved without thinking, wrapping my legs around his waist. A soft moan pulled from my throat, and he grunted when my core pressed against his belly. The point of no return was fast approaching, and I was helpless against it.

"Vy–"

"Hush," I scolded.

I threaded my fingers behind his neck, bringing my face to his. He turned away at the last moment, refusing to let our lips meet. I let out a frustrated growl and nipped at his ear. He hissed and spun, pressing my back against the stone.

"Vy, don't–" he started, but this time I caught him.

My eyes fluttered closed, and I pressed my lips against his. He froze. I pulled back, just enough to feel his quick breaths tickle my skin, to see his dark eye alight and burning with need. That was what I had seen in him, that desire that I hadn't understood. It's what I felt now.

Need.

I needed him.

He let out a fierce growl and ducked his face to my neck, cursing.

"We can't," he rasped against my throat, teeth nipping at my skin.

"I know."

I tightened my hold, bringing him closer. I tilted my chin, facing the sky, full of want and desire. His lips explored my skin, biting first, then kissing the sting away. A Shadow could show up, and I couldn't care less. I needed Rafe, consequences be cursed.

He snarled and drew back, resting the top of his head against my chest, heaving for breath. It put the smallest amount of distance between us, and I hated it. I slipped my hands under his tunic and down his back, dragging my nails against his skin as I pulled up.

"Rafe," I pleaded.

"What do you want?"

His head shot up with sudden menace. I tried to kiss him again, but he jerked away.

"What do you want?" he growled again, his hands gripping my thighs in a bruising hold.

"You. I want you."

My words sounded breathless and strange. I was on fire. There was so much need roaring through my veins. I was blind to the anger in his eye.

"No."

A crack of reasoning shed light on my poor passion-induced haze. "I—what?"

"No. You don't want me," he repeated.

My eyebrows met in a confused frown as he released me, and I staggered on wobbly legs.

He tugged at his trousers and glared. "You want a life mate."

"I–" I blinked in confusion. Where had that come from?

"You're a woman. Regardless of what you wear, or how you cut your hair, you're a woman. You desire a life mate above all else," he snapped, pacing.

"I want you," I said, not understanding the small ache building in my chest.

"Oh, you think you do," he sneered, coming to stand before me. "You think you want me until you see the real me. Until you realize I'm not some wounded soul, but a dark, twisted thing full of anger and hate."

Venom laced his tone, and I blinked, bringing my hands to the cold boulder behind me to brace myself against his onslaught.

"Rafe, I know you. Have you forgotten what we've been through? I've seen you on your bad days. I know there's more to you than that."

"Bad days?" He laughed, a harsh and bitter sound. "You haven't seen me tear out a man's eyes while he's still conscious. Or beat a man to death with my bare hands until his insides spilled out. You haven't–"

I slapped my hands on his cheeks and used my nails as grapples to pull him down to me. "Rafe of Deomein. I know you—I know who you are, and what you've done." I put every ounce of conviction into my next words. "You don't scare me."

He hissed like a wild animal and tore his face away, resulting in my nails scratching his left cheek. I grimaced, watching him pace.

"If you want to say now is not the time–" I started.

"It will never be the time!" he growled, whipping his head toward me. "You want a life mate. My life could end tonight. Your life could end tonight. We can't promise each other forever."

"Not forever," I whispered.

That wild animal caged inside his body stopped and listened.

"Just for as long as we have."

He offered me a cruel smirk and walked to me. Grabbing my hand, he shoved it under his tunic and over his heart. It beat a frantic rhythm, passionate and angry.

"Do you know how old this heart is? Have you given that thought?"

I tried to pull my hand away, but he held it on his hot chest. It felt like he was searing me with the anger under his skin.

"It doesn't matter."

"Doesn't it? What if you want children? I'm not father material. I'm far too old for that."

"No, Rafe–"

"A home, a life mate, a child—I can't give you any of those things!" he snarled.

"Rafe, stop."

"No, Vy. You've pushed me too far. You–"

"I've pushed you too far?" I hissed. My fingers under his tunic hooked into claws. "I wasn't the only one burning up from desire. I didn't mount you without help. Don't blame this on me."

"You've–"

"No," I snapped, angry now. "If anything, you're older. You knew where this was going far before I did. You knew not only what I was doing, but what you were doing! Don't you dare blame me for this."

He recoiled, and I knew from the look in his eye, I had hit home. He had known about my attraction far before I understood it. His enraged gaze softened and gave way to the Rafe I'd grown to love.

"You're right." He dropped his temple to the top of my head and heaved a weary sigh.

My pulse stuttered. Panic gripped my heart like a vise. Something was wrong. My Rafe didn't surrender. He didn't give in. He fought for what he wanted.

"You're right," he repeated. "I knew better... I used you. I dragged you into–"

My throat tightened. "No!" I choked. I didn't want to wake the others but suddenly my world was crashing down around me.

"It's my fault," he muttered.

"No, it's–"

He cut off my words with a chaste kiss to my temple. "It won't happen again." He turned away.

My heart screamed at the distance between us, and I took a step toward him. I would not lose this.

I would not lose the happiness I had found.

I would not lose him.

I reached out to grasp his vest, but he drew back further.

"Rafe, I–"

A roar shook the ground. My knees gave out, and I slapped my hands over my ears. A gust of wind tore at my hair, whipping it around my face in a frenzy. Through the scattering of snow and cracked branches, a dragon swooped down, claws extended.

Something snared my cloak and threw me. I landed behind Rafe and he drew his sword, facing the creature.

"Bow! Get your bow!" he shouted over the dragon's outraged screech.

I scrambled back, gaping up at it. It pulled up, flaring its wings wide. It was huge—fully grown. Its scales were a dim gray in the moonlight, but its eyes burned—bright and alight like raging flames.

Why did those eyes look so familiar?

It pumped its wings and tucked into another dive. I rose on trembling legs and took off at a run toward the camp. Jamlin and Xzanth were already running our way. Xzanth took aim at the creature but didn't loose an arrow.

From birth, we were taught dragons were special creatures that deserved our love, respect, and gratitude. It would be hard to overcome all that teaching and instinct, to strike at it. I pumped my legs faster, trying to reach them, but my ankle gave way, twisting in the deep snow.

A shadow loomed above me, and terror chilled my soul. A gust of wind knocked me off my feet, and I flailed. Someone crashed into my back and I fought to free my face from the cold snow. A heavy weight rolled off me. The ground quaked, and I pushed myself up. The beast stood just behind me, paces away. It opened its maw, and the world went eerily quiet.

Its hundreds of teeth were sharpened to wicked points, and its tongue flicked in agitation. Everything was unnaturally silent as Rafe's body moved between me and the dragon. It whipped its head back and lashed at him with its tail. He jumped and rolled with the blow. As he landed, the dragon swiped its claws, shoving him away before he found his feet.

The behemoth threw its head to the ground in front of me. Snow flew into the air, drifting down in lazy trails. Its scaled lips twitched and nostrils flared. Wind ripped at me as it sucked in a deep breath, and I grimaced, expecting it to open its mouth and drench me in fire.

It lifted its head, and I rocked back on my knees, staring up at it. It tilted its head as it crept closer, peering down at me with eyes like fire. I swallowed against the terror squeezing my throat. It slowly lowered its muzzle.

I threw my hands in front of me, bracing myself for impact as the great head swung toward me.

I expected to feel physical pain.

I expected the massive head to crash into me, or dragon fire to rain down.

What I didn't expect to feel was the dragon inside me.

My mouth opened in a silent scream as pain tore its way through my heart and mind, as though the giant beast had entered my very soul.

What was that?!

Continue Avyanna's journey in
Following Fate: Book Two of the Fate Unraveled Trilogy!

Rafe POV

Because we all need a little more Rafe

The roar of the dragons grated on my nerves.

I rolled my shoulders, knowing the red dog wasn't watching me. Ruveel was stationed at the front lines, his dragon blasting through the Sky Trees, searching for the Shadow Shamans.

Where I should be.

Biting down on a curse, I slowed my steps and looked up at the stars. I would have Ruveel's head for sending me back to this cursed school.

School.

It was naught but a school for children.

The dorms loomed in the darkness, illuminated by the full moon. The building was tall and brooding, immense, housing several hundred children. Women. Civilians.

Faulkin called me reckless, claiming I needed a break from the war.

Ruveel hadn't been any help. No surprise there. 'Too much bloodshed can warp a man,' he said.

I'd wager his red dog killed more than I ever had. I just killed close enough to see the light die in my enemy's eyes.

As I ducked into the shadow of a tree, I resisted the temptation to rip off the blasted cloth tied around my head. It was stifling and impeded my vision. The old wound itched under the fabric.

'Reckless,' Faulkin called me.

He had no idea.

My hand slipped under the cloth as I rubbed at my eye, blinking. A flash of white caught my attention.

I froze, not so much as breathing as I saw a small figure pull a hood over a mass of white hair. I tried to place the figure as they failed to sneak toward the Dragon Canyon. There were only two people I'd ever seen with hair like that.

One of them was dead.

The other was his daughter.

I lifted my head, pulling the cloth from my left eye. After the incident, it saw far better in the dark.

Avyanna of Gareth crept around a tree—on the fire-blasted wrong side, in full light of the moon.

Stupid.

White fabric peeked between her cloak as she moved to the next tree. Her calf practically glowed in the moonlight, revealed by the short length of her night shift.

Had she not bothered to even dress?

She tripped over a loose stone and stumbled a few steps before darting behind a hedge. She didn't have to stoop far—she was so tiny, but she left half her cloak sticking out in plain sight.

Was she really that bad at sneaking about? Wasn't that what all teens did? How could she be so blatantly obvious?

The hem of the cloak disappeared as she sped down a path, around a boulder and out of my sight. Stupid, foolish, reckless teenagers. She was headed into the Dragon Canyon. The one place a perfect little Chosen like her was denied.

She had been refused—*twice*.

There was no going back after a refusal. No second chances with that dragonling. To be passed up for a Second Chosen was one thing. To be rejected by a Wilding, though? She was screwed. She'd be lucky if they considered her to haul dung out of the canyon.

Scoffing at the idiocy of her actions, I shook my head and pulled the cloth back down. I had better things to do than ogle a pathetic kid grasping at straws. I had a wager to win. A duel with the Master of Men seemed far more entertaining than worrying about some girl chasing dead dreams.

I stepped from behind the tree, keeping to the shadows, embracing them the same way I embraced my eye. As I crept along, I kept my steps light and silent, the only noise being the inevitable rustle of my trousers.

Somehow... I wandered closer to the canyon.

Odd, that was.

Perhaps I was just curious.

The canyon's high, stone walls blocked out the moonlight, darkening the path. Even on the lower level, I wouldn't recommend anyone traverse it at night.

Pursing my lips, I squinted at the thin paths that led along the top levels. An idea sparked in me. If I could get some wagers going, walking those would be quite the challenge. A worthy task for–

"Ah!"

I recoiled at the quiet cry, blinking in surprise as it was followed by the scattering of pebbles.

Surely she wasn't that witless.

I heard a quick sniff as if she had been offended by her own feet tripping. My legs moved of their own accord, deftly carrying me along. I caught glimpses of her cloak as she sped down the winding path. She hadn't learned her lesson concerning speed, then. Dense girl.

A long, controlled exhale followed my deep breath. What was I doing? The brat had the nerve to think she had what it takes to stand up to me in the barracks, and now she thought she could force a dragonling to her bidding?

I wasn't going to rescue her from that.

One could only do so much for a dumb mule. Sometimes, one had to let them fall off the edge of madness.

That, or put them down.

I shrugged at my thoughts, moving silently down the path. Pack mules who caught the magicked gaze of the Shadows had to be butchered. Better to feed the men than feed *off* the men. Now, this addle-brained girl... She might have to be dispatched in–

My boots were inaudible against the stone as I pulled up short. I took a quick step around a bend, blocking my bulk from her vision should she choose to turn back.

Who was I jesting? She wouldn't be smart enough to check if someone followed her.

With a shake of my head, I returned to the path and leaned against the stone wall. She had stopped in front of a cave, and from the quiet snores coming from within, she was admiring the young dragon inside.

A smile flitted across her face, small and bright, but even from this distance I could see it waver. My lips fell into a frown as I studied her. She clutched her cloak, watching the dragon with longing—yearning.

Something painful twisted in my chest.

I crossed my arms. I was here to watch the girl make a fool of herself—*not* to rescue her from her ego.

That look, though... That smile.

She looked like her flaming father.

I closed my eye against memories I locked away long ago, reminding myself I couldn't do anything about the past. I took a breath, forcing it to remain steady and even. Everyone made mistakes. Everyone moved past them.

Some mistakes claimed lives.

And I had moved on.

A familiar ache of hurt and anger warred inside me. It was part of me now. I couldn't ignore the torturous sensation—only embrace it.

When she darted down the path, her hood slipped off, revealing her stark-white hair. Just like her father's. I choked back my groan as she tucked it back up to conceal her telling mane.

As I pushed off the stone, I cursed every fire-blasted thing Gareth ever did for me. Curse the man for being so caring. Curse the man for showing me how to fight—for taking a rebellious monster of a boy under his arm.

Curse him for going along with my plan. Curse him for not staying back when he knew my mission was doomed.

I clenched my jaw to prevent the curses from slipping past my lips. It wouldn't do to let the girl know I followed her now. She might not try to force the bond. Maybe she had a bit of common sense in her tiny brain and would glimpse it and move on for the night.

Perhaps she had another reason for sneaking out. My brows met as I realized that bothered me. Thrice-curse it, why was I feeling all these things? She was petty—determined to get her way like every other woman.

I just wanted to see her fail.

She stopped in front of another cavern, and I tilted my head, watching as she pulled off her hood and entered cautiously.

Here we go. I settled back against the entrance.

"Easy, little one... It's just me. My name is Avyanna."

I stifled a sigh as I leaned my weight against the stone. The foolish girl rambled on for an eternity. I found myself listening to the story of her life with a bit of amusement. It sounded awfully familiar to my own. But then, so would many that called Northwing home.

Orphaned, sent to the school. Told to be good... except she seemed to enjoy it. Aside from being a lone wolf, she thrived here. She had the dragons, and the aptitude for bonding. She loved the classes and Masters.

Didn't have a rebellious bone in her measly body.

Until tonight.

"So, what do you say? Are we friends?"

Drawing myself off the wall, I leaned around the entrance and peered into the dark cave. She was crouched on the floor with her palm extended toward a blue dragonling. A white dragon stood back from them, watching the pair with bright, curious eyes.

Apparently, she approved.

Avyanna slid a boot forward on the ground, and the scraping was jarring, even to my ears. I ground my teeth together as her patiently woven spell shattered like a lantern to the canyon floor.

The dragonling lunged.

I moved at the same time the white dragon did. I reached for the girl as the dragon batted the little blue aside with a roar of disapproval.

Oh, this girl was flamed.

My hand landed on her shoulder and hauled her to her feet. She cried out in surprise and tried to face me, but stumbled on numb legs. I shoved her behind me as the dragon snaked her head toward the dragonling, as if to herd it away from us.

"Go." My command fell flat, and I didn't bother to wonder if she would obey or not.

The blue beast scrambled around the white dragon and tore at us. There was only one way I could save her from her own stupidity. She could cost me everything.

I yanked at the cloth over my eye as the blue sped close, murder in its glowing gaze.

A whimper pulled at my focus. The blasted girl was still behind me.

"Go!"

I couldn't wait until she cleared the entrance. Dropping to a crouch, I blinked, adjusting my vision to the dim light. I clenched the cloth in my hand, throwing all caution to the wind.

"Be still."

The blue's eyes flashed to meet mine, and I drew out the black, twisted thing that grew in place of my heart. With my stare locked on the dragonling's, I pushed the darkness behind my words and the strangely familiar strain on my mind.

The blue skidded to a stop as the white jerked up with a hiss. She would know this—the power I wielded. She would recognize it and tell her Rider.

I had to deal with her.

"Be silent," I ordered the blue.

It opened its mouth as if to roar its displeasure, but no sound came out. Thrill filled me as a smile spread over my face.

Dragons and their magic.

Pah.

Turning to look at the white dragon, she shrank back, tasting the air nervously. Her pink tongue flicked out, and a fleeting wonder crossed my thoughts. What power did she hide within her flesh? I blinked, and the thought was gone, replaced by my own.

"We were not here." I threw the black, twisted thing inside me behind my words.

She gaped as if tasting something foul and shook her head frantically, eyes closed.

I only had a moment.

Jumping to my feet, I dodged out of the cave and almost collided with the flaming girl. My fingers fumbled to secure the cloth around my face as I hurried her with my presence at her back. She moved far too slow for my liking. She went along, stumbling as the black thing in my soul lashed out at me, wrapping around my mind and squeezing. I clenched my jaw against the pain and tucked it away.

I wouldn't need it for the girl.

The throbbing pain in my head nearly blocked out the sound of scattering stones.

Nearly.

I grabbed her arm and shoved her into a cave. She landed against the wall, between stacks of crates.

A perfect corner for a mouse.

My hand clamped over her mouth before she could scream. I crowded into the space, pressing my body against hers.

Blast it all, but she was tiny.

I tilted my head, listening for the footsteps, trying to figure out if they were headed our way or not. As the quick steps grew more defined, I leaned down to press my cheek against her temple.

"Play along or you'll be tossed to the dogs." To the dragons or Masters, I didn't care.

I tugged her hood over her white hair, hoping it was enough. With a deep breath, I closed the last bit of distance between us and bent low to press my face to her neck.

Thrice-curse it all, she smelled good.

Her heart raced like a frightened rabbit as she clutched the sides of my tunic. A faint whimper was all that escaped her as I fought the urge to move my lips against her smooth skin.

Just to rile her.

Not because I wanted to.

She might be small, but she was soft in all the right places a man would want. Something dark stirred inside me. A craving—a *want*.

A sharp intake of breath snapped me out of my thoughts. I pulled up, trying not to swallow the lump that had formed in my throat. I wouldn't seem weak. I was a General for love of the sun. Moving my hand to cup her cheek, my thumb stroked her face as I hid it from view—a mere coincidence.

The man who approached was dressed in naught but a cloak and trousers he'd laced in a hurry. It didn't appear as though he was about for an honorable stroll. He cleared his throat, eyes dancing between us. I glowered in response and he nodded to me, darting back down the path.

Was he the white's Rider? Did the magic hold?

"Who was that?" she whispered, her voice breathless.

I snapped my glare back to the girl pressed against me, angry that her hands on my tunic felt so... *right*. She needed me. She relied on me. I protected her from discovery, and something inside me relished that feeling.

Fire-blast it all.

"Someone doing what we only pretended," I grunted.

Her eyes widened, and the realization of our proximity painted her cheeks a faint red. Pleasure thrummed through my veins. I did *so* love making people uncomfortable.

"What do you think you were doing?" I pulled my hands off her, knowing if I left them, it would only lead to them wandering.

I braced myself on the wall behind her, boxing her in, relishing the fear in her eyes. She jerked her hands off my tunic and her throat bobbed in a swallow.

She *should* be afraid.

Foolish girl.

I leaned low to press my lips to her ear. So close she would feel my breath against her skin. "What were you thinking?" My voice caught on syllables as it came out lower than I intended.

Dung heaps, I knew why boys chased girls like whipped puppies. I knew, and still, I stood here towering over a girl that... smelled of... what were those yellow flowers?

"You wouldn't understand."

My eye closed in resignation. She was pathetic. And here I was thinking of flowers. A weary sigh escaped me as I pulled back. The corner of my mouth twitched as she panted like a dog in heat.

That—or she was terrified and felt like she was suffocating.

"I will only tell you this once, so look at me," I rumbled, crossing my arms over my chest. Better that my hands were tucked safely away from her. "Gareth of Beor once saved my skin."

Oh, that got a reaction from her. Her gaze sought mine.

"I never got the chance to repay him, so saving you from your little stunt back there, I consider my debt settled."

Because I got him killed.

Her lips parted as a question flashed in her eyes, and I snapped a hand out. Her mouth slammed shut with a click and I smirked, tapping a finger against her lips as she shivered in outrage.

Run little rabbit, run.

Shoving those thoughts to the side, I continued, "Good girl. Let me finish. I'm no rat, so the Masters won't hear about this from me. That said, if you make another dung-brained decision like this again, I won't be here to save you."

Thoughts spun behind those forest green eyes of hers, and I wondered what she was thinking. Would she use that backbone she was growing and push against me? Part of me wanted that. Let her test her mettle against me. I would show her what to do with her attitude.

Or would she crumple like the simple girl I thought she was? Weak and easily manipulated.

She gave a sharp nod, and I dipped my chin in return.

"Glad we understand each other." Good girl. Take your orders.

She shifted her feet as if she was eager to escape the cavern. I fought back a smile. Was I so oppressive, so horrible that she wanted to flee? If she ran, I wouldn't be able to hold back my laugh. She gazed outside with longing and I knew she wouldn't run.

Grew too much of a backbone.

I could remedy that.

"One more thing." I deadpanned.

She looked up at me with those blasted green eyes, glittering in the weak light. I stepped forward, closing the distance between us and crushing her between my hips and the stone wall. I straightened to my full height, hoping I didn't hit my head on the low ceiling. I glared down at her and rested my hand against her throat—her pulse raced against my palm. The darkness inside me hummed at that frantic beat.

So small. So fragile.

"If you ever breathe a word about what happened in that cave, I'll kill you."

My life depended on no one finding out what I could do. My freedom depended on people thinking I had lost my eye. I would have no rest if anyone found out. They would torture me, make a mockery of me. I would be killed as an example—an example of what happened when magic twisted what it wanted and went wild.

As I looked down at her, I didn't entertain the idea that I had any kind of morals. I had no sense of honor. If she dared threaten me, I would throw her over the edge of the canyon now. She held my life in her hands, and I loathed that.

Her throat bobbed under my grasp, and I saw the fear, the answering horror in her gaze.

She knew I could kill her.

Good.

I pulled away and stalked out of the cave, stifling my staggering breath.

It might be my last as a free man.

More Cool Things!

Scan the QR code for more details concerning merch, signed copies and even a top-secret, super-secret, not-so-secret club with bonus content!

The Password is: Pumpernickel.

THANK-YOU

"So you see, you can't do everything alone."
—Rosemary Clooney

Self-Publishing is a hard road filled with insecurities and imposter syndrome. I have been blessed to be surrounded by people who have nudged, pushed, and at times *thrown* me toward my goal. Without them, Forcing Fate would still be a dream.

I am indebted to Jessie. I would have never started this journey without you egging me on. To Ali. You were the first step to opening myself up to readers. To Nick. It seemed so trivial, so petty, at the beginning. You had faith in me that I didn't have in myself. To Sarah Emmer. When I was terrified, too nervous to take the plunge—seeing you publish gave me the courage to pursue my dream. To K. C. Preston and our long conversations about Rafe. Thank you for being my critique partner and helping me through this.

My thanks to my Editor, Erynn who went above and beyond in editing. You are a godsend. I bow to your Editorialness.

There are many others who I owe a debt of gratitude to. Countless other indie authors who I saw struggle and rise victorious. I watched you, I learned with you, I owe you.

Independent Writers... you can do this!

M.A. Frick

M.A. Frick is a mere peasant.

Once upon a time, she wished to be a lost princess... or rather the dragon who snatched the princess away. In her earliest memories, there were always swords, beautiful dresses and villains. There were dashing knights and dragons abounding in her backyard.

Putting those childish aspirations aside, she is now content to chase her three children around with foam swords, cosplay at Ren Faires and cuddle with her own knight in shining armor while reading or writing some new adventure.

Made in the USA
Monee, IL
05 May 2025